BABY SMALL

Book II of I Heart Ed Small

Shirley Johnson

Baby Small

Baby Small

Lyrics from "Breathe" written by Roger Waters and used with written permission from Roger Waters.

No part of this novel may be used, copied, or reproduced without written permission by the author.

All events in this novel and all characters within it are fictional and any resemblance to people or events present or in the past is purely coincidental.

Copyright November 2015 by Shirley Johnson
Cover art Copyright November 2015 by Shirley Johnson
ISBN- 978-1519284501 , 1519284500

Other works by the author:
I Heart Ed Small
The Music of Mary Frances

Baby Small

Chapter One

"I'm never letting Ed touch me again."

I shut my eyes as I confessed this to Petra but that wasn't enough to protect me from the shrieking eruption her weak body was still capable of making.

"You have lost your ever loving mind!" she screeched and swatted at my arm with her long thin hand and missed. "Get over here!" she commanded and snapped her skinny fingers at me till I moved my arm closer and let her slap me.

"How can you even say such nonsense?"

I had never talked to Petra about losing Dan and wasn't going to now, so I just shrugged and winced against another shrieking.

"Ed is such a sex god. Jeez, I get all worked up just thinking of him. Which by the way, I need all the details. You never told me anything at all!"

"Ugh." I flopped back on Petra's white bed spread and felt my aches that were real and solid, low in my belly and in my chest, where I had lost my Dan and where they'd fixed my heart.

"What's Ed think of your declaration?" she asked.

Ed had cried.

Ed had begged.

I had been sitting in the T-bucket watching the cold winter sun set between the apple trees. It was only two weeks before Christmas and I went out there to get away from Daddy. I needed to get away from all the Christmas cards, the shopping lists, the cookies and all the happy music. I needed a few minutes to myself. I needed a moment without Ed and yet I hoped Ed would see me sitting out there and come out to me.

I wanted to tell Ed I had aches. I had aches where they fixed my heart and I had aches because they'd never been able to fix my mama. If they'd only tried to fix her back when I was six, she would have lived. I could have had her here with me right now. I wouldn't have been raised by Aunt Clem and the twins and I wouldn't have been brought up with Ed Small.

It seemed Ed colored every page of my life. There was nothing that was me that wasn't touched by him. I ached for him. I ached to be as grown up as him. I wanted to be a woman. But I ached like I was sure no woman had ever ached.

I hurt for my lost baby. I hurt and knew it was all my fault he'd died. And I hurt for any hurt he might have felt as he died without knowing the world. Without knowing me. It wasn't right that I had lost my own mama and now here I'd lost my own baby. It just wasn't right. And I hurt and it would never stop because it was my fault. Because I made him. I was too young to be doing that. To be making babies. I was too young to even say 'sex' in my own thoughts in my own private mind.

I ached and felt torn in more ways than one. Ed colored every thought of mine. Ed's fingers touched every thought, every memory. There was only Ed and lack of Ed. There were only times with Ed and times waiting for Ed to return.

I had wondered what he was doing right then as I blew out chuffs of air and watched the vapor puff away. I wanted Ed. Yet I was scared of him. I was scared of losing him. I ached at the thought of losing another one of his babies. And I ached between my legs from where I'd birthed the baby while I wasn't even awake. Who knew you could birth a baby when you weren't even awake?

I tried to cross my arms over my chest but it hurt. So I just propped my heels up on the steering wheel of the rusted model T and lay my head back on the cracked old seat and sighed as Venus winked on bright and twinkling, disguised as a star next to the December moon. But I was only out there alone for a little.

"Penny for your thoughts, Blondie," Ed called to me as the wind sighed through the bare limbs of the apple trees.

The T-bucket creaked on its springs as he climbed in and sat next to me.

"Blondie," he sighed with his lips in my hair, his hands cradling my head to him.

"Ed," was all I could manage and I let myself lean my head on him.

He smelled of smoke and pumpkin pie and musk and nutmeg. Being near him gave my head a heavy restful feeling.

The days after Thanksgiving had blurred right into December with leftovers and cold weather and leaf fires in the driveway, and just us.

"No Hunnicutt cousins," Ed stated as if he'd read my mind as he stroked my hair.

"Nope."

"Thanksgiving just us and now Christmas too without all them cousins," he said and paused at stroking my hair. "Here," he said more to

Baby Small

himself than to me and I felt him fiddling with his fingers under my hair where some of it was pulled down tight into the neck of my winter coat.

"Here," he said again barely more than a whisper between his thick lips.

He pulled my long hair up out of my coat and smoothed it down my back.

"That's better," he sighed and I felt the relief of it no longer being lumped up under the back of my coat.

I leaned closer to him and I snaked my arms around his waist and squeezed him to me.

"What's buggin' you, Baby Hunnicutt?" Ed asked and yet pulled my face so tight to his plaid coat that I couldn't talk.

A tear rolled off my cheek and I stared at it where it clung to his jacket as a tiny quivering silver bead.

I didn't answer him. I just squeezed him tighter and willed him to know all my feelings and all my fears and all my aches. I opened and closed my mouth a couple of times, the wool of his jacket scratchy on my face, but I couldn't get any words to come out.

"Here we are in the T-bucket, Baby."

I pinched my eyes shut on a hundred memories of me and Jimmy Collins hiding in the sunflowers while Ed got slapped by various pretty girls from good families as he pawed at them in the old rusted car. Ed was mine now.

I heard the flick of his lighter and smelled the crisp burning of his cigarette.

"Do you love me, Baby?" he asked in between drags on his smoke, and he gave me a squeeze about my shoulders.

"Yes, Ed. I love you."

"Are you sure, Baby?" he whispered and kissed the edges of my hair, the top of my head.

I could hear his sticky kissing sounds as he held my head softly and kissed the crown of my head.

"I'm fine."

Ed froze with my head still in his hands, his thumbs on the tops of my ears, under all my hair.

"Blondie." It was the voice that said I was in trouble. It was the voice that said I'd better get my bee-hind over there. But I was right next to Ed. I was so close to him I couldn't tell where I ended and he began.

Ed was silent for several beats of my heart. I pictured the stars whizzing by overhead in the black night while we sat there quiet, pulling each other closer. And then he gave my head a light squeeze and a final kiss; his breath hot on my scalp and the cold air stole it just as quick as I felt it.

"Tell me Baby. Right now."

I felt him rub his chin on my head, his whiskers fuzzing all my hair up near the part, and before I could think I blurted out, "Remember the other day when you told me you wanted to have lots of babies? Well, I'm too little to have your babies. It ain't gonna work. I lost Dan. I can't lose anymore, Ed. I can't do it. I'm too plum small," and I shuddered out a sigh when it was all finally said.

Ed had shook his head at me slowly and pouted till the cleft in his chin went in way deep.

"Say it ain't so, Baby Hunnicutt," he begged me out in the T-bucket and then he let his hair fall in his face in heavy hanks.

His eyes did get a little moist and he must have licked his lips a hundred times but he sat there quiet and I could see his chest rise and fall as he breathed in hard as if I'd punched him low in his belly.

I scooted back from him on the squeaky old seat.

But then his breathing slowed and he just stared at me hard. He was thinking of something in that head under all that hair as he let his mouth relax and his lips grow fat again. He closed his eyes and his tongue slipped out to touch the fullest part of his top lip.

"This ain't the Baby that I know. The Baby I know isn't scared of things. She doesn't quit," he told me and looked at me hard.

And then he took a deep breath and I waited to hear what he'd say.

"Ah Baby, you are right," he sighed and spread his knees as wide in the little box of the T-bucket cab as he could as he leaned his head all the way back on the seat and smiled up at the black night with his eyes shut.

"I'll give you time to grow. I'll give you time to get bigger. You ain't no bigger than a minute, sweet little Locks. I should a never started nothin' with you, but I did. And now I love you more than anything. We should scoot over to the Dairy Freeze right now and fatten ya up some," he said with his head back.

And then he sat up and when he opened his eyes he saw me just sitting there with my mouth hanging open and he laughed.

"Huh! Ahuh! It's gonna be all right, Baby."

He lay back in the seat and unbuttoned his coat with one hand without looking down and when he got his coat open he rubbed his belly and spread his legs even wider till his knee pressed up against my thigh. His leg shook as he laughed silently up at the sky.

Baby Small

"Shit mother fuck," he whispered and ran his hand through his hair. "I can't wait," he said to the sky. "But I can wait," he said under his breath but I heard him.

"Sexy sex god like Ed won't like any of that, Baby," Petra told me now as she flipped through her yearbook. "There's hundreds of girls who'd let him have his way."

She smacked her lips for good measure as she thought a while with her eyes shut; her finger blindly tracing under all the black and white smiles of the freshmen class.

"He'll wait for me," I told Petra and her black eyes popped open and shined as she smiled at my confidence.

"He'll wait," I said again.

And then I walked over to Petra's window and looked down across the street to the empty porch at Aunt Clem's house. "He'll wait. He said he'd wait. Till June."

I swallowed hard and sat back down on Petra's bed as she tried to pull herself closer to me with her stick arms. All she managed to do was slide the slippery chenille spread off the corner of the bed and on to the floor with a sigh of cloth.

"Till June?" she demanded.

I nodded and swallowed again and hugged one of her pillows to me.

"What's he gonna do in June?" she asked; her eyes glittered as she leaned towards me, her large angular face dwarfed her bony shoulders.

I just shrugged but I knew what he was thinking of doing in June and my face flushed hot as I flashed back on being under the dining room table with Ed. As I remembered being on my old bed back at Aunt Clem's with Ed. As I thought of the very first time Ed climbed on top of me and just got real close to my face and didn't kiss me or anything. That, that first time kept playing in my head over and over in a loop every night before bed. And it colored all my dreams.

I thought of all the dreams I had had about Ed. Dreams about being on his waterbed. Being in the backseat of the Cutlass. The backroom of Tollys. And everywhere else it seemed. It seemed I was obsessed with Ed. Something was wrong with me. It wasn't right. I wasn't right. Maybe I was just sex-crazed like Petra.

I shook my head hard to get it out of my mind but I still heard him. "Baby." That's all he said. My name. And then I heard Petra say it too. "Baby."

She sat back and cocked her crooked body at me in a question mark. "Baby what's he think is so magical about June? What's happening in June?"

She really didn't know and she drummed her slick red nails on the bed as she waited for me to explain.

"I'll be eighteen," I said and popped my eyes wide at her.

She backed up even further and frowned and looked around the room as if examining every memory of me she'd ever had. She looked from the dresser to the desk to the window and back again and when she looked around I could see a faint echo of us as we grew up together; all the talks we had had in here and all the life lessons taught to me via Barbie and GI Joe. I wondered if Petra saw the same memories as me.

"No you won't," she finally came back to the present moment and said and straightened out her crooked question mark self as much as her body allowed her. I saw her tendons straining under the thin skin of her arms as she held herself up.

"That's what Ed thinks," I gulped. "He thinks I'll be eighteen."

"Oh my God."

"Ed's always had my age wrong." I shrugged.

"And now he thinks you'll be eighteen." Petra's eyes were nearly swirling; she was that starstruck.

"Yep."

"How romantic," Petra gushed and fell completely over.

"It's not romantic, Petra! It's serious! It's my health we're talking about here!"

"Where's all this seriousness coming from?" Petra asked between gasps as she struggled to pull herself back up to a sitting position.

I let her struggle on her own a while, her bony arms worked to pull her normal sized torso back up off the bed. She twisted and pushed with her fists into the spongy bed and tried to raise herself.

"Here," I finally said and hoisted her up by her armpits.

"Thanks," she puffed out and blew a damp piece of hair off her forehead. I held her steady without a word while she got herself situated better on the bed.

"So what's got your knickers in a twist, Baby?" she asked me as she rearranged the hem of her shirt which had gotten pulled kitty-whumpis.

"I went to the doctors."

"Oh."

Petra knew all about doctors. She had her own fair share of them.

I'd felt pretty good, inside and out until I went to the doctors. That visit to Rush Hospital had set off all my aches and all my worries. That check-up had gotten me to thinking.

Maybe Mama was right. Maybe Ed Small was crazy, I had thought to myself as I sat in my Mama's old rocking chair after the doctors' visits and tried to remember everything she'd ever told me when she was alive. And I thought maybe she was right; maybe I did stare into Ed Small's eyes long enough and I had made him go plum crazy. Just like she always warned.

That night after the doctors' visits I could hear my daddy being efficient in the kitchen, clanking pots and making our dinner. We'd spent most of the day at Rush Hospital getting me my one month check-up. It'd been one month since I'd collapsed at the sight of Ed at the La Rue Homecoming football game. It'd been one month since the doctors had repaired me. It'd been one month of me recuperating and trying to grow stronger and it'd been a month of me spending every day with Ed. And of course I had a lot of time with my Daddy and Mrs. Small, and even Aunt Clem.

But I had thought after this month of healing up I'd be back to normal. But as the doctor explained, I now had what he called a new normal. Now I had medicines. And those medicines and their affects needed monitored. So now I needed tests every month. And I would for the rest of my life.

After the heart doctor I had to see the baby doctor. And I had to talk about the complication of getting pregnant so young. And I had to talk about a thousand other things I didn't feel like discussing with a bald old man I didn't know while my Daddy sat in a room full of pregnant ladies.

It was a silent ride home. I didn't even feel like stopping by the Dairy Freeze for a special dinner. So here I sat in the dusk of the cold night while my Daddy opened cans and clinked things in the kitchen.

I had sat in Mama's rocking chair and I held her cross-stitched pillow to my chest and sighed deep as I thought of all the ways my life had changed in the past six months.

I'd turned sixteen in June and Ed came home. I was part of a big play and gotten hurt by Allen and fell in love with Ed. I'd lost a baby I'd only had in me a while when I collapsed and died for a bit till Ed revived me. Collapsed the same as Mama when she'd collapsed on the stairs carrying too much laundry.

I could have been in the ground the same as her. The same as little Dan. I shuddered and sighed and hugged the pillow tighter as the fat tears ran hot down my face.

I prayed to my mama.

I should have listened to you Mama. I should have stayed away from Ed Small. I should have, I searched for what I should have done but couldn't think of anything else and just sat there in the dark, blinking away the tears and thinking, Mama, Mama, Mama, Mama, and feeling the weight of guilt pressing on my heart. Guilt for what, I'd be hard pressed to say exactly. But guilty and undeserving to be sitting here with another chance, a chance at life, a chance my Mama never got.

I sat there till my Daddy called me to dinner. But when I got up I didn't go to the kitchen and eat. I went up to my room. I paused on the steps where she had collapsed and died when I was six. I paused there and sniffed and said, "Mama," one last time to myself before I went up to my room and crawled into bed.

That morning after the doctors' visits I felt raw and unraveled as an old sweater as I sat on the wool rug in front of the tv and brushed out my wet hair.

I'd cried myself hoarse and even the hot shower hadn't made me feel better. All I'd thought all night was, Mama was right; Ed Small was someone to stay away from.

In the dark winter night with the ceiling glowing in my room from the glow of the full December moon I felt grateful to be alive. And in the early hours of the night, just past midnight my tired logic talked me into believing it was my own Mama who'd saved me so I'd have a chance to do things right. And by that, I meant not do things with Ed.

"Well good luck with that," Petra told me now and patted me weakly on my back as I saw myself out her door.

She couldn't follow me down the stairs without her grandfather carrying her down, so she just waved at me from where her legs dangled off her bed, and I went home.

**

Chapter Two

"Baby you're giving me a headache," Ed said to me from where he sat on top of the dining room table rubbing at the skin next to his eye with his thick fingers. "Jesus, Baby, this is more than I can handle."

"I was serious Ed Small," I said to him as I furiously ironed my Daddy's work shirts.

"Baby."

"I mean it, Ed Small, I mean it!" I thrust the nose of the iron in his direction.

"Jesus, you're killing me. At least come eat with me at the Freeze."

"All right. If we can get a tree."

"You are a piece of work Baby Hunnicutt, twisting me around your finger like that. Making me do whatever little thing you want and giving nothing in return," he said in a serious voice but had a huge smile on his face with his dimples winking under his beard.

"I told you Ed," I said to him with my back to him as I unplugged the iron. "I told you Ed, I need to wait."

"I know, you're too small to handle me, I know."

"No Ed. I'm too small to make babies right now."

"That's what I said," he said as he helped me shrug on my winter coat.
**

I held the warm greasy packages of cheeseburgers and fries that Ed handed me as if I were weighing them. I felt like I needed to say something, something important, to mark this occasion of us eating as just friends again. I glanced over at Ed with his lips shiny with grease in the light of the dash. He tensed his eyebrows as he thought his own thoughts and I felt satisfied and sure that he knew how I felt; he knew we needed to just be friends, and there was no need for me to say anything. Yes, he knew it was necessary. And so I sighed and unwrapped my sandwiches and ate and wondered why I wanted to kiss him so bad.

We ate in silence and after my first cheeseburger I glanced over to look at him again. He'd stopped eating and held his cheeseburger halfway to his mouth. Steam came off it in waves in the cold car as he just sat there staring at the steering wheel with his eyebrows tense.

But he only sat that way a few seconds and the spell broke and he shoved the entire sandwich in his mouth and turned and grinned at me with ketchup on his chin.

"Baby Small, you better eat."

Ed blinked his lazy bruised eyes at me and sucked the greasy sauce off his bottom lip before shoving a handful of fries in his mouth.

He pushed his hair behind his ears before taking the lid off his shake.

"I'm not Baby Small," I told him and I leaned towards him and dipped a handful of my own fries in his shake.

"You will be, Baby-Locks," he whispered to me and took hold of my wrist that was still holding a handful of shake covered fries.

"Ed!"

He batted his eyelashes at me and kissed my knuckles before pulling my hand towards his open mouth and shoving my fries into it.

"Huh!" he laughed around my fingertips and sucked the fries from me. "Of course you're gonna be Baby Small, Baby Small! You already are! That is if you want to be. That is, I mean you will be, won't you? You'll be my Baby Small?"

And this question, this important question left me so flustered, I couldn't even look at Ed, much less answer him. I wasn't even sure I'd heard him right.

"Baby!"

"What?"

"Don't just sit there!" he reached over and shoved me in a playful way.

"I don't know what to say, Ed. What exactly are you asking me?"

"You know what I'm asking Baby."

"No, Ed, I don't."

He grinned at me with his eyes shut and he held his eyes closed so long and just grinned and I grew nervous waiting to see what he'd do.

"Baby you know what I'm asking," he murmured and slid closer to me.

I gulped and looked up at the dimple in his chin as he came even closer.

"What am I asking you, Baby?" he almost begged.

"You're asking me to," I trailed off as he threaded his fingers through my hair and raised goosebumps up on the back of my neck.

"Asking you what, Baby Small?" he prompted as he rested his forehead against my own.

"To be Baby Small," I breathed out as his lips closed on mine and as he slid his tongue and its salty warmth into my mouth.

**

"Blondie. Blondie I'm, I'm sorry. I'm sorry Blondie," Ed said to me as he gripped the steering wheel and stared straight ahead as he drove us home.

"I didn't mean to hurt ya, Blondie."

I rode home in silence with my legs feeling wobbly. Poor Ed was just as shook up and wouldn't stop apologizing and I couldn't say anything to give him reprieve from hurting me. I had the chills and the goosebumps and couldn't stop shivering.

"Blondie," he now said to me and I heard his lips stutter around the B.

"Blondie, what was that noise you made?" he asked and that was the last thing he said before pulling up into his drive right next door to my house.

"You can't make sounds like that, Blondie," he said more to himself than me.

He put the car in park and just sat there, both hands gripping the wheel. His eyes looked glassy and frozen and he didn't even blink.

"Blondie," he finally said and turned to me. "Baby Hunnicutt. You're right."

"What Ed, what?"

"'Bout leaving you alone," he said and swallowed hard.

I watched him as he ran his hands through his hair and as he tucked it behind his ears again and again.

"You were right," he said again and gulped just as two tears hung from his lashes. "I need to leave. You need to go. That little groan, Jesus God, I'm only a man and that little sound, Baby. Who knew?" he asked himself and I looked over to see him shaking his head and shaking all his hair into his face.

"I might try to steal a kiss from you, so I'm gonna ask you to get out of the car now, because a man is only a man," he lamented.

"Ed?"

"I'm not kiddin' Blondie-Locks. I'm gonna take a kiss if you don't get out. And you saw where that one kiss took us back at the Freeze. And you're not wanting to give me any, any you know, and I, I don't wanna take what I shouldn't be takin'."

And he reached over me without looking at me and opened the door.

I got out quietly and looked back at the car. The Christmas tree we'd gotten from the lot behind Tolly's was still strapped to the top of it. Ed just sat there with his hands on the wheel and his eyes squeezed shut and a grimace twisting his lips.

As I took a half step back towards the car he threw it into reverse and backed up out of the drive with the fat rear tires spinning on the ice.

"Ed, you didn't really hurt me. I'm just a little bit sore," I tried to say without any breath in me and I held up my hand over my heart; it felt light and as if it'd just fly away. But he didn't look at me as he sped away with the passenger's side of the car empty and dark.

Ed showed up later that night when I was sitting on the floor in front of the tv eating cheese puffs right from the bag and drinking a tall glass of Qwik.

"Baby Small," he drawled from behind me.

He stood in the front door where he'd just let himself in and had half a grin on his sleepy looking face. His hands were behind his back.

"I see I'm back to being Baby Small again." I squinted up at him.

"You left a tree tied to my car."

He had a devilish smile on his face and I mirrored it right back at him. This amused him.

"Yep. You're still mine. It's a matter of time before we got the paper that states it as such. But in the meantime, you're still Baby Small to me. And your tree is still tied to the top of my car."

He had a huge grin on his face and he still had his hands behind his back.

"You made me get out of the car, Ed Small!"

His cheeks were red from the cold and his eyes were a pale wintry blue and he grinned at me and brought one of his arms out from behind his back and wound it up and threw a snowball across the living room at me and hit me in the side of the head with a soft splish.

"Huh! Ahuh!" he laughed and left me there picking ice out of my hair as he stepped out the door to go get the Christmas tree.

**

Christmas Eve found me opening presents at my Daddy's for the first time in ten years. I had told him that I didn't think I could do such a long car ride to Uncle Fritz's and that I still didn't feel up to being around all the relatives. It was my suggestion that we have Aunt Clem over Christmas Eve. Jeffrey and Lisa brought her and after Jeffrey helped a very pregnant Lisa up the porch stairs he went back out to Aunt Clem's car and brought in the biggest Christmas present I'd ever seen and sat it on the floor in front of my feet.

"For me?" I asked as Burl Ives played on the record and Ed carried in a plate of cookies from the kitchen.

"For you, Baby," Jeffrey said to me with a huge smile on his face, his eyes twinkling with excitement.

Baby Small

"We opening presents now?" Ed asked as Aunt Clem passed around cups of cocoa and as my Daddy plugged in all the lights to the tree. You could smell the electricity bouncing off the tinsel.

"Go ahead Baby, open it," Jeffrey squatted down next to the large present and looked up at me. His cheeks shone with expectation.

"Is it ok, Daddy?" I asked my dad as he frowned at his cocoa from where he sat on the edge of his old green chair.

"Sure Baby."

I looked all around the room from tiny Aunt Clem, in her green pantsuit to rounded Lisa heavy with the end of her pregnancy, to Ed who was leaning in the doorway and licking green icing and sprinkles off his fingertips as I tore off the top of the paper.

"Oh my."

A million memories came back to me as I slid off the couch onto my knees on the braided rug and I pulled the rest of the paper off and let it float to the floor. There sat Aunt Clem's old green and white doll house, my old doll house; full of wooden furniture and with faded photos of Frank Sinatra glued to the walls. There was my doll family Allen had gotten me from Cloyd's after Ed had hit me with the see saw at Dragon Park on that day it was too cold to swim.

I sat cross-legged in front of all the little tiny rooms of the house and inhaled and smelled basement smell and smelled the dusty starchy talcum smell of Aunt Clem's house. I shut my eyes and breathed in scotch tape and baby shampoo and coppertone suntan lotion.

I opened my eyes and touched all the hair and all the little clothes of all the dolls and they were still in good shape; their eyes still bright blue, their hair still curly and golden.

"My family."

"Yep." Jeffrey grinned and sat down next to me and helped himself to rearranging the furniture that had shifted about and fell over when he'd carried it here. He still remembered where the tv went.

"There's where Gerald the mouse used to chew," Jeffrey said and pointed to the doorway of the blue and white bathroom where Jeffrey's pet mouse used to sit and gnaw when we'd let him run around the house and visit my doll family.

"Where you gonna put that, Baby?" My daddy asked and brought me and Jeffrey's attention from out of the house. I looked at him through one of the windows in the upper story.

"Up in my room, of course."

"Well, ok, I just wondered if you weren't too big is all."

I stared at my dad for a moment and recalled the longing I had had for all my lost toys that had remained back in my room when I'd moved to Aunt Clem's without any notice after Mama had died.

"Baby's not too big for toys," Jeffrey laughed but then caught Ed's eye and stopped.

But Ed didn't say anything.

Later, however, as he stood next to me at the kitchen sink, with his lips close to mine he told me, "I have a special gift for you later." And he squeezed my shoulder and left.

**

"You under the table Blondie?" Ed called to me as I put my socked feet on the underside of the dining room table the day after Christmas. He came in wet-headed with his hair parted straight and his face clean shaven with his lips red and his eyes at half-mast as he peered under the table at me.

I blushed and stared at the white crescents of his thumbnails as he gripped the underside of the table before he dropped to all fours and crawled over to where I was laying.

"Merry Christmas, Blondie," he said and poked me in the forehead with his finger, right where he would have usually kissed me.

"You're all cleaned up, Ed."

His hair was wet and sleek and parted perfectly down the middle and it contrasted with his wide jaw and the fullness of his sad mouth. I tried to sit up under the table to get a better look at him.

"You're leavin' aren't you!" I said to him with a panic sliding into my stomach.

Ed wasn't mine. I realized I couldn't keep him because people I loved never stayed and I had told Ed, I had told him he had to wait because I loved him.

"I'm not leavin'. Not yet anyway. Not today. I brought cookies," he said. "And your present."

He scooted on his butt towards me under the table with a giant Santa Claus shaped plate piled high with assorted bright colored cookies wrapped tight with saran wrap and in his other hand he held a small square box.

"Where'd you get those?" I asked him as we both propped up on our elbows under the table.

"Mom forgot to take them to church."

He smiled at me with his eyes shining with mischief and I could see he already had a milk mustache and had already been at the cookies. "And this, I got out in Colorado," and Ed opened the little white box without giving it to me.

Before I could see what it was, his fingers were in my hair and I heard a snap and felt a barrette being clicked into place. I reached up and felt feathers, light and fluffy against the palm of my hand. Ed watched me as I undid the barrette and slid it out of my hair. It was dark leather with leather cords and on the ends of them were white and brown fluffy feathers.

"It's beautiful, Ed. Thank you," I told him and clipped it back into my hair how I liked it.

"This is our table, Blondie," he said to me as he snapped the head off a reindeer cookie with his teeth and slit his eyes and grinned at me. "Right here," he said and leaned back on his arm and stretched out his legs in his tight old jeans. He munched his cookie and kicked off his hiking boots that he'd worn over unlaced.

I didn't say anything back to him.

"History was made here, 'member?" He flipped his hair off his face and out of his eyes and scorched me with his gaze.

I felt a pulse in my belly quicken when his lips twitched and then relaxed to their full pout. He didn't say anything else but stretched out on his back and shut his eyes. His shirt rode up over his tan stomach as he sighed.

"I'm torn Blondie," he said as he blindly felt around for another cookie. "I want to take you right here, get you under me, take your sweetness, make love to you all afternoon, right here, where you nearly pulled my hair off my head. I want to take you now, Blondie. Right now. Wear you down. Touch you where you're so sweet. So nice." His words made me shiver and I shook my head to shake my mind clear.

He began to roll his head from side to side. I watched a small tear swell out of the corner of his closed eye and roll down his cheek and disappear into the crisp golden curls of his sideburn.

But he didn't say anything. But I knew. Something was coming. Something important. Even if he did reach out for another cookie.

I watched his fingers fumble over the pile of pretty cookies and I put my hand on top of his and stilled it and I picked out a fat snowman covered in thick sugary white icing. I touched his top lip with the cookie and I smeared a little icing on his cupid's bow and giggled.

I watched his eyes move a little under his bruised lids. And then his tongue parted his thick lips and he licked a slow dip out of the frosting.

I fed Ed cookies under the dining room table and I touched the leather barrette and the feathers attached to it. I watched as a couple more fat tears rolled down the side of his face and I waited for him to tell me the bad news. But he never said anything at all. He just lay there on his back and let me feed him cookies and after he'd had about seven of them I said, "Daddy's not coming home tonight."

I just sort of blurted it out. And then I rolled away from Ed and sprung out from under the table to get a head start on getting away from him.

"Shit mother fuck!" he barked, his eyes popping open and cookie crumbs falling in his hair. "Fuck Blondie, I'm coming after you for that!"

I didn't stick around to let him get me and I ran upstairs. But I did hear him laugh and as I got to the top of the stairs I heard the dining room table pop as he smacked its top as he came after me.

"Ed! I'm still healing and shouldn't run!" I yelled at him as I skidded into my little bedroom.

"I know Blondie! I'm just glad I get to be here. All night if you want me. To watch you do your things, your Blondie things. Just to be here, to see you do your stuff," he said as he came into the room. He looked bigger than life compared to all my old things.

He sauntered into the room in his tight jeans and flopped on his back onto my bed and stretched out with his head on my pillow. Seeing him there made me ache. I was lonely so often in my Daddy's house and I just wanted Ed with me all night long to hold, even though I knew it was wrong. I had to look away from him but had to turn back because he had got my curiosity up.

"What sort of stuff? What are you thinking I'll do?" I asked him.

"Oh I dunno. Doin' Blondie stuff."

But Ed could see I was nervous.

"Keep your shirt on, Blondie. Just Blondie things. Reading books and flipping your hair about and wearing weird dresses that look like quilts and hankies and watching Bing Crosby Christmas movies on the tv and wait," Ed paused and slitted his eyes at me. "What are you wearing, Blondie?"

"What?"

He looked at me even harder and he even shut one eye.

"What?" I asked again and walked away from him some.

"You cold, Blondie?" he asked and pressed his lips together and cocked his head to the side.

"No, why?"

I pulled at the hem of my red turtleneck sweater and shifted around in my thick socks.

"What are you wearing?" Ed sat up on the edge of my bed and grinned.

"Nothin'."

"Nothin'? That don't look like nothin'. That looks like about fifty layers of a whole lot of somehtin'."

"It's cold." I shrugged and turned my back to Ed and pulled the quilted flannel shirt of Daddy's I had on over my turtleneck around me tighter.

"You look off, Blondie," Ed mumbled and scratched his head.

"What's that supposed to mean?" I snapped and turned back around so fast to face him my hair flew.

"Come here, Baby."

His lips curled up in the smallest of smiles but his intentions were all glowing in his shiny eyes.

"No." I tried to say it firm but I couldn't help but smile at him. His eyes were infectious.

Even still, I planted my feet on the braided rug and squared my shoulders at him.

"Baby."

"No, be good!" I pointed at him.

"I'm gonna get to the bottom of this," he said more to himself than to me and he stretched out his legs in his tight old jeans and stood up. He gave me the old look he used to do which was a warning he was about to play too rough.

"No," I told him but it was useless because he'd do what he wanted and I didn't mean it anyway.

"Now I don't think this qualifies as being a Blondie thing. This is not what I had in mind when I said I wanted to watch you do your things," he grunted. "I thought I might see you brush your hair or wash some pots and pans or something. But if this is what you want, Blondie, if this," he trailed off and reached out and rubbed the flannel of my shirt between his fingers and thumb.

Ed was quiet for a while as his eyes ran over me and I almost didn't hear him when he finally spoke.

"What's wrong, Blondie?" he asked and tilted his head to the side a bit.

"Nothing." My voice just a rasp. I looked down to see he still had a hold of the material of my shirt.

Ed slid his fingers around my wrist and pulled me to him.

"Blondie, have I hurt you so bad?" he asked as he pulled me closer to him and slid his arm around my waist. "Have I permanently hurt my Baby?" he asked as he pulled my hair away from my ear and kissed me there.

"No, Ed, I'm fine," I answered and leaned into him and wrapped my arms around him too.

"Blondie, you're not the same. You're all covered up in forty-leven layers and it ain't like you," he said softly, his lips in my hair.

"I'm the same Ed. I'm the same as I ever was. You didn't, you didn't hurt me. I'm fine, really I am."

"Why you so covered up? Where's your Blondie things? Your crazy dresses? Your patchy pants? Where's my heart necklace I gave you?"

"I have it on. I have it. I always wear it." I felt ashamed and couldn't look at him. I stood on his feet with my thick socks and flexed my toes against him.

"Did I ruin you, Blondie?" he asked and I felt his fingers on my chin.

"I don't think so," I said to him but I wasn't even sure what he was really asking.

He pulled my face up to look at him. And when my eyes finally met his, his face relaxed into a grin so wide he shut his eyes, and his lashes were as long and dark on his face as they ever were and I instinctively stood on tiptoe and kissed him there.

"You're ok, Blondie?" he finally opened his eyes and asked. He stared down at me with a soft grin on his lips and his eyes blazing and cool in the winter sun coming in my window.

I was dazzled for a while just looking up at him and didn't answer.

"You in there Baby Small?" he giggled and gave me a little shake.

"Yes, Ed." I reached up and tucked his hair behind his ears.

And that, that reaching up to him was all he needed to encourage him to bend down and kiss me. And we kissed like that with me standing on his feet and our arms wrapped around each other, there in my bedroom.

"Now, Blondie. I don't ever boss you around but," Ed said to me some minutes later when he broke away from our kiss and held me at arm's distance.

"You've bossed me around my entire life, Ed Small. Even from all the way in Colorado when you ran off, you were bossing me around in your letters!" I reached out and pinched his arm.

"Now Blondie, we're having a tender moment, don't go and ruin it."

"I'm not the one ruining it you're the one getting ready to boss me."

"Now woman, just listen to what I have to say. I want you to change out of these fifty something layers of Elmer Fudd clothing and put on one of your kooky dresses."

And at this Ed led me by my hand to my closet.

"Is that what you want?" I asked him and squeezed his hand hard and began to bend his fingers backwards.

"Damn woman! Let up!" he hollered as I squeezed his big fingers with my smaller ones.

"No, Ed! I will not change into one of my kooky dresses!"

I twisted at his fingers harder till he dropped to his knees in front of me.

"Shit mother fuck, woman! Let up! You know I can't fight back Baby Small, you know I'd never ever take advantage of you and it ain't fair!" he hollered from where he knelt in front of me and hung his head as I pulled on his thumb a good yank.

"Baby Small," he panted, "I just thought, I just thought one of your dresses might look nice with my barrette I got you, is all." He looked up at me and grinned and I let go of his hand and went to the closet.

"Jesus Christ, woman," I heard him whisper as he rubbed his fingers as I flipped through the dresses in the closet.

"That's more like it," he said to me some minutes later when I came back into the room after changing into a wool plaid pinafore handed down to me from my cousins. "Nice knee socks," he added as he folded his arms under his head and lay back down on my bed.

"You think you're so smart," I started to say to him but he bounded off the bed without warning and grabbed me and pulled me down on the bed and pinned my arms down.

"I ain't never been that smart, Blondie. But I'm smart enough to hang on to you. I'm at least that smart."

Ed was quiet for a while and just lay on top of me, with my wrists captured in his hands. He didn't say a thing and just stared into my eyes. I was too shocked to say anything and only when he let go of me did I realize I'd been holding my breath. He touched my hair and my face with his fingers but he never stopped staring into my eyes. I don't think he blinked at all and his eyes looked vast like pale blue frozen solar systems. I was completely enchanted.

He stroked my hair once more and kissed me between the eyes and whispered against my forehead, his lips wet, "Ok let's go do Blondie things now." And he rolled off of me. And I followed him down the stairs.

Ed watched me do 'my things' as he called them, all day. And he helped me as well. He carried baskets of laundry for me up and down the stairs and he watched me fold it. He lay under the dining room table by himself and whistled and sang Christmas songs while I ironed Daddy's clothes. I stole glances at him as he lay there with his arms over his eyes. All I could see were his lips and I watched them as he talked about children and kittens and dogs and flying helicopters and mountains and things he'd never spoken of before. He rolled his head from side to side while his eyes were covered and I paused in my ironing to watch his hair as it flopped back to expose his sideburns. When I moved away from the ironing board, he came out from under the table and trailed after me, rubbing the stars from his eyes.

I turned around and looked at him as the winter sun came through the long windows and blazed a crown on the top of his head where his hair was parted and had fuzzed up in the back and it felt as if a million years had passed since I dragged Ed to my house that afternoon my Mama collapsed.

I shook my head to get rid of the memory and went on to my next task.

Ed pecked around on the piano and made up melodies while I dusted the front rooms. I peeked in on him to find him standing at the piano with his brow furrowed, his sweatshirt too tight across his back, with sweat stains under his arms as he ran his fingers through his hair and hummed a melody with his eyes shut and picked at the notes.

He completely disappeared when I cleaned up the kitchen and the house was quiet except for the water and the scrubbing of things. But I found him later asleep in my bed completely covered up and snoring.

"Did I miss anything good?" he asked as he rubbed one eye with his knuckle when I sat on the edge of the bed to wake him.

It felt good to have him up in my room, to know he was there even if he wasn't down there with me as I did my chores. It felt good to know we weren't rushed; we had all the time in the world to spend together on that day. Daddy wouldn't be home all night. Ed could stay over. What would happen then, I didn't know. But for now Ed was hungry.

"Baby Hunni," he said to me through a mouth of fries, later at the Dairy Freeze. "I think this is our place."

"The Dairy Freeze?" I asked as I ate my own hot salty fries, covered in shake.

"The Dairy Freeze," Ed gestured with his fries. "The front seat of this car. This little town. Me and you. I think this is as close to heaven as they'll ever let me."

"You think you'll go to hell?"

"I don't know about that but I can't imagine Heaven being better than any of this." He reached over and kissed my forehead with a wet loud swak and leaned back and dumped his shake into his open mouth.

"Yes, this is nice," I agreed and looked around the dark car and ate my dinner.

"Too bad I have to leave," Ed said as he wiped his lips with his fingers and stared straight ahead out the windshield. "Maybe you'll be ready to handle me when I get back, Baby. But maybe you won't. That's ok. I ain't staying away forever."

And this was it; the thing I knew was coming, Ed was leaving.

**

That night he indulged me and let me wash his hair in our kitchen sink. Daddy would have died and would have killed us both if he'd a come in and seen it.

Ed and I had passed the evening eating Easy Cheez on Ritz crackers and watching Christmas movies on tv in front of the Christmas Tree. But as the night got later and the house got darker and quieter, we both felt something. It felt serious and made us both fidgety. And on a whim I asked Ed if I could wash his hair.

"Not in the shower?" he asked me as I pulled him out of the bathroom; him with his sweatshirt half on and half off and stuck completely on his head, covering his face. It was all I could do to not run my hand across his broad back when he had his sweatshirt stuck on his head.

"No, Ed," I said and pulled him by his hand down the hall to the kitchen.

"Not out in the back yard, I hope!" he hollered at me as he struggled to get all the way out of his sweatshirt.

Ed let me wash his hair with what he called girly shampoo in the kitchen sink and for a moment I froze as I held the sink sprayer in the palm of my hand. I stood there and felt the weight of it in my palm and felt my heart ramp up in a crazy rhythm that scared me and I shut my eyes and waited for the memory to go away. Ed was silent and unknowing as he bent over with his head in the sink and waited for me to begin.

"What's the hold-up Blondie? You forget to pay the water bill?" he asked. And I heard him laugh with the wet nose sound of an upside down laugh. And that reminded me of Ed holding me upside down with water running down my nose and how I'd choked when I had tried to yell.

"Blondie?" he called again. And when I didn't reply, he stood up. "What?" he asked. He looked down at me and I almost crumbled under the pressure from his stormy eyes. "What?" he asked again and pooched out his bottom lip at me.

I shifted my weight from foot to foot and looked away and remembered a thousand things all at once in a rush.

"Nothing, lean back over," I told him and put my hand on his bare shoulder and guided him back over.

His skin was hot under my palm. I took a breath and I began to spray his head and all that hair, and worked in the shampoo with my fingers.

"I know what you were thinkin'," came from the sink five minutes later as I was rinsing out the soap.

"What?" I gulped.

"You're thinking about our first time."

"What?" My mind zoomed from Aunt Clem's sink to the dining room table and my hand went up to my eye absently and touched where it had been swollen and blackened so many months ago.

"That's what you were thinkin'. You were thinking about spraying me and runnin' away from me in your patchy dress made out of old jeans."

I dropped the sprayer and it landed with a metallic smack on the sink and I started scrubbing my fingers through all of Ed's thick hair to make sure the soap was out. I scrubbed him so hard his shoulders shook.

"Owww, Blondie! Gentle. Be gentle," Ed crooned to me and I scrubbed softer.

"'Member that? 'Member our first time?" he said from deep in the sink. It sounded like he had a cold when he talked upside down.

"That wasn't our first time," I whispered and wasn't sure he heard me.

"It was too, Blondie."

He rolled his shoulders and flexed all the muscles in his bronze back while still bent over in the sink till I took my hands away. Ed stood up and shook out his hair and stood looking down at me without his shirt on, water dribbling down his belly.

"That was our first time, Blondie."

"We didn't," I shook my head up at him.

"We didn't?" he grinned at me, his face flushed and his hair wet.

"No, Ed, that wasn't," I trailed off.

"You don't think that was our first time, Blondie?"

Baby Small

I couldn't answer him. I couldn't get my mouth to close. I just stood there, backing up out of the kitchen with my hands out in front of me, shaking my head at him.

"What'd we do then?" he asked and winked at me, still grinning and came towards me as I continued to walk backward.

His eyes never left mine as he ran his fingers through his dripping hair and he tried to part it and tried to comb through the wet tangles.

"I know what you're thinking, Blondie."

His eyes burned cold in the dusky glow of the sleepy house. He picked at the dimple on his chin as he waited for me to answer.

"No you don't." I gulped.

"I do. You're thinking of our first time," he nodded at me, his pupils huge in the gloom.

The tv was still on in the living room but we could only see the flickering blue on the ceiling and couldn't hear it as we went past.

"You're thinking of the first time Baby Blondie."

He tilted his head down at me and smiled.

"We just, you just, you chased me."

I shook my head at him and walked backwards away from him.

"Yes, and what else?" he asked and now his eyes were lidded and looked bruised and sleepy.

"You, you wanted me to scream and I wouldn't."

"But you did." His eyes popped open wide to me and his grin was now a huge smile, his teeth white in the dark house.

"I, I, you picked me up but we didn't." I continued to shake my head at him and began backing up the stairs.

"Where you going, Blondie?"

"I'm just going, Ed." I didn't like how my own voice rose high. I gripped the bannister blindly as I went up the stairs backwards.

Here he stopped following me up the stairs and his smile faltered. His eyes almost closed and his lips became thicker as his face went slack and he stood still and looked down for a bit. A thought flicked here and there under his eyelids as he thought something over. A thick strand of wet hair fell over his forehead and the water from it ran down the side of his jaw. I watched it till it dropped onto his shoulder and then I remembered to keep going up the stairs. I didn't trust myself to not touch him as he stood there defenseless with his eyes shut.

"I'm coming up too, Blondie," he said as he gazed up at me and his mouth curled up in a grin. "I'm coming up too because I want to hear how you remember it."

His hair continued to dribble water down his shoulders and his chest as he hunched over a bit and looked up at me through his eyelashes and asked me, "Don't you remember what we did?"

"I remember what you did!"

"I bet you do," he chuckled and his face flushed deep red.

I just stared at him with my eyes all the way open.

"We did it that day." He winked at me.

I just kept shaking my head.

"No, we didn't!" I protested and held my hands out at him. Now we were in the hall and I backed up to the door of my bedroom and stopped.

"What'd we do, Blondie? I want you to tell me. I want to hear a bedtime story." He reached over to take my hands in his.

"You carried me!" I yelped and smacked at Ed's hands, but didn't mean it.

"Yes, and?" he asked and smacked right back at my own hands with his thick fingers, but not hard. And when I looked up at him and met his eyes, he took my hands in his own and everything went calm.

"And, and you put me down on my back on the bed," I whispered to his bare chest.

We'd never really spoke of it and sometimes I couldn't be sure if it wasn't all in my imagination.

"And what?" he asked and squeezed my hands.

"And, and," I swallowed hard and shut my eyes and turned my head to the side. I felt dizzy and breathless and stood there quiet.

I felt Ed stroke my hair where it fell down my shoulders and I leaned in to his touches.

"What else, what else?" he urged me on as he began to kiss the part in my hair from the back of my head to the front.

"And you got on top of me, and you touched me places I'd never even ever touched myself."

I blushed hot and covered my face. But he pulled my hands away and held my wrists down at my side.

"Yes Blondie I did."

"And you ripped my dress and!" I said up to him with my eyes shut and trailed off and couldn't catch my breath because now he was kissing my jaw from my ear to my chin and down my neck. Little sucking kisses with his thick lips that worked their wet magic on my skin. I could feel his teeth nibbling me as he went.

I remembered that day. Now that I was here with Ed in my room it was all coming back to me. And I remembered being scared but excited. I remembered being scared at seeing Ed in a different way. And I remembered being scared that things were happening so fast. And I remembered being scared that I liked those things. I wanted to slow down and experience those things slower. But I also wanted it to hurry up and yet also never end.

"What else, Blondie? What else?"

He stopped kissing me and let go of my arms and walked right on past me with a blinding smile on his face and his eyes looking crazy. He walked on past me with his hair wet and dripping down his back in slow rivulets and he laid down right on my bed on his side and propped himself up on his elbow.

"What else Blondie? Get to the good parts!"

"And, and something bad was in those Frosted Flakes, Ed Small!"

"Huh! Ahuh! Making me hungry ain't gonna change the topic!" he guffawed; not remembering eating Frosted Flakes right before chasing me.

I shook my finger at him now and couldn't say a word. But he reached for me and with a big laugh and he pulled me onto the bed with him.

"I love you so much, Blondie," his voice sounded thick as he kissed me high on the cheek and drew me back into him.

"What are you gonna do, Ed?" I asked as I snuggled backwards into him.

"I'm gonna wait, Blondie. We're gonna wait till you're bigger. Till you can handle me, huh! Ahuh!" he laughed and squeezed me tight to him and was quiet for several breaths.

"You mean till I'm big enough to handle you?" I kidded him.

"Oh you can handle me, Baby. You know you can. Matter of fact you handled me earlier today." His voice came to me in the dark and I blushed.

I squirmed to get away from him but he pulled me tighter and I felt tired from all my chores and I felt at home next to him and just let myself go limp against him.

"Will you wait, Ed?" I asked him after we'd settled down a while.

"Course I will. I'll pass the time with just doing Blondie things with you. And of course I'll be back in Breckenridge here in a couple of days and when I come back," he trailed off and squeezed me again and kissed my hair.

I fought the tears as long as I could as I stared out into the black room. I swallowed them back and squeezed my eyes shut and was just quiet there with Ed. My eyes burned with tiredness and strained to see something, anything in the dark. I could just make out the moonlight on the edges of the closed curtain and I sighed.

"When? When do you go?" was all I could ask Ed.

"A few days," was all he answered.

Chapter Three

That winter was record for snowfall and Daddy said that it was so fierce a winter that it was going to scare spring away altogether. And I think he was right because spring did end up being late that year. Or at least it felt that way to me.

Winter had brought with it a melancholy New Year's and a farewell to Ed as he returned to Colorado on the bus on New Year's Day. It was a morning of exhaustion and dehydration; my eyes open wide despite having stayed up the entire night at the kitchen table just staring at Ed. We both drank Pepsi's till we thought we'd burst just to make sure we stayed awake all night.

The evening had started happy enough.

We went to Tolly's and I realized we had become the hippies my Mama had always warned me to not stare at.

Ed looked at all the different chips for sale and stood stroking his chin where his beard was beginning to grow again; I looked at him as my Mama would have and I saw then myself reflected in the doors to the freezers and realized I had become a hippie too.

I glanced around and wondered if there were any mothers warning their kids to not stare at us; that we were dangerous.

Ed stood there in the middle of the aisle singing almost silently between his thick lips about moonbeams and night breezes while scratching his head and looking at bags of chips, and I thought, how could anyone ever think he was dangerous?

"Baby?" he called to me without taking his eyes off the bright bags. "We ought to get these because they look like party hats. But I don't think one bag will be enough." He stroked his chin and rubbed his lips and sized up the bags.

A little girl peeped around the corner of the aisle and stared at Ed as he popped a bag open and crammed a handful into his mouth and crunched with his eyes shut.

"Yep. Gonna need more than one bag."

I watched him lick the salt off his lips.

He dusted his hands off and threw seven bags in the cart and noticed the little girl staring at him.

"What?" he asked her and looked back at the open bag still in his hands. "You ever have these?" he asked her, wiping his mouth with the back of his hand, causing her to squeak and look at me with wide eyes.

Baby Small

      I walked to Ed and helped myself to a handful of Bugles and I winked at her and smiled and caused her squeak again. She spun around in her snow boots and ran back around the corner.

      "What?" he asked and looked around and began placing the little salty party hats on his fingertips as he sauntered on down the aisle singing about stars fading.

      The night started off happy enough. We brought home lots of salty snacks and pop for the night. Daddy told us a hundred times he'd be going to bed at nine just like normal; no sense staying up late. We watched Dick Clark without him. We watched various scary movies on the tv and we ate a load of snacks. We were camped out on the couch with quilts and tv trays and we must have put five hundred Bugles on our fingertips and eaten them off. Aunt Clem called to say she thought Lisa was going into labor but that she wasn't in the hospital yet. Mrs. Small came by carrying a platter of chipped beef rolled up with pickles and cream cheese and a six pack of Fresca. Daddy could be heard in the basement sanding something and hammering something else. And still Ed and I sat on the couch together eating chips and flicking the tv from Dick Clark back to the scary movie and counting down the time.

      After midnight and long after Daddy had gone to bed, and Ed had gone home only to sneak back over after we were sure Daddy was asleep, we sat at the kitchen table.

      For a while we talked. Ed told me about helicopter school. He told me about the mountains. He told me about the avalanches and the skiers and the updrafts and the downdrafts and the ice until I asked him to stop.

      After that we were silent for long stretches.

      I took Ed to the train station at 4 AM. He hugged me and kissed me and cursed himself for letting me bring him because I wouldn't stop crying and hiccupping.

      "Now get home Baby Small and don't wait for this train to leave because I'm just gonna get settled on there and fall asleep. You get on home to bed."

      But I stayed. Even if he was going to go right to sleep, I stayed. And soon I saw him five cars down from where I stood, I saw him in the window waving at me and I ran to him. If I could have, I would have pulled him right back off the train. But all I could do was wave back at him because the window was too high for me to get close to him. I waved once. And he did too. And we just stood there and stared at each other. Him with a huge sad smile on his tired face. And me with just tears rolling down my cheeks until he began to make his silly faces he'd always made for me. He clowned and batted his eyes and made fish lips right on the

Baby Small

window of the train until it began to pull away. Only then did he get serious. And he waved one last time and blew me a kiss.

Chapter Four

After Ed left for Colorado, the dull grey sky dumped fat wet snowflakes for days and kept me inside. Each day brought doubt into my heart that I'd ever done anything right in my life. Doubt and homesickness. Homesickness for my time with Ed. Homesickness for Aunt Clem, for my room there, for Allen, Jeffrey and our times together. And although I missed Ed the most, I doubted our future together. I doubted everything about myself.

We had wet snows for four days after Ed left on the bus. But on the fourth day, it warmed up and the sun came out bright and promising and I decided to walk over to Petra's.

"Petra, I've got cabin fever," I told her. "Let's go down to Cloyd's. Get a pop or something. Get out."

Petra didn't answer. She just squinched her black eyes at me and looked at me hard. Finally she said, "In the snow?"

"Can you do the snow?"

"Yes. Of course I can."

There could have been four feet of snow outside and Petra would have never admitted she couldn't get around in it. But as it were there were only a few inches of melting slushy snow on the sidewalks. But Petra now had to use a walker everywhere she went and even on dry land she was a slow shuffler. She'd have to shuffle her walker through the slush.

"I can do it," she said from where she sat at the kitchen table with her thin hands folded on its top. "Let me get my coat."

I stayed seated as I watched her lean on the table with her elbows and push herself up.

It was slow going down the sidewalks with their ruts of footprints in the slush and ice with Petra pushing her walker. She no longer really picked it up and just shoved it through the melting snow. I watched her black galoshes as they kicked through it all and didn't say anything. Every time I started to say something a car would go by and as it went by us it'd slow and the people in it would look at us. We couldn't get to Cloyd's fast enough.

The smell of cinnamon and bubblegum and candies of every sort was a caress right from my childhood as I pushed open the door to Cloyd's and the little bell tinkled above us as we slid in the store. Two of our schoolmates stopped in the doorway to stare as we went in and they went out and I glared at them for being rude to Petra.

Baby Small

As we wandered the store I remembered all the times we'd stopped there on our way to the pool. All the Pepsi's we'd bought, all the bags of BBQ chips we'd purchased. I thought of all the barrettes Allen was always bringing me and packets of Juicy Fruit gum. And I put these different things in my basket now as if buying all the right things together at once would bring back the past. Petra asked for red vines and a Coke, not Pepsi and I put those in my basket too.

I noticed the store felt different. A quiet seemed to blanket it just like it had our neighborhood after all the snow. I noticed people peering around the corners of the aisles at us and I wondered what their problem was. Petra had had troubles walking since she was a kid, why were they staring so much at her? Finally I snapped and said something to her.

"The heck are all these people staring at you today? I have half a mind to say something to them!"

"It's not me they're looking at," she said to me and I stopped in the middle of the aisle.

"What?" I looked at her in her red wool coat with her black hair perfectly flipped this way and that; her red nails glossy and pointy as she gripped the handles on her walker.

"It's you they're staring at."

"Me?"

I looked around the store. I could hear Barry Manilow on the speakers and I could hear the register bell up front ringing someone up. And I could see people at the end of the aisle peering at me over their baskets. Some of them stared at me outright with nothing in their hands.

"You didn't think this would stay quiet, did you?"

"What?" I asked Petra.

As sure as winter brought heavy snows that quieted the neighborhood, it had also brought the story of unborn Dan to all the neighbors and to all the kids at the high school.

"Nothing goes unnoticed in a tiny town, especially a birth to a sixteen year old girl and especially the death of the unborn baby," Petra informed me.

No one said anything to me directly but I felt their looks and I heard their whispers. I felt their curiosity. I felt their judgment. I felt them form a thousand unspoken thoughts about me and Ed. Their eyes told me everything. Some looked curious. And some even looked sad like they had pity on me. And some looked pinched and harsh and judgmental and I didn't like that at all. I didn't like the pity either. I didn't like any of it.

"I," was all I could say and I shook my head back and forth and looked at the basket of talismans I had collected and knew it was

Baby Small

worthless. Nothing could bring everything back together. I could buy all these things and put them all on the pearly kitchen table and mix them together or burn them in a pile in Aunt Clem's alley and they wouldn't bring us all back together like we were before we all fell apart. I sat the basket down as I continued to watch the few shoppers around me.

"You want me to carry it?" Petra asked.

"What? No, you can't," I told her.

"Then why are you setting it down?"

"I, I'm ready to go. That's all."

"Then, let's go," Petra said as she slid a five out of her coat pocket. "I'll help pay," she said as she leaned over and grabbed a box of Red Hot Dollars off the counter and threw them in the basket. "For Ed," she said and nudged the basket with her walker.

I chewed over the curiosity and speculation of the gawkers as I chewed a mouthful of the spicy hot little coins on the way home. Petra pushed her walker through the grooves with more determination, fueled no doubt by the small town gossips, and I walked behind her to avoid being soaked at the ankles from her wake.

All the gawking and whispering and wondering was made worse when I recalled the looks of pity on their faces; pity that I'd been taken in by Ed Small, long haired lay-about and small town lothario.

I wrote to Ed immediately in those first few days he was gone. But I didn't tell him about the stares. I wondered if maybe it was just happening because Cloyd's was in our neighborhood. Maybe only the people that lived near me knew. So I went to Tolly's the next day, just to see how far the news about me had travelled. I walked all the way to Tolly's and when I finally got there my boots were leaking and my feet were cold and I was sweaty under my coat and I realized I couldn't get too many things because I'd have to carry them all the way back.

I plodded through the store all too aware of everyone around me and I ended up staring at them much more than they stared at me and I couldn't tell who had looked at who first and I abandoned my basket and left after three aisles.

But I did write to Ed. I wrote to him and told him nothing of heading back to school. Of the looks and the whispers and the laughter that I got behind my back as I walked the halls. I told him nothing of my loneliness or sadness. I only told him good things. Like I passed my driver's test at the DMV and that Daddy let me drive him anywhere I wanted in his truck and I took us all the way out to Dragon Park on the slick roads. I even used the four wheel drive gear.

Baby Small

I told Ed about playing Parcheesi with his mom. I told him about Lisa having the baby and how I drove Jeffrey to the hospital over in Rush to visit her and the new baby daughter Olivia. I told him they said something was wrong with the baby. And I told him that maybe she looked a little different than some babies, but that she seemed perfect enough to me.

I told him that I had become my Daddy's caretaker; making his breakfasts before the sun rose, ironing his shirts, and washing his things. I bought all the groceries and cooked and cleaned after school. I was feeling stronger, I told Ed.

I wrote and told Ed the most exciting thing. That how one night when the snow was falling again that Daddy stayed up late, even after I had gone to bed.

I had gone to bed early, tired from school, from cleaning, from fending off all the questions and stares at school, and so I was asleep when around midnight I was woke by the sound of loud truck engines and big tires in our drive and I peered out my long window. I saw my uncle pull up in his old Travel-All and a black old rounded truck blubbering and blatting pulled in behind it. I wondered who had died because it was after midnight on a Friday and why would Uncle Fritz and the cousins drive two hours in the dead of winter to come here unless someone had died.

I took a mortal headcount of Mrs. Small, Aunt Clem, Jeffrey, and Lisa and knew they had to be okay. The cousins wouldn't come for that. Ed. Ed was in Colorado learning to fly helicopters in the mountains. He could have crashed. My heart squeezed flat just like the doctor warned me about. The doc had told me to not get too worked up. Told me I needed to be calm. Maybe Ed crashed and there were no remains to be found. My heart squeezed a little tighter and I dug my fist into my chest right where it hurt. "Shhh shhh," I told myself and began to rub my scar on my chest through my nightgown. "Shh shh," I said again. If Ed had crashed, the cousins and Uncle Fritz wouldn't care or know. They wouldn't be here.

I wasn't dead. Daddy was outside opening the hood on the truck. He was here. Mama was in the ground ten years. Who was left? Aunt Frances? I asked myself.

Meanwhile, the cousins had gathered around the engine of the black truck while it continued its rested rumbling in the milk white moonlit drive.

Before I could even get the courage to go down there and see what was the matter, just like that they all piled back in the Travel-All. My dad dropped the hood closed again on the truck and jumped in and moved it so Uncle Fritz could back out. And once he was gone, my daddy pulled that truck back in. A big black old truck with one wobbly headlight shining in the middle of the night. It didn't make sense. I stood there at my window and watched my daddy alone in the night as he pulled out an old rag and rubbed at the rounded old fenders in the cold moon light.

I went back to bed after using the bathroom and getting a drink right out of the sink and in the morning I wondered if it weren't all a dream. But the keychain on my placemat at the little kitchen table told me everything that my daddy couldn't tell me himself. I had a truck.

I wrote Ed about it all. The snow, the truck, my school classes and grades and how I drove around in the loud black truck. How I felt like a grownup toolin' around town and around the country shifting low on curves and observing things I'd never seen before. How old our town looked, how the houses looked as if they were sinking right into the wet spring earth as the snow melted. I told Ed everything except I left out how the town all knew about me. And about him. And worst of all about Dan.

And Ed wrote me back but he didn't say much. He sent a narrow box and in it a pair of brown moccasins with little beads sewn on them. He sent postcards of mountains almost every day; mountains covered in snow, mountains covered in trees, mountains in high altitude sunshine, but he never said when he was coming home.

I just assumed it'd be summer. When spring came in with a heat wave and a heaviness that felt like summer, I began to get anxious for Ed and I found myself doing anything I could to not think about him; I decided to plant a garden and I began to dig up the earth out back. I made lists of the veggies I wanted to plant. I kept busy. But it was hard because the letters kept coming and no mention of his return.

He sent one envelope with a stack of three square photos inside. The first was a picture of the mountains; the trees looked tiny and the sun splintering off the lens of the camera completely obliterated all the color out of the left corner. The second was a picture of Ed close up and a little blurry. He'd held the camera out himself and the arms of his jacket were visible on the sides. His face was mostly clear but his hair was out of focus. His forehead was tan and his pale eyes lidded and almost sleepy in the sun, his teeth blinding white and his lips red and full. I ate up every ounce of color and every detail of the photo immediately. I stared at it a long time, a sharp pain in my throat, before I looked at the third photo. It was Ed in a flight suit standing broad-shouldered and bearded, next to a red and white helicopter on a mountaintop, his face lit up with a huge

Baby Small

smile, a helmet under his arm. In pencil, on the back of the photo, he'd written, I PASSED!

Ed was a pilot now.

When would I see him again?

I kept those photos plus all of Ed's notes and postcards in a box in my dollhouse with it turned windows facing out to my room so no one could see them in there. I would have been hard to say why, just that I wanted them somewhere safe when I wasn't around. And some silly part of me thought of the dollhouse as special, as magical. It was the only logical place I could think of to store Ed's photos and notes where I could easily get to them. It was where I could smell my past and look at pictures of my present at the same time. The two things were tied together so tightly; my past at Aunt Clem's and my present with Ed.

I was clinging to talismans of the past wherever I turned. I thought of the basket of things I'd gotten at Cloyd's and how they'd seemed promising and magical at the time, but when I got them home they didn't add to much more than some junk food piled on the table.

But I did want Ed's photos. And I didn't want Daddy to find them. For now, mostly I wanted to know when Ed would be home. I decided I would call him. I'd never called anybody long distance. I didn't know anyone far away. I was a little nervous thinking about it but I was determined and I went over to Mrs. Small's and let myself in to find her and ask her for Ed's phone number. But Mrs. Small wasn't to be found in the kitchen. Nor was she in her bedroom or the bathroom. I peeked down in the basement but it was dark as pitch but still I looked down the stairs from where I stood in the hall and I gripped the bannister and strained my eyes. Just as I was about to give up, there at the bottom of the stairs I could just make out the faint yellow glow of Caesar's eyes. I gave up that day on trying to call Ed and I went home and sulked.

I knew something was different even though I had been keeping my head down and my days full of school as whispers and stares followed me. I narrowed my focus to just homework and housework and making dinner for Daddy. I tried to keep moving, keep doing, and keep my head in a book or headphones on my ears to keep myself safe from the loss I felt. To keep myself safe from the talk of the town. At night I would lay under the dining room table with the headphones on to keep myself from hearing the gossip in my head.

"People just want to know is all," Petra said to me every day after school when we would ride home in my truck.

She loved the truck. She would pat the side of it as she ambled up to it after school, and she would speak soft words to it as if it were a big black heavy hipped horse instead of a big black machine. I picked her up every morning for school and gave her a ride home every night unless she had pep squad practice. Then I would hurry away from school and try to avoid all the looks from the girls and the calls from the boys.

With Petra by my side no one dared say something impolite, no one dared cat call or whisper behind their hands. Petra would not hesitate to sling herself with her walker at them and give them a dressing down that could singe their hair.

"The boys all think you're loose now," she told me one day and I flushed hot and bit back the tears.

"Of course any boy that says that around Jimmy Collins is asking for a butt kicking. Because for some reason he's taken it upon himself to be your champion." And this was when Petra would give me the calculated look. "But of course I know you aren't loose."

This was also the day she'd informed me that Kai had asked her in study hall if it was ok to call me.

"Petra, I don't know what I would say to him and I don't want to know what people are thinking of me!" I had yelled at her as I flung her walker in the bed of the truck. "I just want summer to be here is all," I said as if that was that and I turned the ignition and hoped the truck roaring to life would end all conversation that made me uncomfortable.

"You just want Ed to come back."

"Yes," I admitted and leaned on the wheel.

"You just want to stick your head in the sand," she continued as she arranged her legs in the truck by pulling on the knees of her pants and not looking at me.

"Petra." I looked over at her.

She wouldn't look at me.

"Petra are you mad?"

She examined her nails and was silent so I threw the truck into gear and lurched us out of the La Rue High School parking lot in a cloud of black smoke.

"It's just that you never even told me what happened. I'm your closest friend and I don't even know things. I can't even put on a genuine smug face when these pissants on the pep squad pepper me for the details. Come on Baby. I known you since you were knee high to Ed Small's bee-hind!"

Petra looked fit to boil over and nearly ready to bawl which was a dangerous combination.

I started to smile as I let her talk herself down. I loved Petra.

Baby Small

"I known you since Ed Small was telling everyone he was your daddy. I known you since before you got your period. And you've done everything in the book there is for a girl to do and haven't told me anything about it. Now I'm patient, Baby. But I'm also stubborn and I ain't getting out of this truck till you tell me," she said to me as I pulled up in her grandparents' drive.

So I threw it into reverse and backed up without a word and we went to the Dairy Freeze and I told her everything over fries and cokes. Well, almost everything. There were certain details I couldn't share and for that I endured many of Petra's feeble slaps because she knew I was holding out.

When I got home Daddy was already there and was dipping chicken in flour and egg and making dinner.

"Baby," Daddy said to me that night as he took a piece of fried chicken off the platter.

We were in the little kitchen eating a late dinner. The windows were open and a warm spring rain was coming down steady.

"Baby, it's time for you and I to talk about something."

I thought he just wanted to talk about me being late. About me not getting dinner on. But I knew when he set down his chicken leg without taking a bite, I knew it was about something bigger. And deep down I knew something bad was coming. I hoped it wasn't about Ed.

"Baby."

"Yes, Daddy?"

He just sat there with his mouth clamped tight together and didn't say anything.

I let go of the spoon in the corn and waited with my hands in my lap for him to gather himself and say what he had to say.

"Baby, can you go live with your Aunt Clementine a while?"

I flicked my head and wondered if I'd heard right. Before I could ask why, Daddy held up his hand to me and explained it all.

"Aunt Frances has a brain tumor. I'm going to go run the farm while she takes treatment. While Fritz takes her to St. Louis."

St. Louis, I thought. Too serious for Rush Hospital, she was going all the way down to St. Louis. I thought of how Aunt Frances had started every morning of her life getting up at 4:30 am in her farmhouse way out on the western prairie and how every morning she had her coffee on the couch in front of the big window and not at the kitchen table with all her kids, just so she could watch the sun come up and the deer graze in her yard. What would she see from her window in St. Louis?

"When will she be home?" I asked Daddy as he began to scrape potatoes into his plate.

"Don't know," he said and ladled gravy over everything.

"Do I have to go to Clem's?"

Daddy took a drink of iced tea and then poured pepper into his palm before sprinkling it on his dinner.

"No," he finally said, "but I'd prefer it. So you're not so alone."

"I was wanting to put in a garden here, Daddy."

"Aunt Clem's got better sun than we do," he cocked his head to the side at me and scratched at his blonde flat top.

"Aunt Clem say it's ok?"

"I don't see why she'd care if you planted a few things."

"No, I mean about my staying there."

"Yes. She agrees. You should come there."

"Can I keep a key to this house?"

"Yes, that'd be good."

And he reached over and took my hand in his and held it a while.

**

"Ed, I'm moving back in with Aunt Clem," I told Ed on the phone.

I'd got up the courage to track down Mrs. Small and ask her for his number the next afternoon after school and I called him before Daddy got home.

I didn't think he would answer. But he did and that was the first thing that popped out of my mouth. No hello or nothing. Just, "I'm moving back to Aunt Clem's."

"Whoa there little Blondie-Locks, who died?"

"No one Ed! Sheesh! Why would you say that?"

"Well, the last time you got dumped there it was cuz your mama died."

"No one died. And no one dumped me there. Sheesh! That is my DADDY you're talking about, Ed!"

"Baby," was all he said and I knew he was grinning from ear to ear over the phone.

"Ed, someone is sick, try to be serious!"

"I am Blondie, who's sick?"

"Aunt Frances."

"That the one that makes all them crazy dresses?"

"Yes. She makes them for her daughters and then gives them to me," I trailed off because it sounded worse when you said it out loud. I was hoping Ed wouldn't say anything about it and he didn't.

"She gonna be ok?"

Baby Small

"I don't know. She's going to St. Louis."

"Wow."

I leaned on the door of the living room and cradled the phone to my cheek and thought of Ed doing the same and I swallowed hard.

"Hope she'll be ok because lord knows you need more hankie dresses."

"Ed. Come home," I blurted out.

"I can't. But I'll be home soon enough, I passed!"

He sounded excited. He sounded too far away. There was too much air between our words.

"Come home for my birthday," I pleaded.

"Baby. I'll try."

Chapter Five

"You're moving back," Petra said to me as we sat on the steps of Aunt Clem's front porch. "You're coming home, school's almost over, and you got a job," she said before she took a huge suck on the straw of her rootbeer float I'd brought home from the Dairy Freeze.
"Yep, I'm coming home. It feels more like home than home does. And I'm excited about my job. Things are good." I sighed and just thought that things were almost perfect.
I'd driven by the Dairy Freeze and seen the help wanted sign three times before I stopped and asked for an application. The old manager brought me an apron as I sat at one of the outside tables and he said to me, "You got the job, Baby Hunnicutt, you just need to fill this out for our records."
Old man Mr. Sosos brought me out a rootbeer float and large fries just ten minutes later when he gave me my first schedule.
"You got a truck, you got a job, you're moving back here, you got Ed coming back, you've got everything. You're across the street again but I ain't ever gonna see you because you'll be working or off with Ed."
"I'll only work nights. And if you want, I'll see if I can get you on too! And during the day when we aren't working, we can go to the pool!"
Petra's face lit up huge as she smiled at me. "The pool," she sighed.
"And Ed won't be home till my birthday."
"That's just a couple of weeks," Petra complained to me, her voice sounding thin.
Just like I had whined to Ed on the phone.
"Two weeks?" I had asked him.
"Two weeks, Blondie."
"Why Ed?"
"Well I passed my flying tests but now I been asked to stay on and learn some engine repair on the small planes."
I didn't know what to say to him.
"It'll help me find a job once I get back home, Baby."
And now here I had a job too.
"Baby," Petra squealed to me, "we'll have to go shop for swimsuits!" She sucked on the straw to her float until it gurgled and she nodded her head to me in excitement.
"Oh no Petra, I'm not shopping with you! You're dangerous!"

"You're still mad about that strapless dress I had you get last year!" she laughed and we both caught each other's eyes and were serious for a minute before laughing again.

**

Later that night after Daddy went to bed, I called Ed again.

"Ed," I whispered into the phone, "it's me."

"Blondie, two calls in one week, you miss me much? Why you whispering? You in church? Huh! Ahuh!"

"Ed. I miss you," I told him with my hand cupped around the phone.

"I'll be home in time for your birthday, Blondie. The sixth, just like I told you. Huh! Ahuh!" he laughed loud in the phone and I was scared Daddy would somehow hear him clear upstairs.

I held my hand completely over the earpiece for a second.

"Blondie? Blondie, you there?" I heard Ed's voice come from under my fingers.

"Ed. I don't have much time to talk. Long distance is expensive. I gotta say it fast."

"Then say it fast," Ed drawled out.

"I don't know what your life is like there," I blurted out.

He was quiet for so long I didn't think he understood me.

"Ed?"

"I'm here. I'm making burritos. I'm hungry, Blondie. Hold on."

I heard pots clanking and I heard Ed breathing as if he were holding the phone with his jaw against it.

And when I thought he'd forgotten me and when I began to panic about how much this was going to cost, he came back on the phone with a grunt and said to me with a soft mouthful of food, "Now what's so urgent Blondie? What do you need to know?"

"What's your place like? What do you do all day? Who, who do you hang out with or do things with?"

What I wanted to ask was, are there any girls, Ed?

I gripped the receiver tight in the dark hallway and waited for him to answer.

"Well," he said and belched quietly. "I live in a one room apartment above a ski shop. It smells like socks and it's too cold and I can't control the heat. I got a couch that folds out into a bed and it ain't the waterbed let me tell ya, Blondie. And I got a little sink and stove and what-all you need to live right here in this one room. I got," he paused and I imagined him scratching his eyebrow and looking around his place in the dark.

"I got," he continued, "a tub and no shower, and a toilet that leaks. I got a little tv and sometimes I can get Charlie's Angels on it but only when the tv is in the bathroom. So," Ed sighed, "I watch it while I take a bath. And uhhh, I got one friend named Patrick and that's about it. We get a beer after class sometimes. And that's about all I know, Blondie. I ain't got the money to ski much or the time either. I do go up the slope when I can. I do odd jobs to get a lift ticket. Basically though, I do school and some odd jobs and I sit around and play the guitar. People always come by when I'm outside on the stoop and they talk some. But mostly I'm just homesick Blondie. I shoulda packed you up and brought you with me. We coulda been cold together."

Here we were both quiet and I needed Ed more now than I ever had.

"I need you Ed," I said it without thinking.

"I need you too Blondie. You move back in Aunt Clem's yet?"

"Not yet. This weekend."

"Who's helping you?"

"Petra."

"Petra?"

"Yes."

"Petra can't even walk, Baby. Huh ahuh!"

"Well Jeffrey's busy with the new baby," I shrugged to the darkened living room.

"Blondie, I gotta get back home to you cuz if I don't, ain't nobody ever gonna take care of you."

"I got Petra!"

"Petra can't even carry a record Baby. If she drops one of your Pink Floyd albums, you'll kill her! Huh! Ahuh!"

"Shoosh!" I hollered at him and covered my mouth and glanced up the black stairs. "Daddy's gonna kill me when he gets the bill for this, Ed! I gotta go!"

"All right Blondie. I'm sure glad you called."

"I miss you Ed."

"I'll see you soon, Blondie Locks."

"Okay," I told him but he'd already hung up.

**

At least I had Petra to keep me company until Ed returned.

"You can't drive me everywhere, Baby. I need to walk to keep up my strength," Petra said as she bumped her way down the stairs in her house.

Her legs jutted straight out ahead of her, locked in that position by her metal braces. Her thin arms didn't have the strength to scoot her gently down the stairs so she had a thin cushion from a kitchen chair under her rear to pad her as she free fell from step to step scooting and banging along down the stairs.

"Besides," she sighed as she banged on down the last step and wiped sweat and a lock of hair off her forehead, "walking to Cloyd's is part of going to Cloyd's. It's the walk that's interesting."

Petra hauled herself up and checked that her braces were locked at the knees and grabbed her walker. With swinging legs and pure grit she swayed and scooted herself out the door and down the ramp of her front porch.

Petra went so slow I had time to look at everything twice.

"Petra what's so interesting about the walk to Cloyd's?" I asked her after we'd only gone a half a block.

"Well there was a moving truck down here last Saturday and I want to see who finally moved in."

"Down where?"

"Linda Kirby's."

At that we both locked eyes, our faces grim instantaneously. Linda Kirby was a thirty year old divorcee who had committed suicide three years ago and they'd never been able to sell the house on account of she'd killed herself in the bathtub.

"I wonder who moved in?" Petra mused as she shoved her walker along.

When I didn't say anything, she continued.

"I wonder if they kept the same tub?"

"That's morbid."

"Why's that morbid?" Petra asked and pulled away from me on the walk.

"I dunno. Thinking about where she died."

"Where people die can be haunted. Or can have a trace. A trace of them can be left behind in that space forever."

I thought about the steps where Mama had collapsed. I thought of how I sometimes paused there and the memory of it all would flare up sharp and bright in my eyes. Maybe Petra was right.

Then I thought of Mrs. Small always painting the trim in her kitchen. The trim Dale had drawn on in marker before getting killed in a car accident. Maybe memories flared up for Mrs. Small every time she looked at that spot in the trim.

"Do you think if there's a bit of that, of her, of that sad event left in that tub that just anyone could see it? Or would it have to be someone close to Linda Kirby in life, to see her after her death?" I asked Petra and was embarrassed that my voice sounded weak and close to crying.

"I don't know, Baby. But maybe we can get in there and get a peek and see."

As we got closer to the Linda Kirby home we could see lots of white boxes stacked up on the curb.

"Mother's Choice Crib" and "Mother's Choice High Chair" and an assortment of the white and green Mother's Choice boxes that had held everything you'd need for a new baby; from diapers to a wind up swing that played music were all stacked up on the curb.

"Wow! Someone sure has a lot of stuff!" Petra said and bumped her walker into the empty boxes.

I thought about Jeffrey and Lisa's baby Olivia and how she slept right in the bed with Jeffrey and Lisa and how during the day she rode around in a sling on Lisa's chest, whether she was awake or asleep. Olivia slept, rode, and fed from that sling. It seemed Lisa could manipulate that paisley cloth to make it become anything she needed for Olivia. Daddy had joked and asked Jeffrey if he was gonna wear it.

"I never knew you needed so much stuff for a baby," I gasped and nudged a box with my toe.

"Maybe they had a shower and everyone chipped in and bought them all matching things! How wonderful! But who would want to raise their baby in the Linda Kirby house?"

I looked over to find Petra's eyes shining in delight as she gaped at all the boxes but then I saw her face turn to horror as she looked up at the house.

"Well, let's go on to Cloyd's," I said and started to walk away.

"Wait!" Petra was breathless. "Wait," she said again and reached out blindly toward my arm and missed. "Someone's coming," she whispered.

"Who? Where?"

I was looking at the front door so at first I didn't see someone come from the carport. Someone round and pregnant in a bright red dress and with red curly hair pulled back in a bow.

"Oh my God," Petra breathed out and covered her lips with her slack hand.

"It's Miss Polkadot," we both whispered at the same time.

"Well hello there," Miss Polkadot chirped to us as she carried yet another white and green cardboard box to the curb.

"Hello Miss Pollock," we both chimed.

Baby Small

Petra's eyes were bulging out of her sockets and near to popping out as she took in Miss Polkadot's tight red dress, the perfectly round tight belly, all the boxes, and roamed back up to the Linda Kirby house.

"Miss Pollock, Miss Pollock," Petra gestured feebly.

"Mrs. Anderson now, Mrs. Todd Anderson," she gushed as she held out a swollen and freckly hand where she wore a skinny gold band and one tiny diamond.

"You, you," Petra gestured with one hand while clutching her walker.

"Pregnant and ready to burst! I know!"

"No, no, you bought the Linda Kirby house!" Petra interrupted her in awe and let her mouth hang open.

Miss Polkadot's happy face fell and she crossed her arms over her swollen chest and she turned and looked at me with her eyes squeezed tense just like she used to do when I'd come in from the playground sweaty and scraped up all those years ago. She looked me up and down just like she had when I was in kindergarten. She took my measure. And I took hers and saw that she had a whole roadmap of tight little wrinkles around her mouth and eyes now.

"Well it's my house now."

She looked at me and gazed pointedly at my flat stomach in my hi-waisted bellbottom jeans and my tight old Pink Floyd shirt and she tsked at me and shook her head.

"That's too bad what happened to you, Baby," she emphasized my name.

I didn't know how to reply. She hadn't said she was sorry and she hadn't asked a question and I just stood there and felt my face burn as I looked down at the metal and leather fasteners on Petra's ankles and felt for sure she'd just insulted me.

"You ever hear from that, that Ed Small or did he leave for good?"

"I hear from him," I said down to the ground.

"Well it's not like there was a reason for him to stay," she said and dusted her hands off after handling all those green and white boxes and assembling what must have been a houseful of baby furniture.

"Let me give you a piece of advice, Baby Hunnicutt. Don't ever get in relations with a man until you get a ring on your finger. And don't ever get in relations with a no good long hair like Ed Small, who is way too old for you."

I looked up at her as she said this, and I couldn't help but notice that her face had turned red hot when she said Ed's name.

"Well let me give you a piece of advice, Miss Polkadot," Petra snapped me out of my shock when she shoved her walker into all the stacked up boxes and knocked them down in the street. "Be careful in that tub of yours in your new house because that dead Linda Kirby will come right out of the plug hole and snatch your baby right up and make it hers!"

"Petra!" I yanked her by the arm towards me but she wasn't done and she snapped right out of my grasp.

"And I know for a fact," Petra snapped at Miss Pollock, her eyes black and shiny and her jaw set tight against her smooth skin, "I know for a fact that you didn't have that two bit piece of tin on your fat finger when you got knocked up with Polkadot Jr. here. The whole town knows Todd Anderson was engaged to Merry Lee Walburn till you turned up preggers and claimed it was his. So you might want to add a leash to your list of things to get, to keep hubby at home, because it seems like he likes to roam!"

"Petra!" I tried to pull her away but she was just getting warmed up.

"And I also know," Petra bit off the words as her lips got tighter and tighter and her jaw tensed up and she pointed her finger at Miss Pollock. "I know for a certifiable fact that Ed Small loves Baby more than anything in the world and there is not one thing wrong with that!"

"Well you are one disturbed little girl if you think that anything between them is all right. Why what they had together isn't nothing but, but," and here Miss Pollock paused and looked me up and down as her face turned crimson and she held her breath for a couple of seconds before nearly shrieking, "statutory rape of a minor!"

Petra and I both stood back for a moment. I was close to tears and completely ashamed that all that kept me from running home was the fact that I knew Petra couldn't keep up with me.

"Statuatory rape is it?" Petra snarled.

"That is all it is. Ed Small is a rapist pedophile and he ought to be in jail! And you are sick and disturbed if you think what he has done to her is ok. I ought to call the law right now and press charges on him and have him arrested as soon as he shows his ugly face back in this town. You can dress it up and call it romance but it ain't nothin', I repeat nothin' but rape of a minor and I think I'll call the cops right now and register my complaint."

"So help me God you do," Petra started to say but not before I cut her off.

"You leave Ed alone! He's done nothing wrong! We're going to get married someday and it's none of your business! What we do doesn't involve you!"

But this wasn't good enough for Petra.

"So help me God," she hissed at Miss Pollock, "you start any trouble around here and I'll come up out of that plug-hole myself and poke you in your fat freckled ass like Satan himself!"

I thought Petra was going to throw her walker at Miss Pollock, pregnant or not for at the end of this last threat, Petra picked up her walker and with all her might and all the balance she could muster, she shook it in the air as the frightened teacher waddled off back to her carport and disappeared into her house.

"She's probably calling the law right now," I said shakily.

"She is not. She's in there changing her pee pants, the old hag."

Petra sounded brave but I saw how her arms trembled when she steered her walker around.

"I don't want to go to Cloyd's anymore, Petra. I just want to go home."

Petra looked at me with a mix of curiosity and fear and anger on her face, but she would never look at me with pity and for that, I loved her.

"Let's just go home, ok?"

"Ok. But living in that house is nothing but asking for bad luck if you ask me, and threatening to hurt you or Ed is guaranteeing bad luck," Petra said and swung her walker around to face the way we had come and to head back home.

Miss Polkadot brought me down very low and I was glad to have my new job as a diversion in the next few days. I was even happier when Mr. Sosos agreed to bring on Petra as a cashier and would have her work when I worked.

She couldn't believe it when I brought her the hat and apron. I looked away when I saw her looking down at her skinny legs in their braces. She never felt sorry for herself out loud but at that moment, for the first time ever, I swore doubt rippled over her face for just a moment and I didn't want her to know I saw.

Petra always took up for me and protected me my whole childhood and she was still fighting for me. I guess that was what had fueled me to work so hard to persuade Mr. Sosos to bring her on.

**

Baby Small

Chapter Six

"Baby Small."

"Ed?"

It was Friday night the first of June and I was settled in at Aunt Clem's and eating popcorn with her on the couch and watching Charlie's Angels. I'd just been thinking of Ed and wondering if Charlie's Angels came on the same time in Colorado as it did in Illinois. I was feeling down because my birthday was coming up and I wasn't sure Ed was going to be there. I was wondering if he'd send me something, when the phone rang.

"What time is it there Baby Small?" Ed asked me.

He sounded serious and I pictured his eyes clear and fixed on some point far off in the mountains and his eyebrows heavy and tense. How I wished I were with Ed in Colorado. Seeing Miss Polkadot had shaken me up for days and I was still feeling it.

"It's 8:15, Ed." I swallowed and waited for him to respond.

"In eighteen hours I'll be there."

"Oh my god!" I jumped up and down on the spot.

"You excited, Baby?" Ed asked me.

He was eating something. I heard the spoon hit his teeth.

"Yes Ed." I was almost panting. One hand was squeezing the phone tight and the other hand was a sweaty fist clamped over my heart.

"Breathe, Baby Small," Ed told me and again I heard his lips smacking against some soft food.

"I can't believe it Ed."

"Believe it Baby Small. I'm coming home," and here he sighed. "I'm coming home and I'm staying home. I'm coming home and I'm not sure I can wait for you. I'm like a starving man, you understand?"

I blinked my eyes several times while I tried to soak it all in.

"Yes Ed. I do. I'm pretty hungry myself."

"Well there's hungry and then there's hungry, and then there's no sense letting good chow go to waste."

"Are we talking about food now, Ed? Or the other thing?"

"Huh! Ahuh! The other thing."

"Me too, Ed," I told him and my face burned and I faced away from Aunt Clem and stared at the wall.

"I have to go now, Blondie-locks. Speaking of food, I gotta eat as much food as I can from my ice box before I move out. But I'm getting on the train in an hour, pants buttoned or not," and here he belched. "But

I'll be there in about eighteen hours. And I'm coming to get you, Blondie. And I'm gonna steal a kiss. Because I miss you Blondie. I miss my Baby," and he sighed again and gulped another huge bite of something and smacked his lips.

"Oh my gosh, Ed! I'm so excited I'm freaking out!" I jumped up and down till it hurt my feet right there in Aunt Clem's dining room and caused all the plates in the china cabinet to rattle and Aunt Clem to turn around from the tv and look at me. "Two o'clock tomorrow my time, Ed," I said into the phone behind my cupped hand.

"Blondie I'm not sure what it'll be your time, hell I just got used to mountain time, but I'll come find you. Don't leave town and don't lock the door. Huh! Ahuh!" and he laughed and shoved another spoonful of whatever he was eating into his mouth. Ice cream I imagined. And he hung up before I could tell him one hundred times that I loved him more than life. And before I could tell him I'd be at work at 2 pm Saturday. He didn't even know of my job at the Dairy Freeze.

**

"Petra, Petra, Petra," I must have said her name a thousand times the next day as we finished working the lunch shift in the blinding summer sun.

"Three fifteen Baby, same as it was twenty seconds ago when you came flying in here and knocked all my straws on the floor."

Petra popped her gum and continued stocking her condiment station with her back to me. She was lining all the salt packets up perfect as could be after us carhops had ransacked her little cubbies during the lunch rush.

"I hope Ed knows where to find me. I hope Ed remembers I moved back in with Aunt Clem. I hope Mrs. Small remembers to tell him I'm working. I hope Ed gets here ok. I hope I can get off work early."

"Jeez Louise Baby Hunnicutt take a pill, calm down, or go mop the parking lot or something but get out of here. You're giving me heart palpitations!"

"Customer Baby, slot 12," Mr. Sosos called to me from where he sat at a little desk counting dimes.

"Welcome to Dairy Freeze, may I take your order," I said into the little speaker.

"Uhh, yes, I'll take four double cheeseburgers and two vanilla cokes and four fries and two chocolate shakes and better throw in some onion rings because this little blonde hell cat that's meeting me here eats more than she weighs! Huh! Ahuh!"

"Oh my God! ED!" I screamed into the speaker box and threw my pen and pad and ran out the door as fast as I could to the black Cutlass sitting low on its fat wheels parked in the back corner slot.

And there was Ed hanging out the window with a giant blazing smile on his face and his hair long and golden with a full beard on his happy face. He was hanging out the window, clutching the biggest bouquet of daisies you ever did see. He hung out the window and just nodded and smiled at me as I ran to him. And as I got closer he climbed out the window, daisies, hair and all and got one of his hiking boots stuck in the window and fell on the pavement right on his butt.

He was wearing bib overalls over a white t-shirt and as he lay there on his backside, still holding all those flowers, I fell on him and wrapped my arms around him.

"Baby Small, where's my tray? I need gut-waddin', I'm darn near starved!" he cried as he squeezed me around my waist as I clung to his neck and lay on top of him right there in the parking lot of the Dairy Freeze.

Chapter Seven

"I love you," I whispered in his hair as I kissed his sideburns, his jaw, his lips. "I love you Ed." I told him again and again. "You're home in time for my birthday. What'd you bring me?"

"Baby Small, hold on there," Ed mumbled to me as I held his face in my hands.

We were on Aunt Clem's front porch in the warm night and I held his face in my hands and kissed him under his jaw where his neck was warm.

"I missed you Ed," I whispered and bumped my lips over the beard on his chin. I knew his dimple was under there somewhere but I couldn't find it.

I ran my fingers through his long hair and felt his sweaty scalp under my fingertips and closed my eyes and listened to the night.

"Take it easy, Blondie. I'm home."

I stopped kissing him on the face and rested my cheek on his shoulder but the fastener to his overalls dug into the skin on my face.

I couldn't get comfortable next to him. I wanted in his lap. I wanted his arms around me. I wanted under him. I wanted Ed.

"I've changed my mind. I know what I want for my birthday," I said with my eyes closed.

"Blondie. I know now you ain't but turning seventeen and I ain't sure that's legal. So I'm doing my best to be good," he said and nodded his head with each word. His hair swayed in the light from the front room window as he said it. "I'm trying Blondie to not, to not, you know," he trailed off with his eyebrows pinched and serious as his hair fell in his eyes.

He looked innocent for once as he rubbed his nose with a finger and rocked back and forth on the step.

"I'm just doing what you wanted, Blondie," he pleaded and held out his hand.

For a minute I was hurt and scared that Ed didn't love me anymore. I sat on the step and stared at him and felt crushed until just as sudden he turned and smiled at me. His eyes bright as star's light and his smile wide; he set my heart to pounding hard and slow.

"Blondie-pants," he said to me and batted his lashes. "Let me be good." He licked his lips and scratched at his armpit and looked everywhere but at me.

Baby Small

"Ed?"

"What?" he asked and pooched out his lips in that familiar old tic of his.

"Ed? Don't you?"

"Don't I what, Blondie?"

My face flushed hot and my eyes stung.

"What is it you want, Blondie?"

"You know, Ed. I want," I gulped and faltered.

"What?"

Even in the shadowy moonlight on Aunt Clem's front porch I could see his eyebrow point up in a teasing slant.

"What, Blondie? Tell me what you want."

And now he had a hold of my face in his big hand; his thumb on my chin, his full lips open and rubbing mine. "You want something Blondie?"

"Yes."

"You want me to go to jail?" he giggled.

"No," I gasped and pushed his hands away from me.

"You want the neighbors to call the law?"

"No!" I said and scooted further back from him.

"You want to tempt me Baby?"

"No Ed, I don't."

"What do you want then, Blondie?" he asked and scooted closer to me.

I could smell his old familiar scent of smoke and hair and sweat and sunshine and I licked my lips as if I could taste him in the air. But I refused to look at him. I stared up at the ceiling of the porch; at the white slats above me and I swallowed hard and closed my eyes.

"I'm lonesome for you Ed," I finally said and winced at how pathetic it sounded.

"You want to wear me down, Blondie?" he asked with his lips thick and soft on the corners of all the words.

"I don't know what you mean," I lied and kept my eyes shut but could feel my pulse throbbing in my lids.

"You are trying," Ed said with his mouth near my ear, "to wear me down, Blondie-locks."

I kept my eyes pinched shut but I felt his body come closer and I pressed my back against the side rail of the porch steps.

"Wearing me down," he mumbled with his lips in my hair.

I tried to move away. I tried to sit up straight. I fidgeted with my hair and kept my eyes clamped shut. Ed's hand found my own as I fussed with my barrette and I heard him tsk tsk me and it gave me the goosebumps as I felt him pry it open and slip it from my hair.

"Ed," I complained to him as he shoved the plastic barrette in the pocket of his overalls. "Ed I'm trying to be good," I started to say but he was on me, sliding his arms around me, pushing me on my back on the floor of the old porch.

"Ed," I blinked as the back of my head landed on the old wood and my heart erupted as he climbed on top of me.

I strained my eyes to see him in the dark but all I saw was an old moth flutter its way out of the dim porch light and fly out in the night.

"Ed, hold" I told him but my lips were covered by his hair as he pressed closer to me right there on Aunt Clem's front porch and pushed my knees apart with a grunt.

"You there Blondie?" he whispered down to me with his hair hanging around his face. "You ok, Blondie? It's quiet and dark and you feel so small under me."

"I'm here, Ed," I said up to his face in the dark.

I saw that his eyebrows were set in a serious angle as he tucked his hair behind his ears.

"You wore me down, Blondie."

"I didn't."

"You're doing it right now, right here, laying there quiet and beautiful with your eyes all wide. I'd do anything for you Blondie. Anything. You name it. Let's go back to my place," he whispered and time felt urgent.

"Just wait for me Ed," I said up to him.

"I am waiting, Blondie."

"Wait for me to grow up a little more. Wait for me right here." I pulled on his hair to get his attention.

"Right here?" Ed asked and glanced around at the dark porch from where he was propped up over me.

"Right here Ed, in La Rue," I said and pulled on a hank of his hair a little more. "Don't go back to Colorado." Just saying it, just asking him to not go back, just mentioning Colorado hurt me in the back of my throat and I had to swallow the panic away.

"Well about that," he said and he looked away. The dim porch light made his eyes shine aquamarine in the moonlight. "About that, Blondie, I won't be in La Rue much."

I couldn't look at him. I couldn't open my eyes after he said that.

"Penny for your thoughts, Blondie."

"Nothing," I shrugged and held him at arm's length above me.

Baby Small

    I wanted to go in Aunt Clem's and back to my old room and collapse on my bed. I wanted my headphones on and I wanted to listen to records until I was grown; until I could do whatever I wanted. I shut my eyes and willed my bottom lip to not shake. I wouldn't cry over Ed. I wouldn't cry over his refusal to stay in town I wouldn't cry over him leaving town whenever her felt like and leaving me behind.

    "Baby."

    "What?" I asked and still wouldn't open my eyes.

    I felt ready to fight. Ready to let him have it. I squeezed fistfuls of his shirt as I held him.

    "Baby." He ran his thumb over my bottom lip and I opened my eyes to find him grinning at me as if I'd done something silly.

    "What?" I asked and stuck out my chin at him. I failed to find anything funny.

    "Baby. I'll be living right here. But I'll be working over at Rush. I'm the on-call helicopter pilot for the hospital and a mechanic at the Rush Airport."

    "What?"

    "I'm not going back to Colorado, Baby."

    "Oh."

    And here he laughed at me and when I asked "What?" again, he punched me in the arm with what he must have thought was playfulness but I lay there under him and rubbed my arm and thought of Ed never leaving again.

    "I'll be right here, Baby," he said and rolled off me and stood up and reached for my hand and pulled me up. "I'll be right here like a good Ed, waiting for you to grow up a little."

    He pulled me over to him and slung his arm around my shoulder and squeezed me to him.

    "Gonna be hard," I heard him whisper and glanced at him to see him shaking his head and his hair falling in his eyes.

    "I'm about beat, Baby Small," he sighed. "And as much as I'd like to sleep on your rug like old times' sake, you and I both know I'd never stay there so I'm gonna head back to mom's. But I'll be over tomorrow. You can bank on that. And we'll catch up after I get off work." And he sighed again and seemed sad.

    He kissed me on the side of my forehead and gave my shoulder a last squeeze before leaping over the railing on the porch and heading back to Mrs. Small's. I watched his long hair dance between his shoulder blades as he jogged across the yard in the dark.

    **

Baby Small

    The next afternoon was a hot one and the Dairy Freeze was packed from lunch time till the end of our shift and everyone seemed to know Ed Small was back in town.

    "How long's he here for?"

    "Where's he staying?"

    "Why is he back?"

    "How do you feel about it?"

    "Have you seen him?"

    "Was he in jail out there?"

    The whole town had their questions about him; from the kids I went to school with, to the local beat cop, to the owner of the La Pierre restaurant.

    "I'd take him back on as a waiter," Mr. Jackotea of the La Pierre said to me and he smiled and smoothed down his mustache as I hung his tray on his window. "He'd be good for business!"

    "He's got a job. He's got two jobs, Mr. Jackotea," I told him as I tore his bill off my pad and handed it to him.

    "Are you sure? What kind of jobs?"

    And I filled him in and everyone else too as they called to me from their car windows and wanted to know all about the return of Ed Small.

    Girls came in by the dozens. Girls in convertibles. Girls in beaters. Young girls and older girls. Girls Ed's age came in a pack in a new Monte Carlo and they specifically asked for me to be their server. The cook said he was gonna stand me on a coke crate with a megaphone and have me give the Ed speech to everyone at once so I could actually get some work done and stop having to answer so many questions to everyone.

    The girls in the Monte Carlo had gone to high school with Ed and I felt too young when I looked at them. I knew a couple of them were divorced and had kids. And I knew Karen who was at the wheel had never married at all. It was her who asked me if it was true that Ed was working at Rush Hospital.

    "Well, not really at the hospital," I said to her as all her friends strained to poke their faces out the window at me and hear the gossip on Ed.

    I shifted from foot to foot and bent my order pad in half and hoped they'd order soon.

    "I heard he's working at the hospital," Karen tilted her head to the side and looked up at me from where she sat behind the wheel of her new car.

    She twisted her lips and looked smug.

The eyes of the other girls flicked to Karen and then back to me, click click, as they looked at my face for my response.

"Well he's on call for the hospital. When they need a medi-flight, then they radio him. But other than that he does," I started to explain but was cut off.

"But I heard he was moving to Rush," Karen interrupted. "I heard that he has to be closer to the hospital. Is that true?"

Flick flick, the girls looked again at Karen and then to me.

"No. No, he's living with his mom. He's not moving." But my voice sounded unsure. It sounded young compared to hers and I felt stupid and I felt Ed slipping away from me, from my hand and into hers.

Ed had come over that morning around nine while Aunt Clem and I were putting away the cereal and washing up our bowls. I had rinsed my bowl and spoon just to have Ed take it from me just as he took the Frosted Flakes box from Aunt Clem as she put it into the cupboard.

Ed hadn't said anything about moving to Rush. He'd only sat there looking bleary eyed and tired as he ate two bowls of cereal and drank a tall glass of Qwik and told us how his mom was doing. He hadn't said anything about moving. He'd told me about the radio he had to carry with him at all times when he was on call and that he needed to be ready to drive to Rush Field where the medi-copters were. He'd never mentioned moving closer to the hospital.

"What can I get you?" I now asked the girls while I was at their car.

"Oh we don't want anything here," Karen's lips curled as she told me this and her friends all sneered and sat back in their seats. They had nothing else to ask me about Ed. Karen looked down her nose at me as she flicked the button on her electric window and then tore out of the slot right in front of my eyes.

The whole town knew Ed was back. And everywhere I went everyone was talking about him.

"I need to get out of La Rue," I told Petra after work.

It was close to 90 degrees out at 4 that afternoon and we were both shiny from sweat and smelling like French fries.

Petra's eyes lit up as she slung her walker into the bed of my truck. The only way she had the strength to get it back there was to heave it with a twist of her entire body. I winced when it landed in the bed of the truck but I would never offer to put it back there for her. She'd be mad at me for weeks if I did.

"Rushing Waters!" she squealed at me after she dusted her hands off.

"What?"

"The new water park Rushing Waters is open!"

"New water park? What about the pool?"

"Closed," Petra stated as she yanked the door of the truck open.

"Closed?" I asked her as I slid into my seat and watched her haul herself up in the cab.

"Closed," she said and coughed. "Crack in the pool last summer and a slow leak. They sold it. Remember? And built Rushing Waters out by Rush Lake this past Fall."

She looked at me as if to say, where you been? But she thought better of it and began to bounce up and down on the squeaky old seat. She looked as if she could barely contain her excitement.

"They're open till midnight!" she clapped her hands. "We can go there and then cruise Rush for college boys before heading back to town! Thank God you have this truck or we'd be stuck in town yet another summer!"

"There won't be any boys at the college, Petra. It's summer!"

"Oh," she said and her face darkened a bit.

"I need to call Ed," I told her as I put the truck in gear and began to pull out in traffic. "But we'll go sometime and it'll be fun!" I tried to cheer her up.

She was quiet while I drove.

"I have to see him, don't you understand?"

But she didn't understand.

I knew Petra was looking at me with her side-long glare without even having to glance over at her and I heard her growl her disapproval and I pumped the gas and shifted low to drown her out with the loud engine. She wasn't happy with me calling Ed. She was afraid I'd ditch her for him. But she didn't have anything to worry about.

"Ed's at work dear, and won't be home till six or seven and then he's on call," Mrs. Small told me when I called over there, which meant he was working as a mechanic at the airfield and also on call to fly the helicopter for the hospital. "His first night home and he's on call," she said and I could picture her shaking her head at the kitchen table.

I didn't have the heart to tell her that it was really his second night home. I just asked her to tell him I'd called and that I'd be at the pool.

"I hope Ed knows what pool we're at," I told Petra as we bounced on the bench seat of the truck as we flew down the black-top out of La Rue and on our way to the edge of Rush and the Rushing Waters water park.

Baby Small

    Petra didn't even care. She was decked out in her new black and white checked swimsuit and matching flip flops. She'd even managed to somehow paint her nails to match her new suit in the short time we were home after work. She sat on the bench seat now with her fingers splayed out in the air, letting the polish dry the rest of the way.

    She didn't have a care in the world. If she was worried about getting around the water park with her walker she didn't show it. If she was worried about people staring at her new plastic leg braces she had to wear, she didn't mention that either.

    What she was worried about was boys. What I was worried about was people staring at my scar on my chest and I fiddled with my swimsuit top under my cover-up as I drove.

    "I hope there's some decent boys there," Petra interrupted my thoughts and brought my eyes back to the road. "Maybe some boys from Rush. Maybe some boys who aren't jerks. Maybe I need an older boy like Ed." And on and on she went as we drove through the hot corn fields with the wind whipping through the cab of the truck.

    Rushing Waters was nothing like the old public pool. It was crowded and hard to people watch because no one was sitting still. Everyone was always moving; people were moving in line for the slides or carrying tubes for the wave pool, or in line for snacks. As the sun went down the slides lit up with flashing blue lights that made everything look as if it were moving faster than what it was.

    Petra parked her walker at the bottom of the first slide and enlisted three football players from school to help carry her up the slopes to the top of the slides. They bypassed all the crowd and all the lines. I watched her as she sat atop their shoulders like Cleopatra.

    "Handicapped girl coming through," I could hear them calling and the crowds parted for them.

    "Hush now! I ain't handicapped!" I could hear Petra scolding them. The last I saw of her before she got to the top of the slide was her slapping them on the shoulders.

    I stood there and held my breath as I watched her fly down the steepest, straightest slide; her body sleek and tiny but from where I stood, for just a moment she looked normal. But she looked tiny and helpless without her walker when she slid into the pool. I took a step towards her but before I could jump in, she was pulled out by another football player and taken to the side of the pool.

    I watched her go down the slide three times as people jostled me on all sides as the sun went completely down and the crowd grew noisier and tighter and the rock music was turned up louder on the speakers.

Baby Small

    The third time she slid down the steepest slide like a sleek squealing bullet, I followed her and the football players up the concrete slope and I bypassed all the waiting teenagers and with no regard for my heart or its special condition, I went down with Petra again and again till we were cold and starving and exhausted and were told by the pool loudspeakers to leave as it was midnight and they were closing.

    Petra booed the speakers and then later said in the orange glow of the cab of the truck, "I don't care if I die tonight. I had the time of my life tonight." She patted her slicked back hair with a beach towel as we bounced home and I heard her sigh.

    "I did too," I said and I meant it even as I mashed the throttle to the floor and I sped us home with only thoughts of dropping her off and going to see Ed as soon as possible.

    Petra was sound asleep and sliding down in the seat with only the seatbelt keeping her from sliding down in the floor by the time we pulled up in her drive.

    "Oh my gosh, Petra. How am I going to get you up to your room?"

    The Post's house was completely dark and quiet. It was half past midnight and I didn't see how I could get her up the porch stairs and into the house without dropping her or making a ruckus. I couldn't bear to think of waking her. I was exhausted myself from working all day in the heat and water sliding all night. I got out of the truck and listened hard to the quiet night for a sound or some idea but all I heard were crickets and all I saw were dark curtained windows. Mr. and Mrs. Post were sure to have gone to bed hours before.

    And still Petra slept in the cab of the truck with her mouth slightly open. I was just walking over to her side of the truck to wake her up when I heard "Huh! Ahuh!" and stopped dead.

    The lights were on across the street at Aunt Clem's. I strained my eyes to see Ed on the front porch but I could see nothing in the dark except the flickering of the tv on the ceiling of Aunt's Clem's living room.

    "Huh! Ahuh!" It came again and I jumped, torn between staying with Petra and with leaving her in the dark only for a moment to go get Ed.

    With a parting light pat to Petra's hand which was resting in the open window of the truck, I dashed across the street to get Ed.

    Aunt Clem's living room was loud and bright to my eyes that were used to the dark and to my ears that had heard nothing but the engine of the truck and the sigh of the tires on the blacktop the past half hour.

Baby Small

Ed was propped up in Aunt Clem's recliner, barefoot and shirtless with an exploded foil ball of Jiffy Pop popcorn on his lap. I could see the buttery shine on his lips and fingertips as he watched tv with a huge smile on his face and laughter lines on the corners of his eyes.

Aunt Clem, small in her house coat was asleep on the end of the couch; her face slack and her teeth out.

"Baby Hunni," Ed called to me, "bout time you got home. Staying out all hours making me feel like you ain't even glad I'm home," Ed grinned and wiped his fingers off on his jeans and began to get up without folding the recliner back up so as to not wake up Aunt Clem.

"Ed," I whispered and darted a glance at Aunt Clem. "I need your help."

I beckoned for him to come out on the porch.

"Is that so?" he asked and smiled his old wolfish smile and winked at me and came out on the porch. His smile made me feel like I had popcorn butter on my insides.

"What is it you need help with Baby?" he asked after he came down the porch stairs on silent bare feet.

"I need you to carry Petra up to her bed," I whisper-called at him as I walked backwards back across the street to my truck where Petra still slept.

"Shit mother fuck," Ed growled as his hair fell in his face and his walk faltered in the middle of the street.

"Please Ed? I can't do it myself," I waved to him to come to me.

"No way," he rasped at me after he peeked in the truck window and saw Petra slumped over and snoring.

"Please, Ed," I pleaded to him and began to open the door to the truck.

"No fucking way," he said and backed away from me with his hands held out.

Work him, I thought to myself. Work him, wrap him around your finger.

"Please, for me?" I stepped towards him and batted my eyes up at him.

"No Baby Hunnicutt, turn it off, stop, that's not fair." But he'd already changed direction and was now taking long steps back towards the truck. With a determined look pinching his forehead he looked at me one last time as he tucked his hair behind his ears and leaned into the cab to scoop up Petra.

**

"I coulda been killed."

Baby Small

"Oh, Ed."

"That old man," Ed shivered and shook out his hair.

"Oh Ed he didn't even hear us."

"I risked my life. Thank God she didn't wake up. That girl is dangerous in all ways."

"Petra?" I asked. "Petra's harmless," I said up to Ed and pushed away from his bare side. We were walking back to Aunt Clem's and he pulled me close to him as we crossed the street.

"She's sex crazed. She always has been. Gives me the heebies the way she stares at me. She's kooky as ever."

"Well yes. I agree with all that." I smiled up at the moon in the dark summer night.

"But then again so are you, Blondie."

"What?" I tried to shove away from him as he pulled me into a headlock up on the porch and began dutch rubbing my head.

"Baby? Ed?" We heard Aunt Clem call from the living room.

"You home Baby?" I heard her small voice and I sighed.

"Yes, Aunt Clem," I answered from where Ed still held me under his armpit with all my hair in my face.

"It's all right, Blondie. It's late and I gotta git. I gotta long day tomorrow working and I suspect you do too." And he let go of me and helped me get all my hair out of my face.

"But Ed, I," I trailed off.

"Hush girl," he told me and pulled me to him and put his salty hand over my lips. I looked up at him and was quiet.

I wanted to go home with him and sleep in his waterbed next to him.

"Hush," he said again like he read my mind. He leaned down to me and kissed my lips lightly. "You smell like pool, Blondie and you've let your hair dry in a tangle. I'll leave you to your bath and I'll leave you to your sweet dreams."

But he didn't leave. He kissed me, his lips just brushing mine and then he ran his fingers over my bottom lip.

I tried to push his hand away from my mouth but he held firm, his fingers hot on my lips.

"We have all the time we need Blondie." He pulled me closer and with his hand.

I blinked and he let go of me and was over the rail of the porch and in his car before I could even follow him with my eyes in the dark.

I left my truck at Petra's and went into the house. I could hear Aunt Clem in the kitchen filling the tea kettle. Without saying anything to her I went to the bathroom and filled up the tub and sunk into the warm suds

and a hundred memories as I washed away the pool smell with the baby shampoo.
**

"Ed doesn't love me anymore."

"Shut up and get your french fries before Marcie steals them."

"He didn't even give me a kiss goodnight."

"You're forgetting I'm not talking to you. French fries, go."

Petra slammed two fistfuls of French fries on my tray and turned her back to me.

"Why aren't you talking to me, again?" I asked her after I delivered the tray of food.

"You had Ed carry me up to bed," she stamped her foot at me as she counted dimes in the register after I delivered the order.

"You were asleep!"

"I know!" She raised her eyebrows at me and threw the dimes back in the drawer and slammed it.

"You should have warned me you were gonna have Ed carry me. You know I'd want to be awake for that!" She spun away from me and scooted her walker toward the condiment stand and began straightening the straws. Everything always had to be neat with Petra.

"Next time I'll wake you!" I followed her on to the ketchup. "Promise!"

"Oh," she sighed. "Next time." And then her eyes glittered and lit up. "There's always tonight!"

"Petra."

"What?"

"I want to spend time with Ed tonight."

"Darn it I wanted to go back to the pool. And besides Ed doesn't love you anymore, remember?"

"Were you even listening?"

"Of course I was. Come on you and Ed have each other for the rest of all time. I just want one more night at the pool."

"Ugh."

But I called Ed after I dropped Petra off at her house.

"Baby, I'm plum worn out."

"Ed," I whined into the phone where I shifted from foot to foot in Aunt Clem's dining room. "Ed I want to see you. I miss you. Can you come over"

Aunt Clem wouldn't be home for another two hours and I wanted to make plans with Ed right away. I wanted to be gone before she got home.

Baby Small

I didn't want her to see my face before I left to be with Ed. I was afraid of what it might give away.

I didn't want to go to the pool.

I'd been running orders all afternoon, waiting on teens who were either on their way out to Rushing Waters or had just come back to town after spending the day there.

Petra had bugged me all day; asking me if we could go. Telling me we should go. Begging me to take her. Threatening to ask the next carload of boys that drove up to take her. I'd almost drove home without her.

"You just want to be with Ed. That's all you care about. I don't blame you. I wouldn't hesitate to ditch you if I had an Ed myself," she groused all the way home as I drove in silence.

"Just let me call him!" I hollered to Petra after I helped her out of the truck and I watched her scoot her walker into the front door of her house. "Just let me see what he's doing, Petra!" I yelled from the window of my truck as I backed across the street into Aunt Clem's drive.

But Ed wasn't interested in seeing me.

"I'm starved and I'm tired and I want to take a nap. I think I got jet lag."

"But Ed you came home on a train!"

"Well train lag then."

"Well come over and take a nap and I'll watch you sleep. I just miss you Ed."

"Baby."

"Please Ed, or you could go to the pool with us and that'll wake you up!" That was a great idea and I was glad I thought of it. But he didn't think so.

"I'm worn out Baby. I worked all night and was on call today too and I just want quiet and besides, the pool is for kids. I ain't a kid anymore, Baby Small," he said to me and it felt like a punch in the heart.

"Is that so? Is that what you think in that head of yours, Ed Small? Is that what you think underneath all that hair?"

"It is, Baby Small. It is," he said and I could hear him drinking something in one big long swallow. Probably milk right out of the carton.

"Fine." And I hung up on him and before I could even begin to cry I unplugged the phone so he couldn't call me back and say words like, come on Baby hell-cat or anything like that.

"I'm not your hell-cat and I'm not Baby Small," I said to the dead phone and I went and changed into my bikini and grabbed a paperback book.

Baby Small

      Petra found me in the back yard scooting my chair to follow the 4 o'clock sun that was still strong and hot in the sky. She rammed her walker into the gate and shook the whole fence and hollered for me.
      "Come on Baby let's go! Time's a wasting and you're already dressed for it!"
      "Ok Petra."
      With a nervous backwards glance in the rearview mirror I took us out of La Rue and out past Rush to another evening of water slides. I kept looking over my shoulder after we got there. I'd ditched Ed. Something I'd never ever done. Even as a kid. But what did it matter? He was too good for the pool. He was all grown up and we were just kids.
      I frowned and crabbed as Petra and I dipped fat salty pretzels into cups of cheese as we sat on top of a table surrounded by football players in the snack area when I heard him.
      "BLONDIE!"
      I looked around but didn't see him at first.
      "Blondie! What in tarnation are you wearing?"
      And when the football players scattered, there was Ed.
      "What?" I asked him and crossed my legs from where I sat perched on top of the table with Petra balanced carefully next to me.
      "What?" I asked again and dunked my last bit of pretzel in the cheese and ate it.
      "Jesus. If you don't look half naked. And goshdarn if them cheeseburgers don't smell good," he turned away from me, distracted, and sniffed and looked around at the grill and the concession stand.
      "By God we're getting some food and then you're coming home!"
      He grabbed my arm and started to pull me off the table.
      "I am not!" I snapped and I pulled my arm away from him.
      "Blondie. I'm getting a sack of food and you better be ready to get your behind in my car."
      "I will not. I drove myself. And Petra too. I can't leave her."
      "You can go, Baby. Go!" Petra whispered with her mouth hidden behind her hand. "I can get a ride. I'll be fine. Go ahead." Her eyes were huge as she stared at Ed as he lumbered off to the concession line. He looked like a tan wildman when he stood next to all the teens in their bathing suits and he in his faded out old jeans and work shirt that said Ed on the left pocket.
      "Really Petra?"
      "Yes and oh my gosh look who's here! It's Kai!"
      There in the sea of clean-cut football players gathered around our table was Kai. Quiet and smiling, he shyly came up to our table.

Baby Small

"Hi," he said and gave us a half wave.

"Kai, you and Baby can play catch-up another time because she has to go, now!" Petra pinched me and shooed me off towards Ed.

"Are you sure?" I asked her and couldn't stop looking at Kai.

"I'll get a ride with Kai and give you the scoop later."

**

"Baby Small I just want to love you. I don't want nothing between us. Hanging up on me on the phone and all."

Ed trailed off in deep mumblings I couldn't understand as he rubbed his lips with the back of his hand. His eyes had dark smudges under them and he looked completely exhausted, yet he still had a curl of a smile on the corners of his lips. Maybe he was thinking about the cheeseburgers he'd just devoured on the ride home.

"Ed you embarrassed me."

I was mad at Ed yet I was so pleased he'd come out to find me at the water slides.

The whole time I was driving Petra and I out to Rushing Waters I'd felt a nagging in the back of my heart that kept telling me to go back and plug in the phone. Go back and call Ed and say sorry and beg him to come over. If he just knew how important it was to me, he wouldn't be so tired.

But the further away from home we went in the truck, the more impossible it seemed to do just that, till finally we were at the water park.

Ed showing up had embarrassed me, even though I was happy to see him. I felt like everyone in the water park had froze to stare at us. And then there was Kai who I didn't even get a chance to talk to.

"How'd I embarrass you?" he asked, interrupting my thoughts.

"Showing up at the pool and hollerin' at me like I, like I," I couldn't finish it.

And I didn't have to.

"Like you're my own true love child?" he asked as a smile as bright as the mountain sunshine lit up his face.

"Yes," I blushed.

"You hung up on me with that temper of yours. I had to come out there and get you." And here he hung his head and shook his hair in his face and we were both quiet for a bit.

"You worried about Petra?" Ed asked me, coming out of his thoughts and reading my own.

"No. Well. Yes. Maybe."

"He's pretty harmless. She'll be ok."

Ed was referring to Kai. Kai who'd shown up at the pool just as he did. I'd not even seen Kai at school this past year and here he had just popped up out of the crowd of strange faces with his familiar brown eyes and curly hair. He had smiled at us like nothing had ever happened between him and me; between him and Allen.

I had a hard time looking at his face. Even though it'd been months since Allen had beaten him, I was afraid his face would still show signs of being beat. I was afraid his eyes would show it as well. But he looked like sweet Kai; my old Kai I'd known since kindergarten, and he gave me hope that maybe my own eyes didn't reflect everything I'd been through the past year.

"Of course I can help get Petra home," Kai had said. And I'd left him there rubbing his peeling nose, standing next to Petra.

"How will he get her home?" Ed mused now and I heard the laughter in his voice and shot him a look. He was running his fingers through his hair and letting it all fall in his face and not even looking at me. He scratched his chin as if thinking about it and I heard his fingers scrape on his whiskers.

"On his bike?" Huh! Ahuh!" he snorted.

I didn't say anything but I shot him another sharp look.

"Huh! Ahuh!" he laughed some more and rocked back as he sat on my rag rug in my bedroom at Aunt Clem's.

I shushed him and began to brush my hair as I sat on the edge of the bottom bunk.

Ed kicked off his boots and he relaxed on the floor as the giggles rippled through him. His stomach rolled with each wave of explosion of laughter.

"It's not funny."

"It is," he said as he coughed a few times into his hand. "It is Baby. It is. I can picture him pulling her with her walker behind him on that bike of his."

"Don't make fun of Kai or Petra!"

"I'm not making fun of your friend." And here he sobered up fast and sat up straight. His eyes got round and dark and he pushed his hair behind his ears and looked at me. "I wouldn't Blondie. I wouldn't."

Ed got on his knees and crawled over to me where I sat on the bed. "God's honest truth, I would never make fun of your kooky friend. But that boy on the bike, I might."

"Don't Ed."

"That sandal wearing little man with his curly hair, I can make fun of him if I like."

"Ed don't. I've known Kai all my life."

"Excuse me?" he asked with his bottom lip stuck out and his hands gripping the mattress on either side of where I sat.

"I've known him since forever, Ed. Since kindergarten. Remember?"

"Baby Hunnicutt." That was all he said as he narrowed his eyes at me.

"What?"

"I don't believe it."

"What?"

Ed was shaking his head back and forth at me as if he couldn't believe what I'd done, whatever it was.

"What?" I asked again.

"You known him since forever," he mumbled and shook his head at me some more.

"I have."

"Baby Hunnicutt I known you since you was born. I was there when your mama and daddy brought you home. I was there since the beginning. I was there before you came home; I was there when you did come home. I'm the one that's known you forever. I'm the one who was there when you got your period, for Christ's sake."

"Don't blaspheme!"

I reached out to grab his arm hair but he pushed away from me and lay back on his back with his eyes shut.

"Oh my God, Blondie," he sighed, "I still don't like that little whelp."

I watched Ed as he cracked his knuckles and rubbed the corners of his eyes with his fingers. His hair flowed all around his head and his chest rose and fell under his work shirt.

"Kai's all right." I shrugged but Ed didn't see me.

A frown twisted his lips while he still lay on the floor. "He's ok," I said in an attempt to get him to quit frowning. "He's just a kid."

And at that a storm rippled over his face. Lines formed like thunderheads on his forehead and pressed heavy on his eyebrows. His eyelids tensed and darkened and I knew if he opened them they'd be full of frost and would bore through me.

"Just a kid," he grumbled and rolled on to his side.

I watched as he pushed up off the floor. His arms flexed and his shirt pulled tight across his back. With a swinging of his hair he got up on all fours and came to me like a broad backed bear.

"He ain't just a kid, Blondie."

Ed gripped the mattress hard and pulled close to my face as I sat there. My arm went limp and I dropped the hairbrush with a thock on the floor that drew Ed's attention away from me for just a second. I looked away from him in that moment to break away from the tension coming off of him. The early evening sun blazed like liquid gold between the window curtains and I let it warm me before looking back into Ed's cool eyes.

"Kai ain't just a kid and neither are you Blondie," he said and came closer on every word.

He touched my chin with his thumb and tilted my face up to his own. With his eyes fixed on mine he brushed his lips against my mouth. His breath was warm against my skin and I shut my eyes.

"Not just a kid, Baby," he said with his lips bumping mine on the beginning of each word.

"Ed."

My own lips rubbed against his just barely and shivers ran clear to the tips of my hair.

"Blondie."

He pressed his forehead on mine and I breathed him in. The scents were as familiar as my childhood. As my mind raced ahead a hundred miles an hour and my heart beat clear up in my throat, I reached out and took a hold of his rough shirt.

"Aunt Clem will hear," I warned him as I looked up into his eyes.

He grinned down at me as his hair cascaded into his face and he quickly pushed it behind his ears. He licked his lips and then ran his tongue over my top lip while he stared down at me. Still he kept his fingers pressed under my chin and his thumb on my jaw.

"Then you better be quiet," he warned me and slanted his mouth over mine and slid his tongue in.

"Ed, what are we doing?" I asked and pushed his hair out of my face as he nibbled my lips.

"Kissing, Blondie. Can't make babies by kissing."

He was kissing me again and again; slowly entering my mouth with deeper and deeper swoops of his tongue. His rhythm was making me dizzy.

"Ed, kissing leads to other things," I told him when he paused.

"Does it Blondie? Like what?"

He nudged my nose with his and licked at my lips as he ran his hand under my hair and up the back of my neck.

"Tell me where it leads, Blondie. Tell me," he commanded me as he began to rub circles on the back of my neck.

"Ed," was all I could say and when my mouth was open he took possession of it again and completely filled it with his tongue for just a second.

"Talk to me Blondie."

He ran his hand up the back of my neck and into my hair and grabbed a hank of it and wrapped it around his fist a couple of times and pulled my head back.

"Talk to me Blondie," he said again and began to kiss my exposed neck. "Where does kissing lead? Tell me. Tell me now," he told me and kissed the length of my neck as he pulled back on my hair, exposing my neck, making me arch my back more.

But I couldn't talk. And Ed didn't wait for an answer. He just gently nudged me backwards and climbed onto the bed.

"Tell me where Baby," he whispered as he pushed me back and stretched his long body next to my own.

"It leads, it leads," I said as I scooted backwards on the bed and I felt Ed come with me. I ran my hands down the sides of his neck and over his shoulders and held on to him.

"Cat got your tongue?" he asked and propped up on one elbow as he slid one leg over both of mine and climbed on top of me.

As he settled all his weight on top of me he returned to nuzzling and kissing my neck. His whiskers and beard scraped at my sensitive throat.

"It leads where, Blondie? I'm just kissing you. Though I can tell you're still not wearing a bra," he whispered and ran his hands over my ribs and I shivered.

"It leads to making babies, Ed. It leads to us getting in trouble." I squirmed under him. I felt naughty for having even said it.

"I won't even take off your panties, Baby," he whispered in my ear and I nearly vibrated from his words. "I promise," he said and ran his fingers up the side of my thigh.

"I'm not even wearing panties, Ed."

Ed groaned out his reaction and slid his palm under my butt.

"I have my swimsuit bottoms on still," I offered up to try to fix my error but he only groaned again and sucked on the flesh behind my ear.

"You're going to lead us there, Baby. All this talk of panties and no panties."

Ed shifted around on top of me and I wrapped my legs around him and shifted around as well.

"Ugh, you're killing me."

"How Ed?" I struggled to move underneath him so as to not cause him discomfort.

"Don't move," he ordered me and wound his hand in my hair and pulled on it again and I arched against him. His rough work shirt pressed into my thin old t-shirt and I became more restless.

"Ed you're doing something to me."

"I'm sorry, Blondie, someone needs to do something to you," he spoke against my mouth. He let go of my hair and kissed me; his tongue slow and hot in my mouth. He stroked my thigh and whispered as he kissed the side of my face and encouraged me to relax.

"What is Aunt Clem doing?" he asked urgently in my ear and snapped my eyes open.

"She's, she's probably watching tv or getting ready for bed. She has work tomorrow."

 "What do you have tomorrow?"

"I don't know."

Ed was asking me all these questions and I was finding it hard to find enough air to answer them all while he was on top of me, stroking my hair, kissing me. Every time he touched me my pulse sped up and my breath grew more ragged.

"You don't know?" he squinted down at me with his hair falling all around his face.

"No," I panted.

"Maybe I can help you remember," he teased and ran his rough thumb over my bottom lip and began to lightly sing, "Happy Birthday to you."

I followed his eyes as he looked down at me and as he considered my left eye and then my right and as his thumb slid hot and dry over my bottom lip just as he sang, "Happy birthday, dear Baby."

The house was completely silent and we could both hear my little intake of air as Ed slid his thumb over my bottom lip and in my mouth to touch the tip of my tongue.

"Your eyes are big as saucers," he breathed out to me as his fingers gripped my chin. "What do you want for your birthday?"

I couldn't answer. I couldn't nod because he was holding my face firm in his hand. And I couldn't speak because he was slipping his thumb slowly in and out of my mouth and every time he touched the tip of my tongue, I tried to suck on his thumb. The roughness of his skin on my lip excited me and I opened my mouth a little more for him and he slid it in deeper.

"I have to work on my birthday, I have to work tomorrow," I finally managed to say.

"Looking up at me like that Blondie, you're gonna completely undo me. Poor Baby has to work on her birthday, so do I Blondie."

I didn't know what he meant exactly about undoing him except maybe he was feeling like I was. I didn't know what he was doing to me, but I didn't want him to stop. His eyes dilated as I sucked on his thumb and I grew restless under him as he pulled it away and rubbed it back and forth across my lip. I begged him with my eyes to end this pressure I was feeling inside. I took a hold of his wrist with both of my hands and as I watched his face, I guided his thumb back into my mouth and I rubbed the rough underside of it with my tongue.

Ed grunted from deep in his chest and pressed into me tighter and the bed squeaked below us in the dark bedroom.

"We need some place to be alone, Ed," I told him.

"Don't I know it."

"Touch me now," I pleaded and took his hand from my mouth and guided it between my legs.

"Jesus Christ, is this allowed?" he asked as he slid his hand down the front of my swimsuit bottoms.

"Yes," I said as I pressed my head back into the pillow. "It's my birthday."

"You want me, Blondie," Ed said with his lips against my jaw. It wasn't a question. It was a statement.

"I do."

"You want me bad, Blondie," he said a few seconds later.

"Yes," I said in between breaths.

"Is this too much Blondie?"

"Yes."

He froze for a second and stopped touching me and stopped kissing my jaw. I opened my eyes and saw him for a second before shutting them again.

"You ok Blondie? You're still so," Ed trailed off for a moment before finishing his sentence. "Tight."

"Don't stop."

"Ugh. You like this, Blondie?"

"Yes, but why do I, Ed?"

"Ugh," he grunted and pushed my knees open wider. "I'm starving," he said with a growl under his words. "You're starving me, Blondie."

I couldn't answer him. I was beginning to breathe harder and I clenched two handfuls of sheet on either side of me. As I opened my eyes I only saw the part of his hair as he pulled away from my face and his head disappeared between my knees.

"Happy Birthday, make a wish," was the last thing I heard him say for a long time that night and the last time I saw his face that night for a while as well.

**

"You had sex," was the first thing Petra said to me the next morning when I picked her up for work.

"I did not," I denied it and felt my face flash hot.

I watched Petra struggle to get her walker over the side of the truck to put it back in the bed and after she banged the truck a couple of times, I took it from her and placed it back there gently.

"You did. Your lips look crazy," she told me in the cab of the truck.

"Crazy?"

I grabbed the rearview mirror and pulled it down so I could look in it. My lips were red and chapped and swollen and my face was pale and blotchy and there were purple smudges under my eyes.

"I think I'm getting sick," I said and touched my lips with my fingertips and winced. "And just in time for my birthday."

"I think you got some, just in time for your birthday. Happy Birthday by the way," Petra said and slammed her door.

"I'm tired."

"Do tell."

"Ed stayed over."

"At your aunt's?"

"Yes."

"And? You had sex," she said after I didn't offer up anything.

"We did not."

I threw the truck into gear to take us to work.

"Did he spend the whole night?" Petra asked as she struggled to roll down the window and gave up after she could only get it to crank down two inches. I glanced over at her to see her hands laying limply in her lap.

Petra was getting weaker. But I didn't say anything.

"So what did you do then because every inch of you looks completely ravished."

She snapped me out of my thoughts as we sat at a train crossing and waited for the longest soybean train ever to pass.

"We just kissed, and kinda almost had sex," I shrugged. That was all I was going to tell her.

"Almost sex," she grumbled.

"Did Kai take you home?" I asked after the train passed, to change the subject.

"No," she sighed and slumped against the seatbelt. "He was on his bike," she explained and raised her hands palms up and let them drop again in her lap.

"Then how'd you get home?"

"Some guys from the team." And here she just shrugged again so I dropped it and just downshifted and got us to work.

But we weren't at work very long.

"Baby you don't have to clock out. You're not the one I'm letting go," Mr. Sosos pleaded with me fifteen minutes after we'd gotten to work.

"I just don't think she can do the work," he said to me as he followed me to the back room where I took off my hat and little apron and hung them on a peg by the bathroom door.

Petra had thrown her hat hard from where she'd been standing at the register and it'd landed in the frying vat full of bubbling grease on accident. Then she'd shoved her walker hard across the parking lot and gotten in the truck without me. I wanted to give her a couple of minutes alone before I went out to the truck.

"I'm sorry Mr. Sosos. I like working here, I really do. And I hate leaving you in the lurch. But if Petra can't stay, then neither can I."

"But why not? You're my best hop!"

"Because Mr. Sosos," I turned to him as I stopped at the door near the empty register where Petra usually stood balanced with her walker.

"Because someone has to give Petra a ride out to the pool now. Goodbye Mr. Sosos."

I handed him my order pad and greasy pen and I walked back to my truck. Petra looked small like a child as she leaned against the rolled up window as I walked up to the truck.

I got in and didn't say anything and didn't look at her till we were almost home.

"Better stop at Cloyd's," was all I said as we pulled into the little lot.

"What for?" she asked and wiped her nose on the back of her hand.

"We'll need some Pepsi's for the pool and maybe some snacks. God knows we ain't getting lunch at work."

"Well at least you'll have your birthday off." She tried to sound cheerful but her eyes were still watery.

Chapter Eight

Petra and I spent every day the rest of that week at Rushing Waters. I nearly wore out the bottom in my swimsuit going down the slides so many times and had to run to Montgomery Wards one day and pick up a new one. We went out to the water park so much I had to call Daddy and ask for gas money because now that I wasn't working I didn't have any of my own. Daddy must have felt guilty for pretty much leaving me to my own for the second time in my life because he gave me the Shell card, his only credit card he had, to use as I needed. He just left it on the kitchen counter with some small bills in cash for me and a card with a yellow kitten that said, "Happy Birthday". I found them when I went over there to clean the house and check on things that Saturday.

Daddy was pretty much staying at Uncle Fritz's farm full time. Between working at the factory and helping Fritz farm, I never did get to see him. I had to leave a message with my cousins just to get a hold of him.

Ed was working just as much too. Between fixing plane engines and helicopter engines and also being on call for the medi-flight, he couldn't come over that whole week.

Saturday, after I checked in on my old house to see if Daddy was there and after I ran the dust mop all around the hardwood floors, I hurried back to Aunt Clem's without even stopping next door at Ed's. I figured he was working. I'd called there all week just to hear Mrs. Small tell me, "He's working, Baby." Every single time I called there. Morning, afternoon, evening, late at night before bed. He's working or he's sleeping. I wanted to yell, "Wake him up!" But I didn't.

Mrs. Small was due to go in for her tests and scans next week and I knew she had enough on her mind as it was. So I didn't push. And I didn't whine. And I didn't sneak over there at night and crawl into his waterbed.

I kept busy going to the pool every day with Petra. Petra and I went down the waterslides a million times. And you would have thought I'd be used to them by now but I still shrieked like mad every time I went down the steep straight one.

By the end of a day on the slides my voice would oftentimes be hoarse. But I didn't care. Petra and I were having one of our best summers together. And if Kai was there, well he didn't bother me.

Besides, he talked to Petra more than me. He was big enough to carry her in his arms up the slopes and he would do it all day for her.

"So is he just doing this just to get closer to you?" Petra asked me when we were both in front of the mirrors in the girl's locker room putting on lipgloss.

"No."

I paused in putting on my gloss.

"Don't be silly," I told her.

"He was pretty wrapped around you. Is there a chance you'll go back to him? Any chance at all?"

"No. Of course not."

"I just wondered."

"Why?"

"You've not seen Ed for a few days."

"He's working." I shrugged and threw my gloss in our beach bag we shared and I took Petra's and threw it in as well.

"Well, you just don't tell me anything, Baby."

"You still want more details on me and Ed, don't you."

"Yes!" and her eyes lit up.

"I'll tell you tonight on the way home."

Kai was waiting for us outside the locker room. We put Petra's walker near our chair and he picked her up in his arms and back up the slopes we went.

"There's Ed!" Petra called to me over Kai's shoulder as they went up in front of me.

"No way! Where?"

But I couldn't see him in the crowd and I couldn't hold up the line on the slope to the slide either so I went on up it to take my turn.

As usual, I shrieked and whooped all the way down the slide and when I climbed out of the pool I was out of breath and panting and finally saw Ed.

Children were jostling and bumping around him; a river of bright swimsuits and sunburnt shoulders swirled past him as he stood in their midst. He was tall and wide shouldered with his hair in a greasy golden tangle down to his shoulders. But I couldn't see his face. The sun was was too bright. I could see where the mountain sunshine had turned his mustache and the tips of his beard blonde. But I couldn't see his eyes until he took a step towards me. And just as I thought I'd be able to see his eyes, he pulled his shirt up from his waist and over his head and instead of his eyes I saw his muscles roll under his tan stomach.

"Baby hell-cat," was all he said when he pulled his head out of his shirt as I walked towards him.

"Hi Ed." I looked up at his face but all I saw was the blinding sun and the flash of his teeth as he addressed me.

"You gonna go and give me a heart attack." He sounded stern and he looked away from me as he mopped his forehead with his balled up shirt.

"What?"

"Coming down that slide."

He just stood there shaking his head.

I didn't answer him.

"Your daddy know you do that?" He motioned at the slide just as tiny Petra came jetting down it sleek and dark behind Kai. She never screamed coming down it. Nothing scared Petra.

"Daddy wouldn't care, Ed. It's not dangerous."

"I heard you screaming clear back in La Rue. Clear back at the house."

"Did not," I laughed and slapped his arm.

"Your doctor think it's harmless?"

"What? Why would he care?"

"Screaming like that. You must be half out of your mind with fright."

"Shoot, Ed. I'm used to it. It's ok. Nothing scares me." I smiled at him playfully.

"Nothin' huh? I bet I could find something to scare you." And his eyes scorched me as he dropped his gaze on me and winked. "And besides, you have to be careful, Blondie," he got serious again. "You don't want to hurt that heart. That heart belongs to me."

"Oh Ed," was all I could gush and of course I did it just as Kai was carrying Petra up to us.

"Oh Lord if it ain't the dirty hippie!" Petra called from where she lay in Kai's arms.

"Oh sweet mother, if it isn't Baby's kooky little friend Petra," Ed called back to her and he made me so happy because he was smiling at her.

But then he saw Kai and it dimmed and flatlined. "And that guy," he mumbled.

"You remember Kai."

"Yes, I remember, Blondie."

And I swear he growled at Kai.

"You can't take Baby home!" Petra scolded Ed.

Baby Small

"I can. And I will. Blondie getting a fright like that on that slide might be bad for her heart."

"Oh my God. You're right. Let me down Kai! I have to get Baby home right away!" Petra ordered Kai and began to struggle to get down.

"You have to get me home? I drove!"

"I'll take her," Ed grabbed my hand and pulled me to him.

"I have my truck." I pulled my hand back.

"Well I'm starving."

"Imagine that," Petra said and rolled her eyes.

"Me too," Kai put in.

"Fine. You can come too but you ride me with me, boy. We gotta talk about some things on the way back to town. Baby, you give your kooky friend here a ride and we'll meet up at the 'Freeze."

Ed wouldn't tell me what he talked to Kai about on the ride back to town. He said I didn't need to worry my little head about it. Kai didn't give any hints either as we sat at a table together back behind the Dairy Freeze and ate. He was his usual quiet self just like he'd been for as long as I'd known him.

"Baby, you need to eat."

Ed said it to me so many times but I couldn't stop stealing glances at Kai. I wanted to know what he and Ed had talked about but Kai's face told me nothing. I also wanted to examine his face again for a trace of Allen having beat him. But he mostly looked like the same old Kai I'd always known only with longer sideburns.

I wasn't the only one not eating. Petra barely picked at her food as she too stared at Kai. We frustrated Ed with our lack of eating and lack of conversation but still he wouldn't tell me what he and Kai talked about.

"Baby Small, you will not go back on those waterslides," Ed told me later that night.

We were sitting in the T-bucket out behind his house. The apple trees were in full bloom and the air smelled sticky and sweet. Even in the dusk we could still hear the late working honey bees buzzing nearby.

"I will too be going back. It's summer. Petra and I both got fired from the Dairy Freeze, and what else are we gonna do?"

Ed rolled his eyes at me and lit a cigarette. I could see his eyes sparkle in the evening sun. But after he lit his cigarette, he kept them hidden from me with his long lashes. He was in a playful mood as we sat in the T-bucket together at the end of a wonderful day.

We'd left Kai at Petra's; the two of them seemed to have forgotten Ed and I after dinner and neither of them seemed too worried about Kai biking home to his house in the country after dark.

"I'll be all right," was all he'd said as he grinned and pulled his bike out of the back of my truck. Ed and I shrugged and followed each other back to the Small's house.

Now here we sat in the T-bucket and Ed was strangely quiet.

He always used to scare me a little when he'd get quiet when I was small. That always signaled he was about to pounce or tease me or something.

He eased back in the seat and rubbed his belly; his shirt pulled tight over it and pulled up a little so I saw his tummy. I sat and watched him and wondered what he was thinking and waited for him to talk. But he didn't say a thing.

He smoked his cigarette and blinked his long lashes as a smile twitched at the corners of his lips. He stretched his legs and let his eyes droop.

It was like I wasn't even there.

"Penny for your thoughts, Ed."

"Huh!" he laughed quietly and still he gazed off into the trees and didn't say anything.

"You still think you can stop me from going to the waterslides?"

"I already have, or didn't you notice? You came home didn't ya?"

"I did. Because I was ready. But I'll be back out there again tomorrow," I told him and crossed my arms over my chest.

"Hm," Ed rubbed his lips and looked past me.

And still he looked like he was about to break out laughing or at least smile.

"What's so funny?" I demanded and pulled at his arms to get him to quit rubbing his lips and look at me.

He looked down at me with his bruised tired eyes and just then the evening sun lit on him; right on the crown of his head. The sun's last bright rays for the day chose to light up Ed and he turned his eyes heavenward and let whatever was amusing him ripple across his mouth.

"You think those slides don't scare you, Baby?"

He froze me with his gaze as he waited for me to answer.

"They don't."

"You think it's ok to get a fright like that? To put your heart through that?" he asked and shifted in his seat to face me.

"I do. It's ok. A little fear won't hurt my heart. A little excitement can't hurt me." I gulped and backed up from him and crossed my arms tight over the front of my t-shirt.

Ed scratched at his beard and ran his thumb over his bottom lip and shut his eyes.

"You got so afraid when you saw me last fall, your heart stopped," he whispered. "Remember that?"

"No. I wasn't afraid. I was. I was shocked."

I saw the snow and the field and the crowd in the stands and I saw Ed in his cowhide coat and his Colorado suntan and the snowflakes swirling all around. I remembered that day when the sound was turned off in the world and everything in me ceased to be. I clenched my hand in a fist over my heart at the memory and took a breath.

"I wasn't afraid of you Ed," and here I smiled at him. "I was just shocked."

"Was that what it was?" His eyes opened a slit and shone their light on me and just as quick they shut.

"Yes. That's what it was. That's all. Not scared."

He sat there relaxed and stretched out in the seat, breathing slow. And just as I was getting ready to ask him something else, his eyes opened and he sat up and reached out and took a hold of my face with both his hands.

"Remember this?" he asked and slid his thumb across my bottom lip and parted my mouth a little with it.

I gulped at the question in his eyes and I immediately blushed hot. My pulse beat hard in my chest and a knot formed in my lower belly. I couldn't answer him with his thumb almost in my mouth. I couldn't stop trying to taste his thumb with my tongue.

"Does that frighten you?" he asked and shook his head in a flick and said, "I mean shock you?"

His eyes left mine and glanced over my hair, my mouth and back to my eyes.

When he looked back at me, I just shook my head no.

He widened his eyes at me and slid the tips of both his thumbs around the edges of my bottom lip and in my mind's eye I followed their slow journey. Just when I thought he was done, and going to let go of me, he slid them just slightly into my mouth both at the same time. They were thick and rough and hot and dry on my wet bottom lip and he pulled them out as soon as they touched my tongue.

I felt sweat beading up on my forehead and my hair felt heavy on the back of my neck.

"Does that shock you, Blondie?"

"No," I said up to him. I gulped and tasted his salt and said again, "No." I shook my head for emphasis but I trembled at the end of it.

"You sure?"

And here he grinned at me and batted his lashes just once, real slow.

"Should it?" I asked.

I felt stupid. I felt I was missing something. Something because he was older than me and I was too inexperienced to know what it meant. It must have meant something because my breathing was hard and my lungs felt as if they were dragging in as much air as they could. I knew it didn't have anything to do with my heart problem.

"Let's try it again, Blondie."

"Ok."

He sat still for a moment, his hands gentle on my jaw, his thumbs rubbing small circles under my cheeks.

"There's those eyes Blondie. Huge as Caesar's. Black as night. Are they frightened eyes or the watchful eyes of the cat?"

"I don't know, Ed." I hardly had enough air to make a sound. "They're just my eyes." I shrugged.

Ed's circles he was making on my skin were hypnotizing and my breathing fell in time with their rhythm. And still he just stared at me. Stared down into my eyes.

"Maybe they're shocked eyes," he said and slid his thumbs in my mouth, almost all the way and I opened up for him.

He watched my reaction and I kept looking up at him. I couldn't look away. But when he began to make his little circles with his thumbs; in and out, and around and around, wider and wider on my lip, then, then I squeezed my eyes shut.

"Let me see, Blondie. Open up."

I opened my mouth wider and sucked on the rough pads of his thumbs and only opened my eyes to see why he groaned.

"Blondie, I'm trying to shock you; you ain't supposed to be trying to shock me."

He pulled me closer to him and bending down he pulled free from my mouth and kissed me. His tongue was much softer and wetter than his salty hot thumbs.

"I'm not trying to," I said against his mouth.

The night was quiet and we both shifted around on the old leather seat. I pulled away from Ed just so I could pull one leg up then the other off the seat. The backs of my thighs were stuck to it with sweat.

"What is it you're wearing tonight, Blondie?"

I shrugged. "Nothing."

I had on an old T-shirt of Jeffrey's. It was powder blue and had a sparklie picture of a Mustang on the front and the sleeves were ripped off because they were too tight on me.

"It's something, Blondie," Ed chortled and squeezed my knee.

His hand was hot and huge on my knee and I tried to move away but there was nowhere to go.

"Is that a dish towel of some sort?" he asked.

"No! It's my skirt."

"Is that what it is? Looks like dish towels to me, Blondie."

"They're tea towels."

"Tea towels?" Ed asked and slid his palm up my leg a little above the knee.

"Yes."

I had to take a big breath after I answered him. His touch was sending millions of ripples through my stomach and it felt natural to relax my legs open just a little with his touch.

"Mmm," he let out a moan and slid his hand higher. "You sure have some nutty clothes, Blondie."

"Why do you say that?"

"Who makes a skirt out of tea towels? Huh! Ahuh!"

"I like the tea-cups on them." I swatted at his hand and tried to pull the hem down further.

"Are you wearing anything under it, Blondie?"

"Ed!" I shrieked and slapped his hand and thought of all the girls past he'd had in the T-bucket and shivered.

"Did I shock you then?" he asked and his face was delirious with amusement breaking across it.

"No," I told him and turned my face away and closed my legs as tight as I could get.

"I think you are. Shocked that is."

Now he had a hand on each of my thighs, squeezing them and making his little circles with his thumbs.

"I think you really are," he said to me when I didn't answer and when I wouldn't look at him.

My face was hot and my hair was sticking to my forehead and my neck. I rocked on the sticky seat and Ed pushed my legs apart just a little; just enough for a little night breeze to get to me.

"Is it ok out here? Are we ok?" he whispered right in my ear.

He ran his nose through my hair and blew on my scalp as his hands continued to inch upwards and the urge to lie back as far as I could in the T-bucket and open up for him was overwhelming.

"We could be seen out here, Ed," I whispered to the clouds in the star-filled sky above me as Ed kissed my neck and I didn't even realize I was holding my breath until he sat back away from me.

Baby Small

My sigh went up in a wisp in the night sky as my hands rested lightly on his shoulders.

"Fine," Ed said and looked around in the dark before hopping out of the old car and pulling me out with him.

"We'll go in the house, to the waterbed," he said and leaned down and picked me up and threw me over his shoulder.

I shook with the giggles as he carried me over the bumpy ground of Mrs. Small's garden and was still giggling when he opened the side door.

"Shhhh, you'll wake mom," he warned me.

But I couldn't stop and I had to cover my mouth with my hand and stifle the giggles.

**

Chapter Nine

"Ed made me promise to not go on the slides," I said to Petra the next day and then I took three steps back from her.

She already had her swimsuit on with her cover-up over it and her beach bag packed and ready to go.

"Well what Ed don't know won't hurt him. Get your truck, change your clothes."

"Petra I can't. I promised him."

"Baby."

Petra clenched her lips in a tight line and gripped her walker till her bones shone white against her skin.

"Baby. I promised Kai I would meet him out there."

"Petra."

"Quick backin' up from me."

She was shoving her walker at me in choppy bursts of resolve to get to me and make me do what she wanted.

"No Petra, you're gonna slap me."

"Damn right I am."

"Petra I promised."

"Is it because you don't want me hooking up with Kai?"

"Are you hooking up with Kai?"

"Well I hope so. But I don't know! I've never hooked up before."

Petra slumped over her walker and I knew the fight was out of her and that she wasn't going to try to slap me anymore, but it didn't make me feel better.

"Petra, if I take you, I'll just have to drop you off because I promised Ed."

Petra's face fell completely and she sagged loose at the shoulders and wouldn't look at me.

"No, I don't want that. I need you there with me," she sighed. "I guess I'll just have to call him." And she began to scoot her walker across her room and out in the hall to get the phone.

"Petra?" I called to her.

"Yeah?"

"Do you think we could go out to Kai's? And bring him back here? He could hang out with you all day here."

Petra looked at me with her eyes shining like black buttons.

"Bring him back here?"

"Yes. And you and him can do what you want. And I'll get out of your way."

"But what are you gonna do all day?"

"I don't know. Work on the garden I was starting back at Daddy's."

"We'll come too. But I don't like dirt."

"Petra. Gardening is all about dirt."

"Whatever," she snapped and examined her red nails. "I'll come but I'm not touching dirt. Or worms. And I'll need a lounge chair. And I better find my wide brim hat. Gonna heat up so I better get some snacks and drinks," she ticked off all the things she needed on her fingers and then she began to make her way back towards the bedroom closet, shoving her walker between her bed and the wall.

"Kai," I pointed. "Call."

Driving down the gravel drive at Kai's was a trip I'd rather have never made again. Too many bad memories from the last time I'd been out there.

"I'll just stay in the truck. And maybe you should too," I told Petra when I looked out at the gravel walkway and all the tall grass between us and the house. No way could she get her walker through all that.

"Then who's gonna go up to the door?"

Petra gazed wistfully up at Kai's tall white old house.

"Maybe no will have to. He'll hear the truck," I shrugged at her and pumped the throttle to make the truck engine roar.

Kai waved to us as he came out the door and disappeared around the side of the house, wading the deep grass like the sea.

"Where's he going?" Petra asked me and leaned to one side and strained to see where he'd gone and what he was doing.

"Heck if I know."

I laid my head on my hands on the steering wheel and thought of Ed in the T-bucket last night.

"You're not spending the night alone in that house," he'd said to me when we were done fooling around on his waterbed. I was planning on staying over at Daddy's but Ed didn't like that idea.

"But Ed. I don't think I can spend the night here," I trailed off as I wrapped my arms around his neck and inhaled the deep aroma of his sun glazed hair.

"I'll take you back to Aunt Clem's," was all he said to me as he carried me out of the back door of his house and past the apple trees.

It wasn't until the dome light came on in the car when he dropped me off that I realized how tired he looked. And it was because he'd looked so

Baby Small

weary, and also because I was becoming even more wrapped around him than I ever thought possible, that when he made me promise to not go to the waterslides, that I gave in and I promised instead of putting up a fight. It was also because what he'd done to me in his bedroom; how he'd made me feel, that I would have promised him anything he would have asked.

Now here we were picking up Kai and what would Ed have to say about that?

"Why aren't we going to the waterslides?" Kai asked after he lifted his bike in the back of the truck and climbed in.

"Baby can't go."

"Oh, ok."

Kai was happy to leave it at that but Petra was not.

"Ed has forbidden her to go."

I ground the gear shift and glared at Petra.

"Oh."

I could hear the downturn in Kai's voice and attitude in just that word and so did Petra.

"It's because her heart. She's not supposed to strain it," Petra piped up like Kai shouldn't be disappointed because after all, we wanted me to be healthy. When just before she was willing to risk my health to have me go down the slides.

"Oh." And his attitude went right back up.

**

"You guys really gonna just sit there and watch me garden?"

"Garden?" Kai asked and looked around at the muddy back yard.

"Yes. Garden. That's what I'm doing today."

"I can help," Kai shrugged. "You have great sun back here. You can grow all sorts of things." Kai was in his element; outside in the sun; planting things.

It was surreal and it was golden; the two of us working side by side.

I kept looking over my shoulder all afternoon as Kai helped me put in the garden. He used to mean so much to me. But now he was just someone I used to be good friends with. What were we now? I didn't know, so I just put my back into my work and was thankful for his help.

He built stakes and a couple of trellises for me from scraps of wood from Daddy's shop and together we planted the beans and peanuts around them. I wondered if the beans would ever sprout and if the stakes and trellis would ever be needed even.

Petra sat in the shade when it got too hot to be in the sun. She fanned herself and complained about not being able to go to the water park. But I knew she was happy right where she was.

"The waterslides aren't as much fun as the pool used to be," Kai said as he wiped sweat from his forehead. "I like to swim at the lake better. At Settler's Beach. You ever been there? It's a lot of fun but so is putting in a brand new garden."

"Kai, stop trying to be polite to Baby. This is not fun," Petra said and she gestured about at the mud puddles in the soft ground.

But I knew she was having fun. Even when I squirted her with the hose. Even when Kai shot her with the hose a little after I did. I knew she was happy.

We worked till afternoon when Petra managed to get herself up the back step of the house and make lemonade for us by herself. She handed it out the back window and we all stood in the shade and had a rest.

The planting of the garden took up most of the day and at the end of it Kai and I were sweaty and coated in dirt. But for all the work we did, and all the work Petra did not do, it was Petra who was exhausted. By the time we were hosing off the spades, she was asleep in the lounge chair with a package of red vines in her hand.

"What did Ed talk to you about?" I blurted out as Kai and I were hanging up the tools in the garage.

The smells of grass and gasoline were thick in the cobwebby old garage. I couldn't read Kai's face as he stood with his back to the sun-filled door.

"He," Kai cleared his throat, "he wanted to know if I was ok."

Kai's voice sounded high and wavery.

"Ok?" I asked.

"Yeh. Ok," was all he said as if that explained everything.

"Oh."

I was confused but didn't know what to say.

"You know. From Allen." Kai shrugged and hung up the spades and rakes for me.

"Oh."

We were both quiet but didn't leave the garage.

"Why did he want to know that?" I finally asked him.

I couldn't imagine Ed caring if Kai had healed up ok or not. Besides, it was obvious that he had. He looked just fine.

"Well because Allen's back. I guess that's why." And he shrugged again and just blinked at me.

"Allen's not back," I corrected him.

"Oh. Well Ed said he was but maybe he's not."

Kai's silhouette shrugged again and he turned around and walked out of the garage.

Baby Small

**

"Kai told me Allen is back. Is that true?" I questioned Ed as soon as he got home.

I was sunburnt and tired and still had dirt under my fingernails and still had on my bib overalls and dirty shirt from earlier.

Mrs. Small had told me Ed would be home around five and I was sitting on my porch with my stomach growling, waiting on him; waiting to ask him.

"That little piss-ant," Ed growled and sat down next to me. "When'd you see him?"

"Today."

"Where at?"

Ed looked tired and tan and his hands had grease in all the creases. He smelled like jet fuel and his tangled up hair was puffing out from under a blue bandana that was tied tight around his head.

"Where at, Blondie? Where'd you see him?"

"Here," I said and bit my lip and scooted away from him a bit.

"Here?" he yelled.

"Yes."

"The fuck was he doing here?"

"Ed, language," I said to him and sounded just like Allen used to.

"Sorry Blondie. What the heck was he doing here?" Ed asked and reached over and took my hand.

"He was helping me put in the garden," I tried to explain but Ed exploded again.

"Why was he doing that? By God I'm gonna bust up his bicycle." Ed stood up and gritted his teeth and pointed down at me, "Let's see how easy it is to get in town on a busted up bike!"

Ed stomped off across the yard, swinging his arms and hunched over like an ape in his flight suit.

"I'm gonna kill him," I heard him mumble as he punched the palm of his hand.

"Ed, he was here for Petra," I called out to him.

"What?"

And he stomped back to me, the legs of his flight coveralls making sharp little swish sounds.

"He was here for Petra. But he helped me put in the garden."

I shrugged and started to get up from the porch but my back was stiff from bending over all day and it was slow going.

"Nope," Ed said more to himself than me. "Nope, still don't like it."

"Ed, is Allen back?" I asked him while he still wore a confused look on his face as he either thought about killing Kai or tried to work out if him being here for Petra was ok or not.

He didn't answer me right away. He sighed and sat down on the porch step and reached up and grabbed my arm and pulled me down next to him.

"Yes," he hung his head. "Yes, fuck," he sighed again and ran his grimy hands through his hair. "Sorry Blondie," he muttered and looked at me and yanked the bandana off his head and threw it out in the grass.

I watched his face turn dark as he looked out at the yard.

"So he really is here?"

"Yes, dammit he's back."

He wouldn't look at me, but I knew he wasn't mad at me. But he sure was mad at something.

"Where's he at?"

I poked Ed in the shoulder to get him to look at me.

I knew Allen wasn't at Aunt Clem's because that's where I was most of the time. And besides, I was pretty sure Aunt Clem didn't know about his return or she would have definitely said something about it. And she might have even wanted him to stay there at her house. Unless she was worried about me being upset.

"Does Aunt Clem know?" I asked and poked him in the shoulder again as he rested his arms on his knees and hung his head.

"Yes, Blondie. But you weren't supposed to know."

"Why not?" I demanded.

"Because Blondie," and here he peeked up at me. He had a smear of grease across the bridge of his nose and I reached out to wipe it but he grabbed my wrist.

"Don't! I cut it. Don't touch it."

"Ed, you need to wash that out." I could see blood oozing out of the dirty cut that ran diagonal across his nose.

"Blondie, I didn't tell you because I'm not even sure how long he's staying or how he is or anything. But mostly because he just now came back and Jeffrey made me promise to not upset you."

"Where's he staying?"

"You're not going over there."

"I know that. Of course not. But where's he at?"

"He's over Cloyd's." Ed shrugged and sat up and took a deep breath. "He's working at Cloyd's and he's renting a room above there."

I shivered at the close call at imagining running into Allen there unexpectedly.

Baby Small

Baby Small

Chapter Ten

"Doesn't Ed realize you would have found that out eventually?" Lisa asked me as we sat on her couch the next afternoon.

I was holding a very plump baby Olivia who sat on my lap like 15 lbs of warm sugar while Lisa folded the laundry. Ed and I were visiting them in their new apartment. They were finally able to move out of their one room they had above the donut shop that was across from the tractor factory. Now that the baby was here they needed a bigger place. They needed a nicer place.

They now had three rooms in an old Victorian house right next door to the First Methodist True Blood Memorial Church just one block away from Aunt Clem's and it was the most magical apartment ever. Jeffrey with his love for critters had two pet mice, a tank of silver and black angelfish, and another tank with a water turtle. He even had a beautiful beta fish in a tiny bowl sitting on the sill amongst all the vining plants that were hanging from macramé hangers.

Jeffrey and Ed were in the kitchen. They had volunteered to make the dinner and I could smell something burning and could hear Jeffrey cussing at Ed as pans banged about on the stove.

"Do you smell fire?" I asked Lisa and I sniffed the air again.

She sniffed and looked at me with huge eyes.

Later that evening after we'd all gone to the new Kentucky Fried Chicken and had dinner, we'd come back to the apartment to hang out.

"Look at him," Lisa said to me.

Her eyes were on Ed who was on his back on the shag rug. His hair spilled around his head and he was batting his eyelashes and alternating between making kissy sounds and raspberries while he held Olivia up in the air over him. She swatted at him with fat grabby star shaped hands as she cackled and reached for his face. The white bandaid across his nose stood out against his tan skin and he winced whenever she got close to it.

"That's a good way to get an upside-down nose-full of baby vomit there son," Jeffrey said to Ed.

I looked to my cousin, tall and lanky in the doorframe and couldn't remember him ever looking so happy.

"I'm going out for a smoke. You coming?"

"No way. I can't stop," and here Ed broke off into blowing loud raspberries and shaking his head at a squealing Olivia.

Baby Small

    I remembered what Daddy had said about her and I couldn't help but look at her with concern.

    "What's the matter Baby?"

    Lisa was sitting Indian style next to me and she nudged me with her foot.

    "Oh nothing," I forced a smile at her.

    "No really. What is it?"

    Lisa cocked her head to the side at me and smiled. She was always so calm and so grounded, I felt as if I could tell her anything.

    "Well. I was just wondering if the doctors were wrong about her, is all."

    Olivia balanced in Ed's hands and was squealing with glee and making her own raspberries on the back of her fist to match Ed's.

    "Wrong about what?" Lisa asked.

    "Well. What I mean is, it don't look like anything's wrong with her. I think the doctors made a mistake."

    "Ain't nothing wrong with this baby!" Ed growled and lowered her down to his face and blew a loud blubbering raspberry onto her belly. She wiggled and cackled and smacked her chubby hands together and pumped her fat thighs in her yellow jammies.

    "Don't hurt her Ed."

    "Hurt her? Heck she keeps reaching for my nose! She's the one trying to hurt me! Me, I'm just getting me some sweet sugar! Gimme that fat baby sugar!" he growled and plopped her on his face.

    She instantly had two handfuls of his hair and began to yank and squeal and kick with utter delight.

    "I think she's perfect," I said to Lisa and wished more than anything that we hadn't lost little Dan.

    "So what is wrong with her?" Ed asked me later that night as he drove me back over to Aunt Clem's.

    "Daddy says she's mentally retarded." The words tasted bad in my mouth and I cranked down the window and moved my face into the hot night air.

    Ed didn't say anything but I could see him tense his jaw as he stared ahead and drove.

    "I just think she's a little different is all," I told him.

    "She's cute as hell. That's what she is and I can't wait." And here Ed sighed and looked over at me. "I can't wait Baby."

    "What's that mean?"

    "Well."

    "Yes?"

Baby Small

"I been thinking."

"Yes Ed?"

Ed licked his lips and gripped the steering wheel tight.

"Baby, I'm ready."

"For what Ed?"

"To make us a house."

"You mean like build one?"

I was picturing a little home out in the prairie with a stone fireplace and hardwood floors.

"Naw, Baby! Make a home. You know. Find a place. Fix it up. Put up wallpaper and buy some plates. Get it ready."

"Ready for what?" I couldn't help but giggle. I was picturing Ed at Sears buying plates and the looks that the saleswomen would give him.

"For you to move in. For our babies. For when you're my wife, Baby Small."

"I ain't Baby Small yet."

"You will be."

**

That summer I was the one driving out to the countryside every day. Ten years had passed since that first summer when mama died when Allen drove us out to the pool every day and now here it was me doing the driving. Petra and I went out to either pick up Kai from his house or to take all three of us out to the lake. I spent the days swimming while Petra and Kai sat on a blanket and held hands. Quitting my job when Petra got fired turned out to be a pretty good decision, I thought.

I'd never had so much fun during summer ever. I felt in control for the first time. Ed however wasn't having that great of time. Working two jobs wasn't sitting well with him. And me not getting to see him much wasn't sitting well with me.

"I'm plum beat Baby. I'm crashing."

He said this to me so often that it began to irritate me. I was tired of being a third wheel with Kai and Petra and also with Jeffrey and Lisa as well. I spent so many evenings at Jeffrey and Lisa's that Baby Olivia took to me just as easily as she did to her own mama. I spent so many evenings there, feeling like the odd man out that I would encourage Jeffrey and Lisa to go out and leave the baby with me.

"Just don't leave the house with her," Jeffrey always told me before they'd go; excited to get away for a bit.

They never paid me. I knew they couldn't afford it and honestly I didn't do it for the money. I did it so I wouldn't be alone at either my Daddy's house or Aunt Clem's. I also did it because I couldn't keep my hands off that baby. She was such a sweet giggly cuddly baby. I loved her so much. She helped take some of my aches away.

Ed was either too tired or too dirty to get together. He either wanted to go right to bed or he was on call or being called out on emergency flights of an evening.

"Ed. Don't you even care that I'm spending every day out at the lake with Kai?" I asked him on the phone one night at the end of June.

"Baby, we both know your kooky friend is out there with you and she's the one he likes now."

"But I'm in my swimsuit," I teased.

"Baby. Baby I'm too tired for you to be taunting me. Don't think I won't go out there and put the fear on the boy."

"Shouldn't you be putting the fear on me?"

"Baby I could never scare you. I never could, remember?"

I paused there because I remembered all the times in my life Ed had scared me with how unpredictable he was. And I missed those times.

"Ed, you're working too much. Here it is June all gone and I ain't hardly seen you."

"I'm off for the Fourth. Unless there's an accident and they need me to fly. So we'll have all day, Baby. And I'm working on a surprise for you."

"Ok."

"Ok? What's that supposed to mean?"

"We're having a big hoorah at Aunt Clem's," I told him but I was not excited.

"Well can't I come?"

"Of course. But we won't be alone."

"Oh. You want to get me alone do you?"

"I just miss you Ed. I miss talking to you. I miss you. I think I'm ready."

"Ready."

Ed was silent on the phone and I could hear the clock tick on Aunt Clem's stove seven times before he spoke again.

"I'll be there Baby."

I couldn't wait to see him there even if we wouldn't be alone.

But on the day of the Fourth, Ed was late.

"Where is he Mrs. Small?" I asked her when she came over carrying a tupperware full of green fluffy marshmallow salad.

"He had an errand he had to run off and do, dear. He said it was very important."

"What was it Mrs. Small?" I asked her as I followed her in the side door to the kitchen.

"I'm not sure, Baby but he'll be here," she said to me as she squeezed into the kitchen to get a spoon for her salad.

Aunt Clem's yard was filling up. Mr. and Mrs. Post were there. Jeffrey and Lisa and Olivia brought over bubbles and brightly colored plastic lawn toys. Kai and Petra were cool in their dark sunglasses on lounge chairs in the grass sipping cokes. Daddy brought Uncle Fritz and Aunt Frances who although she was bald and weak, was happy to be out of the hospital.

"I would have much rather been at my own house, but your dad insisted I come here."

I knew why. Daddy had been staying at their place trying to keep order on the farm and work at his job too while Aunt Frances was in St. Louis getting her treatments and he'd confided in me that it was a mess.

"Well anyway, the girls all got together and put together this box of things for you Baby." She'd had Uncle Fritz bring a big box full of clothes in and set it on my bed.

"Thank you Aunt Frances, I'll have to look at them later." And I dashed back out to the sunny backyard but still no Ed.

We cooked out and ate and watched Olivia swat at the bubbles that Kai was making using a huge piece of string and the garbage can lid full of suds. Later we got out sparklers and firecrackers as the sun went down and I held an exhausted Olivia. She sucked her fist and fell asleep against my shoulder and I was comforted by her weight. The town fireworks had just started exploding up in the sky and I'd just given up on Ed when he pulled up.

"Oh my God Baby!" he called to me as he ran up to the fence and vaulted right over it in his worn out jeans. He was a blur of beard and boots.

"Ed, what happened to you?" Jeffrey asked with no small amount of alarm in his voice.

As Ed got closer I could see what he meant.

All of Ed's hair was slicked back and parted deep on one side. He had on a blue dress shirt tucked into his jeans and a wide green tie. His fingernails were scrubbed clean of the diesel fuel and plane grease. He looked mildly tamed around the edges for Ed.

"What have you been up to, boy?" Jeffrey asked him and tossed him a can of beer from the old cooler.

"I got big news," Ed panted out of breath and smiling. He popped open the beer and took a pull and wiped his lips off on the back of his hand.

"Baby Small?" He turned to me and so did everyone else in the backyard.

"Yes Ed?"

Ed handed the beer back to Jeffrey and came over to me and dropped down on one knee. I was still holding Olivia who clung to me in her sleep and nuzzled her face closer to my shoulder.

"Baby Small?" Ed said from down on his knee in front of me.

I glanced over at my Daddy, scared for Ed at this moment and saw Daddy had a grave look on his face and his body looked tense.

"Baby Small, look at me." Ed's voice sounded serious; commanding. "Baby Small, you want to come see your future home?"

His eyes grew wide as he knelt in front of me and he held his hand out for me to take.

"My future home?" I cried so loud Olivia popped her head up and blinked her wide eyes several times, and she looked around as if trying to decide whether she should cry or not. She saw Ed and reached out for him and grunted and whined for him to take her.

"Baby Small," Ed said to me as he took Olivia and she grabbed handfuls of his hair and cuddled up to his chest and went back to sleep with little satisfied grunts of tiredness. "I got us a home. Well I ain't got it yet, but I will have. And soon, you'll move in with me."

It was all too much to fathom. There were too many people looking at me, judging my reaction. I didn't know what to say. I was scared to speak. Scared I'd heard Ed wrong. I wanted a house with him so badly. I wanted one place to live in and to stop going back and forth between my Daddy's house and Aunt Clem's; never being comfortable at either one. But I wanted to do it right. I wanted Ed to say the magic words.

"Baby?"

"Yes Ed?" I sat on the edge of my lawn chair as Ed handed Olivia back to Jeffrey and then knelt down in front of me and took my hand.

"Baby, do you want to go see it right now?"

"Right now?"

"Yes."

"Yes Ed!"

"It's just a block over," Ed said to me as he pulled me up out of the lawn chair.

Everyone started to follow us but Ed waved them back. "It's just a block away. Stay put everyone. Sheesh."

And they listened to him. Although I did turn around and saw them all come to the fence and watch us go as Ed pulled me down the sidewalk.

"It's just right down here, Baby. Wait till you see!"

He pulled me down the sidewalk I'd gone down a hundred times to Cloyds as a kid.

"It's not across Main Street, is it Ed?" I asked as I tried to keep up with Ed's long strides as he pulled me behind him.

"No, Blondie. No."

And still he pulled me till we were getting very close to the Linda Kirby house. The house where Miss Polkadot now lived.

"It's not the old Linda Kirby house is it Ed?" I asked with a waver in my voice.

"No, Blondie! Look!" And he stopped right in front of the Linda Kirby house but pointed next door and in the pink dusk I could see a little for sale sign out in front of the little white house.

"Oh Ed, did you buy it? Are you moving in?"

"I made an offer," he said and he stood up straight and pulled on his tie as we both gazed at the house.

"You like it Blondie?" Ed asked as he pulled off his tie and ran his hands through his hair, trying to repart it in the middle.

"I love it Ed," I sighed.

It was a tiny white house and the entire front of it was a sun-porch. And I knew from walking past it all my life that the front porch would be lit up all day by the sun. I knew that in the spring daffodils and tulips and resurrection lilies would pop up in thick rows in the front yard. I knew that the old lady who lived there grew ferns and vines and herbs on the front porch and I knew her cat slept in the window all day.

"Where did she go? The lady who lives here?" I suddenly asked Ed.

"Well I dunno, Blondie. But it's for sale."

"I hope nothing happened to her."

"Now Blondie, it ain't like it's the Linda Kirby house. Nothing like that happened here I'm sure."

"Well I love it Ed." And I sighed again. I wanted to live there. I wanted to live in one house and not travel in between two. I wanted one place to stay. But I didn't know how I'd ever end up living there with Ed. I stared hard at him and willed him to know my thoughts.

"Blondie! Stop!" Ed giggled, as he noticed me staring at him. "You're gonna bore a hole right in my forehead! Huh! Ahuh!" he guffawed and rubbed his forehead.

"Come on Blondie, let's head back! It's been a long night and I'm about starved," Ed said to me as he slapped my palm and grabbed my hand and pulled me behind him back to Aunt Clem's.

Baby Small

"Well?" Petra demanded when we got back to Aunt Clem's backyard.

"Well what?" I asked her and I noticed that Kai was also waiting for an answer.

"When are you getting married?" She hissed at me with her hands on her hips.

"I don't know what you're talking about."

I looked over at Ed as he slid two hotdogs onto a wire and grabbed another can of beer and came back to me. He was nodding his head and smiling with his eyes half shut and looked very satisfied.

"Blondie," was all he said as he sat by me and leaned over the fire and began to roast his dogs.

"You have to get married, Baby. You can't just move in with him," Petra whispered in my ear as she leaned over to me.

I had nothing to say back to her. As if I didn't know that already.

**

Chapter Eleven

"Ed you have to come over right away," I said into the phone as I stretched the cord from the hall into the kitchen to try to look out the back window.

I was at my Daddy's house and had been weeding the garden. The beans were coming in nicely as were the peanuts but they still looked skinny and fragile in the bright sun and it was hard to tell the plants from the weeds.

I pulled a few weeds and had decided to get the rake to break up the dry cloddy earth before watering it. The rake was in the garage but when I went in there, there was something else in there too.

"Baby. I'm at work. I can't just leave this plane engine and come over when it suits you, huh ahuh," he chuckled.

"NO. You do. Right now."

"What is it?"

"There's a giant dog in Daddy's garage and he won't come out." It all came out in a glob and I wasn't sure if Ed would even understand me.

"What?"

I could hear engines and banging in the background where Ed was at the airport machine shop. I'd never called him at work. But this was an emergency. The dog had looked as tall as me.

"There's a giant dog in Daddy's garage," I repeated slower.

"How'd he get in there?"

"I don't know."

"Do you really want him to come out? Right now?"

"Well," I swallowed. "Yes. He can't stay in there."

"How big is he?"

"He's as tall as me."

"Was he standing up like a human on his back legs? Huh! Ahuh!" Ed guffawed till I imagined there were tears in his eyes.

"No, Ed. He was standing regular like a dog."

"I'm sure he ain't that big, Blondie. It's just you ain't bigger than a wisp."

"Ok. Ok whatever you say."

"Now Blondie, don't be difficult. If he's as big as you say you go on in the house and wait for me to get home and deal with it. I'll shoo him out for you when I get home."

Baby Small

    I had to count to ten before I could answer without losing my temper.

    "Ok," was all I could manage.

    "You do it, Blondie. Get in the house and stay there. Do your Blondie things till I get home."

    "Oh I will."

    And we hung up.

    But I didn't stay in the house. I went and peeked back in the garage and I could see his tall outline in the back of the dark building. He was sniffing and snuffing around and licking the floor of the garage and when he heard me he stopped and raised his head at me and I could hear a low growl coming from him as his ears went flat. I stepped away when I saw the glint of his two eyes.

    "Well ok Ed Small, you want me to go in the house, I will," I said to myself as I went in the back door with a glance over my shoulder.

    I dug around in the fridge for a snack and finally settled on a bowl of cold apple sauce. It tasted so sweet and cool to my hot stomach I decided to get a refill and with it in hand I went back outside without thinking and sat on the back porch.

    As I spooned up my apple sauce I looked at the little peanut plants and the little vines of the beans and wondered if my garden would ever produce anything to eat when the big dog poked his long snout around the corner of the back of the garage and looked at me. I froze with the spoon midway from the bowl to my mouth and looked back at him.

    Cold rippled over the back of my neck as I put the spoon back in the bowl. The dog's eyes followed the spoon back to the bowl then he blinked and looked at me and licked his lips several times. He was tall and had a square head and a long snout. His fur was light brown with white marbling and I could see he had once been fluffy but was now greasy and clumpy here and there. He lowered his head and began to crouch. My calves tensed to spring up and I thought of throwing the bowl at him but instead I set the bowl of applesauce on the step below me.

    He looked at it and then up at me. Then he hung his head and began to crawl towards me. As he got to the bowl he sniffed the edge of it and looked up at me.

    "Go ahead. Have a taste," I told him. And he did.

    **

    Ed was completely speechless for once in his life. I watched his mouth open and close as he stood there behind the garage looking at me and the dog.

Baby Small

He absently scratched at his head, remembered he had a bandana tied around it and pulled it off.

"Baby Small," he said in the quietest voice and leaned on his hand on the garage and stared at me.

"Baby Small," he whispered but didn't come any closer. "Baby Small you have lost your cotton pickin' mind, child."

"Shhh, he's eatin'," I said to Ed.

"What is he eatin'? Baby food?" Ed asked and came closer on quiet feet.

"Applesauce."

"Applesauce," he murmured and shook his head. "Who is he?" he asked me and never took his eyes off the tall dog as it bent over and lapped up his third bowl of applesauce.

"Applesauce," I shrugged. "I've been calling him Applesauce. He likes it. He looks like it, too."

"He looks like a she, Blondie."

"She?"

"She."

"I want to keep her."

"Your daddy won't like it."

All I could do was shrug. Ed was right. I knew without asking that Daddy wouldn't let me keep the big dog. I wouldn't have even let it eat out of one of our bowls if Daddy had been home.

"What am I gonna do?"

"Is it friendly?" Ed asked and walked all around the dog as it licked the empty bowl so hard it clinked against the concrete step. When Ed got a little closer to it, it began to wag its tail but it kept right on licking.

"I think so."

"I hope so," Ed sighed but changed his tone when he saw how sad I was about the whole thing. "We'll think of something, Blondie. Promise."

Ed reached out and rubbed the tall dog between its ears as he walked around it one more time and it wagged its tail harder. "Sure is a big beast," he chuckled to himself.

"I really want her."

"I know, Blondie. I know."

"I can't keep her, can I?"

"No, Blondie. Not this one."

**

Ed and I took Applesauce out to Kai's a couple of days later after we earned her trust enough to get her to go with us. She rode in the back of

Baby Small

my truck and I could see her from the rearview mirror as she stretched her head out and smiled into the sun with her tongue blowing in the wind.

"Kai. Thanks for taking Applesauce." I could barely talk and I couldn't even look him in the face. I just watched Applesauce bound around sniffing the tall prairie flowers.

"Not a problem, Baby. Um, Ed, there's no smoking out here. The prairie, you know, it's very flammable."

With a parting growl Ed pulled me reluctantly into the truck and we left Applesauce with Kai.

I held my hand out in a frozen goodbye to no one in particular out my window as I backed us down the long gravel drive.

"Poor Applesauce."

"She looked happy," Ed said and cocked back in his seat.

He put his bare feet up on the dash and stuck his head partially out the window and let the wind whip his hair as he smoked his cigarette as I drove us back to town.

**

"Something's wrong with Baby," I heard Ed tell Jeffrey the next night as we sat out back at Aunt Clem's. "She's down. She's not Blondie," Ed told Jeffrey as he chewed the skin on his thumb and looked at me across the yard.

Jeffrey listened to Ed and stole glances at me as he sliced up a long watermelon on the picnic table out in the backyard. It was too hot to be inside.

"What do you mean?" I heard Jeffrey ask.

"She's like she was when you and Allen got drafted." Ed stood next to Jeffrey and his eyes glazed over and he spaced out for a moment as he chewed his bottom lip. "She's just like that. Remember that?" Ed's eyes glowed pale in the summer evening as he remembered years past and gone.

Jeffrey paused with the long knife hovering over the melon and turned to look at me in the dusk. I pretended to not hear them and I even looked away when Jeffrey wouldn't stop staring at me.

"She don't look that upset."

"Well she is. But now she hides it better than when she was a kid. I'm telling you, something is wrong with Blondie. Christ, look what she did to me!" Here Ed gestured to his hair which I had braided into two plaits and secured into two long pigtails.

"You let her do that?" Guffawed Jeffrey and he went back to slicing the watermelon.

"Yes. I had to. I couldn't tell her no. She's not the same Blondie, I'm telling you. It was that dog. She got wrapped around that dog bad and me getting the house hasn't even cheered her up."

"Hmmph," was all Jeffrey replied.

"We got to do something," Ed urged Jeffrey and he stepped away from him because Aunt Clem came over to continue an argument that her and Jeffrey had started inside the house.

"I'm telling you Jeffrey, they voted. Right after the fourth and the city said we can't have a fire anymore on account of its pollution."

Jeffrey stopped slicing up the melon and walked away from Aunt Clem as she continued to argue with him. But he didn't say anything and just went out by the garage and began picking up dry timber.

Aunt Clem stood up as tall as she could as Jeffrey stared down at her grinning with his skinny arms full of timber and limbs.

"Against the law?" he asked down at her.

"Yes, it was in the paper."

"Well if it was in the paper, it has to be true." He grinned and the sun shone off his sunburnt nose.

"Jeffrey, I don't write the paper."

"No, but you sure do read it." He shook his head and walked away from her.

"I'm not making it up. It's against the law now and the neighbors are likely to call the cops."

"Hell. Let the law come," Ed said and flopped down in a lawn chair next to me and we watched Jeffrey build the bonfire.

But the cops didn't come. But Petra and Kai did.

"How's he get out here?" Ed asked me as we watched Kai help Petra come across the street slowly with her walker.

I swallowed before I answered.

"He bikes."

Ed looked at me like I was nuts.

"Really. He bikes."

"Hmmph," was all he said.

"What?"

"Hmmph. I don't remember him ever biking in to see you."

"Why would you say that, Ed?"

I was hurt and I twisted away from him and went and sat in my lawn chair to look away from him.

"I'm glad he never did, Blondie," he said as he came and pulled me back around.

"Hmmph."

Baby Small

"Blondie."

"Hmmph."

"Get over here," I heard Ed growl as he yanked me out of my chair and over on his lap.

"Ed," I said up to him as I sat sideways on his lap.

"Yes Blondie?" he asked down to me and batted his lashes playfully.

"Let me take out your braids and braid your hair again?"

"Jesus no, woman!" he hollered and got me in a headlock on his lap. He growled and rubbed his knuckles on my scalp until I yelped and squirmed so much the lawnchair turned over and almost flipped us into Jeffrey's fire.

"Shit mother fuck!" Ed yelled as we rolled together with his arms around me. For a moment I felt happy tucked into Ed's arms and I squeezed close to him as he pulled me away from the fire.

"Calm it down, kids," Jeffrey laughed and threw more limbs on the fire. "You're the reason they're trying to outlaw fires in this town!"

I was a little hurt that evening as I watched Kai and Petra. I wasn't hurt that Kai was with Petra now. But I was a little hurt that Kai had never biked into town to see me. Ed had always said if he was that into me, he'd have found a way to get into town to see me. And now here he was biking into town nearly every day to see Petra. And biking home at night in the dark country to boot. I shook my head at it all.

"We should offer Kai a ride home, Ed," I said to him as he loaded his graham crackers up with marshmallows and chocolate squares.

"Hmmph," he said to me with white goo melting into his mustache.

"You look adorable in your braids, Ed," Petra called to him across the fire.

"Hmmph," was all he said back and continued to smack his lips with a mouthful of s'more.

"You feelin' better?" he asked me after he wiped his mouth on the back of his hand.

"I feel fine, what are you talking about?"

"You ain't been right Baby. You ain't been yourself lately."

I just shrugged.

"What is it you want, Baby?"

I thought about Ed getting ready to move into the little white house. I thought about how half my stuff was at Daddy's and half was at Aunt Clem's and that there wasn't that much stuff to begin with. I had a new box of hand me downs from the cousins, half of which was maternity clothes that I couldn't even bear to look at and I just shrugged at Ed.

"Kai says Applesauce is doing good. You should go see her," he said to me.

I just shrugged again.

"Blondie. Don't do this. I want to fix it. Whatever it is. But you have to tell me whatever it is."

"I'm fine."

"Ugh!" Ed cried and dropped his head in my lap.

But the more Ed pushed and pulled at me the more I felt myself closing up. I couldn't even put it into thoughts what I wanted to say to him. I walked over to his new little white house every day the first week after he bought it and I helped him clean it and we painted all the walls white. And as we sat on the front porch drinking sun tea I thought of how I really really wanted to marry Ed and move in to the house too. But if Ed didn't feel the same way, there was no way I was going to ever admit those feelings to him.

I could hear Miss Polkadot's baby crying next door and it only made things worse.

"Baby Small, I think I know what's wrong."

"With what, Ed?"

"With you!"

"I'm not Baby Small, that's what's wrong."

It was like a lightbulb went on in Ed's head. I watched him as his eyes lit up and a thousand watt smile broke across his face as he slowly stood up and pointed at me.

"That's it," he whispered.

"What's it?"

I was hopeful that he finally got it.

Ed began to pace back and forth in the glassed in porch. I watched his bellbottoms swish over the tops of his long brown feet.

"That's it."

"What, Ed?"

"You want a baby!" he snapped so loud I jerked.

"What?"

"I'll be right back," he called to me and ran out to the car barefoot.

"A baby ain't something you can just run out and buy at Cloyd's!" I yelled after him.

**

"I have someone for you to meet, Baby Small," Ed called to me.

Baby Small

I had drifted off to sleep in the rocking chair on the porch of his new house. He'd been gone that long. But now he was back. And he was grinning and I could see his dimples even through his beard as he came up the steps.

"Someone for me to meet?" I asked and stretched as I sat in the rocking chair.

"Meet Thunderhead."

He pulled and detached a little meowing furball from his shirt and plopped a big headed black and white kitten in my lap. It immediately looked up at me and mewed. His blue eyes looked watery and sleepy.

"Thunderhead?" I cried out with joy and confusion.

"Yeh Blondie. You need a baby. One not so big as Applesauce. So. I saw a sign on the way to the airport the other day. A sign at a farm. 'Free Kittens'. So. Here he is. Thunderhead. Or she. I can't tell." And here Ed pulled up the little pointed tail of the kitten and glanced at its bottom. Thunderhead mewed again and Ed let go.

"I love him."

"I thought you would, Blondie."

Ed sighed and sat on the floor by my feet and looked up at me as I held and kissed Thunderhead.

"He's perfect Ed. I'll always love him."

"Or her. Too furry to tell. Huh! Ahuh!" and Ed's laugh scared the kitty and made him fuzz up and hiss a spitty little hiss.

**

Chapter Twelve

"What did he give it to you for?" Petra asked me the next day.

We were at Daddy's and had just spent the past few hours supervising Thunderhead as he ran around Daddy's house pell-mell.

"Do you need a reason for a kitten?"

"Well," Petra said as she watched the kitten walk slowly in a circle around a couch pillow that had been knocked on the floor.

"Well," she said again as she scooted her walker closer to get a better look as Thunderhead let out one final mew and a giant yawn and collapsed on the pillow sound asleep.

"Well, I think it means something," Petra said with her eyes popping wide on the 'something'.

"Of course it does."

I crossed my arms and sat down on the couch.

"It means Ed loves me."

"It means Ed's giving you a baby without giving you a baby," she told me as her eyebrows disappeared right up into her hair.

"It. Well. Maybe."

I couldn't take my eyes off Thunderhead as he slept; his little tummy vibrated out and in as he purred. He was that cute that I couldn't look away. His head seemed too big for his body. I loved the way his face was black but his whiskers were white and so were his eyelashes.

"You love him," Petra accused me as she sat down.

"Of course I do," I sighed. "He has blue eyes just like Ed."

Petra rolled her eyes but didn't say anything. She didn't melt over Thunderhead like I did.

The next few days as Thunderhead grew and as I doted on everything he did whether exploring Aunt Clem's or my Daddy's, I told Petra all about it, and she equaled everything with a tale about Applesauce or as the dog was now called, Saffron.

"Is that what Kai really calls him? Saffron? Why didn't he like Applesauce?"

"He just didn't," she shrugged.

We were drinking lemonade in Aunt Clem's backyard, sitting on lounge chairs.

"Saffron's a girl, by the way," Petra informed me, "And Kai felt Saffron just sounded more natural."

"And your grandpa lets Kai bring her in the house?"

"Yep."

We were quiet and sipped our drinks and let our heads rest back on our chairs and watched the dry cottony clouds sail past.

"He doesn't really like Kai," Petra said in a faraway voice.

It was as if her mind were examining things across the street back at her house while her voice and her thin little body were here with me.

"He doesn't like Kai a whole lot nor the dog for that matter," she continued. "But he lets them in. He tries to be pleasant," she trailed off with her eyes shut.

I couldn't help but feel a little pang as I thought of Kai biking into town with the dog at his side. He'd never biked into town to see me. Did he like Petra more than he'd ever liked me? It didn't matter. I was happy for her. But something about it still poked at me in a place I couldn't reach or soothe.

"What?" Petra asked. She was sitting up and had taken off her sunglasses.

"Nothing," I said guiltily.

Petra only raised her eyebrow at me. And when I didn't say anything, she said again, "What?" but now it was like a sharp little demand.

Petra knew me too well. I wouldn't have been surprised if she could read my thoughts as they unwound and tangled themselves up in my head.

"Nothing. I was just thinking."

Petra's glare grew flintier.

"I was just thinking about Kai riding his bike into town to see you is all. And. And how it'd be nice if I could visit Applesauce. I mean, Sage."

"Saffron."

"Saffron."

"Of course you can. But what about Thunderhead?"

We both looked at the kitten whose legs were getting longer every day. He was pawing at a big yellow dandelion in the grass and watching it wave back and forth.

"What about Thunderhead?"

"Well he's about a mouthful for Saffron is all."

"Well. I can leave him in the house if he's scared."

"Does Aunt Clem mind you having him here?"

"Well he's not always here. Sometimes we're at Daddy's."

I didn't want to talk about it. I knew Aunt Clem didn't like having him in the house. And I knew Daddy didn't like him either. I didn't want to have to let him stay at Ed's. I wanted him with me.

Petra shook her head at me like I was pitiful and I guess I was. I was staying at Aunt Clem's some. Staying at Daddy's some. And carrying that kitten around with me in the cab of my truck.

"Aren't you worried he won't know which place is his home and get lost? His brain can't be no bigger than a pebble. What's he think, moving about, riding around in a truck?"

Thunderhead was pulling on the dandelion with his teeth and eating it bite by bite and at Petra's words he paused in his chewing to look up at her.

"He does fine. He stays by me all the time and that's all that matters."

Petra looked at me and then back at the kitten just as he began puking up the plant he'd just eaten.

"I don't know," Petra sighed and shook her head. "Going from this house to that has got to be hard on him."

I swallowed back a hurt in my throat and said, "He's fine. Besides, someday I'll have my own home and won't be moving about."

Petra looked me up and down.

"In the meanwhile," I continued as the little cat did a somersault, "he just goes where I go. I look after him."

"Well, maybe leave him here tonight and let Ed babysit him because Kai's coming over and you can come see Applesauce. I mean, Saffron."

I did go see Applesauce and I saw that she was Kai's dog now. And Petra's too. That giant dog never left Petra's side and never took her eyes off Kai. Of course she had hugs for me after she crawled to me with her big dog elbows whacking the hardwood floor and her whole body wagging.

"Oh Applesauce," I wrapped my arms around her big neck.

"Where's your kitten, Baby?" Kai asked me.

"Back at Aunt Clem's."

"Why isn't Ed watching him?"

"He's working."

"He's always working."

"Well, he has two jobs."

"He should quit one."

"But he likes them both and besides, he can't. They both need him."

And they both did.

Ed was serving on the only medivac team in all the western part of the state. He flew people to Chicago and he flew people to St. Louis. He picked up people from accidents and people for transplants. He flew them to bigger hospitals for all sorts of reasons.

He also repaired small plane engines and in the middle of farmland there were lots of small plane engines to work on all the time.

Ed had his house now and he said he was putting away for our future when we'd be together. Thing was, we weren't never together now.

Thunderhead was my constant companion.

I sat on the floor at Petra's and hugged Applesauce and breathed in her scent of prairie grass and watched as Kai pulled Petra away from her walker and onto his lap. They giggled and whispered and clung on to each other as I sat there and got licked in the face by a dog I couldn't keep because I lived in a house I didn't really live in.

I sat and let Applesauce who wasn't Applesauce anymore, lick me more and I felt out of place. I felt guilty for thinking thoughts of how I'd found the dog and how she should have been mine. I couldn't sit there and mope over thoughts that Ed should have been pulling me onto his lap and should have been whispering in my ear while I giggled. But mostly I just wanted him to give me a solid home where I could live permanently.

Besides, I thought as I kissed Applesauce on top of the head, I couldn't help but smile and think that it'd probably be Ed who'd be the one giggling.

**

Chapter Thirteen

"Baby," Aunt Clem said to me when I came in the door the next afternoon. She had her arms full of stockings and was holding them up high and ignoring Thunderhead as he slowly climbed her slacks.

"Aunt Clem, I'm so sorry!" I ran to her and untangled the kitten's claws from her pants.

"Baby, your daddy came by," she said as she tried to shake Thunderhead off her shins as I tried to pull his claws out.

"He wants you to come over."

I followed Aunt Clem to her bedroom and watched her shove the stockings in a drawer.

"Was he attacking your stockings in the bathroom, Aunt Clem?" I asked her.

But she didn't answer.

I followed her as she walked briskly to the kitchen and she almost ran into me when she grabbed the dust mop and turned around.

"Aunt Clem, can I help do something?"

Thunderhead and I both followed her in to my room where she began swabbing the wood floors with the lemony cloth mop.

"Baby," was all she said, her lips tight.

"I'm sorry Aunt Clem, it's just because he's a kitten," I said as I scooped him up as he attacked the yellow mop.

"Baby, your dad needs to talk to you. You better head over now."

Aunt Clem wouldn't look at me. Her eyes wandered over my white iron bed and the yellow quilt and I heard her sigh as her shoulders slumped.

"Oh Aunt Clem," I whispered and wanted to go to her but didn't.

I took a mewing Thunderhead out to my truck and drove home.

Daddy was in the kitchen sitting at the table. His fingers were black with grease from the lawn mower engine that was sitting in front of him on top of some newspapers on the kitchen table.

"Baby. Pull up a chair," he rumbled at me as he pulled at a gasket on the engine.

Thunderhead stiffened and flexed his claws into me from where he sat on my shoulders.

"What's wrong?"

"You're moving back home," he said as he pried at the gummed up cylinder in his hands and didn't look up at me.

Baby Small

I swore under my breath and sat down at the table so hard it caused Thunderhead to jump off my shoulders, his claws raking me as he went.

"Now what?" I grumbled and caught a reproving glare from my dad.

"Allen's moving home, back to Clem's," was all he said as his face lost all its bluster and he quit prying at the stuck part.

"Oh."

"Oh is right."

He looked me right in the eyes. "I don't want you going over there, got it?" he asked but it was more of an order as he pointed at me with the flat head screw driver.

"What about Aunt Clem? What about visiting her? What about going to Jeffrey's?"

"They can come here. But no Allen."

"What about my stuff?"

"I'll get it."

"When?"

"When I can."

"When's he moving back?"

"Soon. Tomorrow, I reckon since you're here now. I don't know for sure."

He went back to his part he was fiddling with; now he was wiping it with an orange rag and twisting it in his hands and still it wouldn't come apart.

I stared at him hard, thinking of my bed and my quilt, my records and my clothes. I wanted what few things I had back here with me but I wasn't ready to see Allen. But I'd go over there if I had to. I stood up to go.

"Sit down. I'll get it," Daddy said as if he read my mind.

"Now?" I asked him because he still sat there and was still prying gunk out of the gasket with the screwdriver.

"In a bit," he said without looking up at me.

"Ok," I said and when he didn't respond I left the room and headed down to the basement to find boxes.

**

"Blondie."

Ed was in the yard of Aunt Clem's a few hours later when I pulled up. My face felt hot and I knew I was inclined to cry or fight or maybe both.

"Ed, get out of my way," I told him as raindrops began to fall on my outstretched arms.

"No Blondie, go back home."

He was smiling and barefoot in tight jeans and an old tie dye shirt with a big red heart on the front.

"Why?"

"Just do as I say. You can't come in." He held his hands out to me as I went to walk around him.

"Why not?"

"Allen's inside."

I thought about that. I thought about seeing him after so much time had passed. After he'd beat me. After he'd beaten Kai. After he'd walked off and disappeared and after he'd spent time in a mental hospital. I couldn't picture him in there. I couldn't remember his face but I searched my feelings for him and I found those.

"I ain't scared of him," I told Ed and stuck out my chin and started to push past him.

"I know you ain't. But you don't need to come in. I'll bring out all your stuff. I'll bring it over later."

He grabbed me around the waist and swung me around clear off my feet. It felt good to be in his arms and I fought to remember I was here for a reason.

"I want my things now," I wailed and smacked at his hands where they held me.

"Quit wigglin' and go home, Blondie!" Ed grunted at me as I struggled to get loose.

"I want my things! I want my dresses! I want my laundry out of the dryer! I want my Pink Floyd albums! I need my medicine!" I yelled and smacked at him on each word.

"I'll get all of that, Blondie," Ed strained to push me toward my truck but I dug my heels in.

"Go home! Go back home to your kitten and wait for me to come over later," Ed pushed me towards the truck on each word.

"Oh my God, Thunderhead!"

I ran towards my truck so unexpectedly as Ed was pushing me that he almost fell down in the gravel alley.

"Oh my God, Thunderhead, I left him alone with Daddy!" I yelled as I ran around to the door of the truck and the waver in my own voice scared me.

"I'll get your things, Blondie. I'll get your albums and dresses and every little last thing, don't you worry," Ed told me.

"Move Ed, move! I have to go now! Thunderhead!" I pushed at him as he leaned in the window of the truck to kiss me goodbye.

Baby Small

How could I have forgotten Thunderhead? I asked myself as I backed down the alley of Aunt Clem's. I felt my stomach drop as I pulled away; black cinders spitting against the truck as I punched it.

**

"Baby? That you?" Daddy called when I came in the door.

"Daddy!"

"Don't be mad, Baby, I called Clem and told her to not let you in," I heard him say from the kitchen.

"Daddy!"

"I told her I don't want Allen near you," he said as he came down the hall.

"Daddy, where's Thunderhead?"

"Where's what?" He stopped wiping the engine part in his hands and stood still.

"Thunderhead. My kitten."

He looked around the edges of the dining room from where he stood as if certainly the kitten was right there. He looked up and down the long polyester curtains where Thunderhead liked to climb, but he was not there.

"Heck if I know."

"Daddy, I left him here."

I was trying to stay calm. I was trying to keep my words from flying up higher and higher the way my heartbeat was.

"Well," he said, "it's gotta be somewhere. Hope it's not crapping in the basement. I'm heading out to the farm," he said and turned to go back to the kitchen.

"He's a he Daddy. He's my baby and I gotta find him. I should have never left him here. If you would have taken me over there to get my things like I wanted," I stuttered. "If I wasn't constantly moving from one house to another, if you were a better dad, I'd be a better parent myself!" I hissed at him, scared to raise my voice. Scared of frightening Thunderhead more than he must already be. I couldn't believe I'd left him. I hadn't even thought of him. I had just cared about my things.

Now I looked over every inch of the house. The couch, under the couch, the laundry, the piano, under the dining room table, my bedroom, Daddy's bedroom, all over the house, but no kitten. I was sure I'd find him sleeping in a little ball somewhere, but he was nowhere to be found.

"Daddy, did you go outside at all while I was at Aunt Clem's?"

"I don't know, Baby."

"How can you not know?" I didn't wait for him to answer.

The kitten could be anywhere. I had to find him now.

Baby Small

**

Chapter Fourteen

"Blondie!"

I was in the basement looking for Thunderhead when I heard Ed call to me from outside the kitchen door at the top of the stairs.

"Open this door or I'm just gonna drop your kooky friend right here, I swear! You owe me for this Blondie! Open up this door!"

Ed was at the back door and he was holding a very embarrassed and very tiny Petra.

"Don't you dare drop me, Ed Small! Don't even think about it!"

She had her arms around his neck and was staring up at his face. I wasn't too sure she wasn't going faint; she looked that pale and that weak next to a very tan and broad-shouldered Ed.

"What's going on?" I asked as I let them in.

"Here," was all Ed said as he deposited Petra on the ground in a loose shambles of skinny legs and arms and leaned her against me.

"I brought her to help you look for your kitten and help keep you at home."

"Oh. You didn't have to do that," I trailed off as I helped Petra stand up without her walker.

"Yes, yes I did. Coming over to your Aunt's all in a frenzy," he grumbled and went out the back door.

"Where are you going?" I called after him but he didn't answer.

"Oh my God! Oh my God!" Petra panted when he left out the door. "I'm gonna swoon! Oh my God! He's so dreamy! I gotta calm down in case Kai comes."

"Kai?"

"Yes. I was on the phone with him when Ed showed up and I have to say I nearly died to see Ed standing on my porch asking me to come help you look for your kitten! Oh my God Baby! I will never get used to how attractive Ed is."

Ed came back in as I was helping Petra sit on a kitchen chair and I eyed her to see if she was going to act weird around him.

"You'll need this," he said as he banged her walker through the screen door.

"But stay inside," he ordered us. "Storm's coming." He stood in the door of the kitchen pointing his finger first at me and then at Petra and then back at me. "Where's your dad?" he asked and looked distracted.

Just then we heard crackling from the radio on his belt and a voice speaking in codes and numbers burst in spurts through the static.

Ed took the radio off and held to his ear.

"Possible tornado, hail, flash floods," the radio warned.

"I wouldn't want to be up there flying tonight, but I'll probably have to go," he said and flashed his eyes on mine, the teasing and silliness all evaporated from his face.

I said a quick prayer that Ed wouldn't get called in. That he could stay with us. Then I remembered Daddy saying he had to head out to the farm. He hadn't even said goodbye.

There were too many worries on my mind at once.

"We'll stay in, Ed. I don't think Thunderhead got out. He's gotta be in here," I said in an attempt at calming myself down more than anything.

I felt calmer with Petra and Ed both helping me. I was glad to know I wasn't the only one who cared the kitten was missing.

"He's probably scared to death," I said as I looked behind the curtains. "He's probably hungry," I told Petra and Ed as Ed as I crawled around the living room looking under the couch and chairs.

"He's probably asleep, the little stinker," Ed mumbled with his face under the couch.

"If he is, it's because he's given up on me finding him."

"Just so long as he isn't outside," Petra's dark voice brought us out from under the furniture and over to the front window where she stood, holding the curtain back.

"It's all right," Ed said as he glanced up at the sky.

It was only sprinkling but it was turning dark as night and it was only two in the afternoon.

Ed stared at the doubt in my face.

"Just a thunderstorm rolling in. I don't think it's going to get as bad as they say. Now if it suddenly turns green out there, get to the basement. Don't wait around."

"Green?" Petra asked.

"Yep. Green means tornado. Or if it hails. Or of course if the sirens blow. Get in the basement." He was all seriousness.

Petra and I both looked at her walker at the same time and then back at Ed. If we had a tornado, Ed would have to carry her to the basement. Our stairs were so steep down there, I don't think she could have even scooted safely on her butt down them.

Ed's radio crackled and we listened to the thin mechanical voices talk about weather systems and fronts and air traffic as we all three looked out the window.

"I don't know Baby but I think I'll head into the shop to be closer if they need me."

The medi-flight copter was housed at the airport, not the hospital.

"But you're helping us look for Thunderhead."

"I want to be close if they need me."

"But Ed they haven't even called you in," I complained and pulled on his hand.

"I know. But they will. People never stay home when they should." He gestured to the dark sky and the blowing trees in the front yard. "It gets bad and people suddenly decide they have to be out. Have to get out in it." He shrugged. "Why can't they wait? Wait out the storm?"

"I don't know," I told him and followed him to the door.

"Now Blondie," he suddenly turned on the porch back to face me. "Blondie," he said and he tucked his hair behind his ears as the wind blew it in his face. "Blondie, you sit tight here with Petra. Play some cards or watch tv or watch the storm roll in. But stay inside. Promise me."

"Ed. Where would I go? I'm not leaving till I find Thunderhead."

"Just make sure you stay in this house, Blondie," he said then he ran for his car.

Petra pulled a dining room chair up to the window and sat and watched the sky and yelled out reports to me as I continued to look everywhere for my little kitten.

"It's raining harder now!" she called to me as I came down the stairs.

"He wasn't anywhere upstairs," I said to her as I pulled my own chair up to the window next to her.

"Look at the grass," she said with her forehead almost pressed against the glass.

"What?"

"Just look. It's creepy."

I looked and saw what she meant. The long dark grass was rippling like water. It didn't look right. I studied the sky to see if it had turned green like Ed had warned and saw it was still dark gray.

"Smells like a bait shop," Petra said as she inhaled. "Worms, coming up for the rain."

I sniffed and smelled it too; a dark earthy smell.

"Gramps always says if you hear a sound like a train during a storm to get to the basement," Petra told me with all seriousness.

"Do you hear anything?" I asked her, scared.

"No. Just the rain and um, the wind," she said as she cocked her head at the window. "I hope Kai stayed home all the same."

"I hope Ed made it to the airport ok," I said and we looked at each other.

"Oh he's so sexy, Baby," Petra looked at me and her face was soft and glowed double; her reflection pale in the window as the rain ran down it. "I was completely awake this time when he carried me! MY God Baby, are you still not letting him touch you?"

"Kind of. A little. "

"Kind of?" She nearly screamed.

"It's difficult; I don't want to get him in trouble."

"In trouble?" She looked at me confused.

"Arrested!"

"Arrested?"

"Yes! I'm only seventeen!"

"Oh who cares," she waved me away and went to looking back out the window.

"Or pregnant!"

"Pregnant? How would that get him in trouble?"

"People would know then that we, you know!"

Petra looked back at me, her eyebrows knitted together.

"Know what?"

"You know."

"People think you're doing that already! Hell, you're crazy for not doing that!"

"They do not think that!"

"Do so! Everyone just assumes it. My God, I would be. I'm all turned on just from him carrying me. He's so strong and so ugh. He's so, Ed."

She rubbed her palms up and down her bare arms and shut her eyes a moment before focusing on me and nearly howling, "Doesn't he turn you on? Don't you want to have him? I've been trying to seduce Kai but he'll only kiss. Ugh."

An image of Kai and Petra kissing formed in my mind and I shook it off as memories of kissing him myself floated in front of my eyes. That had been two lifetimes ago it seemed.

"I want Kai to be my first," Petra confessed next to me.

Baby Small

I couldn't look at her. I didn't want to break the spell on whatever she was going to say next. I let my eyes be transfixed by the rippling grass in the eerie afternoon gloom.

"I think he's the one. The one, Baby." She reached over and took my hand.

"Is it ok if he's the one?" she asked me.

"Do you want him to be the one?"

"Yes. But only if it's ok with you." She squeezed my hand and waited for my answer.

"Petra, you don't have to worry."

I squeezed her hand back.

"I think I'm sex-crazed," Petra admitted baldly and sighed.

"Oh lord, tell me something new."

"I am."

"You've always been."

"It's worse now." She sounded resigned. "Don't you feel that way?"

And here I sighed too. "Yes, I do." I let go of her hand and hid my face in embarrassment.

"Ugh let's do something about it!"

"What?"

"I know what."

Now I was afraid because Petra had her focused look on her face. Her eyes were dark and flinty and even though she was looking out the window I knew she wasn't seeing the storm. I knew she was seeing her plan as it organized itself in her mind.

"What?" I asked afraid to hear it.

"We should seduce them."

"Oh my."

"Yes. But first you know what we should do?"

"Look for Thunderhead some more?"

"No, silly. Go on the pill. Together. Let's do it. Life is short and we are young and we need to seduce them."

She used the window sill to help her stand up and looked ready to go right then.

"Petra, there's no way Daddy will ever let me go on the pill! You've done lost your mind! Plus the doctors. No way."

And even as I thought of all the obstacles between me and the pill, I too stood up because it felt urgent; it felt like the answer I didn't even know I'd been looking for.

"The pill," Petra said and nodded and smiled. "We could go over to Rush clinic. They have one of those Planned Parenthoods."

"Petra, it's storming." But even as I said it, I was planning when we could go. I was planning when I could seduce Ed.

"We need to go as soon as possible. I'm going to seduce Kai right off that bike. And you, well you, I don't even know how you're not on Ed 'round the clock."

She shook her head at me like I was pathetic.

"We can't go now, it's storming."

We both looked out the window.

"Looks like it's clearing up."

"It does look brighter."

We squinted out at the lightening sky. It did look sunnier but the wind was getting stronger and green leaves were flying in the air.

"I think it's gonna rain harder soon, look at that cloud," Petra said and began to push her walker towards the kitchen. "I'm gonna call home," she told me and disappeared into the kitchen.

I waited for her in the dining room and thought about the pill. It sounded like an easy solution to so many of my worries, but I couldn't imagine my doctors letting me go on it. Did they even have doctors at Planned Parenthood?

I would ask Petra, she would know. I waited for her at the window. Even though it looked like the sun was coming back out, the wind was blowing even harder.

"Petra!" I called to her without taking my eyes off the window. "Petra! I think it's hailing!"

Tiny little white balls were bouncing on the sidewalk, the porch, my truck. They were rapidly piling up in the grass.

"Baby, we have to go!" Petra called to me from the kitchen.

"Down to the basement?" I asked her in a panic.

"No. Back to my house."

"But the hail, the storm!"

"Kai is on his way! Grandma told me!" she countered and grabbed her walker. "Help me get down the steps! We gotta go! Kai is on his way! His mom called and asked if he'd made it yet!"

"Petra! Ed told me to stay inside!"

The wind was whistling around the eaves of the house now and pouring rain had replaced the hail.

"Baby, Kai will be there any moment. The storm is almost over, Grandma said so. Run me over there quick. We'll be alright."

But we weren't. We were soaked to the skin by the time I carried her into the truck. She was so wet by the time we made it into the cab of the truck that she nearly slipped out of my hands.

The rain came in great gouts flooding everything. The streets were deep with it. It ran thick over my windshield with the occasional hail bouncing off the hood.

"The sky is lightening up, see," Petra said to me from her side of the cab.

"It don't look right. It looks green to me."

"Just get us there. I gotta get there before Kai or Grandpa won't let him in."

"How's he even getting in to town? I hear sirens!"

I squeezed the steering wheel tighter and sat as close to the windshield as I could in hopes of seeing out better. The windshield wipers were working furiously but the rain was still coming steady.

I was scared to mash the throttle down even though I felt panicky and scared to be driving out in it. The water in the road was so deep, I was scared of stalling out in it.

Petra just shrugged like she didn't have a care as sirens wailed all over town.

"That ain't the tornado siren is it?" I asked her as we pulled into the drive.

Petra sat quiet and listened.

"No, it's just a fire truck."

"Sounds like a hundred of them!"

The clouds raced away above us and the sun blasted through a pink clear sky as the rain slowed to sprinkles and the wind quieted. We could hear the sirens even louder now; wailing and bleating their urgency.

"See, it's over," Petra said and got out of the truck.

My shoes and socks squished with every step as I walked her up to the door.

"Now let go of me, I got it," she commanded me. She batted at my hands as she opened the door. "Thanks, Baby. And remember, we'll get on the pill. Together." Her black eyes glittered as she looked at me one last time before going in. "Hey, look," she said and pointed at the sky. "Is that Ed?"

I looked up as the sun splintered through the last flimsy cloud in the watery sky and saw the red and white helicopter, small in the sky. I couldn't hear it over the sirens.

"Maybe," I said and couldn't stop looking up at it.

"Where is that?" Petra asked distractedly.

"I don't know. Towards the edge of town I think. But it's getting further away."

"Wonder what it was?" she asked as she went in.

I felt odd standing on her porch alone in the now blazing sun with water running out of my shoes; my dress wet on the backs of my legs.

**

Baby Small

Chapter Fifteen

"Baby Small! Where are you?"
Ed's calling for me jerked me awake where I lay in the tub.
"I'm in the tub!"
I was sunk back into the tub with the water up to my chin; my hair fanned out all around me.

After taking Petra home and getting soaked, the storm had blown in a cold front and by the time I got home I was chilled. I'd even boiled the kettle and the pasta pot full of water to add to the tub because we never seemed to have enough to get the tub really full.

The door came open a crack and I saw Ed's shoulder. I peeked up to see him frowning down at the kettle and the empty pot but he kept his eyes off me. "Baby. We need to talk." And then the door puffed shut.

Ed was waiting for me in the hallway when I came out of the bathroom wrapped in a towel.

"Baby," he whispered to me as he leaned his back against the wall.

I stood there in my towel with my hair dripping down my back in a wet tangle and looked up at him. He pressed his palms into his eyes and sighed.

"Ed? Are you ok? You look exhausted."
But he didn't answer.
I just stood there and waited and listened to the singing of the birds who were rejoicing that the storm was over and the sun had come back out if just for a little bit before night. Tomorrow would be a clear day and Petra and I could run over to Rush and get on the pill. It solved so many problems in my mind and I felt relaxed. But now as I stood here in the hall with Ed, I wondered if it was even worth it. He was always so tired. Or maybe he just wasn't interested in me in that way anymore.

"Ed?" I asked him again.
He kept his eyes shut and ran his fingers through his hair and tucked it behind his ears.

"Ed you all right?"
I heard him sniff and saw his bottom lip quiver.
"Ed?"
He opened his eyes for a moment and he looked so heartbroken; just for a moment. Then his eyes ran over my towel, my bare legs and shoulders, my sopping wet hair, and I shivered where I stood.

"I had a hard day at work, Baby. The hardest," he said barely opening his mouth and then he licked his lips.

"Get dressed, Blondie. I got something to tell you," he told me and started to rub his eyes again but he froze when I stepped towards him.

I didn't need to ask him what he was going to tell me. I knew what his bad day at work was going to mean for me; him leaving me again. He was going to tell me he had to go back to Colorado again and I wasn't having it.

I stepped closer and heard him gulp. He still had his hands near his eyes, his elbows bent out at the side of his head.

"I don't want to hear anything bad Ed," I told him and stood on tiptoe and pressed my bare thighs into him.

"Blondie. Stop." He backed away from me into the wall. His eyes looked watery as they locked down onto mine and he blinked several times.

"Blondie, I have something to say." He tried to back up more but he had nowhere to go.

"Is it about Thunderhead?" I asked and suddenly felt like crying.

"No, it's about work," he shook his head and swallowed hard.

"Then it can wait."

I dropped down from my tiptoes and walked away from him, pulling the towel tighter around me and hoping he'd follow.

I couldn't wait for the pill. I needed to seduce Ed now. I needed to make him unable to leave me. And I didn't mean by getting pregnant. I just needed to remind him that for the most part I was ready and able to handle him, and God help me make him see that without me getting pregnant again.

I didn't know what I was planning on doing but I was pretty certain I could just drop my towel and let Ed take his course. He'd know what to do.

"Damnit Blondie," I heard him curse as he followed me up the stairs.

I looked behind me to see him lumbering up the stairs with his head bowed and his hand running up the handrail.

I exaggerated my walk a little and swayed my hips in my towel and coughed to get him to look up. I smiled to myself when I heard him swear again.

"Christ Blondie."

"Don't blaspheme, Ed. It ain't right."

"What you're doing ain't right either."

But I didn't stop or answer him. I just kept going till I got to my room.

"What are you doing?"

"I'm seducing you."

"Seducing me?" he asked and shut the door and leaned against it. I nodded at him. "Yes, I'm wearing you down."

"Wearing me down?" his voice hitched up high on the end.

"Yes," and I stepped closer to him and stood on the top of his boots with my bare feet and threw my arms around his neck.

He grunted and threw his arms around my waist and pulled me into him. But he wouldn't look at me. He stared above my head, his eyes watery and focused on something else. He held his jaw firm and his body tense even as I let my own softness push up against him. Once again he swallowed hard and I just shut my eyes and kissed his neck, the highest part of him I could reach.

"Are you really going to seduce me?" he asked as I kissed his jawline.

"Yes Ed." I pulled on the back of his neck, pulled him down towards me and whispered in his ear.

With a growl he picked me off my feet and lay me on the bed. I threaded my fingers through his hair and tried to kiss his mouth.

"No, Blondie," he growled and pulled both my hands out of his hair. "Not yet," he ordered me and captured my wrists and held them down above my head.

I felt all his weight on me with only the damp towel between us and I wriggled to get my arms free.

"Now ain't the right time," he grunted and pressed me harder into the bed.

"Why not Ed?" I whined under him and gave up trying to get my arms free and just concentrated on getting my legs around him.

"You're not big enough to handle me, remember?"

"I am, I am," I panted and wriggled and felt my towel starting to come untucked at the top.

Ed froze and was still, his face red and strained above me as he continued to hold my wrists pinned to the pillow. I swore I saw two emotions war with each other on the surface of his face. Sadness touched his eyes and the corners of his lips and then he flushed even deeper and came towards my own face. I could feel the flush of his blush. I closed my eyes ready for his kiss.

But he pulled away from me too soon. And he rolled away on to his side.

"Baby."

Baby Small

He lay next to me with his back against the wall and cradled his head and hid his face away from me.

"Ed," I touched his arm and he flinched.

"Baby, I can't do this right now." His voice cracked as he begged me.

I lay immobile as I watched him wipe almost violently at his cheeks as the tears ran down his face.

"Ed?" I couldn't get anything else to come out. My throat closed up and my mouth just open and closed as I gasped to ask a hundred questions at once.

Ed just lay there rubbing his fists on his face as the tears fell faster and faster. I scooted over to give him more space.

"It was the worse day at work ever," he began to tell me as he lay on his back and stared with fierce focus up at the ceiling.

I watched him as he steeled his face and yet his lips still shook and his shoulders quaked. I was finding it hard to wait and I realized I was biting so hard on my lip it was almost bleeding.

"Ed," I prompted him as the tears fell harder and harder from his pale blue eyes.

He was seeing things I wasn't. He was remembering something and I saw the pain deepen on his face as he lay there.

"Baby Small," he said so strong it frightened me and he turned to me and grabbed me by the shoulders and pulled me on top of him. "Baby Small," he said again and held my face between his and pulled me down closer to him. "I don't know how to tell you this. This is the worst," he trailed off.

"The worst what?"

"The worst news of your life," he told me, his face grave and his eyes just a space away from my own and I felt my own tears beginning to fall without even knowing what he was going to say.

"What is it?" I asked my voice barely a croak.

He brought me closer to him and pressed my forehead down onto his own. And when his eyes were locked onto mine and his pupils were all that I saw until I felt as if I were falling into him he said, "It was the worst call of my life."

I blinked back the tears and nodded that he should go on.

"I knew when I got the call. I knew who it was." Ed bit his bottom lip and looked away from me. "I knew, Blondie," he said. The tears ran out of his closed eyes and into his hair. He sighed and put his arms around me and pressed my face into his chest. I heard the rest as if it came right from Ed's own heart.

"I am so sorry Blondie. I am so very sorry. I would never do anything to make you sad Blondie. I would never do anything to bring you sorrow. I would never ever break your heart, Blondie. But I'm going to break it now." And Ed squeezed me hard and sighed. I trembled as I lay on top of him, afraid of moving, afraid of crossing some invisible sad line that divided me between now and not knowing and after and knowing whatever it was that was tearing at Ed.

I didn't want him to tell me. And I think he knew that and he kissed me on the top of the head and gave me another squeeze and I heard him with my ear against his chest as he took a deep, dragging breath.

"Darling."

I bit my lip and squeezed my eyes shut.

Ed sniffled and stiffened under me.

"I knew it was him when I got the call."

I felt Ed's chin against the top of my head. I felt his whiskers rub against my hair and scalp.

"I knew it the whole time I suited up; the whole time I flew to him. I knew it was him when they said, when they said kid on a bike."

Ed's body quaked beneath me and for a horrible second I thought he was laughing. But no, he wasn't. He was completely sobbing. His chest was heaving up and down and I could hear his hitching breath as he cried and as I looked up I saw his face crumple under the reality of what he was saying. The last part of what he said echoed in my ears.

"Kid on a bike?" I asked.

Ed's eyes tightened but he didn't say a thing.

"No!!!!" I shrieked, more angry at Ed than I had ever been my entire life.

"NO!" I screamed and smacked at his shoulders with both of my hands. "No Ed!" I yelled as I smacked blindly with both hands wildly all around me.

"Blondie!" Ed cried and twisted away from me as he grabbed my wrists and flipped me onto my back and pinned my arms down again.

"Blondie, I'm so sorry," he cooed and tried to kiss my cheek but I wrenched my face away from him.

"No!" I yelled and shut my eyes.

"Blondie I'm so sorry. I'm so sorry. He didn't make it Blondie. We tried. We tried so hard but it was already too late when we got there he," but I cut Ed off.

"NO! Shut up! I don't want to hear it!" and I began to shriek and I wrenched my wrists out of Ed's grip and tore at my hair and covered my ears.

"Blondie. It's ok, you're ok, I'm so sorry, we tried so hard, it was no use Blondie. We thought if we could just fly him out of there we'd help him but he was gone Blondie. He was so gone he never even knew, Blondie. He never even knew he was gone," Ed whispered in my hair as the sobs ripped out of me as my heart completely tore in half and I knew there was not one good thing left in this entire world.

"Blondie, I'm so sorry, I know you loved your curly haired sandal man."

"Ed. Ed. You can never leave me."

"I won't Blondie. I won't, Baby Small. I promise."

The room was much too quiet after all my screaming and my throat burned and I couldn't stop crying.

"I'm so sorry," Ed said and sat up straddling me.

He pulled his old small white t-shirt over his head and rolled it into a ball and wiped my face with it.

"Should I call your dad, Baby?" he asked me when he was done sopping up my tears.

"No. Not yet." I felt angry. I felt the sting in the back of my eyes and I stared hard at the ceiling for a moment.

"Ok."

He nodded at me and started to stand up but I reached for his hand and pulled him down towards me.

"What?" he asked. His eyes burned into mine and he pooched his lips out in that tic of his and then he did it again like he used to do when he was nervous, and in that moment I saw sixteen year old Ed. I saw him as he was when I first came to spend all my days with him and I pulled him down to me and this time he came. The bed squeaked under our weight.

"Blondie," was all he said as he gently covered me with his body. Only the damp towel was between us.

"What is it you want?" he asked with his lips in my hair.

I shut my heavy eyes and thought about his question and just lay under him and let my heart slow down, let my mind slow down.

"It's not right for me to be here now, Baby," he said quietly and moved away a little.

"Why not?" I asked him and my eyes popped open and I stared at the ceiling while I waited for him to answer.

"Because, Blondie, because I want you right now and I shouldn't."

"Oh," I said and felt disappointed.

"I want to make love to you."

"But love is a good thing, Ed."

"It is and I love you so much," he told me and gripped my face in his hands.

"I love you too."

I ran my hands through his hair as he kissed along my jaw on up to behind my ear.

"Blondie you have so much hair," he murmured as his mouth moved down my neck.

I was sweaty under the towel and I pushed Ed up off me and pulled it out and threw it onto the floor.

"Hmmm," Ed told me as he looked down at me.

"Ed, be gentle with me. Please don't pull my hair."

"I won't baby. I'll be gentle. I will, I promise. You'll like this. If you don't, I'll stop."

"Ed," I said, my voice tight as I looked up into his face as his hair fell all around.

"Relax Blondie, let it happen," he coaxed me and slowed down rubbing my shoulders with his powerful hands and moved them down under me to my backside and I felt faint.

"Spread your knees a bit," he urged and pushed my legs apart a little. I raised myself up a little more and spread my knees wider. I felt my breathing fall in time with his rubbing my body.

"You're my Baby Small. My sweet Baby," he crooned as he rubbed little circles down the insides of my thighs.

"Oh Ed."

"I'm being gentle."

"Yes."

"I'm being very gentle with you."

"Yes Ed."

My face began to heat up and I felt sweat trickle down the back of my neck.

I arched my back and scooted down the bed to be closer to him; I felt his beard on the inside of my thighs. One of Ed's rough hands ran down the side of my ribs and he rubbed his face on the inside of my thigh as he whispered words of love and tenderness as he began to touch me again.

"I love you," he told me.

"Yes," was all I could answer and let my hands relax out of their fists. I dug my head back into the pillow and shut my eyes.

"I love you, you're so sweet."

"Yes, Ed."

"Am I being gentle Baby?"

"Yes. Yes you are."

"Is this gentle enough?"

"Oh yes Ed."

"You like this?"

"Hmm. I like this very much."

And I heard his pants unzip and felt both of his hands on my butt for a moment and then he was right on top of me.

"Ohh," I gasped.

"Are you ok? Should I stop?"

"I'm ok," I panted.

"I love you for all time, Baby," he said with his breath coming in chuffs, slow and whispery in the dark.

"You're never leaving me ever again, Ed," I suddenly yelled and surprised us both.

"No, I'm not. But I'm 'bout to! Hurry up!" he suddenly yelled, his voice filling my small room with its power.

**

"Let's get out of here, Baby," he said after we lay there a few minutes and held out his hand for me to take.

"Where will we go?"

"I don't know, let just," he said and pulled me up off the bed.

"I need to tell Petra."

"Not yet. We're going for a ride." His voice was thoughtful as he slipped on his jeans.

Ed drove us around in the country on the wet black roads and I leaned back in the seat with the windows down and listened to the tires sigh in the night. I didn't look up to see where we were going and Ed didn't talk. I felt the rise and the fall of the old roads and thought of all the places I had gone with Kai out in the country; with Petra and before Petra. And even though it was only a little more than a year since then, now that I looked over at Ed, it felt like two lifetimes ago since I had been with Kai.

**

Chapter Sixteen

Kai's funeral was out in the country but not in the big old house that was a funeral home out on the western prairie where my Mama and little baby Dan's services were. Kai's funeral was way out behind his own house. I looked at his parents as we walked through the prairie grass and wondered how they'd be able to look out there and see their son's resting place every day for the rest of their lives. I looked back at Ed in order to get the courage to keep walking toward the casket that was covered in a wreath of prairie flowers.

When we'd gotten to the funeral we parked behind Petra's grandparents and got out just as her grandfather was telling her she wouldn't be able to make it up to the service because of her walker and without saying a word, Ed swept her off her feet and carried her as I led the way. Her tear stained face burned with embarrassment at being carried by Ed in front of nearly the whole town but there was no way we were leaving her. My own daddy helped Petra's grandma stay balanced on the soft path back into the prairie. Mrs. Small, Aunt Clem, Jeffrey and Lisa with little Olivia, hundreds of kids from school, Shakespearian actors, and just about everyone from town filed in and filled out a huge circle in the grass all around Kai's final resting place.

We sat under the tendrils of the willow trees as the preacher talked of faith and God and the kingdom of heaven and how Christ used to say, let the children come to me. I couldn't really follow it because my heart was broken; not just for the loss of Kai but also for the loss that Petra had to bear. And for his poor parents and of course for him, for himself and all he would miss of this world. I hoped the preacher was right. I hoped he was up with God right now and maybe with my own mama, She'd look after him. Just like I was sure she was looking after me and Ed's son, Dan.

Just as they were lowering him into the grave a swirl of yellow butterflies flew down to the casket and the crowd all gasped and held their breath to see it. I could have sworn they all touched the lid of the casket one at a time in a rapid downward swirl before they flew off up into the trees. I stopped myself mid-wave as I waved them farewell.

"Look!" Petra hissed to Ed and I and for a moment I thought the butterflies were coming back but I didn't see them.

"What?" I whispered back to her.

"Allen," she whispered back to me and held her hand in a fist over her mouth.

Baby Small

I didn't see him.

Six men helped lower the casket down into the grave as Kai's parents stood at the lip of the hole and watched and hung on to each other as they said goodbye to their son.

"Allen?" I asked Petra and she pointed to which one he was.

He was the one in full military dress honor guard uniform. White gloves and white belt and shiny boots and everything. Ed squeezed my hand as I stared at the back of Allen and watched him work with precision movements to help lower Kai down in the ground. The sun glinted off his pale blonde hair that was shaved short on the back of his head.

"Are you sure?"

I didn't understand how Petra could spot my cousin before I could.

I looked over to see Jeffrey crying now and realized he'd just recognized his twin. Aunt Clem was blowing her nose and shaking her head as my dad put his arm around her. Even he had tears in his eyes. Almost everyone was broken up. Next to Jeffrey, Lisa was kissing Olivia and talking nonsense to her and holding her up in the air as she waved her chubby hands above her head. I looked up at the happy baby girl and kept on looking up at the sky and saw the tops of the trees were full of yellow butterflies flying up high.

"I'm sure," Petra said, never taking her eyes off the scene.

I wiped her tears for her as she gripped her walker so hard she shook.

Allen stood at attention near the grave, balanced on his cane as the five other men threw dirt down on it. His face was red and serious and he seemed to see nothing at all as his eyes scanned all the faces around. And then he saw his mom and I watched his eyes speed up looking all around us, frantic, until he found me. When his eyes found my own he glanced for a second up at Ed next to me and then came back to me; his eyes brimming with tears that wouldn't fall.

Without thinking of anything but myself and my own needs I let go of Ed's hand and ran to him.

I held onto Allen and he held onto me till after the casket was covered with dirt and half the people had left the meadow. He held on to me as my family, Ed and my best friend surrounded us. I felt a hand on my back and then another and looked up to see Kai's parents pass behind me; touching me as they went.

I looked around at everyone's sad face and took Allen's hand and Ed's hand and we left the clearing together.

**

Together, Aunt Clem, my Daddy, and Mrs. Small had made enough corn beef sandwiches to feed the whole neighborhood. Kai's parents didn't want a dinner or a reception or anything but my family all silently agreed that that was just what you did when someone died. You made food. You made coffee and people brought cake and salad and nuts and candy and you sat around and ate in quiet voices until late afternoon when the mood became happier and everyone went home.

Our mood was cautious as we hosted half the town and most of the high school in our house. The weather was pleasant so many of the men and the boys sat outside in mismatched lawn chairs, on the front porch or just gathered standing in clumps in the yard.

Petra had completely collapsed in her grandparents' car on the way back to town and they had taken her on home. I hoped she'd be ok and was worried about her but for now I just wanted to see Allen.

"Now take it easy, Baby," Ed told me as he held my hand tight as I led us into my house.

I ignored him and pulled him back through all the crowd towards the kitchen where I knew Allen would be.

"Take it easy. I don't want you getting upset."

"I won't," I said as I looked around.

The kitchen was full of ladies from the neighborhood brewing coffee and stirring sugar into pitchers of tea. Jimmy Collin's mom was slicing a tall pink cake and using the wide knife to lay slices of it on paper plates. Women were zooming in and out of the kitchen with trays of coffee and Aunt Clem and Mrs. Small were their own little assembly line of making corn beef sandwiches and between them, helping with the mustard, was Allen.

Ed and I sat with Allen on the back porch the rest of the afternoon. Allen said sorry to me one thousand times and I tried my best to accept his apology but it was a hard day to do it on. Ed sat with us the whole time except when he ran home to his mom's for a minute and came back with his guitar. While he played quietly behind me, Allen and I talked.

"Baby I am sorry for last summer. There's nothing I can say to repair what I did to you."

He started to touch my face but he changed his mind with a glare from Ed who suddenly stopped playing.

"Baby. I was sick last summer. That doesn't make up for it, I know," Allen said as he stared out into the backyard at the runner beans that were beginning to climb up the trellis that Kai had built for me out of scraps from Daddy's garage.

I looked down at all the mud puddles and remembered that day that Kai and I put in the garden while Petra watched from her lawn chair. It seemed so long ago. I couldn't believe he was gone and began to sob afresh all over again.

"I think that's enough for Baby for now," Ed told Allen and began to get up.

"Look who I found!"

We all looked up to see Jeffrey come out of from behind the garage. His face was red and his eyes were excited and he was cradling something small in his arms. When he got to the bottom stair of the back porch I saw that he was carrying Thunderhead tucked in his arms.

"Came out to have a smoke and get away from it all and heard this guy," Jeffrey said with his lips tight around the cigarette in his mouth. "Little dickens was down by the cellar over at your mom's," he said and nodded his head at Ed.

Ed helped me up and I went to collect Thunderhead in my arms. He was damp and cold and shaking. He must have been out all night in the rain.

"So that's why Caesar was making all that noise the other night," Ed said and rubbed his beard.

"Oh Thunderhead," I murmured to him. "Did Caesar hurt you?"

Allen held the door open for me and stood back as Ed followed me in. I bypassed all the neighbors and friends, went past Mrs. Small, my daddy, Aunt Clem, and Lisa and the baby and went up to my room with my kitten in my arms. It had been a long day and I was done. All done.

I put Thunderhead down on the bed where he began to lick his paws and wash his face while Ed helped me untie my sundress and pull it over my head. He had my pajamas out of the drawer before I could even get my slip and undies off.

"Get some sleep Baby," he told me as tears still continued to flood hot down my cheeks. "Get some sleep and try to not be so sad. Kai wouldn't have wanted you to be sad for very long."

"I don't know how to stop," I told him and cried even harder.

Ed held me in the dark of my room as I cried. We stood on the little braided rug and held each other and swayed while I cried. I wrapped my arms around his neck as tight as they would go and when I was empty and all cried out I looked up at him. I could see his eyelashes silhouetted in the moonlight from the window as he looked down at me.

"You need to get out of this town. You never go anywhere." His voice broke through the stillness and I shivered in his arms.

"I can't leave Petra right now."

Baby Small

I pulled tighter to him and stood on my toes to reach his lips and began to kiss him. I kissed him gentle again and again and when he opened his mouth for me I let my tongue touch his.

We stood and kissed until my knees began to tremble from being locked so long from holding me up on my toes to reach Ed. I sunk back down to the floor with my feet on the old rug and walked backwards to the bed.

I crawled under the covers and Thunderhead curled up on my feet. I waited for Ed to get in with me. But he went to the window and opened it and stood looking down at the street. My eyelids began to grow heavy as I tried to count how many car doors I heard as people began to leave.

"You can't be sad forever and neither can she. She's stronger than we give her credit for," he said from where he stood and when I didn't answer he continued, " I'm gonna get you out of here."

"But where would we go? Dragon Park?"

I was falling fast asleep and as I shut my eyes I thought of all the places Ed and I could go such as Dragon Park or Rush Lake and all of them were places I had been with Kai and I didn't want to go to any of them.

"No, Blondie." And I heard him chuckle.

One last look at the window showed me that Ed was still there, deep in thought with one hand holding open the curtains and the other one rubbing his thick lips; his stare a million miles away. I could hear him sigh but other than that he was still. As far as I knew, he stood there all night while I slept.

**

Chapter Seventeen

"He was the one."

"I know Petra, but if you don't sit still your whole fingertip is going to be red."

"He was going to be the one. We were going to go to Planned Parenthood, remember and he was going to be my first time."

She tried to pull her hand away from me but I wouldn't let her.

"I know," I whispered to her and held on to her wrist. "I know, Petra."

I sat there and felt helpless as I watched tears leak from Petra's dark eyes. I had to do something.

"Let's go visit him," I said.

"What?" She almost looked angry at me.

"Let's go visit him. Right now. Get up. You can dry your nails out the window of the truck."

I thought this would cheer her up but she cried even harder.

"He's supposed to be here. He's supposed to carry me down the stairs. You can't carry me down the stairs!" she howled and pointed at me and it scared me because I'd never seen Petra be scared before.

"Watch me," I told her and I slung her over my shoulder and carried her out to the truck.

**

Petra needed to be alone at Kai's grave. I could see that as I looked at her as we drove down the hot roads through the tall corn out to his parent's house.

 I carried her past Kai's house fine but after I got her to the back meadow I had to set her down twice to rest. I finally got her back to the grave that was still covered in fresh flowers. I set her right down on the ground by what I hoped was the head of his grave. There was no stone. I made sure she was stable and comfortable and then I walked away into the fields and the flowers and tall grass till I was sure I was on my own and could cry by myself without upsetting Petra even more. I sat down right in the deep grass where it was hot and moist and full of crickets and things that crawled. I shut my eyes and started to cry but was interrupted.

I heard a sound coming through the grass towards me slow. In between the tall prairie grass I saw her.

"Saffron?" I called and saw her drop her head and stop. "Saffron?" I called again and tried to make kissy sounds but just couldn't do it.

She wouldn't come.

"Come on Saffron. Come here girl."

Still she wouldn't come. I got up on my hands and knees and began to crawl towards her. "Saffron," I said and she backed up from me and put her head down on her paws with her butt still in the air. A breeze made its way through the thick grass and pulled my hair up off my neck and a ripple of fear shivered down my spine for a second. What if she didn't remember me?

And then it hit me.

"Applesauce?" I called to her and she dropped her bottom down to the ground so she was now laying down and her whole body began to wag as she crawled to me through the prairie flowers.

"Applesauce, come here girl," my voice wavered and she cocked her head and came to me.

I hugged her huge head. It was warm from the sun. I hugged her close to my chest and rested my eyes on her forehead.

"Applesauce you all right baby girl?" I asked her and she wagged all over and laid her long body into me with her tail thumping hard on the packed dirt.

**

I peeked around the big dog as she bounced next to me as we drove down the old blacktop back into town. Petra had her arm around Applesauce and was leaning on her. She kept patting the dog on the back absentmindedly while we drove.

"You sure you don't want her, Petra?"

"I do want her. But Grandpa will never let me keep her."

We were quiet with only the sound of the wind and the dog panting in the cab.

"Will your daddy let you keep her?"

"Probably not. But. I'm not asking." And I patted the dog myself.

**

Chapter Eighteen

Ed found me in bed the next morning with Applesauce on my feet and Thunderhead curled on my pillow. The room was dark and when he came in I couldn't tell if I was dreaming or awake.

"What are you doing here?"

"Watching you. Thinking."

"About what?"

Ed just shrugged and I stared at him as the morning sun came through the curtains and lit up the fuzzed up part in his hair. He stood there shrugging with a huge grin breaking across his face.

"Ed?"

I began to stick my legs out of the covers and started to sit up.

"I'm just wondering if you're starting some sort of family without me? You got kitty here," and here he rubbed the cat's head, "and this giant thing here," he laughed and rubbed the dog's belly as she rolled over.

I didn't know how to answer Ed. I was ready to start a family with him right then but I just had to catch up with him in age. If only he could wait for me or time could speed up. I was just waiting to finish my last year of high school.

"You could be starting one right now, Baby," Ed said to me and rubbed my arm with his rough hand. "You know we could have, the other day, Baby."

Ed's eyes were soft and yet so serious as he looked at me. I'd thought the same thing but I could tell I was getting ready to start my period. I could feel the cramps coming on as I lay there in bed even.

"I'm not sure I'm ready for that," I told Ed and immediately regretted it because he looked crushed.

"I don't mean it like that, Ed. I just meant the doc said my heart needed time to get stronger!"

"I'm ready to start a family, Baby. I'm ready for you to spend the night in my house. I'm tired of sneaking over here whenever your dad is gone. Which is pretty much all the time."

"I can't. I can't stay in your house." I told him and sat up and hugged my knees to my chin.

"Why not?"

"I can't stay there till I'm Baby Small." My voice sounded weak in my own ears.

"But you are Baby Small!" Ed complained.

Baby Small

I thrust out my left hand at him.

A huge grin erupted across his face and he even blushed in the morning sunlight.

"Are you asking me to marry you, Blondie?"

"I'm telling you to, Ed Small."

I stood up on the bed and stamped my bare foot and grabbed him by the neck of his t-shirt and shook him.

"Yes, Baby Small, yes, I'll marry you!" he howled and grabbed me and pulled me down to him right there on the floor.

**

"How many pancakes are you gonna eat?" Ed hollered at me from where he stood at the stove as he watched me take the entire stack off the plate next to the cast iron skillet.

"What?" I asked him as I sat at the table and pulled the butter closer. "What?" I asked him again as he stared me down. "Pancakes are burnin," I warned him as smoke came from the pan.

"Dang it, Blondie I think you are pregnant!" Ed yelped as he scraped at the skillet. "Now mine have gone and burned."

Ed put the charred and smoking skillet in the sink and ran it full of water.

"Budge up and give 'em up, Blondie," he told me as he sat down and elbowed my hand away from my stack as I was cutting into them. "Give me some," he pouted.

"Aww poor baby Ed," I crooned at him and guided a sticky forkful of pancake to his lips.

"Jesus, Blondie, you're not gonna be happy until I'm dead," Ed sighed on his back on the kitchen floor ten minutes later. "Dining room floor, bedroom floor, now kitchen floor. Jesus, woman," he said to me as he found his shirt crumpled on the floor and fished around in it and pulled out his cigarettes and matches.

I looked over at him and saw his hair was sweaty and damp on his forehead. I watched as he shut his eyes and licked his lips a few times before putting the smoke in his mouth and lighting it.

"Jesus, woman, we gotta get married," he said and exhaled smoke up at the underneath side of the kitchen table.

"Ed."

All I could say was his name. I felt like I needed to go back to bed and sleep a few more hours. Or eat another stack of pancakes. Or both.

"I gotta get a ring. We gotta get this done. You're my woman. We should be doing this on our own floor. Huh. Ahuh! Baby hell-cat," he said and coughed.

Baby Small

"Ed, we only been foolin' around."

"We should be foolin' around on our own floor, Blondie. Not on your daddy's floor. Jesus woman. My heart can't take this," he said and sighed with his eyes shut.

I watched him as he clamped his smoke between his teeth and as he ran his fingers furiously through his hair.

"I mean really Blondie," he said as he struggled to find the right words. "What are we waiting on?" he complained with his eyes still shut, his shoulders pressed into the kitchen floor as he wiggled his butt against the floor and pulled at the crotch of his pants. "What's holding up this here rodeo?"

And here Ed flashed his eyes on me and made me almost jump.

"I'm being good Blondie. I'm waiting. For what? Well for you to take your panties off, huh ahuh! But no really, I'm waiting for you to be my wife. I guess I'm trying to do right. But you're wearing me down, again. I'm like a wolf ready to spring."

"Ed."

"You're a fine little rabbit." He shut his eyes and sighed.

"I thought I was a sheep, Ed. A sheep let loose without the sheepdogs."

"You're more dangerous than a sheep. But whatever you are, I'm coming for you. I'm coming for you soon." He trailed off here and inhaled on his cigarette.

I shivered where I lay under the kitchen table at the thought of Ed coming for me.

**

"When did you first love me?" Ed asked me from where he sat next to me in the T-Bucket a few nights later after he came over after work.

"I don't know," was the first answer to come out of my mouth as I closed my eyes and thought. I closed my eyes and a hundred visions played from my memory and Ed was patient with me as I narrated them all.

"When you comforted me as a child all the times I was hurt and alone. All the times I was starved for affection and you held me and brushed out my hair," I took a breath and sighed and leaned into him.

I felt his chin on top of my head as he folded me in closer to him. I thought for a moment and snuggled into him and said, "All the times you listened to me talk about nothing. All the times you asked me what went wrong at school and then you came and straightened things out for me.

Baby Small

All the times you shared your candy and pop with me. All the times you just let me be around just to watch you shoot pool or play your guitar."

Ed was quiet and didn't speak for a while.

"All the times you watched cartoons with me," I said and I felt him shift around behind me and heard him lick his lips and start to say something several times only to remain silent till finally, "But when did you fall in love with me? When did you know that?"

His voice reached for me as the sun sank and though I hated to make him wait for an answer, I again had to shut my eyes and think on it.

"In love," I said to myself and remembered things that I did not narrate to Ed.

Ed dark tan and without his shirt in Aunt Clem's back yard with me. Ed crazed and chasing me around Aunt Clem's dining room table with milk in his mustache. I remembered those things and thought about them and was pretty sure I was in love with him before that. Before he ever touched me. Before we ever kissed or anything. I was pretty sure I was in love with him before I even thought of him like that.

Maybe I fell in love with Ed when he held me in his car at the Dairy Freeze and threatened to kill Kai. And now I felt an almost overwhelming guilt for that. And my mind scrambled for another memory to grasp on to in its place.

Maybe I fell in love with Ed with each letter he sent me from Colorado. Or maybe before he left for Colorado the first time. Maybe that's why it hurt so bad when he left town. Maybe as a kid I was falling in love with him with my childish heart. Was it possible? Ten years was a lifetime when you were a kid. And to some people ten years were a horrible gap between Ed and I. And maybe it was difficult for people to understand with me only being seventeen now. And him being ten years older. But what would it matter in the long run? And wasn't that what older people were always talking about? The long run?

"All I know is," I said to him now in the T-bucket as I turned to face him and grabbed him by his t-shirt and pulled closer to him, "is that I've always loved you. It's not been any one thing but many that have tied me to you."

Ed didn't look too satisfied with that answer so I distracted him with one of my own.

"When did you fall in love with me?" I asked him and expected him to laugh it off or say something smart.

But he didn't. He looked thoughtful for a minute as his eyes drifted shut till finally his face colored even in the dusky light and I saw him blush and smile and he opened his eyes and said, "I fell in love with you the moment I came back from Colorado and saw you in that strapless dress. Something hit me then. That's when I fell in love with you. But I'd always loved you in some sense."

"What do you mean?"

"I mean I loved all your little things. I loved when you watched the same Flintstones over and over and laughed at the same gags every time. And I loved you when you helped Jeffrey feed his mice, and every little critter he ever brought home even though you were a little scared of some of them."

"I was not!" I protested and smacked his arm.

"Were too. You were scared of those snakes, remember? Just like you were always scared of me, yet you'd never run away." And here he hugged me close to him and squeezed me hard and kissed my head.

I remembered the snakes. And I shivered in his arms.

"Blondie," he whispered with his lips bumping my ear and made me shiver again.

"Yes?"

"Is it bad that I'm so older than you?"

I pulled closer to him and balled his shirt in my fists as I clung to him.

"No," I said and shook my head, my forehead grazing against his chest, my hair mussing up against his beard.

"People think it's bad."

"Not everyone," I told Ed and looked up at the bottom of his jaw, his beard.

"I know. Not everyone."

"Do you think it's bad?" I asked him and was suddenly afraid of his answer as if he'd changed mind.

"No. But maybe I only see the future. I mean, I see right now. But I see our whole lives and a few years won't make much difference. Will it?"

I didn't know. And I didn't answer. But I didn't think it'd matter. Not at all.

"Blondie, unzip your pants for me."

The sudden change in subject threw me and I coughed and laughed both at the same time.

"Why?"

"So I can see if you still like me," Ed's low grumble vibrated my ear, my heart, the tips of my toes and made my eyes close.

"You know I do."

"Please, Blondie. I know you like me. I want to see how much," he purred and licked my ear lobe with slow flicks of his tongue.

"Out here in the T-Bucket?" I asked and shivered.

"Yes, out here in the T-Bucket. Just unzip your pants for me."

"Why can't you do it yourself?" I asked him and felt smart.

"I want you to do it, Blondie. I want you to want it."

"Ok," I agreed and untwined myself from him and sat back a little on the old car seat.

I looked down at the button of my jeans like I'd never seen it before and I took a deep breath, looked up at Ed to see him lick his bottom lip, and then I unbuttoned my pants. My hand froze on the zipper. I looked up at Ed one more time and could not read his expression for the life of me. His mouth was almost hanging open and his eyes were dark and almost glaring at my hand. And while he stared at my hand, and while I watched his face, I pulled down on the zipper, notch by notch and saw his nostrils tense as he inhaled and tensed his mouth.

"Ok," I stated. And I sounded as if I'd just run from the Dairy Freeze to home and couldn't catch my breath.

Ed didn't say anything but he leaned over and kissed me soft. His lips were gentle on my own as I felt his hand warm on my belly and then felt him slowly slide his thick calloused fingers down the front of my panties.

His breath quickened on my neck and I relaxed all the way back against the door of the old car as my legs went limp.

"You still like me a lot," he said with his lips on my jaw.

"I told you."

"You like me a whole lot Blondie."

I could hear the grin in his voice but I couldn't reply. I leaned back in the seat as far as I could.

"Don't be shy."

"I'm not," I said up to the sky.

"You like me here, and here, and," Ed whispered as his free hand wound its way up the back of my neck and grasped my hair.

My heart hammered hard and I thought to myself that if I died right now, that that would be ok. But my heart stayed steady. Even when Ed began to knee my legs open wider.

"You like me so much Blondie. You're so sweet for me. You're so sweet. So soft. So warm for me. How does it feel?"

I could only moan quiet and small in the back of my throat.

"Put some words to it, Blondie."

"Calloused. Rough," I managed, my voice ragged.

"Does it hurt?" he asked and he paused in his movements.

I took a hold of his wrist and set him to moving again.

Baby Small

"No," I said and my tongue felt too thick to speak, my mouth felt slow.

"You feel heavenly, Blondie. You feel ready."

"I am ready," I panted in the twilight a few minutes later.

"I'm ready too." Ed's voice was grainy and serious and I trembled all around him and squeezed his wrist till I felt his tendons stand out.

"You still like me Blondie," he laughed and his mood was light again as he pulled his hand away and zipped my pants back up.

My face was damp and so were other parts of me; my armpits, my scalp, the back of my neck, and behind my knees. Between my legs felt completely unrepairable. I wanted to just collapse in bed and slip into sleep.

"Time to go in, Baby," Ed told me and helped me climb down out of the old car on shaky legs.

"Time for me to talk to your daddy," he said as he pulled me to the back door of the house.

That jolted me awake and the panic dried all my sweat with a rippling of goosebumps that chased away the way I was feeling.

**

But Daddy wasn't ready to talk right away. He'd just come home from the store and was efficiently organizing everything in the kitchen and wouldn't look at neither Ed nor me, which was fine because I couldn't face him just yet, and neither could Ed.

The waiting made me nervous.

"What?" Ed asked me for like the third time.

He was sitting on the floor in the living room, his hair wet from splashing cold water on his face several times in the bathroom. Now he looked completely calm and normal and he had just grabbed the new can of cashews off the counter in the kitchen before Daddy could put them away. Daddy followed his new can of nuts into the living room and Ed looked from him back to me before scooping up a handful and pouring them into his upturned mouth.

"Somethin' the matter?" he asked me and winked and then his eyes darted back to my father.

"Ed," I laughed at him. "You took the whole can before we could even put them in a dish!" I giggled at him.

"We don't need a dish, Baby Small." Ed shook his head at me as he ate another handful. "These are salty," he told me and began to lick his fingers and I had to look away with embarrassment.

"That's it," Daddy said and swooped down and took the can away.

Baby Small

"You got any soda pop?" Ed asked me as my father stomped off to his chair with the can of nuts gripped in his hands.

"I'll get you an iced tea," I told him.

"Yeh, that'll work too," he said as he rubbed the salt off on the legs of his tight jeans and stood up. "Take your time getting it, Blondie. I got something to talk to your dad about."

"What?"

"Just get my tea."

I took my time getting Ed an iced tea and I got Daddy one too. But they were still discussing something when I came back to the room.

They were both sitting tense on the edges of their seats, with Ed reaching towards my Dad with both of his hands. His pleading arms almost looked comical if not for the serious focus in his eyes; his lips in a firm pout and the color high on his cheekbones.

"Oh um I'll just go upstairs and listen to a record then," I said to them after I handed them their glasses of tea.

I heard Ed say, "She can finish high school as my wife," and I skipped up the steps two at a time to get away from the raw growl in his voice.

Finish high school as Ed's wife? I thought about this and had to suppress a giggle wondering if the back of my gym suit would say Mrs. Small on it.

I crept down again later after the record was over but they were still talking.

"No, I haven't given her a ring," I heard Ed tell my Dad. "But I will. She knows I will."

I held my breath on the stairs and I held onto the bannister tightly as I waited for them to say more.

"Just let her finish high school Ed. Please. Just let her live here one more year with me." My Daddy's voice was thin in the dark room and I peered around the corner to look at him and saw him with his elbows on his knees, rubbing his hands over his short hair.

"It's important to me," I heard him say. "It's what her mother would want and I owe Baby one more year at home."

Ed was also sitting with his elbows on his knees and his hands on his head and all his hair in his face. But now he looked up at my Dad. He started to say something but stopped.

And then he finally said, "But Mr. Hunnicutt you're never here."

"I will be," my dad said and stood up and yawned.

I stepped back from the doorway and then peeked around the corner again.

"Frances is coming back home. There's nothing else can be done for her." He pinched the bridge of his nose and shut his eyes. Ed stood up too and looked tall compared to my dad.

"How long?" Ed asked.

My dad just shook his head.

"Don't know. Not long. I'm coming home in a couple of days. They need to be together alone."

"I'm sorry," Ed said and drank his watery tea.

"You can tell Baby goodnight. She's waiting on the stairs. I'm going to bed. You can get married soon as she graduates. I'll give you my blessing. Then. Till then, well you know."

Daddy hugged me as he walked past. I couldn't help but notice how tired he looked.

"Goodnight Daddy."

"Be good, Baby. Think of your mother."

"I will," I told him as he went up the stairs.

Ed told me what my dad should have said.

"Congratulations, Baby Small, because you're gonna be Baby Small legally real soon. Soon as you graduate. Now come here and kiss me," Ed growled at me and pulled into a one armed hug as he kissed me.

Chapter Nineteen

"Your Daddy says to be good, Blondie," Ed told me. But he had a mischievous twinkle in his eye and a shine to his bottom lip as he said it and after he said it, I forgot what he'd even said.

"Blondie!"

"What?"

"Did you hear what I said?"

"I think so."

"Blondie!" he hollered but had a blinding smile on his face.

"What?"

"Jesus woman, you're supposed to be being good."

"I am!"

I spread a blanket out on the back yard behind Ed's little white house; the house that would someday be mine too. Ed, Applesauce and Thunderhead all watched from the back steps where Ed stood with a beer in his hand and a cigarette hanging out of his mouth.

"What are you doing then?" he demanded as he stood there and stared me down.

"I'm being good," I told him and picked up my paperback book and lay down on the blanket in the sun to read.

I glanced back up at Ed after reading one page to see him just standing there still; his mouth slightly open and his eyes blazing in the sun.

"Ed, are you ok?" I asked him.

He stood there in his bare feet and turned away from me and blinked up at the sun. I watched him for a moment as he seemed deep in thought, just smiling up at the sky.

"Ed? Are you ok?" I asked him but still he just stood there.

"Blondie," he started to say and then cleared his throat and coughed several times.

I waited for him to gather his thoughts.

"Dear God, Blondie," he said and then, "Dear lord." He shook his head and just smiled at me as he reached out and rubbed Applesauce's head.

"You should be good, behave when you're over here or you won't be allowed to visit me anymore."

He tried to be serious. I watched him as he tried to keep his face rigid, but his lips kept curling up on the corners. He wagged his finger at me a couple of times before just giving up and collapsing on the blanket next to me.

"Ed, I'm just laying here. Reading. I'm not doing anything wrong."

The rest of the summer we were mostly good. We kissed. Here and there. And held each other close all the time. But we were good like Daddy asked us to be. Though for all the effort we still got stern looks from my Daddy. His distrust even made it hard for me to have a private conversation with Petra.

"Baby," Petra said to me on Saturday morning towards the end of August.

It was only 8 in the morning and already 85 outside. I was sitting on the porch trying to catch a breeze and thinking that the summer must have saved all its hot days for right when school was going to start, when the phone rang and made me jump.

"Hi Petra, gonna be a hot one today. What are you doing calling so early?"

"Baby, can you come get me? "

"Right now? It's a little early," I started to say but she cut me off.

"Baby, it's an emergency," she whispered into the phone.

"Is everything ok?"

"Yes. Just come over quick. I'll be waiting."

"Ok."

Petra was waiting in her drive when I pulled in. I glanced in the rearview mirror and saw Allen sitting on Aunt Clem's porch across the street. He was smoking and reading the paper and he looked up at me and gave a wave as I got out of the truck.

"What's going on?" I asked Petra after I helped get her in the cab of the truck.

"Back out first, get us out of here before he comes out and starts up again." She rapped her fist on the dash and clinched her jaw tight as I threw the truck in reverse and lurched us out of the drive.

"Who comes out?"

"Grandpa."

"Well where we going?" I asked her as we stopped in front of Cloyd's.

"Downtown. Clarkson Building."

"Clarkson Building?"

That was where the main city offices were.

"What are we doing there?" I asked Petra and looked over at her and noticed she was dressed very sober for her in a black sleeveless A-line with white Peter Pan collar.

"We're dropping out of school."

"We are?" I was shocked and yet felt a kick of excitement in my stomach.

"Well I am. But when you think about it, you should too."

"But why?" I asked as I parked in a slanted in spot and turned off the truck.

Petra just shrugged. "There's nothing there for me anymore. There's no Kai. There's no friends for me there. There's no job I can prepare for. I can't hardly walk at all anymore. I'm just a cripple." She shrugged again and looked close to crying.

"But Petra! What do your grandparents say?"

And here she shrugged again and didn't say anything but I waited.

Finally she said, "Grandpa is mad. Grandma didn't say anything but I know she agrees with me."

"Holy cow," I sighed. "Quitting school," I said and let out a whistle.

"You should too. Then you could marry Ed. It's not like I won't have my diploma. I'll get my GED."

The GED. You always heard older people talking about the GED but you never heard of anyone our age getting it or thinking it was something to be proud of.

"Petra I don't want to be at school without you!"

"Then quit," she said and got out of the truck.

Petra filled out all the forms for withdrawing from school and I stood by and watched in awe at how easy it was.

People in the office looked from her to me with disapproving faces; disapproval at Petra for withdrawing from school and also for just being disabled, and at me with recognition, pity, and also disapproval. The whole town knew about me and Ed and the baby we'd lost.

I watched Petra fill out every bit of her forms just to keep from having to see all the looks we were being given.

"Well that's done," Petra finally said and dusted her hands off and turned in her stack of papers. "Whaddaya say we go home, change clothes, get lunch and head out to see Kai and then head over to the waterslides for one last hurrah?"

"That sounds like a plan," I told her, knowing Ed was at work and the day was my own, but I didn't tell Petra all that. "We have any flowers for Kai?"

153

Baby Small

"We can pick some there. He'd like those best I think."

We were both quiet and then I said, "Yes, he'd like those best."

When we pulled up to her house she didn't get out of the truck. She just sat there with her eyes pinched shut.

"What?" I finally asked her.

"Ugh," she sighed and I waited for what she had to say.

"Will you go in and get my swimsuit and things?"

"Sure. Why though?"

"I don't want to see Grandpa."

"Well, you'll have to eventually," I told her but she was already folding up all her paperwork from quitting school and putting it in my glove box.

"It's all upstairs in the middle drawer and my bag is in the closet. I can borrow a towel from you!" she called to me as I let myself in her house.

When I got back out to the truck, Allen was there talking to her. Seeing him felt like seeing a ghost I never knew. I froze on the walkway with Petra's beach bag in my hand and just stared at him a second. He stood there in the late morning sun with his hands in his pockets talking to Petra and it sounded as if they were catching up on old times.

"Yep I just quit school," I heard Petra say from inside the truck but I couldn't see her face. "I'm not going back. What's the use?"

"Well, what's your plan?" Allen asked.

And it was like someone had grabbed the big clock of time and turned the hands back ten years when Allen had always had a plan for us. I did a double take as if I expected to see him with his hair pulled back in a curly pony tail like he had when I was small. But he was still Army Allen. Allen with his curls shorn off almost completely on the sides and tapered at the top. Not my old Allen after all. Not the same.

"Well," Petra sighed as I got in the cab of the truck, "the plan is to get my GED."

"And then what?" Allen wanted to know.

Petra just shrugged and she looked like she was going to cry again.

"Well, we better go," I said across Petra to Allen and put the truck into reverse.

"Where's that dog of yours?"

"At Mrs Small's."

Applesauce liked to sleep on Mrs. Small's back porch or out in her garden when I wasn't home. She'd follow Mrs. Small around all day out back there when I was gone and sometimes even Thunderhead would be with them too.

"Where you guys going?" he asked again as he continued to lean in Petra's window.

"The waterpark," we both answered.

"Oh. Yeh. They tore down the old pool, I heard."

For a moment I thought he was going to ask to go with. He stared off for a moment. But then he stepped away and patted the door of the truck.

"All right kids, have fun," he told us and headed back to Aunt Clem's.

"So we gonna visit Kai?" I asked after we'd both changed into our suits at my house and threw together a quick picnic.

"Yes," Petra said as she gazed out the window as we barreled down the country road. "Just for a little bit but maybe after the pool."

It seemed as if everyone had the same idea about going to the pool today because it was packed with teens even though the gates had just opened when we got there.

"See anyone?" I asked as I helped us push our way through the crowd.

"Ugh. No one I want to see."

"I know what you mean. Oh gosh, look the other way, it's Jimmy."

But it was too late.

"Hey girls, how's your summer been?"

Petra shot him a look that made all six feet of him quiver and cower.

"Real great," she snapped.

"Oh I heard about Kai. I saw you at the funeral. Remember?"

Petra just stared at him; her face firm, her thin jaw locked.

"Well ok. I'm going down the slides now."

"You do that, Jimmy Collins."

We got away from him and it was Petra who suggested we leave and we go see Kai after only going down the slides a couple more times. The pool wasn't doing it for either one of us. It just wasn't fun anymore. I knew Ed wasn't going to come drag me home and Kai wasn't ever going to show up for Petra again.

We sat in the sun in the grass near Kai's grave as the wind dried our hair and our swimsuits. It didn't feel nearly so sad to visit him in the sunny hot afternoon while eating Cheetoh's and drinking Pepsis. But it didn't feel great either.

"What are we doing later?" Petra asked me and a wave of guilt crashed on me and I nearly choked on my Pepsi.

"Ed wants to take me somewhere," I told her.

Baby Small

"Oh," was all she said and she looked out over the prairie flowers waving in the sun.
**

Chapter Twenty

"I'm scared Ed"

"Don't be scared. It's supposed to be romantic."

Ed pulled on my hand and I drug my clumsy feet across the tarmac.

"You won't get in trouble for this? You won't get fired?"

"No I already cleared it. I told you that already."

And Ed had told me that. Five hundred times at the Dairy Freeze as we picked up our food and he explained what we were going to do.

"Bag it up!" he had told the carhop. "Cuz we ain't eatin' it here!"

"Where are we eating it?" I had asked him.

"Up in the air! Well, you are. I might be busy flying." And here he'd grinned huge with his eyes absolutely devilish on me.

"Up in the air Ed?"

"Up in the air. I got permission to take you up in the bird."

"Oh my gosh," I'd said then and was saying it again now as we ran across the black tarmac.

The wind whipped and pulled at my hair and my heart throbbed in time to the rotors that were spinning on the white and red helicopter.

"Is it gonna cut my head off?" I asked as we got closer.

"No, but hold onto your hair," Ed told me and I pulled all my hair down right to my head as Ed guided me under the rotors and pushed me up towards the door.

I almost didn't recognize Ed with his hair pulled back in a ponytail and a helmet on his head. He had a radio mike, headphones and dark sunglasses on his helmet and he looked completely unknown to me until he smiled and the dimples popped out even through his beard.

"What do the women you save think of you, Ed?" I asked as I let him guide me into the front seat.

"Think of me?" Ed asked as he strapped me in the seat and pulled the buckles tight. "They think," he said as he pulled on all the straps and double checked them. "They think- get me to the hospital fast boy, if they think of me at all."

"They probably fall in love with you."

"Shoot, all I ever see of any of them is the bottoms of their feet or the tops of their heads, depending on how they slide 'em in the back. I just fly, Baby."

I looked in the back past the two little jump seats at the gurney. It was low to the floor and went back into the tail of the helicopter. It was enclosed on all sides with cords and tubes and compartments and I thought how frightening it would be to be hurt or ill and be back there flying in that long tight space. It gave me the chills so I looked back over at Ed and when I did, he slid a helmet on my head too and adjusted the chin strap for me.

"Bill and Ken are coming up with us," Ed told me and I heard him through the headset on my helmet and his voice made me smile.

I felt the copter dip a little and I turned back to see two older men climbing into the little seats and start to strap themselves in.

"They're coming on account of I need more hours in order to be able to take a passenger like you up. Bill's my supervisor and Ken's my co-pilot. But they're gonna allow you to sit up here with me for now."

"Oh. Ok." I glanced back at them again and they smiled and gave me a thumbs up.

"Here's your dinner, Baby," Ed said and sat the bag of food on my lap as he started going through a checklist of clicking switches and knobs on the dash and saying things I didn't understand.

"We usually have a couple of medevacs back there or an EMT, and just me and Ken up here, but we're not picking anyone up this time," Ed told me as he continued to get ready for take-off. I just nodded my head with its heavy helmet on it and stared around at everything.

"You gonna eat that, Baby?"

"I don't think I can."

My stomach was already beginning to feel sick as the engines began their whine and whistle and the rotor was building up speed above our heads.

"You scared, Baby?"

"Yes, Ed. I am."

"Roger that," he said and grinned at me. "You'll be fine, you're gonna love it. Just let go and lean back."

**

"Oh my God, you had sex!" Petra screamed at me the next morning when I came up on her porch.

"You always say that!"

I frowned at her as I sat down next to her on the step.

"You're always doing it!" she exclaimed.

She was drinking coffee and had a plate of donuts sitting next to her. They looked freshly made and were sticky with thick glaze.

"We aren't," I complained and earned a look from her.

"You did something. You're absolutely glowing. What is it?"

"This!" I squealed and splayed my fingers in front of her eyes.

"Ohhh my God! Oh my God!" Petra shrieked in the early morning quiet and grabbed my hands with both of hers.

She examined every inch of the ring, even the underside of the band. And then she began squealing more.

"Oh my God! It has a diamond and everything and oh my God it has these tiny little emeralds! Oh my God, where did he get it? How much did it cost? Where did he ask you? Oh my God!" She dropped my hand and picked up the plate of donuts and offered me one.

"I want to hear all about it."

"All about what?"

We both turned to see Allen had come over without us noticing.

"Oh um," I stuttered and took a little bite of the donut that was still warm and I looked at Petra.

"Ed asked Baby to marry him properly," Petra emphasized.

Allen's eyes squeezed tight in the morning sun as he looked at me and I couldn't tell if he was smiling or just squinting.

"See!" Petra exclaimed and held my hand out.

Allen glanced at the gold ring and back up at me.

"Donut?" Petra offered the plate and when he hesitated, "Grandma made them this morning." She raised the plate higher and finally Allen took one.

"So, details," she said and turned her attention to me.

"Well," I started, "We picked up food from the Dairy Freeze."

"Oh my lord don't tell me Ed Small proposed at the Daiy Freeze!"

"Sounds like Ed," Allen smirked.

I stopped telling my story to frown at them both just as Jeffrey came striding up the walk.

"Hey Jeffrey, come here boy!" Allen called to him.

"Hey y'all."

Jeffrey had his fishing hat on and his tackle and his pole in his hand.

"Ed proposed to Baby," Allen grumbled to his twin and helped himself to another donut. I caught Petra smiling at him as he did so and noticed she looked happier than she had since Kai died.

"What do you think of that?" Allen asked Jeffrey and waited for his answer before taking a bite.

Jeffrey looked thoughtful and stroked his goatee with his long fingers for a while before looking at me.

"I think it's wonderful. I think it's 'bout time, right Baby?" But he didn't wait for me to answer and he helped himself to two donuts off the plate, leaving just one.

"Speak of the devil," Allen drawled and we all turned and looked to see and saw Ed jogging up to the porch across the street in front of Aunt Clem's.

Baby Small

"Hey you hippie, we're over here," Allen and Jeffrey both called to him at the same time.

"Hey! Something smells good. Donuts!" Ed sniffed the air and smiled and then frowned when he saw there was only one left.

But just then the door opened and out came Petra's grandma with a plate of hot glazed donuts.

"Don't worry, there's more," she said to us as Ed took the plate.

"God bless you, Mrs. Post. I know your husband don't have no use for me, but by God you're a sweet woman," he told her and caused the old woman to blush.

"You're welcome."

"What's going on out there?" We heard Petra's grandpa shout from in the house. And then we heard him yell, "Goddamn layabouts, all of them!"

Mrs. Post went back in and shut the door.

"He's still mad I quit school," Petra shrugged and then took the donuts away from Ed because he had four of them on his fingers like rings and was taking bites out of them all and trying to keep his long hair out of the sticky glaze.

"Jesus, Ed, you never change," Allen criticized Ed and Jeffrey giggled.

"Thanks, man," Ed said in between licking his lips.

"Be quiet, y'all, Baby's giving me the details of Ed asking her to marry him!" Petra hushed them all and turned her attention back to me.

I quickly glanced at Ed and would have sworn he was blushing above his beard.

"Oh well let me tell it because I'm sure Blondie will leave out all the good details!" Ed's face shone with mischief and his impish grin.

"Ed!" I smacked at him. "I will not leave out details!"

"You will too, you had your hands over your eyes nearly the whole time and you probably wouldn't even tell them how you nearly puked and how you dropped my ring at ten thousand feet in the air! Huh! Ahuh!"

He laughed and sucked the icing off his thumb before wiping his hand off on his old jeans.

"What?" all three of them asked me and Ed at once.

"She hasn't told us anything yet!" Petra complained.

"Well let me tell it. I tell it better than Blondie anyway. Sit on my lap Blondie so I can keep you quiet and so you don't tell them how you cried," Ed told me and winked at me and held out his big hand.

"I'm not the one who cried!" I protested, but I came to him anyway.

I couldn't take my eyes off the ring on my finger as I slid my hand into his and let him pull me onto his lap.

I sat leaning into him and every time I tried to interrupt him because he was embarrassing me or making it sound more outrageous than it really was, he'd clamp his hand over my mouth and squeeze me around the waist.

"See I took her up in my helicopter. And she sure was scared, it was all of this 'oh Ed you're scaring me! You're gonna kill us! You're gonna crash us right into the La Pierre, Ed!' and I just about did because she kept grabbing at me while I was trying to control the stick, see," he laughed and told them only parts of the whole thing.

He left out how he took us up in the clouds and into the sun's rays. And he left out how he told me he felt destined to take care of me ever since day one of my life. He told me he couldn't imagine life without me and that I had to promise to never ever leave him, ever. And he left out how he had to blow his nose and wipe his eyes as he flew the helicopter and how he made Bill and Ken in the back turn off their headsets so they couldn't hear him. And I didn't drop the ring. Ed did when he got it out of the little zipper pocket on the chest of his flight suit. But I caught it. I caught it and gave it back to Ed and I helped him slide it on my finger so he didn't crash the helicopter.

"Congratulations boy!" Jeffrey clapped Ed on the shoulder and smiled at us both. "Whatcha doing over here today anyway? You off?"

"Nah, I gotta go but I wanted to find Baby before I went in. Her dad said she was over here."

We all looked at Ed expectedly.

"It's Labor Day weekend." He looked at us like were idiots.

"And?" Jeffrey prompted him.

"And I'm not on rotation on Monday and wanted to tell y'all I'm having a barbeque at my new place and everyone's invited!" Ed smiled and looked delighted as he held his arms out to emphasize everyone was invited.

"Well, all right then. We'll be there," Allen answered for all of us and then looked around. "Right guys?"

"Right," we all answered.

"That goes for your grandparents, Miss Kooky," Ed told Petra.

"I'll tell them," Petra said and she couldn't look at Ed. Again I noticed how she looked happier than she had in a long time and I loved Ed for including her and her family.

"So you ain't going fishing with us, Ed?" Jeffrey asked.

"Nope. Can't."

"All right then, I guess we gotta go," Allen sighed and got up and walked back across the road with his twin.

**

Chapter Twenty-One

The summer was ending and I was excited for Ed's Labor Day party at his new place. But the end of the summer brought with it too many conflicting feelings for me to deal with. It felt overwhelming and it made me doubt if I was really growing up or not. A grown up would be able to handle all these conflicting emotions. And I could not.

I mean I was excited about starting my last year of high school. I was also kind of in a hurry for it to end so I could marry Ed. I also couldn't wait for the other kids at school to see my engagement ring. But I was also sad about Petra not going back to school with me.

I tried not to think about Kai. Even though I was taking Petra out to his grave whenever she wanted to go. I think I boxed up those feelings about Kai and put them far away because I just felt numb when I thought of him.

I felt bad for Petra losing him but she seemed to be doing ok. Was it wrong for us to be ok and to get on living after losing him? I asked myself this as I patted Applesauce on her big boxy head.

"What would Kai have wanted?" I asked out loud and was startled by my dad answering.

"He'd want you to come help shuck all this corn, that's what," Daddy said as he set a big cardboard box full of sweet corn down on the dining room table.

"Where ever did you find all that corn this late in the season?"

"Iowa. But don't tell anyone. But Iowa is where you have to go for the best sweet corn. Sorry Illinois. But there is one perk of living in western Illinois, it's being close to Iowa and the corn," he laughed and began to peel the husks off and I dug in and helped.

"So. Guess this is what we're taking to Ed's?"

"Yep."

"I guess we got a big enough pot for all of this?"

"Yep," he answered and just kept peeling without looking at me.

"I guess you're finally ok with Ed?"

"I guess since you have a ring on your finger, I better be." He finally looked at me. And then he finally smiled.

The party at Ed's was a flurry of food containers being opened, of people unfolding lawn chairs from home, of someone telling everyone that someone needed to run to Cloyd's for more ice, and then running back again for more soda. It was a lot like old times with Jeffrey building a fire pit in Ed's backyard after Allen had walked all over with his cane gripped in his hand, making sure they picked the best spot for it.

Baby Small

It was a night of Ed smiling with pride and excitement at all the old friends and family and coworkers who came over. Daddy brought Mrs. Small and Aunt Clem in his truck with a bed full of lawn chairs and dishes of food in big cardboard boxes. Allen brought Petra but her grandparents stayed home. Jeffrey and Lisa walked over with Jeffrey pushing Olivia in a new stroller. It was a night of Ed giving everyone the grand tour of his house. It was a night of us announcing our engagement and having everyone cheer and toast to our future as we kissed.

It was our own safe little bubble of acceptance in the town. And it was perfect. Even when it was interrupted.

After it had gotten dark and late, the older folks had gone home and only Allen, Jeffrey, Petra, Ed and I were sitting around the fire roasting marshmallows and telling old stories. Most of them were about me and Ed and Ed belly laughed up into the starry sky at every single one. That's what brought over the neighbor; Miss Pollock's husband.

"This is a respectable neighborhood where people have jobs. You all had better be quiet and go home or I'm going to call the law!"

This demand was answered first by Applesauce who let out a series of growls and barks while charging at the fence, causing it to shake and rattle either by the dog or the neighbor. And then the demand was answered by Ed.

"People have jobs here? Well I'll be," Ed chuckled after the dog settled down.

"Who the hell is that?" Allen asked as he twisted around in his chair.

I jumped a little from where I sat on Ed's lap on a blanket by the fire and Ed stroked my hair and said, "hush, ain't no one but the pissant neighbor."

"Who's there?" Jeffrey called out in a friendly voice in the dark.

"It's your tax paying law abiding neighbor!"

"Law abiding neighbor?" We all repeated and giggled.

"Well shit I guess we're in trouble now," I heard Allen say. "This guy pays taxes and is also law abiding."

We all laughed.

"Just ignore him. He's always threatening me," Ed said from behind me as he loaded a fork with two more marshmallows.

"Like what?" Jeffrey asked. "What's he threaten you about?"

"Oh you know, my grass is too tall, my dog is too tall, my pecker's too tall, huh! Ahuh!" Ed laughed and tossed the bag of marshmallows to Allen. "Fix Petra a s'more, she's darn near wasting away over there."

I turned around to look at Ed and he smiled and winked at me.

"I don't need no one to make me a s'more, I can make my own," I heard Petra complain in the dark. I could barely see her in the glow of the fire.

"Fires are not allowed in city limits!" The voice of Miss Pollock's husband snapped in the night and Applesauce barked and growled and charged the fence with a crash again. "I'll call the pound if you don't get this mutt away from me!" he yelled and we heard the fence rattling again.

"Jesus Christ, this guy," Ed groaned and popped his s'more in his mouth. He wiped his hands on his jeans and asked me if I wouldn't mind getting up just for a moment.

"What are you gonna do?"

"Nothing. Just gonna kill him," Ed said nonchalantly and he reached into the cooler on the way to the fence.

"Ed! Don't!"

"Just relax Baby," Jeffrey told me.

"Let's see what happens," Allen said.

Jeffrey lit a smoke and cracked open a beer but Allen stood up slow and shook his leg out before leaning heavily on his cane.

"Hey there, Ted," we heard Ed say.

"It's Todd," snapped back the reply.

"Todd, right," we could hear Ed. We also heard him take a long drink of beer and then a crinkle and a lighter clicking. We could just barely see his cigarette flare in the dark.

I could see the outline of Applesauce right next to Ed.

"What seems to be the problem?" We heard Ed ask quietly and the hairs stood up on my head.

"I need to sleep. I gotta baby that needs to sleep. Time to wrap this party up."

"Probably can't sleep because that house is haunted by Linda Kirby," Petra whispered in my direction and I shushed her in time to hear Ed.

"We'll quiet down neighbor. How old's the baby?"

"Two months."

"Is that right? Well that's something. Boy or girl?"

"Boy."

More sipping sounds from Ed. Us at the fire didn't make a sound.

"Hey man, why don't you come over and have a beer? You look like you could use a beer."

We all waited to hear the answer.

Finally, "All right."

"Cool. Climb over."

"No. I'll go to the gate."

"Whatever."

We could see Ed's silhouette give us the 'who knows' look with his hands palms up in the dark as the neighbor went around to the gate.

"Hey man," Ed called to him and they both came to the fire.

"Help yourself to a beer," Jeffrey called out to him.

"Here, take my seat, man," Allen said to him and came and stood behind Petra who was stretched out on a blanket.

"Cheers!" Ed called out. "To your new son!"

"Hear hear!" We all called out and raised our drinks. Petra and I had huge mugs of warm cider.

Ed sat back down behind me on the blanket and I heard him light another smoke. I turned around to look at him and saw his eyes were tense and tight in the firelight.

"It's ok, Baby," he said to me and stroked my hair.

Applesauce came over and stretched out next to my legs on the blanket, let out and sigh and lay her head down.

"So you came back from Nam all shot up?" Todd asked and raised his can towards Allen.

We all nearly snapped our necks to see Allen's reaction.

Allen didn't answer immediately and his face showed nothing.

"Not so bad," he finally answered and shifted his weight on his cane.

We were all quiet as we watched Todd to see what he would say next. But Jeffrey broke the silence next.

"Two month old son? I have an infant girl, I know how it is," Jeffrey said and smiled at the newcomer.

Todd sneered at Jeffrey and it felt like a slap to all of us. I could feel Ed tense behind me.

"My son ain't nothing like your baby," Todd drawled.

"Whaddya mean?" Allen asked and took a step towards him.

Todd looked Allen up and down and shook his head in pity.

"You the one that busted that kid's face up aren't you? The one that got killed on his bike just here lately? That kid. You do any time for that? For knocking him around like that?"

Allen took another step towards him and I felt sick and set my cider down on the ground. I felt Ed's hands on my shoulders.

"I served my time," Allen told him and leaned in his direction. Applesauce's ears went up.

The two men stared each other down and then Allen asked, "What'd you mean about my niece not being like your son?"

"My son ain't like his kid. His kid is a retard," he said and spat in the grass.

Ed pushed me off his lap and jumped up and Applesauce did too.

"Son of a bitch," I heard Jeffrey hiss and his chair toppled over as he made his way over to the neighbor.

But it was Allen, despite his cane, who got to him first and had his cane pressed against his throat.

"Son of a bitch," Jeffrey said again. "Get off him, let me at him," he told his twin.

"He ain't worth it," Ed growled and pulled Allen off and then had to pull Jeffrey off him too.

"I'm calling the law, Ed Small!" Todd threatened as he held his throat.

"Go on home and do it then, if you can get your square ass over the fence before my dog bites ya!"

"Get 'em Applesauce!" I called from where I was standing. The dog looked at me once and twitched her ear and dropped her head and took off after him in the dark.

We laughed it off. And Ed and Allen even cooked more hotdogs even though it was almost midnight. We chuckled about it even though the mood was changed. Especially when the law did come.

"You call the cops, Ed?" an officer called from the fence.

"Nah. But the neighbors did."

We all looked at Allen.

"What happened?"

"Oh he got his pants in a twist 'bout our bonfire is all," Jeffrey called out to the cop.

"Oh fuck him," Ed sighed.

The cop went next door for a few minutes and when he returned he came into the yard and sat by the fire and took off his cap.

"Fucking idiot," he sighed. "He said y'all roughed him up."

"Huh! Ahuh! Do we look like the type to rough anyone up?" Ed asked and smiled at the cop and rolled his eyes.

Petra and I both giggled and Allen hobbled over to the cooler and chuckled as he limped.

"He said something about underage girls," the cop said and looked at Petra and me.

"Baby and Ed are engaged. This was their engagement party," Allen said and I saw his hands were in fists.

"That guy he's just," Ed trailed off and waved his cigarette in the air.

"That's what I thought," the cop said and got up.
"See you Jim," Ed called to him.
"See ya, Ed."
"See? I'm on the right side of the law now," smirked Ed.
I turned around and looked at him.
"I'm a good guy now," he said and smiled, his eyes closed and he looked tired. "I'm in with the cops and the firemen and all that good stuff, now," he said and yawned.
"Baby's got school," Allen interrupted and brought us back. "Let's get the girls home."
"I don't have school, I don't have to go home," Petra piped up.
"Yes you do!" Allen, Jeffrey, Ed and me all yelled together and laughed.
**
"How was school?" my dad asked me as he came in the door the next day.
I took his lunchbox and his plaid thermos from him and took them to the kitchen.
"I got written up," I told him as I rinsed out the empty thermos.
"Written up? What's that mean?"
"That means she broke the rules," came from Petra. "What'd you do on the first day?"
She had been waiting on the porch when I got home from school.
"How'd you get here?" I had asked her.
"Walked," she said as she pulled herself up on the walker from where she'd been sitting on the step.
"A little far isn't it?"
She shrugged and wouldn't look at me.
Then I saw him. Allen came out of the garage with Thunderhead and Applesauce at his heels.
"Allen walked with me," Petra admitted.
She'd stayed on for supper and Allen had gone home after I got home. He'd said walking was good therapy for his leg and that he might walk over to Jeffrey and Lisa's next.
All that walking wasn't good for Petra though. She was exhausted.
"What rule did you break?" my dad asked me now.
"I ate lunch in the truck," I said with my back to him as I pulled the Shake N Bake chicken out of the oven.
"Why'd you eat in the truck?" Daddy asked as he hung his hat up on the peg near the back door and then started to scrub his fingers in the kitchen sink.

"Because it's quieter there. It's no big deal." I shot Petra a look.

"Hey! It's not my fault!"

It wasn't Petra's fault but it didn't make lunchtimes at school any easier. The weeks passed and I ate alone in the cafeteria every single day.

I'd never really had many friends at school, but now I had none. I watched the clock all day long dreading lunch and yet also counting down to being able to come home. I was in a hurry for time to pass and yet I wasn't.

If Ed wasn't working, I'd go straight to his house. Or Petra's. School was so stressful I'd hug Ed as soon as I saw him. And if he wasn't home, I'd hug Petra.

"I'm worried about you Baby."

"I'm fine. School's horrible but it's not forever."

"Anyone bothering you?" she asked me.

I looked out at the back of Ed's kitchen window where we were sitting at the table where I was doing homework after supper. Ed and Allen were out back working on two motorcycles that looked more like two pieces of junk with wheels than anything a person could ride.

I shrugged off Petra's questions which lead her to ask, "Who's bothering you?" And she scooted closer to me at the table.

I twisted my engagement ring around and around my finger and looked back out the window.

"Do I need to come to school?" Petra asked with an edge to her voice.

"No." And I couldn't help but smile at her.

"Then tell me what's going on."

She folded her arms over her chest.

"Well," it was all I could say for a minute but Petra let me gather my thoughts without interrupting.

"I wanted to tell people I was engaged," I finally said. It was all I could manage to put words to. The pressure in my throat wouldn't let anymore come out.

Applesauce sighed from where she lay below the table and then dropped her head on my feet.

"So why didn't you tell people?" Petra asked.

"I don't know. There was no one to tell and it doesn't matter anymore."

I looked back out at Ed. He was taking some piece of the bike apart on his lap while Allen watched and just stood there with a wrench in his hand.

Baby Small

"Doesn't matter anymore?" Petra echoed. "What's that supposed to mean?" she demanded.

"I don't know."

"It matters."

Petra stared at me and looked fierce.

"Oh it matters," she said.

And here she stood up and went to the back door with her walker. Applesauce jumped up with a clatter and followed her as did I out on the back porch.

"Hey Baby," Ed waved a greasy hand at us and then wiped his forehead leaving behind a black shiny smudge.

"Hey Ed," I waved back.

"Hey kooky friend," Ed called to Petra and waved at her. But she didn't wave or say hey back till Allen called his hello across the yard to her.

"Of course it matters," Petra said to me as I unfolded lawn chairs. "You are in love and more importantly, he is in love with you. That's everything in life that matters, right there."

And here Petra nodded towards Ed and Allen. Allen just stood there rubbing his new mustache as Ed wiped out all these little round pieces of the motorcycle and then gently laid them on the ground where he was sitting. For once Ed was the leader between he and Allen.

"You'd be right if you wanted to yell it for all the world."

"I just thought it would matter at school."

I shrugged as if to say, but it didn't.

"It does!"

I didn't answer but I was thinking, no it doesn't.

"Oh I see," Petra said low.

"What?" I asked as I went back up the stairs of the back porch and helped her come down.

"I see," she said when she finally reached the bottom and sat down in the lawn chair I offered for her.

"What do you see?" I asked her as I sat down next to her.

"You thought it would matter. You thought if you told them all you were engaged it would matter that, that, they would stop talking about you." She looked at me right in the eye.

"I don't care what they say about me," I told her and flipped my hair over my shoulder.

"Oh but you do. You do. And you thought things would be normal at school if you told them. But then you realized you were wrong."

I didn't answer. And she just stared at me a little while she thought her thoughts.

"But now you don't think it'll make any difference if they know." She waited for me to react but I just shrugged again.

"But you know what really doesn't matter? To them?"

"What?"

"That you and Ed had sex. That Ed's ten years older than you. That you were pregnant and lost him. "

Petra referred to Dan as him and not it and for that I loved her and I grabbed her and hugged her to me. But she didn't know that was why I hugged her and she said, "Hell, everyone at school is having sex with whoever all over town and half of 'em will be pregnant come May. It matters to you that you had sex with Ed, and maybe it matters to you that he's older, but not to them. They're all a bunch of clods."

"Thanks Petra."

"Any time. Now which one of these guys is gonna give me a ride home?"

"I will," Allen offered.

It was hard to not give Petra a look of any sort of concern but the truth was she could hardly walk anywhere anymore. And for her to ask for help was serious.

**

"Scooter or wheelchair?" She asked me that Halloween with her palms up as if weighing each choice. "That's what I have to decide," she told me as we sat around the bonfire at Aunt Clem's, watching Ed trying to roast a Snickers on the end of a wiener fork.

The answer turned out to be scooter and as Petra waited for it to arrive we all scrambled to get her "world" ready for it. The Saturday after it was ordered we watched Jeffrey, Allen, and Ed sawing and sanding wood in front of Petra's grandparent's house to make a bigger ramp.

"What about when Miss Kooky comes to visit you at our place?" Ed asked and rubbed Petra's head hard and then ducked away to keep from being slapped.

"Would you build a ramp there too?"

"I would for you, Baby Small, but only in the back of the house so no one knows she's visiting us, huh ahuh!" he laughed and before I knew what was happening he was grabbing me and dutch rubbing me in a headlock.

"Get off me! Your armpits stink!" I complained and tried to pull away from him.

"You like my stink, woman!" Ed growled and let me go.

Baby Small

"You guys don't have to go out of the way just so I can come over. I don't want you to alter your house for me," Petra protested when Ed and Allen began to discuss where they would put the ramp on his back porch.

"If we don't, I'll never hear the end of it from Blondie," Ed teased and laughed and put his safety glasses back on and finished sanding.

Jeffrey gave up trying to help and just sat and gave them criticism while he chain-smoked.

Two weeks later my daddy made our own make shift ramp to our house because Aunt Frances was coming for Thanksgiving with all the cousins and she was now in a wheelchair too.

"For how long does she have to use it?" I asked.

That was when it really hit that she wouldn't be getting better. That she was dying.

That night as Daddy brought up all our folding chairs from the basement to wash them and get them ready for Thanksgiving, I called Ed.

"Is your mom gonna die?" I asked him as soon as he answered the phone.

"What? Who is this? Blondie is that you? That's not a very nice crank call."

"Yes, it's me and I'm not cranking you. Is she?"

"Blondie, we're all gonna die," he answered and laughed.

"No, I mean is she getting better?"

"She's better. What's going on over there?"

"Everyone's dying!"

"Who's dying?"

"Aunt Frances isn't getting any better."

"Who else?" Ed sounded a little desperate.

"Petra."

Ed was silent for five fast heart beats.

"What? Did you say Petra?"

"Yes."

"Since when?"

"She's getting worse, I'm unhealthy, you have a dangerous job, we're all dying."

"Blondie."

"What?" I nearly shouted and my dad eyeballed me as he leaned three folding chairs against the wall in the dining room.

"Are you on your period?" Ed asked and I could hear his huge smile under the words and I felt my face burn.

"Ed, you always say that."

"ARE you?"

I rubbed my side where I had cramps.

"Yes," I finally answered.

"I knew it."

"Oh you think you know everything. Aren't you just an Einstein."

"You got your old Pink Floyd shirt on, dontcha?" he asked and now he really was laughing.

"Maybe."

"I knew it. Well at least you ain't pregnant. But that'd be ok too."

"Ed!"

"Listen, Blondie I'd love to sit and jabber with you on the horn all night but I gotta go into work. Page just came in."

**

Thanksgiving was a flurry of cousins and their spouses, of their new babies and babies who'd become toddlers, and of toddlers who'd become full blown kids. In a last minute panic I got Ed to help me hide my dollhouse up in the attic.

"Now Blondie, you're too big to play with that anymore, you should let the kids have fun with it," he'd said and chuckled as he looked at my dolls.

"Hush, just help me get it up the stairs."

"Jesus criminy, you sure don't share good."

"That doll house is special to me," I'd grumbled at him as I pushed him and smacked his butt up the narrow stairs.

That year we blended my dad's family with my mom's. Mrs. Small came over too and so did the Posts with Petra.

Aunt Frances and Petra both used the new ramp Daddy had built onto the back porch and all the little cousins were agog at Petra's scooter.

Aunt Frances stayed in her wheelchair all day and mostly stayed in the kitchen where she could watch the food preparation. But Petra parked her scooter and sat on the couch in the living room with Ed and Allen and Jeffrey and Lisa while Olivia socialized with all the other toddlers on the living room rug.

We had so many of us we ate at card tables in the living room. Moms held their babies on their laps or passed them around the table, hand to hand, from cousins to aunts to uncles. The little kids ate at our old pearly kitchen table and I checked up on them and made sure they were eating their green beans and had enough butter on their rolls.

Ed made everyone laugh by completely covering his pie in whipped cream and Aunt Clem made everyone cry and laugh by singing old songs while Lisa played the piano.

The news of my engagement to Ed rippled through the relatives and everyone wanted to know the date of our wedding. They wanted to know about my new home. They wanted to know how many kids we wanted. They were excited for us and they were disappointed that we didn't have a date set up yet.

"I'm not sure yet. Soon as school is out," was all I said and hoped that I didn't sound silly or childish.

But they didn't look at me as a child anymore and I knew this by how they acted. I was too grown up for the kids' table. Someone even brought me a cup of coffee when pies were being cut, instead of milk. I looked down at it so long thinking that that cup of black coffee meant much more than it did, that Ed nudged me and passed me the creamer.

"Too black for you?" he asked as he began spooning sugar into his. "I like mine thick with sugar," he grinned and finally quit scooping sugar and began to stir it.

"Leave some for me," I complained and pulled the sugar bowl over for myself.

The evening found us all eating leftovers and throwing tidbits to Applesauce while we watched football on tv and the first snowflakes of the year fall in the front yard.

Finally the goodbyes began. Coats were found, leftovers wrapped up and a sleeping Thunderhead was prized from the arms of a little cousin's arms. Applesauce pounded her tail against the open door in farewell to everyone as they left and to everyone's enjoyment she scampered out on the thin snow that was barely covering the grass and ran around in an excited circle as cars pulled away from the house.

We all let out a sigh to the quiet and uncrowded living room as we sank back on the couch. But the quiet was short-lived for we all belly laughed when Ed asked, "Do you think they deliver pizza on Thanksgiving?" as he rubbed his belly.

He looked around at all of us as he settled back into the couch with his knees spread wide and his sweater tight over his tummy.

"I'm a little hungry," was all he said as his eyes drifted shut and he fell into a doze.
**

After Thanksgiving break came reality for all of us. For me it was back to school and back to being shunned. For Petra it was the lonesomeness of being home all day with her grandparents. For Ed it was lots of overtime because as December began, the snow fell harder every day and the car accidents never ended.

Baby Small

For me it was a countdown to Christmas but even more exciting it was a countdown to the end of school. The year was half over.

Baby Small

Chapter Twenty-Two

We started our Christmas shopping early that year. And for the first time I could recall Daddy took me with him.

The parking lot at the Pines shopping center was a slippery mess and Daddy held my arm as we walked from his truck to the Goldblatts.

"What would Aunt Clem want?" he asked and I stared at him as he rubbed his chin and looked at coffee makers. I couldn't ever remember him getting Aunt Clem a Christmas gift. He also bought a Kermit the Frog for Olivia and he even picked it out himself out of the whole wall of identical Kermits.

"This one," he said and placed it in our cart.

We also got house slippers for Mrs. Small, new Christmas ornaments for our tree and wrapping paper for the gifts, and even a new Christmas record.

Goldblatts was followed up by Montgomery Wards where we split up and shopped for each other. I got Daddy a new set of socket wrenches and I got Ed a set too.

That night just Daddy and I were in the living room wrapping presents and listening to records when the phone rang.

Aunt Frances had died.

The family gathered once again out on the western prairie of Illinois in that big white house that was a funeral home.

Memories of my own mama in her blue pant suit with her dark hair curled tight around her head haunted the back of my eyes and made me more nervous than I should have been. But I had Ed to hold my hand now.

"Ed?" I whispered to him as he pulled a wad of tissues out of the box next to the guest sign-in.

"You need some Kleenex too?" he asked me and I noticed his eyes were red.

"No. I have some, but Ed?"

"What Blondie?"

The service had been long and confusing; full of talk about heaven and eternity and hope and yet also full of a sense of no guarantee we would be united with our loved ones in the afterlife. Aunt Frances' minister was a grim fellow and his angry eulogy gave me no comfort at all. And now as we filed out into the lobby, I needed to ask Ed something.

"Ed?"

"Yes?"

"Were you here when my mama died?"

Ed hesitated for a moment and looked down at me before looking around the furniture filled room, crowded with relatives in their country Sunday best helping themselves to Styrofoam cups of coffee, straightening their tie-tacks and digging in their pocket-books for gum or mints to quell the tired and hungry kids.

"Yes Blondie, I was here."

He squeezed my hand and looked down at me, his eyes sad and his lips in a pout.

"Mom and I came out. It was a lot more crowded than it is now."

He looked around the room again and pointed to a wide doorway that had a thick velvet curtain drawn across it.

"That," he pointed, "that was opened up and I think there was another room on the other side also because so many people came Baby, your mom was so young. Mom and I sat in the back there with your Aunt Clem."

Ed cleared his throat and rubbed his chin and looked thoughtful. His hair was clean and shiny and parted straight down the middle and his beard was trim and neat over his blue dress shirt and tie.

"Aunt Clem, well, she was supposed to sit up front, being your mom's sister and all," Ed said to me now as he guided me away from all the relatives. "But I think it was Jeffrey," Ed said and paused as he guided me to a hard little couch. "It was Jeffrey who could not bear to be near your mom's um, casket." Ed looked at me and dipped his head willing me to understand something.

"What?" I asked.

"Well," Ed swallowed and scratched his head. "Jeffrey was always," Ed paused and I waited for him to say Jeffery was always nervous or different.

"Jeffrey was always so crazy about your mama, he took it very hard. And you know Jeffrey, he's different." Ed shrugged.

I remembered after I'd seen my mama laying in her white casket that Daddy had carried me off to that back room to Aunt Clem and sent me home with her. That felt a hundred years ago instead of just eleven. I pictured her black shiny hair and looked around at all my aunts and uncles, most of them with gray at their temples or all through their hair. I looked around and saw the wrinkled faces, the skin beat hard from the country sun.

"Well where were you and your mom?"

Baby Small

"Well, we were with Jeffrey and Allen. Allen, he walked up to the casket and he shook your dad's hand. I watched, from back there, with Jeffrey. Aunt Clem went up with Allen. I didn't feel I needed to go."

Ed looked away from me.

He looked as if he weren't going to say anything else on the subject.

"Why didn't you feel as if you needed to go?" I asked him, curious, and waited two whole minutes for him to answer.

"Well Blondie, I'd already said my goodbye to her," he said and squeezed me to him or the hard little couch.

"When?" I asked and pulled away just enough to see his face.

"Um," he stalled and wouldn't look at me. "Um," he turned away from me until I took him by the chin and guided his face back to me.

"Well, you came and got me, remember?" he said gently.

"Yes."

I could barely breathe and motioned that he should go on.

"I uh, I said goodbye when, when I looked at her and I had um, you know, listened for her heart," and here Ed's face softened and when he blinked he had tears. He sniffed and cleared his throat and wiped his lips with his fingers.

"When, when she didn't have a heartbeat and I saw her face, saw she was gone, she had just gone, it was like she was there, she had just been there."

Ed snapped his fingers and continued, "Her face looked like she had only just been there and had only just left or was leaving right then, Blondie. And I said goodbye to her then and I think she said goodbye to me." And here Ed dropped his face and ran his fingers through his hair and messed it up.

"Blondie," he said with his head bowed. "Blondie let's just bug out of here after the burial. I can't take anymore death."

I looked around at the crowded room and said, "Yes."

The long line of cars and mostly trucks snaked up and down the country blacktop through a flurry of spiraling snowflakes; fat, wet, and heavy as the country side was blanketed in quiet snow.

After Aunt Frances was buried, Ed and I visited baby Dan, Ed's brother Dale, and lastly my mama's graves.

"I'll take care of her Mrs. Hunnicutt," Ed said down to her headstone as he held me close to his side. "They're in the ground, Blondie. But not really," Ed said to me as I drove us away from the cemetery.

"I don't like to think of them in the ground, under all that snow, and dirt. They're in Heaven," I said with conviction.

"I suppose you are right." Ed nodded a few times and seemed like he was going to say more but he didn't.

"What do you think it's like?" I asked and looked towards the sky.

"Hmmm. It's like what it's like before you're born."

"But I don't remember that."

"Well. You're not supposed to know."

"Why not?"

"Because. Because you need to have faith. Because, you'll remember it once you get there, Blondie."

"I don't know. I don't want to think about it right now."

We didn't talk the rest of the drive to town. Ed didn't say one word till we pulled up to his house.

"We're home."

**

"Did I force you to grow up, Blondie?" Ed asked me as he pulled sweaty strands of hair off my forehead and kissed the moist skin.

My eyes closed and I tried to catch my breath.

"No Ed, no," I whispered.

"Did I force you to fall in love with me?"

I opened my eyes and looked in to his as he lay above me. He too was breathing as ragged as me as he held his weight off of me as he lay on top of me.

"Penny for your thoughts?" he asked and still I thought about his question.

"Did I bring shame on your family? Would your mama be ashamed of me? Of us?" and here he hid his face with his hand.

"No, Ed," and I reached up to him and moved his hand and tucked his hair behind his ear.

The sweat dotted his forehead and his temples were damp. We were both sweaty even though it continued to blow and snow hard outside. We were in Ed's house with the radiators clanking their way through all his rooms. We were in Ed's waterbed with the heat turned up high. And we were holding each other tightly.

"Did I wear you down? Did I use cunning to get my way with you Blondie? What do you see when you look at me?"

"You're trying to wear me down now, Ed!" I giggled from under him and he gave a look that made me put a lid on my giggles. "I see my sweet Ed," I quickly said to him. "I see my world, my life, I see the one who I want to live with. I see, I see, a lot of hair," and I started giggling again as all his hair fell in his face. He laughed and smiled behind it all and I stretched up and kissed him.

"You won't see anything when I flip you over!" Ed growled and rolled off me and with one gentle but powerful pull he flipped me over on my tummy.

"Are you gonna regret this later?" I asked him while laughing hard under him.

I stretched out on my stomach and pulled a pillow up under my face and rested on it as Ed climbed on top of me.

"Never. Not in ten thousand years."

"Did I cause you to," I paused for the right word. "Did I cause you to leave your path, your fate?" I asked with my face against the pillow.

"You are my fate, Blondielocks. You didn't pull me from my path. You pulled me to my knees. But you had no idea of your power over me. It was me who was weak. I'm a scoundrel for taking you. For chasing you around. I'm a scoundrel. But I'll never stray."

He grunted and pushed my knees open and I felt him wedge himself between them.

"You're not doing something weird with my butt are you?"

"I'm not doing that, Blondie! How perverted do you think I am?" he yelped and then laughed, "Huh! Ahuh!" and kissed me behind the ear.

"Jesus, Blondie, I'd never hurt you."

And he didn't. He was gentle as always but I missed being able to see his face and when we were finished I turned to face him, to see him. He was tired and his eyes were shut as he rolled onto his side.

"Ed, I don't think I can stay here all night."

I patted the waterbed and caused waves to ripple through it slowly.

"But it's so warm," Ed murmured and collapsed next to me.

We rolled up and down together on the waves of the bed and he pulled the flannel comforter up over both of us.

"You should be here every night for the rest of forever."

I was asleep when I heard him say, "Besides, your dad will never miss you tonight. The blizzard's just getting started. I'm sure he's staying out at your uncles, and I'm betting school's cancelled tomorrow."

I didn't hear anymore till morning when his pager went off and he rolled out of bed. He looked tall against the morning light as he slid on his pants. I hunkered down into the warm bed, but the smell of coffee pulled me out; that and I wanted to say goodbye before he went to work.

**

Christmas was quiet as we were all still mourning the loss of Aunt Frances. We all exchanged our gifts on Christmas Eve and it was Olivia and her delight with her new Kermit that cheered us all up and a round of hugs went around the room as we wished each other Merry Christmas.

Baby Small

Daddy poured us all eggnog from a carton and Aunt Clem made cocoa for everyone who didn't like the egg nog. As cups were collected and exchanged and taken to the kitchen, Ed and I gave each other our gifts. We laughed when we saw how practical we both were this year; I gave Ed socket wrenches and he gave me a set of tea cups with little yellow flowers on them and a matching tea pot.

New Year's Eve was much happier this year than last; last year it'd been Ed's last night before he went away to finish flight school. This year we had a party at Aunt Clem's with Allen, Jeffrey, Lisa, Petra, me and Ed. Aunt Clem was there of course and so was my dad for a little bit. Petra sat on the couch with Applesauce at her feet while Ed and I cleared away the furniture and tried to learn to Jitterbug. Aunt Clem put on old records and kept telling us how to do the dance but Ed kept breaking out in to The Hustle.

"It's not disco, Ed, it's not disco!" Allen kept telling him but Ed wouldn't stop.

"He can't help but shake that big butt of his," Jeffrey laughed at him.

I noticed Petra checking out his butt and not being discreet about it either.

"Come on Ed, we're jitterbugging," I told him as I tried to do the steps that Aunt Clem made look so easy as Ed kept swiveling his hips in his tight jeans.

Jeffrey even tried to help us pick it up but eventually it was Lisa and I who finally got the steps down. Ed, Allen and Jeffrey and Olivia and Aunt Clem too, laughed and watched us from where they sat on top of the dining room table as Lisa and I danced in between the living room and dining room.

We stayed up till after midnight eating junk food and drinking soda pop then Petra and I said goodnight to everyone and Ed and Allen walked us across the street to Petra's. It was much easier getting over there now that Petra had her scooter.

Ed told me goodbye and kissed me till Allen told him to break it up already and Petra let out a sharp shrill whistle. Ed was a little tipsy and his tongue was warm against my lips in the cold night air and I never wanted him to stop. But he had to go home.

I spent the night at Petra's house and slept on a rollaway bed in her new bedroom in the old den behind the kitchen. But really I couldn't fall asleep. I kept thinking, this is a new year, the year I get married. I kept thinking of Ed's lips.

Baby Small

I woke up early and after I poked Petra awake and persuaded her to get up, I drove us over to Ed's, but not without Allen. He saw us from where he sat bundled up in his winter coat on Aunt Clem's front porch, drinking coffee and reading the morning paper. I looked at him over Petra's lap as she sat between us in the cab of the truck holding a plate of hot glazed donuts her grandma made for us.

"What kind of wedding dress will you get?" Petra asked me after we got to Ed's. We were sitting around the red and white table in Ed's kitchen, eating donuts and sipping his dark coffee.

"Oh I don't know. I haven't thought about it," I sighed and a hundred new worries fluttered into my mind but were shoved away by Ed.

"A white one, duh," Ed said with his mouth full of sticky donut.

Petra looked at me and raised an eyebrow but didn't say anything else.

I spent the rest of the day mad at her and later when Allen had taken her home I asked Ed, "Will people think it's bad if I wear white?"

"Why would anyone think it's bad? And what sort of people are gonna be at our wedding who would think bad thoughts about you? White is what brides wear, Baby."

We were out in the garage with a space heater whirring away and glowing orange in the corner while he worked on his motorcycle. His was resembling a motorcycle more and more everyday whereas Allen's still looked like a skeleton.

"I'm not building his," Ed had told me days before. "If he wants it built, he's gonna have to put in the work. I'll help him. But I ain't doing it all. And I ain't buying the parts either."

Allen didn't like to put in the hours on working on the bike. But Ed did. And here we sat in the cold garage instead of going to the movies or going out to eat and I was fine with that. I had a big mug of hot chocolate and a ball of Jiffy Pop hot on my lap and had been munching and thinking about dresses and weddings and gossipy people while Ed worked on the bike.

"It might be bad for me to wear a white dress," I told Ed now.

"Aw Baby, you look good in white. I'd like a white strapless dress for you," he said and put down what he had in his hands and made a curvy woman shape with his hands. "Va va voom!"

"But white is for virgins," I told him and held the cocoa mug in front of my face while I waited for him to respond.

"Virgins?" he frowned and tucked his hair behind his ears and leaned over and dug in his tool chest. "Shoot, Blondie, I can count on one hand how many times we did it."

He scratched his head and ticked off his fingers, "Under the table, at the lake, in your bed, in my bed, and that's just four times in two years."

He pooched his lips out at me and frowned again.

"You're wearing a white strapless dress, I say so," he said and began working on his bike again, his eyes dark with concentration and his forehead wrinkled.

"You say so?" I asked him and set the mug and the popcorn down on the floor of the garage.

"I say so," he said and didn't even look up at me.

I stood up and wiped my hands off on each other and clamped my mouth shut.

"I'm the man, Baby. I'm older. I know what's right. I know what's best. You're wearing a white strapless dress."

He shot me a fierce look with his eyes focused hard and flashing cold blue that pained my heart.

"Now hold on a minute," I said down to him. "Hold on one stinking minute," I said to him again and his face softened and he broke into a huge smile.

"You know I'm right Blondie. And once we get married, I'm the boss, I'm the head of the house."

"Well we ain't married," I said between gritted teeth and took a step towards him.

"Blondie," he said up to me, still smiling, his eyes shining.

"Listen here," I said, pointing my finger down at him as he sat there on the garage floor in his mechanics overalls smirking up at me. "Listen here, mister."

"Oh lord, you're a hell-cat," he said and grinned.

"You better believe it, Ed Small. No one has ever told me what to wear."

"Petra does all the time," he complained and ducked away from me as I took a playful swipe at his head.

"Petra's been telling me for years what to wear and I've never listened to her, have I?"

"Does this mean no strapless dress, Blondie?" he asked and scratched his head.

"It means, I'll be picking out my own dress, and you won't be there when I do."

"Awww, Blondie-locks," he whined and went back to working on his bike.

We were quiet for a few minutes; I stared hard at him and he ignored me.

"You're gonna look so beautiful," he said without looking at me and without stopping tightening things on his bike.

I smiled at the happy look of concentration on his face.

"You're gonna look like an angel in your white strapless dress," he said and looked up at me and pooched out his big lips at me before winking up at me.

"Huh! Ahuh!" he laughed and ducked as I grabbed the foil ball of Jiffy Pop and dumped it all on his head. "Huh ahuh!" he laughed as he picked popcorn out of his hair and ate a bite and quick as a cat he reached out and grabbed me around my knees and pulled me down on his lap.

**

I was thankful for Ed's light heart and cheerfulness because seeing him made life bearable when heading back to school. I felt like an outcast and even when old friends from the pom-pom team tried to get me to talk or sit with them at lunch, I worried that they only did it to get details out of me about Ed. About everything.

But eventually I gave in to their invites. These girls who reached out to me at lunchtime made school less stressful but even still as January became February; I had a hard time waking up in the morning for school and was constantly late to first period.

Petra gave me a hard time because she heard I was back with the pom-pom team and it took a whole afternoon for me to convince her I wasn't.

"I was lonely at school," I tried to explain to her as we sat at her grandparents' table drinking coffee the day before Valentine's.

Petra looked perturbed. She was snapping pink and red iced cookies in half and putting them back on the plate.

"Won't your grandma be mad about that?" I asked her and she glared at me and snapped another one in half and threw it back onto the plate.

"What's the matter with you, Petra? Are you on your period?" I asked her and secretly felt mad at myself because that's what Ed was always asking me when I was being difficult.

"I am, as a matter a fact! What's you're excuse? You on the rag too?"

"No, I'm not," I snapped back at her.

"You're not?" she asked as she looked at me and one of her eyebrows went up.

She picked up a cookie and bit the point off the heart and continued to look at me as she munched.

"What?"

"Nothing."

"No, what, really?" I asked and picked up a cookie and bit it but it tasted too sweet to me and made my mouth water too much.

But she didn't say anything. She just widened her eyes and nodded her head and looked at me. She rolled her thin hand in the air at me and I could see that she'd pained her nails pink with red hearts on each one.

"What?" I asked again and put the cookie down on the table.

"You're supposed to have your period when I have mine."

"Says who?" I asked and laughed and picked up the cookie again and snapped it in half.

"Says since this whole past year. We've been synced. I've been keeping track."

"What?" I nearly shrieked.

"I have it on the calendar in my room. I've been mapping both of us all year. Especially when I thought," she trailed off and looked away and blinked her eyes real fast.

"When you thought what? You thought I was pregnant again?"

"No!" she yelled. "No," she said much quieter, "I really started paying attention this summer," and here she sighed.

"Why?"

"Because Kai. I thought he and I would, you know, so I wanted to know when it was safe."

"Is it ever safe?" I asked once again amazed that Petra would know so much about our bodies that I didn't even know.

"I don't think any time is ever safe with you."

She looked me up and down.

"What's that mean?"

"I'm on the fourth day of my period and you've not even started yours and we've been locked in sync for nearly a year."

"Well, we got out of sync because you quit school."

"Oh what's that mean? You're synced up with the pom pom team now?"

"No!"

"Huh!" she huffed at me and snapped another cookie in half.

**

"Thunderhead looks fatter, don't you think?"

Baby Small

"What?" I asked and almost jumped out of my skin.

I'd been jumpy ever since Valentine's Day. I didn't even know if my jumpiness was making everything taste off or if everything tasting off was making me jumpy.

"Who's fat?" I asked and instinctively covered my tummy with both hands.

"Thunderhead. Look at him. He looks thick."

I looked on the floor where the cat was laying on his side right in front of the tv at my house. Ed had come over for dinner after work and I had made a roast for him and Daddy.

Daddy peeked around his paper and looked at the cat and then glared at Ed.

"He's probably a she and she's probably pregnant," Daddy said with a snap to his newspaper and he went back to reading.

"Huh ahuh," Ed chuckled quietly and shook his head like that was the craziest thought ever.

"Thunderhead, you been out getting in trouble?" he asked the cat and nudged it with his socked toe. "Bad kitty," he said and I felt my stomach roll and I groaned and gritted my teeth.

"What's the matter with you?" Ed asked me. "You look all pale and sweaty."

"I think I'm coming down with the flu."

"Well, you look plum green."

Another snap of the paper and Daddy looked at me.

"You didn't hardly touch dinner," Daddy said.

"I know. I think I'm coming down with something."

They both looked at me.

"Something's going around school," I shrugged and regretted it; the movement of my head made me dizzy.

"Hmmph," Ed grunted. "Only thing going 'round that school," he started to say and stopped and looked at my Daddy and then looked back at me. "Jesus lord Baby Small!" he gasped as his eyes widened on me and he stood up.

"What?"

Now my dad's newspaper was completely forgotten and he let it slip off his lap and onto the floor.

"Jesus lord, you missed your period didn't you!" Ed breathed out low.

I blushed red hot and with it came a wave of nausea. I looked from Ed to my dad and back to Ed.

"Maybe," I admitted and hung my head.

"You're pregnant!" Both of them exclaimed.

"Ed, that's not it. I'm not. I'm just sick is all."

I stood up to go over to my dad who looked as pale and sick as I felt but Ed intercepted me and pulled me close to him. I let him hug me tight and I hid my face in his worn flannel shirt and sighed and started to cry.

"I'm gonna be a dad," he said with his chin pressing down on top of my head and his beard tangling in my hair.

"I don't know, Ed. I think I just have the stomach bug is all."

"No it's not," he disagreed and squeezed me closer to him. "You're pregnant." He sighed and rubbed the back of my head and stroked my hair from the top of my head clear down my back.

I peeked out from under his arm and looked at my dad who had his elbows on his knees and was rubbing the bristly hairs of his crew cut.

"Daddy, I don't know for sure."

"It don't matter," he said without looking at me. "I asked you to be good Baby, just till you finished school and got married."

"It's okay," Ed whispered in my ear just for me to hear. "It's okay," he said again and kissed my hair above my ear. "You're still good, Baby Small."

"But I might not even be pregnant," I said up to Ed and the tears sprang hot from the corners of my eyes.

"It's okay," Ed said down to me.

He pulled up the tail of his shirt and wiped my eyes and wiped my cheeks.

"I'm here for you," he told me and hugged me tight.

**

Chapter Twenty-Three

We were all nervous at the doctor's office the next week. Ed and Daddy both came with me to my appointment after school. They both took off early from work to go with me. It was a silent ride through barren winter fields to the doctor over in Rush.

"You need a closer doctor," Ed observed as we took it slow around an icy curve, Daddy shifting low in the old truck.

"This doctor is fine!" Daddy barked at him across the cab of the truck and that's all they said to each other the whole ride.

One of them was hopeful and the other one was quiet and nervous and I was stuck in the middle.

I felt embarrassed and out place sitting between the two of them at the doctor's office; Ed tall and broad-shouldered still in his flight suit; his hair long and windblown. He sat next to me with his lips in a thick pout and stroked his beard as he thought his thoughts and worried his own worries. Daddy next to me in his old work clothes with his safety glasses still on, sat on the edge of his seat and cracked his knuckles over and over until every woman in the waiting room glared at him.

"Baby Hunnicutt."

When they called my name both Daddy and Ed stood up while I stayed seated. The nurse eyed Ed up and down and blushed and smiled before she said, "Gentlemen, you'll have to wait out here. We'll take good care of her."

"You make sure you do," Ed called to the nurse. "She's my own true love-child."

"Come on, Baby," the nurse said and shook her head distractedly at Ed as she held her hand out to me.

I felt everyone stare at me as I got up and walked to the door. But then again I had on my old crocheted and quilted dress over a yellow ribbed turtleneck and maybe they were just looking at that.

"You'll be ok, Baby," Ed called to me and I turned around and looked at him one last time before I followed the nurse through the door.

**

"Pregnant! YES!" Ed whooped the entire ride home. "Yes! I'm gonna be a daddy!" he yelled and beat on the dashboard of Daddy's truck. "Take us to the Dairy Freeze Mr. Hunnicutt, I'm buying!"

Daddy just shook his head the entire ride back to town but he had a faint smile on his blushing face.

Baby Small

"I'm happy for you, Baby, but I'm worried about you too," was all he had said to me after the doctor examined me and wanted to meet with me and my dad. I insisted Ed be there too and we all were quiet while the doctor looked Ed up and down.

"Medevac?" the doctor had finally said. "Well that's good, I guess," then the doc had invited us all to sit in his office and he told us all the complications of me having a baby while being on blood thinners. How we would have to plan for my delivery and how closely I would need to be monitored.

But for now, we three sat in the cab of the truck, the labor and delivery and arrival of the baby was too far in the future for us to worry about and it didn't outweigh the happiness Ed was feeling. I think even Daddy was feeling it too because he ordered two cheeseburgers and a large onion rings and I couldn't remember him ever ordering junk food.

The carhop stared at us all when she brought the food. She stared from Daddy to me and then she even craned her head almost inside our truck to get a good look at Ed.

No one else seemed to notice but me.

"Ahh," Ed sighed when the food came and we were all opening our sandwiches and the inside of the truck smelled like good things to eat. "This is the life and we should all be thankful."

"Amen," my Daddy agreed and held up his shake.

By the time we got home Daddy and Ed were full of plans for our future kid; each one trying to out-do the other one. Meanwhile I just had a headache and felt sick to my stomach again and was glad to get home.

Ed and Daddy were talking about swingsets and treehouses and .22 rifles as we went through the front door and didn't even notice that I crawled under the dining room table and cuddled up with Applesauce and fell asleep.

**

"Oh my God! You'll be dropping out of school!" Petra squealed when I told her the news the next afternoon. "Thank God, I was about to lose my mind being home alone every day."

"I'm not dropping out, Petra."

Daddy and Ed had both said the same thing. I didn't even argue with them. I came out from under the table with Applesauce at my side and I pointed my finger at both of them.

"Oh no, here it comes," Ed had mumbled and ducked his head so all his hair fell in his face.

"What?" My daddy had asked.

"You'll see," Ed had warned.

"I'm not dropping out of school. I'm finishing." And that was all I'd said to Daddy and Ed before heading up to my room. And this is what I told Petra now.

"I'm finishing."

"They'll all know," she warned me.

"I don't care."

But they didn't know. Because I looked the same as everyone else still.

Now that I was pregnant, Ed made sure he came over almost every day or I went to his place. And every time we saw each other, he placed his ear to my belly and listened as if he'd hear something besides my tummy gurgling. He'd speak to my belly and the little miracle growing in there.

"Boy or girl, Baby, what do you think it is?"

"I don't know, Ed."

"Can't you tell?"

"I can barely tell I'm pregnant yet, much less what this baby is."

"Aww Blondie, I'm just so excited."

And I was too. But some days I tried not to think about it. But other days it was all I thought about. Some days it seemed as if the baby would be here too soon. Other days it felt as if it'd never get here. I couldn't imagine being huge pregnant. And Ed couldn't wait for me to balloon out. He measured my belly with his hands. He stood me against a white wall and had me pull up my shirt a little and he took a photo of me every other few days.

"When are you actually due?" Ed asked every single day.

"August 16th."

"And how do you reckon they came up with that date?" he'd ask every single time.

"It's based on when I had my last period. And when we, you know. And I actually missed my period in January but didn't realize it until February," I admitted to him and felt sheepish.

"When we you know, you know," Ed would always say and waggle his eyebrows at me like a nut.

"I just hope they got the date right," he'd say a few minutes later, all serious.

"I do too. But I have a feeling I'll know when it's time."

"Well I would hope." And he'd be back to grinning at me again.

I had no doubt I would know when it was time for the baby to be born. It'd have to be pretty obvious.

March came in windy and wet and full of icy rainstorms. March also brought the first tangible changes to my body.

"Whoa, Blondie," Ed said to me and batted his eyelashes and I could have sworn he was blushing.

"What?" I snapped but I knew what he was going to say.

All my clothes and dresses were getting tighter and tighter across my chest. It was like my breasts had doubled in size over night just like Petra always threatened they would. They hardly fit in my bras that I had left over from the last time. I shoved them in the bras as much as I could and they were tender and it made me cranky. I felt like everyone was staring at me wherever I went. Even if I had a coat on, I was aware of my breasts defining my figure.

"Blondie," was all Ed said to me but he made squeezing motions with his hands as he licked his lips and his eyes looked absolutely glowing and crazy.

"Stop it!" I laughed and swatted at his hands but he came closer anyway.

"I can't help myself, I think this dress is gonna blow apart, Blondie."

He laughed and came closer and pulled at the tie at the top of my dress. We were at his house and I had just finished my homework at his kitchen table and he had just finished the dinner dishes. I couldn't wait to marry Ed and move in and not have to divide my time between here and my Daddy's house. Over at Ed's was the only time we had any privacy and I spent as many hours here as Daddy would allow when Ed was off from work.

"Shoo!" I teased Ed and bent his thumbs back till he howled.

"Where's that belly? How come it's not popping out yet?" he asked and pulled his thumbs free from my grip. "Show me that belly."

"I can't show you today I'm wearing a dress," I told him as he pulled playfully at the full skirt of my dress.

"So?" he asked and I realized he was dropping down to his knees.

"No picture today, Ed."

I put my hands over my tummy that felt just a little rounder and a little plumper than usual.

"Maybe it's not a picture that I want," he said as his head disappeared under my skirt.

"ED!" I shrieked and reached for him through the skirt but I couldn't see him.

"I'm just looking for your belly," came his muffled reply from under my dress.

I felt his beard on my thighs; his hands gripped the backs of them.

"Can we have sex, Blondie?" he asked from under all the cloth and sounded pathetic.

"Why?" I asked.

"Because I'm frisky, that's why."

"Ed," I squealed as he kissed the inside of my leg. "That's not my belly!"

"Oh, sorry," he apologized and reached his hands up to my stomach.

He was gentle as he ran his warm hands over my tummy that was just barely beginning to pop out. I felt his gentle sigh puff on my skin and then I felt him pull away and come out from under my skirt.

"Come to the bedroom, Blondie," he told me. "You're feet look like they gotta be tired. I'll rub them. And your back too. And other things."

His hair was a wild fuzzy tangle from rubbing against my dress and he had a sharp focus to his pale eyes as he pulled me down the hall.

Chapter Twenty-Four

The middle of April I finally began to show. I popped out and it felt like overnight. I went to bed early and exhausted one night and woke up and could hardly roll out of bed. I was off kilter and off balance as I made my way as fast as possible to the bathroom. I had a round little ball where my waist had been. That morning as I got dressed I found out only dresses would fit me now. I would need to get out the box of hand-me-down maternity clothes Aunt Frances had given me before she died. I was dreading opening it up, though I would have been hard pressed to explain why.

I told Daddy at the breakfast table early that morning that I needed some money for a few new things because even my dresses were getting snug on me.

"You better head over to Montgomery Wards then," he told me as he filled my glass with more milk.

But it wasn't maternity clothes I came home with.

We looked at all the horrible maternity pants and all the horrible tent-shaped shirts with Winnie the Pooh on the front.

"You're having a baby. You're not becoming one," Petra said as she looked at all the cartoon character shirts. "These are horrible," she said with disgust at all the pastel colored things.

"I can't wear these, Petra."

"I couldn't be seen with you if you did," she said and turned her scooter around.

"Even these pants are horrible," I told her as I browsed through all the stretchy pants but she didn't hear me because something had caught her eye and she was whizzing away from me across the store. I had no idea where she was headed, but I felt compelled to follow her.

"Oh my God," she said when she heard me behind her. "Look at that," she said and sounded out of breath.

I followed her thin hand to where it was pointing at a pure white eyelet prom dress. It had sparkles all over it.

"Petra. No."

"Look at it. It's perfect."

Petra looked starstruck, pale, wide eyed, speechless.

"No."

"Your wedding is one month away," Petra told me as if I had forgotten.

Baby Small

I wouldn't even walk near it.

Petra held out the layers of pure white eyelet in both her hands. She ran her tiny fingers over all the material.

"It's perfect," she breathed.

"It's strapless."

I looked down at her and crossed my arms over my chest.

"I can't let you get married in anything else, Baby. If I don't help you pick something out you'll end up getting married in some sort hand-me-down."

Her little eyes focused on me like two black stones.

"Petra it's a prom dress, not a wedding dress," I said but yet walked around her scooter towards it and felt the material myself.

"Ohhh," I said surprised as I touched it. "It feels like, it feels like," I paused and couldn't think of a word to describe it.

"Like cake," Petra said as she touched the beautiful material.

"Yes!"

I looked down at her and then back at the dress.

"Cake. How strange," we both said at the same time.

"It is pretty," I finally agreed after I took it off the rack and looked at it from all angles; at all the white frothy cloth, the sparkles sprinkled lightly across the skirt. "Oh but look at how much it is." I held the tag over for her to see.

"You're getting it," Petra said and jutted her chin out at me and took the dress out of my hands.

"I don't even know if it fits," I said and took it back from her.

She pulled it back towards her and looked at the tag.

"That's a three," she said and then looked me up and down with her measuring eyes. "You're a five now."

I raised my eyebrow at her.

"You are," she said matter of factly and began to flip through the dresses.

But it turned out that I wasn't a five. I was a seven. And if I got too much bigger I wouldn't be that either.

"Holy cow!" Petra had gasped from her scooter where she was supposed to be sitting on the other side of the dressing room curtain.

"Petra!" I hollered at her as I stood there in my underpants holding the dress in front of me.

Petra's eyes were about to bug out of her face.

"Holy cow," she gasped again. "Let me see your belly again. Please," She added and her face softened and I moved the dress again and let her see.

She drove the nose of her scooter into the dressing room and stretched out her hand and put it on my belly.

"Oh my gosh," she whispered. "I can feel him!" she cried out and when she looked up at me she had tears in her eyes. "Oh my gosh, Baby, you're really gonna be a mom!" And then she really broke down crying with her fist in a curled ball at her mouth.

That was how the store clerk had found us and pulled us apart and then helped me get in the dress and get it zipped up while Petra watched.

"You're getting this," Petra said to me in the big three-way mirror as she tugged on the full skirt of the dress from where she sat next to me.

"Call her father," Petra called out to the clerk. "Tell him to come see his Baby," she sniffled. "Tell him to come buy this dress," she said louder as the clerk ran off to the register.

Daddy came fast. He thought I needed the doctor. But I was fine and it was good that he came and saw me in my dress.

"You really are getting married. And you really are very pregnant, Baby," he said as he stood there amidst all the satin and sequins and layers in the prom dress department of Montgomery Wards. "There's no kidding anyone about your condition," he shook his head and jingled the coins in his pocket. "But everyone who sees you, can see you're in love with Ed Small, and," he paused here and looked around, "And everyone can tell that Ed's not such a lay-about after all, and well, he loves you too."

Petra looked from Daddy to me and back to Daddy with the clerk behind her just as speechless as us both.

"This is a beautiful moment," was all Petra could finally say.

And it was.

"Wait till Ed hears you're gonna wear a white strapless dress just like he wanted!" Petra gushed as I took her home.

"You're not to tell him!" I warned her.

"You better not get any more pregnant or I won't have to. You won't be fittin' in that dress! Only one more month till you get married! You better hope Ed Jr. in there doesn't sprout too big in that time!"

**

That night as I lay in bed, Petra's words echoed in my ears. One more month. Just thinking about it set the baby inside me kicking and rolling.

One more month till I got married. It was with that thought the butterflies kicked up in my stomach and the baby kicked up too and made it hard to drift off. If it weren't for the pure exhaustion I felt at the end of the day- every single day lately, I'm sure I wouldn't have ever gotten any sleep in the next couple of weeks.

"Blondie, two more weeks and you'll graduate and we'll get married and before you know it, August 16 will be here and we'll be parents!" Ed told me as he kicked back on two legs on the kitchen chair in my Dad's backyard.

"You make it sound so simple," I said as I rubbed the sides of my belly. The skin felt tight and it hurt.

"It is simple," Ed said without noticing the discomfort I was in.

He drank a cold can of beer and stared off into the clouds while I snapped beans in a plastic bowl.

It didn't seem simple to me. I had a million worries on my mind. My size for one. It was getting harder to fit in the desks at school. It was getting harder to go down the halls. It was getting harder to handle all the stares and looks from the kids and the teachers. All their stares and all the little comments from them made me sad. It was ok for everyone else to have sex, but it was not ok for me to be pregnant. That's what it felt like as I heard someone whisper 'slut' as I walked past.

I was also worried about the wedding. Ed was all about keeping it loose and small. Just us. At the lake. No big deal. These were the things he was always saying to me.

But the cousins were calling everyday it seemed. The wedding was two weeks away and I was panicking.

"Baby!" Ed's cry shocked me so much I dropped the Tupperware bowl of beans on the back porch and they spilled out everywhere.

"What?"

"Are you in labor? You're breathing really hard!" He was at my side in a second.

"Ed, we're not ready to get married," I managed to say.

"We are too. You're gonna graduate and turn eighteen and you're gonna have my child, and I've loved you a thousand years if I've loved you one," he said as he dropped to his knees next to me and took both my hands.

"But we don't have the cake or the flowers or what about my cousins?"

Ed looked confused and scratched his head.

"What about them?"

"They'll want to be there!"

"Awww Blondie. Can't they just come to the house after?"

"I guess," I sighed. "But what will I feed them?"

"Cake of course. Mom's making a huge cake! Huh ahuh!"

"I didn't know," I admitted.

"You've been too busy being pregnant and perfect and going to all those doctor's appointments," Ed said and chuffed me on the chin.

And he was right. I was going to lots of doctor's appointments. Appointments for my heart doctor. And appointments for my obstetrician. Even an appointment where the two of them actually saw me together at a clinic in between the two different offices. There was much note-taking between the two of them about the best way for me to labor and the best medicines for me to be on before the baby came, while the baby was coming, and what to put me on after the arrival.

Many tests were ordered on my blood just about every single week. I was exhausting myself driving myself over to Rush Hospital for scans and blood draws and monitoring. One Friday afternoon when I'd missed the entire day of school going to appointments and having tests and consultations I was so tired that on the way home I found myself on autopilot in the old truck and I realized that the gentle curves I was taking on the road through the tall prairie grass, was the road out to Kai's.

My feet were swollen and my back was aching and so tight that once I got out to his grave I was afraid if I sat down I'd not be able to get up again.

"Here," I heard someone say and turned around to see Kai's mother. Her long hair seemed faded, as did the freckles from her once young face as she handed me a glass of tea. "You look beautiful Baby," she said and held her hand out to my tummy where the calico cotton of my dress clung to it in the prairie wind. "You're gonna be a mama," she said and I barely heard her voice. "Pregnancy is a beautiful thing and childbirth is a miracle, I'm so happy for you," she said and she smiled. The corners of her eyes looked wet and she wiped at them with her knuckles.

"Thank you," I told her and took the tea and looked over the rim of the cold glass at Kai's grave as I drank it.

"You'll have a natural childbirth, of course," she said and I looked back at her.

"What is that?" I felt stupid for not knowing.

"Well, you know, Lamaze, and handling your labor with relaxation and staying home to labor as long as you can. I'm sure Ed will help you relax," she said and smiled and the color came back to her cheeks.

"Um, I don't think I can do that." I looked down at my wrist and the two hospital bracelets I was still wearing from the day of tests of exams.

"Of course you can. And you can get a midwife to help you if you don't think Ed will be enough."

She took my hand in both of hers and held it and I felt the strength of her broad, warm hands and thought of what a good mom she was, and how nice it would have been to have a mom at a time like this.

"I'm still so sorry about Kai," I said and swallowed hard before looking at her.

"Of course you are. We all are. But we'll get through it. But why don't you think you can do natural childbirth?"

"Well because of my heart," I told her, my hand going to my chest where my scar was. "I'm on all kinds of medicines for my heart now, and they have to make sure I don't, I don't bleed out."

I had hesitated to tell her that. It seemed morbid to say it so close to Kai's grave. But she didn't mind and I ended up spending the rest of the day with her.

"Please call me Sandy," she told me as she sliced a warm loaf of bread for us at their butcher block table.

We spent the afternoon together with me asking her hundreds of questions about labor and delivery and the care of a baby. She answered every single one and never seemed to tire of me needing to talk about so many things that I was afraid of; so many things I didn't know how to do.

"You're going to do just fine," she reassured me as she patted my hand through the open window of the truck before I left. "But consider having a midwife with you, even though your delivery has to be planned, and you have to be monitored so close. You can still do natural, without any drugs."

"I'll look into it," I promised her. But in my mind I couldn't imagine a midwife being in the room with me when the baby came, just because it seemed as if it were going to be packed as it were with all my doctors.

"Where were you just now?" Ed asked me and I was back on the porch with him and he was picking up all the green beans I had spilled.

"Just thinking about everything, Ed. There's so much to think about."

"It's going to be fine," he reassured me but I wasn't feeling it.

"I just am so busy with doctors and school and trying to graduate."

I looked down at my swollen feet and stood up and stretched.

When I looked at Ed he had a screwed up look of concentration on his face I didn't like.

"That's it," was all he said. And he didn't say much more that night.

Chapter Twenty-Five

Two more weeks of school, only two more weeks of school was the thought I clung to as I went to bed that night. And while the promise of that coming soon helped me drift off asleep, it didn't help me wake up and I found myself once again in the attendance office asking for a tardy slip.

"Baby, the vice principal has been waiting for you," the secretary with the hair that had too many frosted tips told me.

"Waiting for me?"

My heart pounded hard and I felt the baby kick and roll inside me, making me feel like I'd done a loopy loop myself.

"Shhhh," I said down to my belly and spread my fingers over the baby that rolled and rolled inside me as I walked into Mr. Vick's office.

"Good morning, um, Baby," Mr. Vick greeted me and stood up behind his desk with a nervous smile over his crooked teeth. His face was flushed and I could see that his forehead was glistening.

"Mr. Vick, I'm sorry I'm late again, I'm just not sleeping good." I hung my head and looked at the floor and held my stomach as it growled. How could I be hungry again?

"I know Baby and that's what we need to talk about."

"I'm sorry," I started to say again but just burst out crying.

"Miss Hunnicutt, please, sit down," his voice wavered as he gestured repeatedly for me to sit down. "I have some papers for you, please Miss," he pleaded until I sat down.

"Miss Hunnicutt, your, um, your fiancé, um, Ed Small came in here this morning."

My head snapped up.

"Yes?" I asked.

"Yes," he answered and reached his hand across the desk, stretching his arm as far as he could to hand me a Kleenex. "Yes, and um we, we think you should consider taking a medical leave these last two weeks of school."

"Medical leave? Why?"

"Why?" he asked and looked flabbergasted. "Because, because of your condition," he said and waved his hand toward my stomach that stuck out under my flowy dress.

"Because I'm pregnant?" I asked him and he blushed.

"Well that," he said and ran his hand through his hair. He started to get up then he sat back down. He started to speak but only opened his mouth and then shut it. His eyes brightened and he stood up all the way and pointed at me, "Your heart condition!" he nearly yelled as if he'd finally found the answer he was searching for.

"My heart condition?"

"Yes!" he said and sat back down as relief softened his face.

"I don't understand. The doctors all said I was fine for finishing school."

"We don't want to risk anything like last time. You were pregnant when you collapsed on the football field," he told me and he whispered the last bit like it was a secret I was pregnant when I had collapsed on the football field.

But I thought about it for a second. I wondered how exactly Mr. Vick had found out I had been pregnant then. I wondered how the story got out. I wondered what words people used when they spoke of me losing my baby.

And then I wondered what he thought of me now. I wondered if he judged me hard like so many others did and I looked into his face and saw that he was mostly just nervous and young and I tried to picture Ed coming in and talking to him on his way to work.

"Ed came in?" I asked and still couldn't believe it.

He nodded and then smiled.

"He told you about my heart?"

He nodded again.

"He said I should quit school?"

"No," he said and smiled at me kindly, "he said you needed to take a medical leave."

"But do I get to graduate?"

"Yes, but Mr. Small said you might be busy on that afternoon. He was pretty certain you would be busy that day." He smiled again.

"Yes, I think I will be," I answered him and stood up. In my mind I was done with high school. I signed all of his papers and he assured me that he would call my dad and have him sign them too, since I wasn't eighteen yet. When all the paperwork was finished, I drifted out of the building without seeing anyone in the empty and quiet halls. I only glanced at the kids sitting in the classrooms as I walked out of the building. I felt excited kicks in my belly as I walked back out to my truck in the morning May sunshine and I never looked back as I left school one last time and went home.

Ed had a huge grin on his face as he got out of the Cutlass that night when he pulled into his garage.

"Blondie," he said as he came to me where I sat with Applesauce.

Baby Small

"Ed," I said back to him.

"How was school?" he asked as he walked toward me.

"Ed," I drawled out his name as Applesauce put her head on my belly.

"Awww don't be mad Blondie, I brought us food," he told me as he pulled out a big bag from behind his back. "I even got you're your own cheeseburger," he said down at the dog as she sniffed the air from where her head still lay on my belly. "I hope you didn't make dinner, Blondie-locks," Ed said as he helped me get up.

"Nope. But I made a cake."

"A cake?" he asked as he held open the screen door and waited for me and the dog to climb the back steps.

"A graduation cake. I'm done with school," I said to him as I climbed the stairs slow.

"That you are," he said and smiled and took my hand and began to pull me inside, but I hesitated because Applesauce wasn't following; she was suddenly racing to the fence, her long legs powerful as she nearly leapt over the gate, all the while barking furiously.

"Who's here?" Ed asked, coming back out on the back porch.

"Looks like the law," I said as a black and white police car pulled in the drive.

Chapter Twenty-Six

"Listen, I shouldn't be having cake, I'm here on business."

"Oh hush and have a slice, it's Baby's graduation cake," Ed laughed and turned the oven on low and put our bag of dinner in there to stay warm. "She's all done with school, and we're gonna celebrate before we have dinner, I guess. Is that ok Baby?" Ed asked.

"Sure," I said and tried to smile but felt nervous with the police officer in the house.

"Slice 'em big," Ed said and chuckled as he took a saucer with the slice of cake I'd just cut and slid it down on the table in front of the officer.

But he wasn't just a police officer. He was a friend of Ed's.

"Listen Ed, I'm out here because I have to be. I have to ask you and Baby some questions. I'm supposed to ask Baby alone," he said and looked at me and back at Ed. "I'm supposed to have a social worker with me, but hell, they're hard to come by so here I am."

"What's this all about? Are you serious Jackson?" Ed asked as he cut himself a thicker slice of the white cake than I had cut for him and then poured us all a glass of milk.

"Well, it could be serious," Officer Jackson said in between taking a bite and wiping the white icing off his mustache. "The neighbors, your neighbors," he inclined his head toward the kitchen windows, "have filed a complaint against you Ed."

"What'd I do this time?" Ed asked and grinned. We could hear Applesauce's tail thumping against the linoleum down by our feet under the table.

"The official complaint is rape of a minor," Officer Jackson said and folded his napkin and set it next to the saucer even though he still had half a slice of cake left.

I watched Ed's face as it flooded with color and as his eyes darkened and his pupils contracted to tiny pinpoints as he cut his eyes over to the windows as if he'd see the neighbors peeking in right then. His jaw flexed and he put both palms on the table on either side of his cake and stood up.

"What are you doing Ed?" I asked in a panic as Applesauce ran out from under the table and went and stood by the back door as if to block his exit.

"I'm going over there and having a word," was all Ed would say as he strode toward the door but I got there before him.

"No Ed, sit back down," I pleaded with him and put my belly in between him and the door.

"Ed, sit back down," the officer told him. "Sit back down and let me ask my questions and get this over with."

"Rape," I heard Ed mutter. "Jesus Christ, what a thing to say," he whispered as he hung his head and came back to the table with his hair in his face.

"It's not a charge, it's a complaint and I have to look into it. And I have to ask you some questions. I don't want to but I have to. And it's better me than someone you don't know."

"Ok let's get this over with," Ed said and straightened up. He seemed to grow in height and width as he sat there next to the cop; as he looked straight ahead at the kitchen stove.

Officer Jackson took his time getting a small notebook out of his shirt pocket along with a dull pencil. He licked the tip of the pencil twice before opening the notebook and clearing his throat. I watched Ed snarl out from under hair and swear I heard him growl.

"I'm ready," Ed said and tucked his hair behind his ears. His face was scarlet and his eyes blazed with pale coldness as he looked over at his friend, the cop.

"Ok Ed. Um. Have you had sexual relations with Baby Hunnicutt?"

"Yes," Ed hissed.

He was breathing hard and his nostrils were flared and I was scared to look at his face too much longer. Applesauce thumped her tail and whimpered from under the table.

"And um, when was the first time?"

"I don't know," Ed growled and wouldn't look at me. His eyes looked glassy from the sides and I held my breath as I waited for him to blink.

The officer sat with his pencil poised over the notebook and looked up at Ed and then over at me. I shrugged at him. I wasn't going to answer if I didn't have to.

"How old were you Baby the first time you and Ed, had," and here he paused while Ed gave him a heated look. "How old were you Baby?" he cut the question short.

I didn't answer right away. I looked at Ed. He was rubbing his temples now and his face was still flushed but a lot of the anger seemed to have already subsided from his face and he just looked weary.

"Sixteen. She was sixteen," Ed answered for me.

"I was sixteen," I agreed and nodded to the cop.

He wrote it down in his notebook and licked his pencil again.

"Jesus. Can we get this over with?" Ed barked at him.

"Did you consent to it?" the officer asked me without looking up from his notebook.

"Yes."

He wrote that down and then he made a deal out of reading the small amount of notes he'd written down before looking up at us and saying, "This is ridiculous, me having to ask all this."

"Is that all you need to ask?" Ed asked and banged his fist on the table.

"No."

We waited while he flipped through his notebook. If he licked his pencil one more time I was going to scream at him.

"How old are you now?" he finally asked me and ran his tongue over his teeth underneath his lip instead licking the dull pencil tip; I watched it travel up into his cheek.

"Almost eighteen. I'll be eighteen in three weeks." The answer left me short of breath. I felt like I was starting to hyperventilate.

"Jesus Christ we're getting married in two weeks, Jackson. Two weeks. Can we cut the crap and can you get the fuck out of my house? There's nothing wrong with what Baby and I have. Jesus. She's pregnant! We're expecting a baby, for Christ's sake," Ed's voice got louder and louder and he stood up from the table.

"Ed, you blasphemed like three hundred times. It's ok," I said to him.

"It is not. And I'm going next door to wring that son of bitch's neck."

"Ed, I'm going to pretend I didn't hear that," Officer Jackson said as he got up.

We were all three quiet and stood in an awkward circle in the kitchen as we each wondered what to say or do next.

"Listen, just hurry up and get married and this can all be thrown out the window, ok? And in the meantime, no bonfires, no ruckus, leave your neighbor alone."

Ed didn't answer. He just grumbled and growled from under his beard and walked the cop to the door.

"You're still coming to the wedding reception, aren't ya?" Ed called to him after he went out the door, but I didn't hear his answer.

"Huh ahuh, it's gonna be all right, Blondie. We're getting married, and you're having my kid and you'll be eighteen soon and it's gonna be all right. Those people can just," but here I cut Ed off.

"Ed!"

"Huh ahuh, all right Blondie, let's eat our dinner. Sorry this happened."

And he pulled me into a side hug up against him.

"I love you," I told him.

"I love you too," he said down to me and kissed the top of my head.

Ed pulled the bag from the oven and set our dinner on the table. I wasn't hungry after the cake and after the questions and for the first time ever Ed didn't seem to be either.

"For the baby, Blondie," Ed said to me and gestured to my belly.

"You eat too," I told him as I unwrapped a burger. "And don't forget the one for Applesauce.

"I won't, here girl," he said and tossed a cheeseburger in the air and we laughed as we watched her catch it and gulp it down.

"Hope that don't come back up later," Ed said to me and we both began to eat our dinner.

"Guess I better get you home," he said to me across the table as we were balling up our wrappers and napkins.

"Guess so."

"Wish I could have a smoke," he said as he stood up and scraped our cake plates in the sink.

"Why can't ya have a smoke?"

"Because I quit, Blondie," he said and looked at me and winked as he ran hot water over the sugary plates.

"Wow," was all I was able to get out, so I hugged Ed from behind as he laughed and did the rest of the dishes before taking me home.

Chapter Twenty-Seven

Ed refrained from choking Miss Pollock's husband Todd a time or two the next couple of weeks. He kept busy working long shifts and also by moving my clothes and the little baby things I had, over to his house.

"How many diapers have you bought?" Ed complained as I folded and refolded all the little white cloth diapers into a box.

"A lot! We're gonna need a lot," I told him and patted them all down. "And we don't have near enough clothes, or bottles, or things," I said to him and couldn't help but sound panicked.

"We'll have a shower for the baby after we're married, I guess," he said to me uncertainly after he realized how little we had for the baby; that all of it fit in just a few boxes.

"Daddy's building some things," I told Ed but we both exchanged looks because we knew there were so many things we didn't have.

"Don't worry, there's lots of time till August 16th, Baby," Ed smiled as he opened a box and held up tiny yellow sleepers. "It's hard to believe it's going to be that small when you're already so big," he told me and his eyes grew round and teasing.

"Hush!"

"I'm just kidding. But when have you had the time to buy all these things?" he asked me and looked at all the little spoons and bowls and teething rings I'd been picking up here and there at the store the past couple of months.

I just shrugged and thought about needing to get so many more things like a car seat and a swing and a cradle and worried that we weren't going to be ready and that I had so much to do still.

But Ed insisted I rest those last two weeks before the wedding and he promised he was taking care of all the plans for the ceremony and the reception. He ignored Miss Pollock's husband every time he saw him over the backyard fence or out in the front yard, getting the mail. And I was proud of him for not starting something with him after we were questioned by the police.

But Ed could not resist throwing a bonfire the night before our wedding and Jeffrey was more than enthusiastic in getting it set up. For once it was Allen who was quiet and in the background; who watched and didn't say anything, though I could tell that he didn't think angering the neighbor was a good idea.

Baby Small

"It's the night before my wedding and this is what we're doing," Ed said with determination as he and Jeffrey piled up the timber for the fire. Petra and I sat together on lawn chairs drinking lemonade and watched as everyone arrived and as everyone else set the party up around us.

"Besides," Ed said as he grinned at me, "No use in callin' the law on me, cuz the law is all gonna be here tonight. Along with the fire department and half the hospital."

But it wasn't really half the hospital though Ed did invite many paramedics and people from the ER along with firefighters and several cops and their families and many in uniform and out, showed up. He even invited all my doctors but I was thankful none of them came.

"All that's missing is the Hunnicutt cousins," Ed told me that night as we sat by the fire and he rested his hand on my belly and giggled as the baby kicked and rolled.

"We'll see them tomorrow night," I said up to the starry sky.

"Tomorrow night you'll finally be Baby Small."

"Yes, I will," I sighed.

As it got later, most of the guests went home.

"Good luck tomorrow and congratulations," they all wished us as they said goodbye. Many of them had early shifts in the morning or even late shifts that night at the hospital or the firehouse. Emergency teams worked round the clock as we knew too well as Ed always had a radio on his belt it seemed.

"Now eat another marshmallow because he's slowed down in there," Ed told me after everyone but close family was gone. He poked a soft marshmallow in my mouth and we waited for the sugar to kick in and set the baby off to kicking and rolling again.

"That child's gonna be born diabetic," Allen warned us.

"Pshaw, he is not, he's Ed's after all," Jeffrey laughed and pulled a toasted brown marshmallow off his fork and made a s'more for Lisa to feed to little Olivia.

"This is the happiest I've been in a long time," Petra said up to the night sky and we all quit horsing around to look at her.

She sat quiet and looked up at the purple sky and her face glowed from the bonfire and the fire danced in her fierce little eyes and I wondered if she was thinking of Kai.

"This is the happiest I'll probably ever be," she said with finality and looked right at me. "You'll be happy the rest of your life, Baby. You have everything," she said and gestured with her little hand at everyone sitting and standing around in the backyard.

Baby Small

"You have everything too, Petra," I told her and tried to get out of the lawn chair and go to her but before I could, Ed was up and grabbing her around the head.

"This isn't the happiest you'll ever be, you kooky kid," Ed said to her and rubbed her head hard with his knuckles and then dodged her swatting hand and loped over to the cooler. "It's not like Baby is moving across the world. She's just moving down the block a ways. And it's not like you're gonna get bored; you got a babysitting job guaranteed for the next eighteen years, huh ahuh!" Ed laughed as he pulled a beer out of the watery cooler, but I looked at Petra to make sure that what he said didn't make her sadder.

"I would love that Baby," Petra said to me as she waved Ed away from getting near her head again as he walked back to his seat. "I can't wait to see the baby, to hold him," she said and smiled and then tried to smooth her hair.

"Shoot, you'll be busy with your own kids," I said to her.

"I don't think so. At least not for a long time but someday I hope so. I hope so," she murmured and looked away from me.

"Oh shucks, all this talk is bringing me down. Jeffrey, help me get something out of the car." Allen winced as he stood up and leaned heavy on his cane and gestured to his twin to come with him.

The twins came back from the car with two fat photo albums and Allen put them both on my lap.

"Early wedding present, Baby, from Mom and me and Jeffrey too," Allen told me and smiled but his eyes looked sad.

"Holy cow, where are all these pictures from?" I asked and slowly pulled open the cover.

"These are all the snapshots we took over the years. And some I got from your dad, and even got some from your cousins."

Allen looked smug and I tried to picture him calling my cousins and asking for photos and couldn't help but smile at the thought.

"We tried to put them in order, but some aren't," Allen told me as he held his cane with both hands and leaned towards me and gazed at the album on my lap.

Ed helped me scoot closer to the fire so I could see the photos and Allen helped Petra move her chair closer to me so she could see them too. Soon my family and Ed's mom was gathered around us as we looked and laughed and reminisced.

"Look, these are of your mother the day you were brought home from the hospital," Mrs. Small said, pointing at the first page. "I remember that day."

Baby Small

"Haha, is that Ed sitting on the porch in the background?" Petra pointed to one of the pictures of my mom holding me in our front yard. In the corner you could see a blurry shape of a boy sitting on the Small's porch holding a football. All I could make out of his face were dark blurs for his eyes and lips. His hair seemed lighter than it was now. But I could tell he was sitting there on the porch without his shirt, and his skin was dark tan.

"Would you look at that? Little Ed, innocent as a lamb," Jeffrey said and snickered.

"Shut up," Ed said and punched Jeffrey in the arm.

"He was a little cusser even back then," Jeffrey confided to me behind his hand.

"You look exactly like your mom," Petra cooed, her voice full of awe as she looked at my face closely from where she sat next to me. "Except the hair; look how dark your mom's hair is!"

"That was the first time I used colored film," my dad explained from where he was peeking over my shoulder.

"Look at Baby in her high chair!" someone else said as we flipped through the photos.

Photos of me and Daddy in front of the truck. Mama must have taken that one. But most of them were taken by Daddy, of me and Mama. Mama holding me on her lap with Goldilocks and the Three Bears book in her hand. Mama and me in front of a fat spruce Christmas tree. Mama and me in the snow; me about four years old and I had mittens that attached to the cuffs of my coat. Mama had on her plaid coat with the fake fur collar and her suede hiking boots and wool pants. Her eyes were big and happy and even in the black and white picture you could tell she had lipstick on. I was starting to have a hard time breathing. It was difficult to see all these old pictures of her and I wanted to turn past them quicker. Sadly enough we got past them to where there were no more pictures of her.

"Holy cow, there's a hundred pictures of us at the pool, if there's one," Jeffrey laughed as I flipped the next page. My breathing slowed as we flipped through page after page of bright sunny photos of the boys goofing in the pool and on lounge chairs.

"Jesus, did I ham it up on the diving board enough?" Ed asked and looked embarrassed.

"Jesus did you have a bubble butt or were those swim-trunks tight enough?" Allen asked and guffawed from where he leaned over our shoulders.

"Who took all those pictures of you?" I asked over Ed's growling at Allen. There were several photos of sixteen year old Ed flexing his arms and posing on the diving board; up close photos of him grinning in the sun, his skin tan and his hair long and wet.

"Where the hell did you get these?" Ed asked Allen with an undertone of annoyance in his voice.

"Karen," Jeffrey answered with a huge grin of glee on his face.

"Karen?"

"Yep, she had 'em. I remembered she was always snapping photos at the pool. She had a whole box of them and was glad to give 'em to me," Jeffrey told us and I was surprised that he had even asked her for them, much less gone and got them.

"Jesus, look at me dive," Ed whispered. "I was so young," he trailed off and we all looked at a blurry photo of Ed diving into the pool, the splash forever frozen.

"Hell, look at Baby!" Jeffrey cried and we all looked at me sitting on a lounge chair with a can of Pepsi. My face was sunburnt and my hair was long and white blonde in the sunlight. Ed was curled up, sitting Indian style on the end of my lounge chair, grinning and looking back at me out of the corner of his eye. I could see two pairs of feet on the edge of the picture that had to belong to the twins who were sitting on the opposite lounger.

"Oh my gosh, turn past that!" I flipped the page embarrassed but it only got worse.

"Baby's first day of kindergarten," Aunt Clem pointed to a picture of me holding a large ugly book-bag with a mushroom on it. I was standing in front of Aunt Clem's porch and looked tiny next to it.

"Remember how we curled your hair with orange juice cans?" asked Aunt Clem.

"Oh lord, I remember that day and Ed and Jeffrey and I walked you to school," Allen laughed.

"And Baby wouldn't sit down because her teacher called her the wrong name!" Jeffrey joined in.

"Oh lord that Miss Pollkadot was a handful and starting trouble even then!" Ed roared with mock anger and laughed and smacked his leg and the baby in me kicked and rolled over.

We looked through pictures from all the family Christmases at my house and at Aunt Clem's. We laughed at all the cousins in their Christmas sweaters and we laughed at Ed with his plate piled high with pie.

Everyone was quiet and respectful as we came across pictures of Kai and me on Aunt Clem's porch; sitting close together holding hands and watching it snow. And we were quiet when we came across all the photos of Ed at my sixteenth birthday party the summer he came back from Colorado.

"You look like the Wild Man from Borneo," Jeffrey said and smiled and shook his head as he pointed at a photo of Ed shirtless in his tight jeans with his chest dark tan and his beard wild. In the photo Ed stood away from everyone else as he watched me blow out the candles on my cake in Aunt Clem's backyard.

"I do not," Ed cracked back at him.

We were all silent, and maybe we even held our breath as we looked at all the pictures the twins had collected from Kai's parents of me in the play out at the prairie theatre.

"Peasebottom," Jeffrey said and touched a photo.

"Peaseblossom," Petra and I both corrected him and I started to smile but then I remembered that was when Allen hit me.

I didn't mean to look at Allen just then. But I did. And he was looking at me too, and I could see he was thinking the same thing.

"It was a long time ago," he said to just me and in the glow of the bonfire it was only his face I could see just then.

"Actually it was just two summers ago," Petra corrected him from where she sat next to me.

"But it was a long time ago," Allen said quietly and just to me.

And he was right. So much had changed since then.

We opened the next album to see me in my La Rue Robin pom pom uniform in front of the football field. Ed wolf whistled and then kissed my cheek.

"There's my papershaker!" he growled and shook his head. "She's too good for me!" he cried up to the starry sky and laughed and drank down his beer.

"She sure is," came from my dad from behind us but we knew he was kidding.

"Petra added these next ones," Allen told me and I looked from him to Petra and backed to Allen and couldn't help but notice both of them were blushing in the firelight and I wondered about Allen going to Petra and asking for photos and I wondered if something was going on between them.

"Oh lands, the two of you in your swimsuits with the whole football team," Aunt Clem said and laughed as we turned the pages.

Baby Small

"You shoulda never been allowed to go to that waterslide," Ed tsked tsked as we looked at all the pictures of me and Petra with her being held in the air by the football team in front of the pool.

"We weren't doing anything wrong," Petra complained and I saw that she had a huge smile on her face as she leaned closer and looked at all the boys in the photo.

But her smile faded when we turned the page and there was Kai. Kai with his brown curls and his peeling nose. He was sitting on a bench at the pool, eating a vanilla ice-cream in the bright sun.

"I miss him," Petra said and everyone leaned in to pat her and hug her. Only Allen stayed where he was, leaning on his cane and looking at the picture from a foot away.

The last few pictures were of me and Ed; of me and my baby bump starting to grow bigger and bigger. The last picture was of me and Thunderhead asleep on Daddy's couch. There were many empty pages after that.

"That's for you and Ed to fill later," Jeffrey told me as he patted the empty slots.

"Oh and we will! Of this little dickens," Ed said and laughed and patted my belly.

"And the wedding!" Petra added.

"And the wedding," Ed and I said together.

"On that note," my dad started to say.

"On that note I should get some rest," I said to everyone and got up and stretched.

My stomach felt nervous as I looked around at everyone one last time before becoming Ed's wife. I felt the tears come and I tried to blink them away but they wouldn't hold back.

"Awww Peasbottom, c'mere," Jeffrey said to me and hugged me.

"I love you guys," I said as I hugged my cousin.

"And we love you," Petra said and stood up and hugged me from the side.

And then everyone moved in closer. First Allen on my other side. Then Aunt Clem, Mrs. Small, my daddy, and finally Ed; who tried to put his arms around everyone.

"It's great to have family," he said with his voice full of laughter and happiness as he tried to squeeze us all.

"Ok, let me go, you're killing me," came from Petra and we all unwound.

Baby Small

My daddy took me home to sleep in his house one last time and even though I was very nervous, I was asleep almost as soon as my head settled into the pillow. Being pregnant was tiring.

Baby Small

Chapter Twenty-Eight

"Do you sweet, heavenly Blondie-Locks promise to love me with long hair or none, with bare feet and my shirt off, with my smart ass mouth and my giving you dutch rubs on the back of your head from this day forward?" Ed asked me as we stood on the sand of Settler's Beach at Rush State Lake, as he rubbed his big, tan hand over my round belly and felt our baby kick at him through my white eyelet, strapless prom dress.

"I do, Ed Small, I do. I loved you since the day my Mama told me to not look into your crazy, pale, hippie eyes, Ed Small," I told him as I stood up on tiptoe and traced my thumb over his pooched out bottom lip. He leaned down and winked at me before he kissed me with all his might in front my twin cousins, Jeffrey and Allen who raised me, and in front of my Aunt Clem who loved me, and in front of crying Petra who was my very best friend, and in front of my Daddy who was offering up a prayer to my poor, dead Mama, to forgive him for not keeping me away from Ed.

We pulled apart for a second and paused as I looked down at his tan bare feet, then up the legs of his new Levis, to his tuxedo shirt and sleek black jacket. He stood there in the summer grass and blinked down at me and waited for me to take a deep breath and then I kissed him with everything I had. I ran my hand through his golden brown tangles that had been shampooed just that morning and were now blowing all around his head and as they caught in both our mouths, he pulled them away and mouthed to me with his eyes wide, shit mother fuck.

The wedding was fast; faster than I ever imagined a wedding could be. But I guess when you only have one bridesmaid and two best men and no ring bearers or flower girls, and no long songs or poems being sung- it goes by pretty fast.

We said our vows and I didn't faint or cry and the pastor announced us man and wife and I kissed Ed with everything I had in me. I kissed him with all the love and desire from all the nights on Aunt Clem's porch, all the nights in the T-bucket, and all the stolen moments we'd had together here and there the past two years as I tried to grow up and as Ed waited for me. I kissed him with everything I had.
Ed was finally mine.

No Colorado, no leaving on a train after a night of sad goodbyes, no more sneaking time together, no more Mr. and Mrs. Polkadot calling the police. We were married. And we were burning with happiness. My face hurt from it and I felt as if I were shining brighter than anything on the planet right now.

"I love you, Blondie," Ed said down to me as everyone around us clapped and Petra and Allen and Jeffrey threw rose petals on us. The sweet scent lifted me off my feet and onto my toes as I inhaled. "I love you Blondie," Ed said again with his voice thick with emotion.

"I love you too, Ed but what are you doing?" I asked him and backed away from him as he began to come towards me bent over a little with his arms out. He looked like an ape.

"I'm coming to get you," he said and ducked his head down a bit and grinned. All his hair blew around his head and covered his face but I could still see his eyes as he came towards me.

"Ed Small, you stop this right now!" I whispered at him as I backed away from him further but had nowhere to go because the lake was behind me.

"I'm gonna scoop you up!" he taunted me as he came closer. "I'm gonna carry you all the way home!" he growled and jumped close to me and picked me up plum off my feet as if I didn't weigh anything. He scooped me right up into his arms with a swirling of my skirt and held me lightly and gently close to him.

"That's a long way to carry me Ed!" I laughed and cradled my bouquet of pink and red roses close to my face and breathed in their rich, sweet scent.

"Aww shucks, guess we better take the car! Huh Ahuh!" he laughed and carried me away from the lake with all our friends and family following and talking.

"I wish we could stay here longer," I told Ed as I looked around at all the prairie flowers blowing in the hot sun around the lake.

"We'll be back soon enough, probably the Fourth of July," Ed said and tossed his hair and looked over his shoulder as he carried me to the car.

I peeked over his shoulder and saw Allen carrying Petra in his arms.

"No way," I gasped and looked up at Ed, to see what he thought. "I think she's just letting him do that because she couldn't get her scooter back here," I told Ed, right in his ear. His hair tickled my nose and I kissed his ear.

"Pfft, that's funny Blondie."

Ed bent down and slid me into the front seat. He brushed his lips over mine and covered my mouth with his thick lips as he buckled me in; careful of my tummy, and then shut the door. We laid waste to the country blacktop as Ed sped us back to Daddy's house and all the awaiting cousins and other party guests.

We formed a reception line under a white tent that was set up in front of the garage and ran the length of the driveway. We stood amongst pink and white balloons and streamers and received hugs and kisses and well wishes from happy faced guests until Ed cut it short claiming I was much too pregnant to stand that long.

"You can shake our hands while we all have a piece of cake!" Ed yelled to everyone as he scooped me up and carried me to the front door and declared the receiving line over.

We followed all the Hunnicutt girl cousins through the house back to the kitchen where the biggest double layer sheet cake I'd ever seen took up the entire kitchen table. There were white balloons hanging everywhere and we could barely get around the table for all the guests.

"Let my Pop through!" Ed hollered as he pulled Daddy through the crowd. "We need pictures of everything today!" he exclaimed as Daddy with his giant flash camera set up a tripod and instructed Ed and I on what to do as he snapped photo after photo; Ed cutting the cake and laughing, Ed getting cake on all his fingers and me wiping them off while he scowled, me feeding Ed and Ed feeding me and then immediately kissing me after. Daddy snapped picture after picture with his flash popping and lighting us all up.

We spent the afternoon sitting outside under then tent at a table full of presents and we took turns opening them while champagne bottles popped all around us.

"Don't tell grandma and grandpa!" Petra giggled as Allen poured her a glass. Ed made sure I had a glass of chocolate milk that he mixed together himself from Quik in the kitchen.

"I've never drank from a glass so fragile," I told him, worried I'd break it.

"Don't worry there's plastic ones for the guests, but you and I get the good ones."

"They even have little wedding rings on them," I said looking at mine and almost spilled it.

"Keep it upright there Blondie!" Ed righted my glass with a push of his finger and then said, "A toast!" and he clinked our glasses together, "May all our babies look just like you Blondie but may they have my sweet disposition!"

Everyone toasted and everyone laughed as we continued to open a mix of baby presents and wedding presents. They gave us things I'd never thought of even asking for; sheets, and towels, and baby wash clothes, and baby sheets, and handmade rag rugs for the house, and a special little seat with tiny seatbelts for the baby to ride in in the car, a battery powered swing, and a highchair.

"You'll need two trucks to get that all home," Jeffrey commented and pointed at all the boxes that were piling up.

"You've got even more than Mrs. Polkadot," Petra sighed as she ran her hand along the top of a box with a baby swing in it.

"Let's take those over to the house," Allen said to his brother and they both loaded them all up in my truck and hauled them over to our house.

"Our house, Ed," I sighed.

"What about it, Blondie?"

"I can't wait to go home and never leave."

"Of course you're gonna leave. What about our honeymoon?"

"Honeymoon? But where can we go with me so pregnant?"

"Somewhere close. Just a short trip." Ed looked mischievous.

"You're not taking her up in that whirly-bird." It was Petra who with the help of my dad and Mrs. Small sat down next to me with a plate full of mints and redskin peanuts.

"Better get some cake, Miss Kooky-pants. It's bad luck to not eat wedding cake at a wedding.

"Is it?" Petra sounded alarmed.

"It is. But sit down. I'll get you a slice." Ed patted her head twice and the third time he gave the back of it a slap that nearly knocked her over.

"Ed!" I yelled.

"Huh ahuh!"

"You!" Petra growled as he ran off to the back door of the house and ducked into the kitchen.

"Be nice, Ed!" I called to him as soon as he came back out and the baby kicked and twirled in me.

"Course I'm not takin Baby up in the 'copter. She's pregnant," Ed said as he came back to the table and slid a slice of fluffy white cake down in front of Petra. He had a huge slice the size of a ham for himself.

"Ed, you're gonna make yourself sick," I warned him.

"Am not, little mama," he answered and I blushed and looked away at all the happy faces sitting around the long white table that stretched the length of the driveway.

Baby Small

**

It was still a little sunny when we moved the party inside the house because the mosquitos were coming out. Everyone was passing our photo albums around and talking about how long Ed and I had known each other. I felt tired from all the excitement and stretched my legs out on the couch and leaned back into Ed's chest where he sat behind me. I was so happy yet I couldn't wait to be alone with just Ed.

I think we were both waiting for a signal of some sort so we could leave and it came in the form of the sun going down all the way.

"Welp, it's dark, we better git," Ed said to me as he helped pull me up from the couch.

We said goodbye to everyone and it was a replay of hugs and congratulations just like when we first arrived at the house, yet somehow it now felt different. Maybe having been married eight hours had already changed me. It hadn't changed Ed much because once again he cut it short.

"Stop hugging my wife or she'll be all hugged out for me," Ed said and I was hard pressed to tell if he was joking or not, he looked so serious with his eyebrows drawn down heavy and his lips pooched out in a pout as he pulled me towards the door.

"We love you all and we're so happy. I'm so happy," I said to the room of relatives who were still popping open champagne and beer and now were also playing cards and eating seconds of cake.

Jeffrey and Allen paused in making their tower of plastic champagne glasses on the dining room table. Petra looked up from where she sat holding a fat Hunnicutt baby boy on her lap and my daddy looked up from where he sat with his brother and several of Ed's coworkers around a table of pinochle. He had a plate of cake balanced on his knee and a mug of coffee in his hand.

"You off so soon?" My daddy asked and got up from the table.

"Yep, we have to go," Ed told him and held tight to my hand as if Daddy would suddenly change his mind and decide he wasn't giving me to Ed after all.

"Well, take care of her," Daddy said and offered his hand.

"I will Dad," Ed told him with a huge smile on his face as he pumped my dad's hand up and down so vigorously it shook us all.

"But you should really stay and have a bite more to eat, we got a ham in the oven and am gonna have hot sandwiches here in a bit," my dad said and I had to look away from how sad his eyes were.

"Thanks but we really need to go and I couldn't eat another bite," Ed told him and then, "We'll grab dinner on the way home," he whispered in my ear just for me.

"I love you Daddy!" I called to him and hugged him one last time.

As he squeezed me extra hard I couldn't help but think, this is the last time I'll call this house home. And it didn't feel that sad, because really it still was my home. My childhood home. And so was Aunt Clem's.

"You'll have to tell me how you like your wedding present," Daddy said as we started to leave.

"Wait. What?" I asked him, confused. I couldn't remember what he got us.

"It's out in front of the curb," he said and grinned.

"In front of the curb?" Ed and I both asked and ran out on the front porch and both clapped our hands over our mouths.

"Oh my sweet God in the sky! It's a Bronco!" Ed said at the same time that I said, "Who's car is that?"

"It's your new car, Baby. For the baby. It's a family car," my dad said and shrugged as he came out to the square little four by four with us. It was dark green with a mint green stripe and had knobby mud tires on it.

"It's perfect for a family, it's four wheel drive and plenty of room for groceries in the back, and it has a solid engine in it," my daddy tried to say but was cut off.

"Thanks Pop!" Ed exclaimed as he crushed my dad to him in a one-armed hug.

"A brand new car," Jeffrey whistled.

"Wow," Allen added.

"Pretty color," Mrs. Small said.

"Daddy, I love you."

"I love you too. Now go on with this layabout hippie boy before I change my mind!" Daddy laughed as I hugged him.

"Go on," he said as I began to cry. "Don't cry, just enjoy it and don't double clutch it."

"But what about the truck?"

"You'll need two cars and Ed can't have his mom's car forever."

"What about Applesauce and Thunderhead?" I suddenly remembered and pulled away from Daddy.

"I've already asked Jeffrey to round 'em up and get 'em over to the house with anything else we mighta forgot, tomorrow," Ed told me as he cupped my chin and kissed me as he pulled me out the front door to the awaiting new Bronco which was covered in white streamers and balloons and 'Just Married' written in white soap on the back glass. We drove away as the family milled out onto the front yard to clap and whoop for us one last time as we drove away. But we didn't drive far.

"Oh my gosh this is too much!" I cried out and laughed out the open window of the Bronco as we pulled into the Dairy Freeze.

"Huh! Ahuh! Mr. Sosos made me promise to bring you by!" Ed laughed as he looked at my face as we pulled into the drive-up.

It was glowing with white Christmas lights criss-crossed across the stalls. One of them, the one in the back corner, the one Ed pulled into, was even decorated with white balloons.

"Our little honeymoon starts here, Baby Small," Ed told me as he turned off the Bronco and slid across the seat to me.

We kissed until the food came. We didn't even order. Ed just put the car in park and turned it off and took me in his arms and kissed me.

"I love you and you are mine and I just want to get you under me but I'll be danged Blondie if you ain't become a little beach ball and we're just gonna have to wait," Ed said and kissed me again and again.

We didn't stop until we heard clapping and cheering and then we broke apart from each other and saw that all of the waitresses and cooks, and even some of the customers were around the car all clapping. They had brought with them a tray heavy with white parcels and we laughed when we realized they'd wrapped our sandwiches and fries in wedding paper. But I was scared for a moment because there were several cop cars that had pulled up around us with their lights swirling and for a moment I had a panic that they were going to arrest Ed in front of everyone and take him away on our wedding night. But then I saw there were also firefighters and EMTS there too and they were clapping and cheering right along with the waitresses and cooks, and that they were just people who worked with Ed.

"What's wrong?" Ed asked, immediately concerned that I was no longer smiling.

"Nothing," I said and shook it off and smiled up at him because everything would be ok.

"This is heaven, Blondie," Ed said as he handed me a cheeseburger wrapped in flowery white and silver paper and a chocolate shake. "This is as close as it gets," he said and bumped his sandwich into mine like a toast.

Baby Small

Chapter Twenty-Nine

"The doctor said it was ok?" Ed asked for about the thousandth time after we got home from the Dairy Freeze.

"Yes Ed, he did," I told him as I tore at the buttons on the front of his shirt.

Weeks ago I had asked Kai's mom. And that was hard for me to ask but I'd done it. And she had said yes it was ok to have sex during pregnancy. I had then also asked my doctor at my next check-up just to be double sure, not that I completely trusted him but I didn't want to do anything to hurt this baby. He had frowned at me but had also said yes, it wouldn't hurt me or the baby to have sex while pregnant. But he had continued to frown at me as if to say, haven't you had enough sex already?

And the answer to that was, no.

Ed was mine. I was his. This was my forever home now. We had told the whole world we loved each other and were committed to each other. Or at least we had told has many people in the town as we could. Aunt Clem even saw to it that announcements were put in the paper. And she also made sure that she got several copies of it to save away for us for our scrapbooks.

"If it's in the paper, it has to be true," Jeffrey had said and laughed when his mom gave us ten copies of the announcement.

And now that it was real, it was permanent and it was forever, and I had no doubts about it being right and Ed didn't either, it was just him and me and I wanted all of him.

"Baby, slow it down. Jesus you're big. Be careful," Ed told me as I unzipped the side of my wedding dress and peeled it off me and threw it onto a chair in the corner of the room. "Good God look at that belly," he whistled and I felt embarrassed at having whipped my dress off like I did and I covered my chest with my hands.

"Awww come here, let me feel the baby." Ed held his hands out for me and took me in his arms and kissed the top of my head.

"I want to have sex, Ed. I don't want to think about the baby for just a moment. I just want to think about you and have sex."

"Calm down there, hell-cat, huh ahuh!" he laughed and ran his warm hands over my tight round belly. "We have to be careful. And I like to think it's going to be more than a 'moment'. I'm not a jackrabbit, you know, huh ahuh!"

Ed stood back away from me and finished taking off his shirt after I'd failed at all the tiny buttons. He stood there in the moonlit room and licked his lips and tucked his hair behind his ears and smiled at me. A shiver shook my hair down my back and I climbed into Ed's big waterbed and lay on my side and pulled the quilt up over me.

"We have all night, Blondie. We have all our lives. We don't need to hurry. Besides," he said and paused and unbuttoned his pants and then looked at me as he unzipped them. "Besides, I think we need to relish this moment, don't you?"

"Ahhh!" I squealed and hid my face and bounced on the waves of the bed.

"I think you're gonna see me nekkid someday, Locks," he told me.

"I think you need to get your naked behind in bed, Ed Small." I patted the waterbed and caused deep waves to run across the surface of it.

"Yes ma'am!" he hollered shook his head and dived in next to me.
**
"Gee whillickers, I need a glass of milk after that," Ed sighed and rolled away from me in the warm bed.

I tried to sit up on the rolling bed and pull my hair up off my neck but lost my balance and rolled gently back onto my side.

"I need some milk and it'd be nice if we'd have been smart enough to bring some of that wedding cake home with us," Ed mumbled from next to me as he lay on his back and rubbed his lips and looked up at the ceiling. "I should put a fan in up there, one of them ceiling fans," he mused and yawned and shut his eyes.

"You want me to get you some milk?" I asked and he didn't answer.

I couldn't help but smile at him as I waited for him to start snoring. But he didn't. His eyes popped back open and he looked at me.

"I didn't hurt ya, did I?" he asked and came closer to me and put his hands on my shoulders.

"No," I sighed and smiled.

"You look sweaty."

"It's hot in here," I laughed at him. It was almost June and Ed had the heat cranking on the bed.

"I'll open a window but I usually keep it closed 'cause the birds wake me up too early. Which reminds me, we gotta get up early."

"Do you have to work?" I asked almost in a panic that the magic was all over with.

"Nooo, silly! Huh ahuh!" he laughed and shook the bed as he got back in after opening the window.

"Am I supposed to go to work?"

"Go to work? You? No Blondie, you're the mama. You're staying home with the little peapod."

"Ok. I was worried. You said we have to get up early. I was wondering why."

"Our honeymoon!"

I looked over at him as he lay on his back and his dark eyes drifted shut.

"Our honeymoon, Blondie," he said and smiled with his eyes closed.

"Where are we going?"

"You'll see. But we gotta get there early."

**

"Fishing?" I asked Ed for the thousandth time the next morning.

"Not just fishin'. But a place to get away. It's a cabin! Our own little cabin. Don't you just love it, Blondie?"

Ed had woke me up at 5am and pushed me to get dressed. "Put on something practical," he kept saying as I pulled on a patchy calico sunback dress and leather sandals.

"Something practical, Blondie, not something fancy!"

"This is a second hand dress Ed, it's nothing fancy!" I had told him with a big yawn on the end.

Now here we were way out in the prairie, almost in Iowa for crying out loud. I had slept most of the way once I saw we weren't getting on a big highway and weren't heading north to Chicago or south to St. Louis. We were just heading west, so I went to sleep. We were so far west in Illinois that I didn't even recognize the land anymore. There were hills and there was just tall prairie everywhere and the sound of crickets was already loud in the morning sun.

"It's too hot. My feet are sweaty," I complained to Ed.

"Don't you want to see the cabin?" Ed asked and pointed to the little yellow house with the faded paint and the sloped roof. It looked dusty. And it looked tiny.

"I want to see the lake you keep telling me about and I want to put my feet in it."

"Well ok, it's not like I'm fishing today anyway, already too hot, so it's ok if you scare the fish," Ed said more to himself than to me as he guided me away from the little yellow house that he kept calling a cabin.

Baby Small

"This is our place Blondie. Our place to get away. There's no phone or tv and no one knows about it, yet. It's just for you and me and the baby and of course Applesauce will love it but it's for us to get away."

Ed's eyes reflected the sky and the clouds as he smiled out at the lake and held out his arms. His hair was a golden tangle down the back of his white undershirt.

"All's that's missing are mountains. Someday we'll take a trip to the mountains," he told me.

I sunk my hot feet into the cold little lake as I sat on the warm earth and Ed sat next to me.

"Happy honeymoon, Baby. This is my wedding gift to you."

"Your what? Oh my!" I covered my mouth and felt stupid.

"What's wrong? You ok? You breathing? Heart going?" Ed asked and instinctively looked down at his radio he always wore clipped to his belt. I imagined him radioing a helicopter to come pick me up and it landing in the middle of the field.

"I'm fine. The baby is fine. Heart is fine," I said and put my hand over my heart. "Your gift to me? I didn't get you anything."

"Not yet you ain't. But August 16th will be here 'for you know it," Ed grinned and leaned over and kissed me.

"I wanted to give you something," I said and looked down at the waves rippling against the muddy bank.

"I got something you can give me, huh ahuh," Ed laughed from where he stood behind me.

"What?" I asked as I turned around to see him standing there with his hands on his hips. He'd already peeled off his tshirt and looked like the wildman of the prairie.

"You can give me your panties and get inside that cabin! Huh AHUH!" he barked out a huge laugh and threw his t-shirt at me and it covered my face.

"Ed Small!" I yelled and tried to get up but the bank was too steep.

"Yes? Baby Small?" he asked as he helped me get up the bank.

"You!"

I wanted to chase him into the cabin but I was too awkward and too clumsy so we just held each other around the waist and walked into the little cabin together.

**

"Ed you have to go in to work tonight?" I asked him that afternoon as we walked through the prairie together. He was showing me everything around the cabin after a morning of showing me everything in the cabin, as he had called our tour inside that ended with the brass bed. I had been pleasantly surprised to find Ed had fitted the bed out with clean sheets and quilts before we got there.

"Blondie, I'm not completely thoughtless," he had grumbled with pretend exasperation at me as he helped me climb up in it.

Now he was showing me the pump for the water and the barn where the firewood, tools, and his fishing gear was stowed.

"Do you have to go in?" I asked him again, worried that our time here was coming to an end.

"No, Blondie. I have two whole days off from work. I told you. Remember?" he asked as he grinned at me and squeezed my hand and pulled me along.

"What if you get called in? What if you get a call on the radio?" I asked him as I looked at the radio he always wore on his belt.

"This?" he asked and cupped the radio with his free hand. "I just brought this for you. In case there was an emergency for you," he said and smiled a crooked grin at me but his eyes crinkled with sadness on their corners.

"Do you always have to wear it?"

It was bad enough that Ed had all my medicines and vitamins lined up on the window ledge and even wrote down what I took and when in a little notebook that he told me I needed to fill out every day.

"You should keep better track of your medicines, Baby," he'd said to me when he'd unpacked our clothes and the cooler of groceries in the little cabin.

"Blondie," he said to me now and he stopped walking and turned to me and cupped his fingers under my jaw. "Blondie, this radio only comes off when my pants come off," he said and flashed me with his cocky smile, his teeth white against his tan face. The sun glinted off the part in his tangled hair and he batted his lashes at me and leaned down to my mouth. His lips were all sweetness and soft against my own.

"Well you better take your pants off then, because I'm tired of looking at that radio," I said to him with my lips bumping against his.

"Yes ma'am!" he declared and he kissed me again more urgently.

I held onto him by his bare shoulders and as we kissed in the sun-blown prairie I heard the slow tick of his zipper as he inched it down.

"Huh ahuh!" he chuckled quietly in my ear as I pushed back from him, giggling myself.

"Out here?" I asked him as I looked around and couldn't see above the tall flowers and grasses.

"You're the boss little Blondie," he told me and winked.

"Let's go back inside," I said but it sounded like a question.

"Whatever you want, wife."

I yanked his hand twice and pulled on his thumb.

"Ed?"

"Yes?" he asked playfully.

"Don't make me beg."

"That's something I could never take Baby. That's something I'd never do," he said and looked into my eyes.

"You have too! Plenty of times!" I protested up to him.

"When?"

"When?" I echoed him.

"Yeh. When?" he asked as he licked his lips as he looked down at me. I looked away from him and I know I blushed.

"When? When did I make you beg? I think I need to hear this so I can fix this right away," he whispered and took a step towards me. "Tell me."

"When this," I said and slowly took his hand and brought it up to my mouth and guided his thumb to touch my bottom lip.

The roughness of his skin surprised me and I flinched back just a little before looking up at him to see his reaction. His own mouth had dropped open and his eyelids were closing as well as he stared down at me and he took a deep slow breath.

I guided his thumb to rub along my lip again and I looked up and watched his face as I did it. He opened his eyes all the way and held his breath as he watched me do it. Then he closed his eyes and shivered and shook his head and all his hair went in his face. I think he even blushed a little as he swallowed and then nervously ran his hand over his hair as I began to suck his thumb a little.

"I remember, I remember that," he told me and he wiggled his thumb just slightly against the tip of my tongue. "But I don't remember you begging for anything. If anything," and here he cleared his throat several times and I watched his face reddened even more. "If anything Blondie, it was me begging you."

"You were begging me?" I asked and pulled his thumb out. I was trying to turn him on but all I was doing was turning myself on and he didn't look moved at all. He just looked very nervous. He even had sweat droplets on his forehead and cheekbones.

"Blondie." Ed took my face in both his hands.

"Yes?"

"I was begging you to do something I didn't have the guts or the heart to ask you."

"What?"

"Something good girls don't do," Ed said as he came closer to my face on every word till his forehead was touching my own.

"What? What, Ed?" I asked and felt dizzy. "What could be so, so bad, you couldn't ask me? Why didn't you ask me?"

"I didn't want to be a scoundrel. I was a scoundrel for thinking it. For wanting it. But I wasn't that bad of a scoundrel," and here he hit me with his full blinding smile, the one where his eyes lit up, his smile wide and his teeth blinding, and then he said, "I wasn't that bad of a guy to ask that."

"Well," I closed my eyes, "well," I opened them again, "you're my scoundrel now. So now you can ask."

I tugged on the waist of his jeans just to get him to move because he looked completely stumped. He was just staring at me with half a smile cocked on his face while he rubbed the beard along his jaw.

"All right. I'll ask. I'll ask you. In the cabin," he told me and took my hand and pulled me through the tall grass of the hot prairie and led me back inside.

**

"Oh my. You want me to what?" I asked Ed in the dusk of the cabin. The air was cool and a relief from all the sun outside. I was sitting on the bed while Ed kneeled on the floor in front of me and rested his hands on my knees.

"That's what I wanted then, Blondie. Then." He added on the end with emphasis and after he said it he pooched his thick lips out in that old tic of his and I heard him gulp as he blinked his eyes shut.

"You wanted it then but you don't anymore?" I asked him and heard the waver in my voice.

"Well. That is always nice to get. But. No. No, Blondie. I don't want that now. You're pregnant."

I cocked my head to the side.

"I don't understand. I can't do that while I'm pregnant?"

"Um," Ed gulped again and bit his bottom lip. "It might be a little hard to do now," he said as he held his thumb and finger close together in front of my eyes. And then he couldn't help but grin and next I knew he was laughing and so was I.

"Blondie! You're a beachball!" he whooped. "How you move at all or tie your shoes or do anything is beyond me! And you're only gonna get bigger! My God, Blondie," he sighed and kissed my hand. "There's time for that, later."

"Oh."

"I love you."

"I love you too."

"You're so sweet. Let me heat you a bath."

"Ok Ed but not too hot."

"I know Blondie."

"I wonder what everyone is doing at home," I said to Ed later as I sunk into the copper tub in the corner of the cabin near the cast iron stove in the kitchen.

"Probably nothing much at all. Probably just exactly the same thing they were doing when we left. And besides, now's not the time to worry about them. Just relax Baby. This is just for us."

Ed made dinner while I soaked in the tub right there in the kitchen. Right in front of the cast iron stove where Ed had built a small but furious little fire.

"Let's have pancakes! I love breakfast for supper, don't you?" Ed called out to me as he banged around in the cabinets.

"I do! But is there syrup and butter?" I asked him as I slid down in the water till it was up to my chin. I peeked at him over the lip of the copper tub as he dug around in the cooler and pulled out eggs and a quart of milk and then peered in a tall cabinet next to the oven.

"Here we go," he grinned and waved a small bottle of syrup and a wooden spoon at me.

Those two days with Ed at our yellow cabin in the prairie were the most relaxed days I'd ever spent since I was a little kid. Maybe even better than when I was a little kid. I had no doubts about where I would end up at the end of the two day stay. I knew I was going to my new home. And our little white house looked so beautiful to me as we pulled up to it in our new Bronco.

"Is that Jeffrey?" I asked Ed and couldn't help but laugh as we pulled up the long drive to the back of the house to the garage.

"Where?"

"Looking out the window," I said but we'd already passed the window where Jeffrey had been looking out at us; smiling a huge toothy smile from where he stood peeking between the curtains. "Why is he here?" I asked Ed.

"He's dog-sitting," Ed told me and winked as he parked in the garage.

"I can't wait to see Applesauce!"

But it wasn't Applesauce who we saw first.

"You're not the only one who got knocked up," Jeffrey chuckled as he held the door open for us as we came in the back door.

Baby Small

Jeffrey had a big cardboard box in his hands and when we came in the kitchen I could hear mewing.

"What is that?" I cried, standing on tiptoe to look in the towel lined box. There was Thunderhead laying on his side. He was big. His fur was rumpled and unkempt. There were six or more sweaty looking balls of fur attached to his belly.

"Oh my gosh! He's a she!"

"He is, Baby. He's a mama."

"We could never tell, with all the fur," I said as I peeked closer to the black and white babies.

"Ed, Caesar's never been neutered has he?" Jeffrey asked Ed as Ed carried in our cooler and things from the car.

"Hell, Jeffrey, why would we do that to a cat?" Ed asked him.

"Oh I don't know, Ed. Most people don't keep a Tom-cat for a pet," Jeffrey smirked and gently put the box down under our dining room table near Applesauce who looked like she was smiling as she thumped her tail against the floor next to the box.

"How's Applesauce taking it?" I asked.

"Oh Applesauce seems damned proud of them as if they were hers."

At these words, the dog whumped her tail even harder against the floor and then rolled over on her back and sneezed a few times.

"Applesauce! Be careful!" I told the big dog and tried to reach down and pet her belly.

"She's ok, Baby," Jeffrey told me quietly.

"She just looks HUGE next to the kittens!" I exclaimed and I worried that Applesauce would be too big and clumsy to ever be around them once they came out of their box. I wanted to sit down under the table with them all but I was too big and too round to get down under there without help and I definitely didn't want to ask Ed or Jeffrey for help doing that.

"You look tired, Baby," Jeffrey said to me as if reading my mind.

"It was our honeymoon, son! Huh! Ahuh!" Ed laughed and clapped Jeffrey on the back as he walked back outside to get more things from the Bronco.

"How are you feeling, Baby?" Jeffrey asked me once Ed was outside.

"Fine. Good," I tried to smile but I did feel tired. My back ached. Again I felt like my stomach had doubled in size in just a couple of days and I was looking forward to sitting down in Ed's big armchair that looked so comfy in the front room.

Baby Small

      The fact was I wasn't feeling fine. I was worried that at the rate my stomach was growing that this baby was going to be way too big for me to birth. I was beginning to doubt God, science, and my own body. I was beginning to doubt if I was ready to do this. There was still two months to go before my delivery date. If I continued to grow like this, I wouldn't be able to move at all much less deliver this child. I was starting to fear he was going to come out a full-sized toddler.

      "Baby," Ed interrupted my thoughts as I sank back into his big brown armchair. "I have bad news," he told me as he squeezed my shoulders from behind me.

      I looked up into Ed's face as he leaned over me with all his hair spilling all around his face.

      "What?" I asked as I looked up at him.

      "I haven't planned your birthday."

      "Oh."

      "Let's have everyone over Friday night, I'm not on call then."

      "Ok," I agreed and shut my eyes and rested my head on the back of the chair.

      "Can you go to the store tomorrow and get what we need?" Ed asked very quietly with his face hovering upside down right over my own.

      "Yes," I said as I drifted off to sleep while Ed rubbed my shoulders.

**

      I was pushing a cart around Tolly's, waddling slow and steady, picking out cans of baked beans and cartons of potato salad and lots of bags of chips and feeling excited that I had a checkbook in my purse that had Ed's name on it and my name on it for me to write my first ever check for the groceries. I was so excited Ed had turned over the checkbook to me and asked me if I would mind keeping track of all the money and all the bills. That was one of my new responsibilities as a wife. I had also told him I was going to do all the laundry and he had whooped and hollered about it and even escorted me to the bright little laundry room and said, "There you go!" with a flourish of his arms towards the matching brand new washer and dryer.

      Petra thought I was crazy to be excited about these things.

      "You are anti-women's lib," she had told me.

      "I am not."

      "You are too. You are willingly putting on the apron of oppression!" she had sputtered at me when I told her how married life was going so far.

"It's not oppression if it's something I want to do!" I had snapped back at her.

And it was something I wanted to do. Just like doing the shopping. I wanted to do that and I was having a good time picking everything out at Tolly's even if getting around the store was slow and my back was cramping up. I was enjoying it. At least I was until I turned a corner to get the hotdogs and ran into Miss Polkadot with her fat, sticky infant in the cart.

"Oh," she said and curled up her lip at me as the red-headed infant banged a long hard biscuit that was sticky and gooey on one end from being sucked on, onto the handle of the cart.

"Hello," I said back to her and went around her.

"I hope you're not planning on throwing another party in your yard," she said from behind me as I picked up six packages of hotdogs.

"What?" I asked and turned around.

"All those hotdogs," she sneered.

"What about them?"

"You must be having another one of your redneck bonfires."

I didn't answer. I was trying to remember how many hotdogs Ed had eaten at past cookouts so I could get an idea of how many to buy. And I was trying to ignore Miss Polkadot.

"Pregnant women shouldn't even eat hotdogs," she said to me.

"What?" I thought I had misheard her.

"Processed meats are bad for the fetus," she told me as she pointed at the hotdogs piled up in my cart.

"Oh."

"So is beer! You're not drinking are you or it'll be born retarded just like your cousin's baby!" she said in a sharp voice.

"Olivia's not retarded," I said to her barely above a whisper.

"She is too," Ms. Polkadot countered and she crossed her arms across her chest as she did so. Her baby stopped banging its biscuit on the cart and stared at his mama with his mouth wide open and a spit bubble shining in the florescent light of the store.

"Lisa didn't drink while pregnant," I mumbled and started to push the cart away. If six packages of hotdogs weren't enough, Ed would just have to come back himself.

"You shouldn't be lifting that beer anyway, in your state."

I yanked the cart to a stop and managed to count to four before turning around.

"I didn't. I had the stock-boy do it for me," I said through gritted teeth.

Baby Small

I stood there and breathed hard through a clenched jaw and felt my temper come out hot in my face.

"You have anything else smart to say?" I asked her as I threw my hair over one shoulder and then the other.

"Yes. As a matter of fact I do," she bit off her words with her tiny little teeth as she came towards me without her cart.

I braced myself for her words and I crossed my arms tighter over my swollen hard belly and stared her down. I'd never felt fiercer in my life.

"Just because you're married," she hissed at me as her face drew closer to mine and I could see every single freckle on her cheeks and nose, "just because you're married doesn't mean it's legal, doesn't mean Ed is protected from being arrested," she threatened as her nostrils flared.

"You leave me and Ed alone. It's none of your business."

"It is my business. I'm not having some cinderblock prairie trash living next door to me breaking every law there is," she growled back at me.

"What law?"

"You're not even eighteen!"

"I will be this weekend!"

"Well you better hope nothing happens to Ed Small before then."

"You better stay away from me and him!" And now I was yelling in Tolly's and now people were beginning to gather and to look. Women in pantsuits and old people in big glasses all peeked and gawked and stared at us.

"You better not have another bonfire or I'm calling the law! And if you think we're gonna allow that big dog to live there, you got another thing coming! That thing is vicious!"

"You leave Applesauce alone or so help me God!" And then I stopped. I stopped and I stepped back away from her because my heart was feeling jittery and my arms and legs felt wobbly. I looked at Miss Polkadot's baby as it contentedly sucked on his teething biscuit and removed it and stared at it before sucking on it again, and I waited till I was calm to move away.

I took several steps backwards with my cart, pulling it with me down the aisle.

"You stay away from me. Stay away from Ed. Stay away from Applesauce," I told her quietly as I turned the cart around and went to the checkout.

Applesauce was waiting for me in the yard when I got home and she followed me in and out the door the many times it took for me to carry everything inside. I opened the case of beer and carried them in four at a

Baby Small

time and it took eight trips and I was exhausted by the time I was finished putting it all away. I checked on the kittens and on Thunderhead and then curled up on the couch with my feet under Applesauce and took a much needed nap.

Chapter Thirty

"Blondie?" Ed called and woke me from my deep sleep on the couch.

I couldn't move my feet. They were completely numb under the dog and my back was crying it was hurting so bad from sleeping in such a tight little ball on the couch. My hands had cradled my belly in my sleep; keeping it from pulling too much on my lower back.

"Blondie?" he called again and I could hear him banging around in the kitchen.

I lay there in the quiet living room and listened to see if I could figure out what he was doing. I lay there and stared through the open front room window as a blazing orange sunset was slicing through the blinds and laying stripes across the wood floor. The kittens in the box were just starting to wake up and I could hear them mewing and scratching around in the box with Thunderhead.

"Blondie?" Ed asked again, much softer this time as he came into the living room on socked feet.

"Yes?" I asked and yawned.

Ed scratched his head and stood against the bright window and put his hand on his hip and said, "I'm confused."

"You are?" I asked and started trying to sit up but all I could do was wiggle my toes under the dog to tickle her belly and get her to get up.

"Get up dog," Ed said to her and pulled her off the couch by her collar and then he helped pull me up to a sitting position.

"Oh Ed, I have to pee, help me get up, quick!" I said to him realizing I really had to go suddenly.

"Jesus, Blondie," he laughed and grabbed my hand and helped me up.

I waddled as fast as I could go down the hall on feet that were all pins and needles.

"So Blondie," Ed said from the other side of the bathroom door that was pulled halfway closed. "Did someone break in while you were asleep?" he asked and I could hear the chuckle under his words.

"Why?" I called back as I washed my hands. My face looked pink with sleep when I looked in the mirror and my hair was a little wild but other than that I thought I looked prettier than I'd ever been. I looked happy.

"Well, Blondie, huh ahuh, I got home from work thinking how great a cold beer would be and I'll be danged but if I don't come home to a full fridge of it. And I remember telling someone," he said as I opened the door see him scratching his head in an exaggerated manner, "I recall telling someone to not buy the heavy stuff at the store when I left for work this morning."

"Hmm..." I said to him and skirted around him in the hall and went back to the living room.

"I wonder who could have put all that beer in the fridge?" he called from behind me.

"I have no idea what you're talking about, Ed Small!" I squealed as he reached out and pinched my bottom.

"I wonder if some tired pregnant woman didn't carry all of that in one can at a time and make twenty four trips to and from the truck," he mused with his finger to his lips and his eyes rolled up looking at the ceiling.

I watched him as he strolled through the kitchen with his long legs making swishing sounds in his flight suit that he still had on.

"I would hate to think that my sweet new wife didn't listen to me and not go and buy heavy stuff at the store, like I told her not to," Ed said as he cocked his head and smiled at me and then he leaned down and picked up two cases of beer; one in each hand.

"Haha!" it was my turn to laugh.

"And that ain't all, Blondie, I got two more out in the back of the truck!"

"Oh my gosh!" I cried and covered my mouth, I was laughing so hard.

"We gonna have one hell of a party for your birthday, Blondie, and you can't even drink!"

"I hope you got something else to drink besides Pabst Blue Ribbon, Ed Small!"

"I did. It'll be delivered tomorrow."

"Delivered?"

"Yup. I got that good chocolate milk that comes in the glass bottles. Milk man is bringing it 5am tomorrow morning. I made him promise."

"Yay!"

"That's my girl," Ed said to me as he pulled me into a hug and kissed me there in the kitchen.

We kissed for a long time right there next to the stove and when we stopped Applesauce was standing there staring at us with her tongue out and her tail whumping against the side of the stove. She cocked her head to the side and looked at us as both as her ears stood up all the way in points like I'd never seen her do before.

"Give mom and dad some privacy, dog, go on now. Go check on the kittens," Ed told the dog and off she went to the dining room and I'll be danged if she didn't peek in the box of kittens just like Ed asked her to.

***

We had plenty of beer for my birthday, we even had more than Ed and I bought because all of Ed's friends seemed to bring a case or a six-pack with them and Ed and I just laughed as cooler after cooler came into the backyard the night of my party.

Applesauce ran around in a barking circle greeting everyone and Ed told every single guest that handed me a present that they were going home with a kitten later.

"They're too young to go home with anyone yet!" I told Ed as he carried one outside, mewing in his hands. "Get that kitten back inside! It'll catch cold!"

"Kittens don't catch cold, Blondie!" he said but he took it back inside all the same.

This bonfire party was our biggest one yet and Ed and I stood and held hands and greeted everyone as they all came in the back yard. Ed kept asking me if I needed to sit down but I felt fine with my bare feet in the deep grass of the summer evening.

The party was a mix of all our family, Petra, several girls from the pom pom team, EMTs and firefighters, half the cops from town, and some of the ER staff. Jimmy Collins even came and I couldn't tell who was more surprised, me, Ed or Jimmy himself. Daddy gave Mrs. Small a ride and Allen brought Aunt Clem. Lisa stayed home with Olivia because she had a cold but Jeffrey came early and got the bonfire going. He even asked her if she was worried about someone calling the law on us for it and her answer was, the hell with the law! Which drew a round of laughs from everyone as there were so many cops in attendance.

Everyone brought me a gift and after our wedding and all those gifts, it felt like an abundance of stuff, even if most of it was for the new baby.

We cooked hot dogs and had a heavily piled table of slaw and chips and water melon and potato salad and plenty of soda and beer and of course my chocolate milk in the glass bottles that Ed said I needed to drink because babies need milk. He patted my belly and sang happy birthday to it till I told him he was going to confuse the baby and make it come out early.

It was the best birthday party ever. Ed told everyone I wasn't really eighteen today.

"Not till midnight," he told everyone over and over. "Tomorrow's her birthday. Tomorrow she's eighteen," he said again and again with a huge smile on his face.

"Well in that case, Ed Small, I'm placing you under arrest," one of his cop friends said to him and grabbed Ed by the wrists and pulled his arms behind his back.

"Huh ahuh!" Ed guffawed but he and I and Jeffrey and Allen and even Petra all eyed the neighbor's house. They'd love to see Ed get arrested.

"That's the Linda Kirby house, you know," I heard Petra say to some girls from the pom pom team. And then she asked them if they knew the story, which of course everyone in town did, and so they discussed all the gory details of it and oogled the house as the sun went down.

I told Petra about Miss Polkadot threatening me at Tolly's and all of the pom pom team listened in and hung on every word as they ate their hotdogs.

"She called you what?" Petra asked and nearly stood up out of her lawn chair in indignation.

"Cinder block prairie trash," I repeated it slowly for Petra.

"Is that even a thing?" Petra asked but before I could answer she declared, "That's not even a thing. We ain't like that here," she said shaking her head and I watched her slit her eyes over at Miss Polkadot's house.

As dark set in we gathered around the fire in lawn-chairs and as people began roasting marshmallows, Ed pulled out his guitar and began to strum and sing. Of course he sang Happy Birthday many times to me in many silly voices and cadences; never really finishing any of them. But when he began to strum a certain chord progression, I froze in my seat.

"Blondie is partial to Pink Floyd, you know," he told everyone and I felt my face color. "She's especially partial to that fella David Gilmour, huh ahuh," he said and laughed.

"I am not," I disagreed quietly.

I wanted him to keep playing. I wanted him to play all the Pink Floyd he could because it reminded me of a bonfire we had had years ago when Kai had come over for the first time. I looked up at the sky and I wondered if Kai was up there. Up there with my mama and Aunt Frances and with me and Ed's lost son Dan. I wondered if he wasn't up there looking down on us. And Ed must have been thinking the same thing because of what he said next.

Baby Small

"I used to play this with Baby's little curly haired friend Kai, God rest his hippie soul," he said as he strummed and then he began to sing, "Breathe, breathe in the air/don't be afraid to care/ leave but don't leave me/look around choose your own ground," and I sang the words with him and closed my eye against the brightness of the leaping bonfire.

Chapter Thirty-One

"That was one hell of a birthday party," Ed groaned the next morning as he staggered into the kitchen.

I was already up and was frying bacon and hashbrowns and had even put on coffee for Ed because I knew he'd need it.

"Lordy. I did not know beer would make me feel that bad Blondie," he said as he sat down and let all his hair fall in his face. A deep gravelly grumble came out of his throat as he sat there and groaned and ran his fingers through all his hair. He leaned on the table with his elbows and pulled at his hair and I stared at him as his muscles bulged and his arms strained the sleeves of his tight old black t-shirt. I almost had to pinch myself to remind myself that I was married to him. It'd only been a week and sometimes I still couldn't believe we were married.

"Poor Ed," I said and sat a mug of hot coffee down in front of him.

"Blondie, we're married now."

"Yes, I know," I told him and remembered last night.

Ed had been drunk and silly but mostly tired and giggly. I had helped him take off his shirt as he sat on the edge of the bed. He'd smelled of bonfire smoke and beer and sweat and all the old familiar scents of childhood and growing up with Ed. He had collapsed back on the waterbed and had giggled as he rode the waves of the bed up and down.

"Take off my socks, Blondie," he'd asked as he held out his feet for me and I had pulled them off easily enough.

I had waited for him to ask me to pull off his pants but he didn't. He just lay there smiling and bobbing up and down on the bed till I'd finally undid his belt without him asking.

"Fasty-pants, I think I'm too drunk," he had mumbled when I'd undone his pants.

"I know Ed, but you don't want to sleep with these jeans on," I had told him as he rolled over on his stomach as I pulled his jeans down. And I laughed in spite of myself at his bare butt as he curled up in a snoring ball in the waterbed.

"You're my wife," he told me now, "and you're supposed to stop me from drinking that much."

Ed had indeed drunk more than I'd ever seen him drink. Him and Jeffrey and all the cops and firefighters and EMTS and even some of the nurses had gotten very drunk.

"Ed, I'm not your mom."

"No, bossy-pants, but you're my wife. You're supposed to keep an eye on me and not let me do things like that."

"We had too much beer is all," I said and I stood there with my hand on my hip and waited for him to look up at me but he wouldn't.

"Ed, I can't tell you what to do."

He growled for an answer and I could barely see his eyes glaring at me bloodshot from behind all his hair.

"Blondie there's a whole list of things you have to keep me from doing now that you're my wife."

"Like what?" I asked with my curiosity completely piqued.

"Don't let me fish with a cane pole, don't let me try to change the clutch on the truck, don't let me get it into my head that Allen and I can roof the house, and don't let me tell the kid how horrible school is."

"I don't know if I can remember all that. I don't even understand half of it," I laughed.

"Just don't let me drink that much on the Fourth, Blondie," he moaned from behind me as I took up the bacon.

"I'll try not to, but I'm not promising. I'm not good at bossing you around."

"Blondie, you know darn well you're the boss of me," he groaned as I set the plate down a little too loudly and he sat there and held his head with one hand as he ate with the other. And then, "Blondie," he said again as he laughed without a sound as I set down my plate that had a tiny candle shoved into a piece of toast.

"Today is my actual birthday," I said to him.

"Finally legal," he said and grinned at me as he tucked his hair behind his ears.

"Yep," I smiled at him because now he was all mine and I was all his and no one could get in between that ever again.

**

That June was the best June of my entire life and it passed in a blur of me getting even bigger, rounder, and the kittens got bigger, and the summer got hotter and hotter.

Petra came over most every morning on her electric scooter. She would zoom up the ramp Ed built on the back of our house and come in and help me fold laundry or hold the kittens. I told her she had to take one home when the time came and she looked at me, dubious.

"Remember last summer and the pool?" she asked one morning, hopeful.

"Yes we had a blast after we quit working at the Dairy Freeze," I said and regretted it because her face fell at the memory.

"I got fired, you quit."

"He was an idiot for firing you."

"You were an idiot for quitting."

"I was not. We wouldn't have been able to go to the pool if I hadn't have quit."

Petra looked thoughtful for a little while she sat and held a sleeping baby kitten on her lap. I knew what she was going to say before she even said it.

"Remember the first time we saw Kai there?"

"Yes."

"Were you surprised?"

"Yes. I think I was."

"I was," she said and smiled with her eyes shut.

But then her smile faltered and a tear squeezed out from under her shut eyes. I sat and was quiet and waited with a folded wash cloth on my lap as her lips began to tremble.

"Petra, don't," I finally said to her.

"Don't what?" she asked and still wouldn't open her eyes.

"Don't think of that, you'll just make yourself feel bad."

"How do you know what I'm thinking of?"

"You're thinking if you hadn't gotten fired, I wouldn't have quit, we wouldn't have gone to the pool all those times and run into Kai and he wouldn't have started seeing you and he'd still be alive today."

"I'm not thinking that!"

"Then what are you thinking?" I asked her softly.

"I'm thinking if he hadn't been scared to learn to drive, he'd been in a car and not on his stupid bike," she said and shut her eyes again.

"He was scared to drive?" I asked.

"Yeh."

"I didn't know that."

"I really tried to get him to learn to drive," she said and opened her eyes.

"Why was he scared?"

"I don't know. He was just Kai."

"Yeh, he was," I said and nodded and knew exactly what she meant.

**

That June was a quiet one; a mellow one. I was so pregnant I could barely go anywhere because it was so hard to move, it was so hard to walk, and so hard to stand very long.

Baby Small

That Fourth of July I was going to disappoint Petra because I asked Ed if he and me could just get away and go to the little yellow cabin. Petra would be upset because she'd be expecting us to have a big party. But I needed to have a quieter celebration so I asked Ed if we could get away.

"Yes, of course, Blondie, that's a great idea and even better, I'm off of work and we can make a weekend of it," Ed agreed and went right out to the garage to get his fishing gear.

He came back in with all his poles and tacklebox of weights and lures and lines and things I didn't really want to have in the house.

"What about the dog?" I asked him.

"She can come with, right?" he said and looked at Applesauce who was under the dining room table with the kittens climbing all over her. She held her head up and looked at us and began wagging her tail slowly.

"What about the kittens?"

"Um, they can't come with us. Jeffrey can watch them."

"What about food?"

"Maybe you can run to the store tomorrow and pick up some things?" Ed asked me and he sounded worried.

"I can do that. I need to get some things for the house anyway."

"Just don't do too much. Promise no heavy things," Ed said to me in all seriousness and took a hold of me by the shoulders.

I stared up into his eyes so long I felt faint.

"Blondie, you're blushing," he said and grinned down at me and batted his eyes.

"Ed, you're giving me the look!"

"What look is that, little 'locks?"

"You know the look," I told him and felt embarrassed.

"Is it the let's go get in bed look?"

"Ed! I'm super pregnant!"

"We can still fool around!"

I sat looking up at Ed, him with his hands still on my shoulders, and I thought about it.

"I have a hard time on the waterbed, I'm so heavy," I complained.

"How about the second bedroom?" he asked and looked absolutely devilish.

"Oh, ok!"

"I'll rub your back."

"Mm…" I said as he helped me up off the couch.

"I'll rub your front," he said and giggled as we went down the hall.

Baby Small

But Ed never made it to my front. I was asleep by the time he got done rubbing my back.

"You fell asleep on me Blondie, so promise, promise you won't carry too much. Just get some pasta and maybe some pudding and milk and cereal for the cabin and that's all we need. I don't even need beer. Just get a handful of things and come right home."

"I will Ed, but I need detergent."

"Ok a small one," Ed made me promise that morning before he went to work.

"When I get home, we'll go to the Dairy Freeze for dinner and then home for early bed, huh ahuh, and then just you and me at the cabin for the weekend."

I was sure grabbing a few things at the store would not be a problem when I left the house that morning. But every step made my back hurt and I was so tired I just wanted to lie down on my side, but with the help of the cart I made it through most of the store just fine. I got the chips, and the pasta and the hotdogs and the pudding mix and the milk and just needed one more thing when I turned the aisle and almost ran right into Karen.

Karen with her frosted feathery tipped hair and her tight jeans with her high heeled sandals and her plaid shirt tied at the waist.

"Well, well, well, if it isn't the newlywed," Karen said through her clinched teeth as she smiled at me. I could see her jaw muscles tense all down her neck.

"Hello," was all I managed and I started to look at the boxes of laundry soap as if they were the most interesting thing ever.

"All's well in matrimony-land?" she asked in an over the top voice.

"Hmm? Yes we are good," I told her and noticed her cart was blocking the whole aisle and that I wouldn't be able to get away without pulling a u-turn.

"All is good," she sighed and looked at a box of dryer sheets and then put them back.

I sighed as well and went back to reading the soaps, thinking that my encounter with her was over.

"Ed has a good job," she said it as a statement.

"Yes, yes two of them really."

"That's not the only thing you have two of, I hear," she sneered and I didn't answer her so she continued, "A little house on Maple Street and a little house out in Schiller County on the lake. And two trucks now too plus Ed always drives his mama's car," she ticked off on her fingers.

Baby Small

"How nice," she said but her face looked pinched and not nice. Not nice at all.

I still didn't say anything.

"Don't you worry about him flying up there?" she asked and she tacked on a brilliant smile at the end of her question. I could see that one of her back teeth was entirely silver. It made her look old.

"No," I lied.

"You don't think about him just dropping out of the sky and getting killed? Those helicopters aren't the most reliable things," she shook her head like she was talking about a naughty child and not a huge machine.

"Nope."

"You and your history of bad luck would make me worry if I were you." She looked smug and satisfied as she stood there with her arms crossed over her flat chest and her leg stretched out in her tight jeans toward me as she tapped her foot as if hurrying me to answer.

"I don't have bad luck," I told her and crossed my own arms over my very ample chest.

"Umm," she rolled her eyes and tapped her teeth with an orange shellacked fingernail. "You do," she said with her eyes widened as far as they would go. "One, your mama dropped dead, two, your cousin is nuts, and three your little boyfriend was knocked to smithereens on his bike. That's a lot of bad luck."

"Well, you're not me and you don't need to worry about Ed. Ed's as safe up there as we are down here."

"As safe as that baby you lost? Don't you think you have the worst luck?" she asked and smirked. "Everyone around you gets killed," she said and examined her nails.

And then it happened. It clicked in my head and a huge smiled rippled across my face until it almost hurt.

"No," I told her with an insane smile twisting my mouth, "I have had great luck. My daddy needed help raising me and I had Aunt Clem and the twins and Ed. I've had Ed since I was born; looking out for me, taking care of me. And when I needed a best friend Petra moved in across the street. And Allen didn't get killed in Nam and he came home alive and is doing fine. I was lucky enough to have met Kai and got a big part in his play and Ed came home and fell in love with me and I fell in love with him. My life has been very lucky. Very good. And now we're married and gonna have a baby and Ed has a wonderful job," I told her and took a deep breath and said, "And let's face it; he's a sex god." This last part I threw in because it's what Petra would have said and it just sort of popped out of my mouth.

I watched Karen as her mouth dropped open with surprise and then I watched as she slit her eyes and began to sneer at me.

I thought I'd really zinged her. For once I hadn't been too astounded to not think nor too shy to speak up. I'd finally spoken back at someone who was judging me, hurting me. But she wasn't going to walk away.

"Ed's just married you because you got knocked up. You'll notice he didn't marry you last time you got pregnant because you lost that one and there was no need. There was no police on his tail then even though you were only sixteen. Now he's got the police after him. Don't you think that's why he married you this time?" she asked but didn't wait for me to answer.

"You'll notice he left town again right after knocking you up that first time and again right after you lost it."

I gripped the handle of the cart and squeezed it tightly as a cramp rippled through my belly and I felt my bladder squeeze and a little dribble run down into my panties.

"Yes, he didn't stick around after you lost that one. And he didn't claim it or you or anything. He just left the state again," and here she paused and pushed her lips together and eyed me and cocked her head to the side as another cramp rolled across my belly and the muscles in my back spasmed. I felt a trickle of pee squeeze out and now my panties were soaked.

Karen smiled and flipped her feathered hair.

"But Ed is Ed and he couldn't stay away from a young piece of fluff like you. He always favored the good girls. He took the cherries of every good girl in school. He always liked them pure and he always made them feel safe enough to give it up," she said and tapped her teeth again as she looked around the store as if ruminating. "But none of them ever got knocked up that I know about. But who knows, maybe there's some Ed juniors toddling around town. Ed would know or maybe he wouldn't. He wasn't ever very bright, just always a good looking piece. But now you've bagged him," she said and eyeballed my belly.

I was thankful she couldn't see the pee running hot down my bare legs under my long patchwork dress and into my leather sandals as the cramps rolled through me and my bladder just let go. I tensed up and tried to hold my water but it still leaked out till my bladder was completely empty. I hoped it wasn't pooling on the floor around my feet and I didn't want to look down to see and draw her attention there.

"I'm surprised he even married you before the baby arrived with your record of losing babies. I'm surprised he didn't wait till it was born to marry you. He's always gotten his milk without buying the cow, I'm surprised he didn't make sure the calf was his before, you know, well. Doesn't mean he won't stray from the yard or jump the fence. I guess he just wanted to shake the cops off his tail," she finally stopped talking and dusted her palms together as if trying to clean them of some unseen dirt and then she touched all the frosted tips of her wing-y hair before smacking her lips one final time.

I struggled to get my cart moving and once it began rolling, I shoved it right past her, forcing her to back up into all the boxes of laundry soap. I pushed my cart right out the door, still full of unpaid groceries, and pushed it right on out to my old truck and there I left it, still full, in the space next to where I had parked.

Chapter Thirty-Two

The phone at the engine shop at the airport rang and rang without an answer. I hung up and redialed as I sat at the kitchen table.

After I'd gotten home I'd changed out of my wet underpants and washed them out in the bathroom sink and hung them over the tub to dry. Then, carefully cradling my belly and waiting for another cramp, I had washed off my legs and feet while I sat balanced on the edge of the claw-footed tub.

No cramps came. But I didn't feel right. The baby felt low. Felt like he was riding right on my hip bones. Felt like he was about to drop right out of me.

I cradled him and waddled to the kitchen where I tried again and again to call Ed but no one answered. I even fiddled with the scanner Ed kept on the dining room buffet but couldn't understand anything I heard on there. I couldn't figure out if he was up in the air somewhere or what.

Finally I called Petra and she answered on the fourth ring.

"Petra, come to the doctor with me," I said to her in a rush when she answered the phone.

"What? When? When's your appointment?"

"I don't have one. But just need to go."

"Is the baby coming?" she asked in a panic.

"I don't think so," I answered but had to think about it for a couple of seconds to be sure. I didn't think he was coming now. "No," I said more calmly, "But I need to see the doctor. Something feels different," I tacked on to the end.

"Are you sure you need to go?" Petra asked in her clipped little voice.

"Yes. I'm sure. Why? What are you doing?"

"Nothing."

"So can you go? Right now?"

"Um. I guess so."

I didn't say anything but just waited for her to clarify that. And when she didn't, I said, "Petra Post, what is going on over there?"

"Allen's here," she finally confessed.

"What?"

"Wait."

I heard her put her hand over the phone and then take it off.

"He wants to come with."

"No." I was firm.

Her hand went back over the mouth piece and came off again with a whoosh.

"Ok. Come get me," she said and was all business and I knew I'd made the right decision by calling her.

"Will the doctor just let you come in without an appointment?" she asked once Allen helped get her settled in my old truck. It was easier to get her scooter in the back of it than the new Bronco. We just had to roll it up on a plank of wood and park it in the bed and then slide the wood up in the truck bed with it to use whenever we got to where we were going. Who in the heck would help us do all this at the clinic, I wondered as I put the truck in gear and drove us away while Allen watched and waved from the yard.

"Baby?" Petra demanded.

"What?" I asked as I ran through the gears to get us out of town as fast as the truck would go.

"Didn't you hear me?"

"Um, no."

"Will the doc just see you without an appointment?"

"Yes," I said as I pumped the clutch with my bare foot.

"Where's your shoes?" Petra asked, her voice climbing high.

"I peed on them."

"Good lord this doctor will think you're nothing but cinder block prairie trash."

"Is that even a thing?" I asked her and laughed.

"It is," she said and crossed her arms.

"Well. He already thinks bad things about me. 'Prairie whatever' can't be any worse." I shrugged and took us down the middle of the blacktop; the engine bellowing all the way to the hospital.

**

"Pre-term labor," Petra puffed out with disgust as she pulled herself back into the truck as a male nurse helped us put Petra's scooter back up in the bed; the same one who had helped us get it down when we first got there.

"Pre-term labor," she said again as she fastened her seatbelt. "Do you agree with that?"

"I guess," I sighed as I sat there and gripped the steering wheel. My belly was so round I could barely fit behind the steering wheel.

I was sweaty and felt sick to my stomach.

"How do you feel?" came from Petra as if she knew already.

"Queasy."

Baby Small

"Hungry?"

I tried to remember what I'd eaten that day and couldn't recall eating anything but some saltines around five thirty that morning.

"Yes, maybe a little."

"What's to eat in this town?" she asked.

"I don't know." I said and rested my forehead on the steering wheel. I suddenly felt very sleepy. Very weak.

The doctor had made me feel like a fool.

"You first time mothers," he'd said. "You think everything is labor the last two months. It's only July 3rd Baby. You have five weeks. Maybe longer till your delivery date. I can tell you right now without even examining you you're not in labor," he'd said but snapped on his gloves and examined me up on the table all the same.

"You're at two," he had said.

"What's that mean?" came from me where I was awkwardly on my back on his too skinny table.

"Two centimeters. You have to get to ten."

"Shouldn't I be at a zero?" I asked in a panic and held out my hand hoping he'd help me sit up.

"Baby," he said as he peeled off his gloves and shot them into a garbage can.

"You could be at a two for months," he finally said and had given me paper towels to wipe myself off with.

"We should find something to eat," Petra said from next to me and brought me out of my thoughts.

I looked over at her to see that she was watching me closely with her sharp little black eyes that never missed a beat.

"Ok, I guess that'd be good," I said and realized I'd been holding my breath and let it out. "My back hurts," I blurted out as I tried to turn from side to side and stretch.

"How come? Because the baby is so big?"

"I guess," I said but wasn't sure.

"Is it sharp pain? Is it your heart?" Petra asked; her voice shrill.

"My heart isn't in my back, Petra," I told her and actually laughed.

"Well they say sometimes when you're having a heart attack," Petra trailed off.

She was all concern and her eyes were going all over me as if to find out what was wrong with me by just looking at me.

"It feels like cramps. But in my back. And," I trailed off.

"And?"

"And even my butt hurts." At this I really did laugh.

"Your butt hurts?" Petra demanded. "That's wrong, Baby."
"Why is that wrong?"
"What did you do to your butt?"
"Nothing!"
"Jesus criminy, being pregnant really must be horrible."

I sat there and felt my back tighten clear down my backside and then felt it release and when all my muscles relaxed, I put the truck in gear and took us out of the parking lot and towards downtown Rush to find a place to eat.

"I wish you could drive, Petra," I said to her in the parking lot of the Steak-N-Shake.

"No joke," she said back to me as she dug in her bag of food and pulled out onion rings. "This food making you feel better?" she asked and grinned at me as she watched me pull two cheeseburgers and a large onion ring out of my own bag.

"Yeh," I said and laughed at how worried I had been before. I had been sure the baby was coming today but now, in the truck, with the buttery fried aroma of food filling the cab, I was feeling better. "I think I was just hungry," I told Petra.

We ate our sandwiches and saved our shakes for the road trip back home. As we rumbled over the blacktop of the country roads with the windows down and our shakes in hand, we sang songs and I drove one handed and barefoot with my hair blowing out the window. It was a beautiful hot day and we took the long way home, looping around the lake and jouncing past the old Dragon Park.

"Hold on to your shake, train track," I told Petra as we neared the top of a rise in the road right before the rough tracks.

"Slow down!" Petra cried and out of the corner of my eye I saw her shake cup fly up in the air when we hit the rough old crossing. I started to laugh because we hadn't even hit the rough second set of tracks yet.

The front wheels of the truck hit the first rail and the jolt hit me in my hip bones and tailbone and my bladder weakened. Then the front wheels hit the second rail and I bounced up off the seat of the truck. I squeezed my shake cup to keep from dropping it and felt the wet cardboard crumple in my hand as my bottom slammed back down on the seat and I felt something give inside me. I took the brunt of the bounce in the hips but the weight of the baby bouncing up and down and then up again and down again smashed my bladder and with an interior relief I let go and wet myself for the second time today.

Baby Small

    I let the truck coast down the rise on the other side of the tracks and looked over at Petra who hadn't fared so well either. Vanilla shake was running in clumps off the dash of the truck and her legs were covered in it too. But she looked fine. She looked angry and I started to laugh but I couldn't because a cramp that started in my thighs pulled and gripped me from my rear-end on up my back and around my belly. It pulled so strongly I had to take my feet off the pedals and let the truck coast and die on the side of the road.

    "Jesus!" Petra cried from next to me. "Look at this mess!"

    I could see her wiping at her legs with napkins and the empty sack from Steak-N-Shake out of the corner of my eye. I was slightly aware that I didn't have my foot on the brake and that the stalled truck was gently and quietly rolling down into the grassy ditch.

    "Baby! We're going down the gulley!" Petra yelled from next to me and I fought against the cramps ripping through me to stomp on the brake. As the cramp coursed through me and squeezed me all around, I felt more wetness leak out of me but now it was more of a soft gush. I looked down and my legs were shiny with it.

    "Petra, I think something's wrong," I told her with my voice shaking as another cramp tightened all my muscles around my middle and a bigger gush of hot wetness squeezed out of me.

    "Oh my lord!" Petra wailed as she looked at my dress that was turning darker from the waist down. "Your water is breaking!" Petra cried and pointed at my knees that had rivulets running down them.

    I gripped the steering wheel and took deep breaths and tried to decide what to do. When the cramps stopped I looked over to see Petra white and chalky with pure panic.

    "It's ok Petra, I'm ok. I think the baby is coming today after all." And then I had to pause and breathe as I felt my hips widening right under me as all the muscles in my back tensed and then relaxed into a dull, steady ache.

    "Turn us around! Go back to the doc!"

    "We're closer to home now, though," I said to her.

    We were at least forty-five minutes from Rush now and only about five minutes from the La Rue town limits.

    "Then, then get us home!"

    "It's ok, Petra. Labor takes a long time. It'll be ok," I reassured her as I stretched out my leg to put in the clutch and start the truck up again. It took two tries but the engine finally roared to life and the big tires got us up out of the grassy ditch. It felt better to get back up on the blacktop and not be leaning at a strange angle in the ditch anymore.

Baby Small

"I can do it," I told Petra as I slowly ran through the gears but as we gained speed and the engine roared louder, another cramp rolled all through me. It felt like it started at my knees and worked its way up my thighs and on up around my middle and deep in my back and I groaned out loud and almost stalled the truck again as the pain squeezed me.

"Pull over, pull over!" Petra cried and I looked up and saw a grain truck coming at us, hogging more than its share of the road and I swerved and almost took us into the ditch again.

"Oh my God," I groaned as I felt the truck shiver under us as the wheels hit the gravel on the side of the road.

"Turn in here, turn in here!" Petra commanded and I saw Kai's lane in front of us and swung the truck in and let the engine shake to a stall too far from his house.

"Just honk the horn. Honk the horn," Petra said and reached over and pressed the center of the steering wheel in a panicked staccato of honking.

Chapter Thirty-Three

"She's having the baby!" Petra cried as she leaned over me when Kai's mom Sandy came to my window to see what was happening. "She's having the baby!" Petra yelled again and again.

Sandy just looked down and saw my soaked dress and put it all together.

"Come in Baby," she said and opened my door.

"No, I can't walk. I can't get out. I'm leaking. I can't walk. I need Ed," I told her and pulled the door shut.

"Where is he?"

"He's at the airport; he's at the engine shop!" Petra told her as she leaned precariously over me.

"What's the number?"

"It's, it's," I pictured the phone in my hand and shut my eyes and told her the number and opened them to see Petra had found a pencil and had written the number on a white bag.

"He's coming," Sandy said to me as she leaned in the window when she came back what seemed days later.

I had been so worried that she wouldn't get a hold of Ed, but mostly I had been worried that I was going to birth this baby right here in the truck.

"How are you doing, Baby?" Sandy asked me as she held my hand through the window.

"You look like you're going to faint!" came from Petra.

"I'm ok. I'm hot," I told them as I rested my head on the back of the seat.

"What medicines are you on, Baby?" Sandy asked gently and I told her.

I opened my eyes and looked at her when she stopped patting my hand and knew that she knew that those medicines while good for me on a day to day basis could cause me to bleed out when I gave birth.

"Is Ed coming?" I asked and heard the keening panic behind my words.

She nodded, "Yes, he's coming. He'll be here soon."

"Good." I lay my head back and concentrated on listening for the blatting roar of the Cutlass as Ed blasted it down the road to come get me.

But I never heard it.

Instead, I heard the 'whock whock whock' of a helicopter right overhead.

"Oh. My. God," Petra breathed from next to me. She was holding one of my hands and Sandy was holding the other one. "Oh. My. God," she repeated. "He brought the Army."

"Ha ha," I laughed with my eyes closed and my head still back on the seat. I felt two tears leak out of the corners of my eyes and run down into my hair.

"Where's he gonna land?" came from Sandy.

"Yeah? Where's he gonna put down?" Petra mused.

I opened my eyes and looked up at him through the windshield to see the red and white helicopter hovering in a circle over Kai's old white house. The whock whock seemed to speed up and I could hear the whistling whine of the engine as it came down closer and closer.

"Right on the front yard!" Petra gasped as the helicopter circled smaller and smaller and then just drifted right straight down on the wide meadow of the lawn in front of Kai's house. A flock of yellow butterflies flittered up out of the grass as it landed and my heart felt light to see them.

The back hatch of the copter opened and two men in white coveralls were out immediately with a stretcher and trotted over to the truck with their heads down.

"Where's Ed?" Petra cried in panic.

"Behind the wheel," I said as a new cramp began to squeeze me without the warning of first creeping up my legs.

"He could at least get out and come see you!" Petra complained.

"He can't, he has to keep the bird going, he has to, be ready to fly," I said in between contractions. I finally said it in my mind, contractions. These were contractions. This was labor. The baby was coming early. I hoped he'd be big enough to live outside of me on his own. I hoped he wouldn't be too small.

The two attendants helped me get out of the truck and I was glad to leave the soaked seat. The wind from the helicopter blew against my wet skirt and chilled me and I felt as if I'd pee myself again as another cramp built up in my back as I stood up all the way.

"Let's get you on the stretcher," one of them said to me but everything else he said was drowned out by the helicopter whose engine was now revving up louder and louder as if Ed was waiting to just punch it and take off as soon as we were inside.

I pulled up my wet skirt a little so that I could free my legs and walk towards the stretcher. When I looked down at my legs I saw blood running down them in bright red rivers and covering my bare feet. The panic that hit me squeezed me all around and I nearly dropped to the ground. I didn't want to die out here in Kai's yard. I didn't want to die with Petra and Ed here. I didn't want to die on this hot summer day. I had never been so scared ever and would have fainted and dropped if the EMT's hadn't been there.

The EMTs picked me up right off my bare feet and got me on the stretcher where they tucked a blanket around me and strapped me in at three different places. Being on my back made me feel claustrophobic but the worst was yet to come when they slid me up in the back of the helicopter's payload area.

"Oh my gosh, it's too small in here, I can't breathe," I said and struggled to sit up.

"Take a deep breath," someone said from over me and snapped a clear cup over my mouth and nose where cool air blew forcefully against my nose and relaxed me immediately.

"Ed, are you up there?" I asked into the oxygen mask and tried to roll my head to see him but could only see the white ceiling of the helicopter with tubes and cords and cables going everywhere.

"I'm here, Baby Small, I'm here. Hang tight and don't birth that baby in the air. We're gonna get you to the hospital."

"Ok, ok. But I'm bleeding Ed, I'm bleeding," I cried out even more scared now that I was in the confines of the helicopter.

"You're gonna be all right, Miss," one of the EMTs assured me.

"I'm on blood thinners, I have a heart problem, I lost a baby once, I don't want to lose this one. I don't want to die," I told him as I took his hand.

"You're going to be ok, you're not bleeding very much, you're going to be fine," he reassured me again. "Just lay back," he said and pushed me back onto the pillow.

"Don't you go dying on me back there Baby Small, I will never forgive you! You cannot die, Blondie!" came from Ed up in the front and he almost sounded angry.

"Ok Ed, I'll be ok, if I could just lay on my side," I said while struggling on the stretcher.

"You can't lay on your side, Mrs. Small, we're taking off," came from one of the EMTs.

And just as he said it I felt the world drop away from under me as the whining reverberating through the stretcher beneath me vibrated fast enough to shake my teeth together. All the shaking made it even more unbearable to be on my back and I felt around for the buckle over my chest and slid it open and pulled it loose as we swayed and lifted up into the air. Once it was loose I was able to move enough to reach the buckle over my thighs and slid it open and then rolled onto my side.

"Can't lay on my back, can't breathe," I said as I felt the muscles around me squeeze and cramp and water gushed from between my legs. "Sorry," I told the EMTs for not following directions and for soaking them as well. I hoped it wasn't a lot of blood coming out of me. I hoped I wasn't slowly dying back there.

"Blondie! You causing trouble back there?" Ed barked from up front.

"I'm not, Ed!" I tried to say but it came out in a yell as the cramp intensified and hurt clear down to my feet. "I don't feel good!" I screamed. "It hurts!"

"Blondie, Blondie!" Ed hollered and I felt the copter sway.

"Don't look at me, don't watch, Ed! Keep your eyes on the road!"

"Good gravy a married couple," one of the EMTs said as he readjusted my buckles and belts that kept me safely on the stretcher as we flew to the hospital.

"Huh! Ahuh!" I heard Ed laugh and I relaxed my cheek against the side of the pillow and tried to breathe slowly and tried to let the contractions flow through me as easily as we were flying through the air.

Chapter Thirty-Four

"Prepare for descent," Ed finally called back to us and I sent thanks up to God over and over that we were almost there.

And even though I had hated the smallness of the helicopter, and hated laying on the stretcher in it when they first wheeled me in, now I hated to leave it. It felt safe. I just wanted to have the baby here. Right here. But that wasn't possible.

No sooner had Ed put us down on the landing pad on top of the hospital than I heard his door open and knew he had jumped out.

"Let's go, let's get her out," came his voice as the back hatch opened and the afternoon heat and sunlight streamed into the back of the helicopter.

"Back up Ed, we'll get her in, you just stay out of the way," the EMTs told him.

The trip through the hospital was a hectic and frightful one as I gripped the side of the stretcher and watched things blur by. People in blue and green scrubs, nurses in white, doctors in suits and doctors in white coats, shiny blue tiled walls and everywhere people were in a hurry.

The EMTs spoke in codes of my condition and the medicines I was on and their complications and further medicines I would need 'stat' as they all said. They were poking me and sticking me and squeezing my wrists and putting sticky bracelets on me and taking my blood pressure and asking me how much discomfort I was in but at that moment I felt fine, because at that moment Ed was right next to me and he was holding my hand as we ran down the hall.

"You gonna be okay, Blondie?" he kept asking me as we rolled down the hallway. He tucked his hair behind his ears again and again as he leaned over to me.

"I'm fine Ed. I made it here. I thought I was gonna be stuck out in the prairie with Petra."

"Lord love a duck what were you doing going out of town?"

"I went to the doctor, Ed. I was in labor!" I said this second part with more urgency because then a cramp was rolling in hard and deep in my back and sides.

"Squeeze my hand, Baby Small, squeeze my hand."
"Ed."
"Yes, Blondie?"
"Ed," that was all I could pant out.
"Yes darling?" he asked with his face close to mine.

Baby Small

I opened my eyes just long enough to see that his eyes looked sad and worried and his lips were pooched out in a pout of concern.

"Ed I think I feel like I need the toilet," I told him.

"Ma'am, that's the baby coming down, we're gonna get you to a room and see how far along you've come."

I turned my head to see who had butted into our conversation and saw a male nurse with a thick neck that ran in a blob up to his chin.

"Blondie, it's going to be all right. I'm going to be with you every step of the way."

"Um, actually sir, we're going to have to ask you to step away and go fill out some paperwork."

"Nope. Not leavin' Blondie's side. Someone else will have to fill out the paperwork because I'm not letting go of her till that baby comes out."

"Call my dad!" I shouted up to the nurse as we turned into a room.

"And you're not examining her!" Ed told the male nurse with a point of his finger in the nurse's big red face. "Get that female in here, she can examine Blondie, but not you!"

The nurse rolled his eyes at us but he did leave on squeaky shoes as the female nurse came in.

"You really need to leave, Mr. Small," the female nurse told Ed as he squatted next to me once they'd gotten me into a fresh bed where I was laying on my side.

"Why?" he asked as he still held my hand.

I just concentrated on his face as I squeezed his hand as the muscles in my back tightened and pulled all around the middle of my body.

"Ugh," I groaned and felt like a tube of toothpaste being squeezed by a giant.

"There's no men allowed in here during delivery and I really need to examine her."

"She's my wife, my wife goddammit. Examine her. Now!" Ed hollered at the nurse as he continued to hold my hand.

"I can't take it, shut up!" I tried to yell but it came out whispery as I panted and breathed hard into the pillow.

"Do it! Woman!" Ed commanded and I couldn't tell if he was talking to me or the nurse but it was then that she began to gently pull on my ankles.

"Baby, I'm going to examine you as soon as this contraction is over."

"Ok."

Baby Small

Thankfully she was quick about it.

"She's at nine. That baby is coming soon," was the last thing I heard the nurse say and then she pulled on a little chain hooked to an intercom and the room was instantly full of people and suddenly Ed was no longer holding my hand.

Baby Small

Chapter Thirty-Five

"I'm not pushing till Ed gets back in here!" I yelled for the second time.

"Baby, please push, you have to push."

"You can do it Baby, and then he can come back in."

I sat up in the bed and glared at everyone all around me. There were at least three doctors and a whole room full of nurses. And they were all pleading with me.

"NO!" I howled and I hoped Ed could hear me wherever he was. And I imagined there was a whole room of people holding him back; keeping him from me.

The pain was unbearable and I felt like I was just going to explode and my legs would fly completely off my body if I didn't push this baby out soon. I was hooked up to all sorts of monitors and gauges and things to measure my heart and my blood-pressure and the contractions and the baby's heart and all of them all started beeping all at the same time.

"We might have to do a C-section," one of the doctors said and I growled at him.

"When's the last time you ate?" another doctor asked me as the beeping grew louder and more urgent.

"An hour ago?" I answered and now I was panting too hard to yell at them.

"How much did you eat?" a nurse asked as she pulled a notebook and a pen out of her pocket and I stifled a laugh because she looked like a waitress. But the laugh turned into an unbearable urge to push and I couldn't hold it back anymore.

"How much?" she asked again

I gripped the handles and shoved my feet back into the stirrups and bellowed, "Two cheeseburgers with everything and a large order of onion rings!" as I bore down and pushed.

"That's my Blondie! Ordering food just like she was at the Freeze!" I heard Ed holler and then he whooped and he was right by my side. "You go Blondie! You do it!" he urged me on and patted my hand as I squeezed the handles.

"I can't do it Ed!" I huffed and grunted and sweat poured down the sides of my face.

"You can do it, Hell-cat, you can do it!" he said and pulled my hair up off my face and blew on the back of my neck.

Baby Small

"I'm tired Ed!"

"I know Blondie, but you're almost there," Ed said and I watched in horror as he bent down and looked between my legs. Three doctors and four nurses also looked on at him, shocked and completely speechless as Ed continued to look and then he said at the same time as one of the nurses, "There's his head!"

"This wasn't meant to be!" I yelled.

"Yes it was! And it is!" Ed yelled back at me and then his eyes widened and his mouth dropped open as I pushed the baby's head out.

"Oh my gosh are we done?" asked everyone in the room as they gestured for Ed to move out of the way.

But the doctors were all scurrying; some were injecting my IV with shots and some were monitoring my beeping machines that were all finally quieting down, and some were pulling in close to me in a place where I didn't want them to be.

"Baby's coming, suction the nose nurse," the main doctor said.

I heard a wet sound and then I felt like I was losing something large.

"One shoulder is out, hold it, hold it, and there's the other and, and, and there's the baby!" the doctor exclaimed as he pulled the baby out.

I felt the baby leave me in a whoosh and I felt my lungs and ribs expand for the first time in months and I took a huge breath and looked at Ed, whose face was shining and red and whose eyes were welling up with tears.

"It's a GIRL!" Both Ed and the doctor announced to the room as deep crying broke out of the throat of the little baby.

"Sweet mother, it's a girl, Blondie. It's a girl. We got us our own daughter. Sweet God I better buy a shotgun right away, it's a girl! Our lives will never be the same," Ed sighed and smiled and sat down next to me.

"A girl? Are you sure?"

"Yes, Blondie. It's a sweet little girl. It's a Baby Small Jr," Ed laughed as the doctor held up a pink and shiny little baby who was already pumping her thick little legs.

"Ed. We are not naming her that," I told Ed as I watched a nurse swaddle her and hand her to me. She was very warm, almost hot through the blanket and she was strong as she screamed with her toothless mouth opened wide and her eyes bright and blue and already smart looking.

"She's perfect," Ed said.

"She is," the doctor agreed with a nod of his head.

Baby Small

"She is," I said as well as I watched her shove her own little fist in her mouth and begin to suckle.

"We'll clean her up right here and give her back to you to nurse," a nurse told me and I reluctantly let her take her from me.

Ed and I watched closely as the nurses cleaned and weighed the baby; as they listened to her heart and examined her.

"Ten fingers and toes?" Ed asked and he sounded scared. I watched him as he licked his lips and tucked his hair behind his ears again and again.

"Yep, ten fingers and ten toes," came from the nurse.

"She doesn't look like a preemie," one of the doctors said as he examined her next.

"I think they had your date wrong."

"Blondie."

"Ed."

"Any guesses on the weight?" the doctor asked and chuckled.

"Ten pounds!" Ed cried.

"Nope, she's 6 lbs and 2 oz. Definitely not a preemie. Look at her color and listen to that heart."

At that, my own heart skidded a few beats and the monitor next to me recorded it in beeps.

"Healthy heart?" I asked the doctor with such a small voice I didn't know if he would hear me over the hubbub of the receding nurses and doctors who were leaving the room.

"Sounds about perfect," he said just as quiet as me as he listened to the stethoscope.

"She gets that from me," Ed said sheepishly and he smiled and leaned over and kissed me on the forehead. "You did good, Mama, you did good."

After everyone but one nurse had left things quieted down and we dimmed the lights and the nurse helped me get the baby latched on. She stayed with me until the tiny baby began to nurse at a good rhythm.

"She'll only take a little to begin with," the nurse told us as she took a step back.

"Huh ahuh! If she's anything like our little Blondie she'll take it all," Ed chuckled as he got as close to me as he could on the bed.

I held my little miracle with her perfect little face and her eyes that were blue as a summer's sky. She watched my face as much as I watched hers and after she had eaten all she wanted and even burped, the nurse told us we would be moved to a recovery room.

Baby Small

Orderlies came in to help move me and Ed pushed a clear little bassinette with the baby in it and we went to a new room down another wing of the hospital. After we all got settled, Ed held the baby in his big arms and I watched as he blinked back a few tears.

He continued to hold her as a nurse brought in a tray of soup and meatloaf and potatoes for me, but mostly I just wanted a large milkshake.

"You and your milkshakes, Blondie," Ed smiled.

"Mine got dropped all over the truck," I sighed. And then in a panic I asked, "What happened to Petra?"

Ed gave me the sleeping baby and said he'd go to the lounge and call everyone and that he'd find out what happened to Petra. It was dinner time and he said he was sure to reach everyone.

Twenty minutes later he came back with a can of grape soda for me, the closest he could get to a shake in this place was what he told me. And twenty-five minutes after that Daddy came and he had Mrs. Small with him.

None of us said much; we just sat quiet and stared at the baby and smiled at each other. Mrs. Small cried and would not be consoled and Ed held his mother a long time while I held the baby and everyone just looked on at me. Finally, Daddy asked to hold her and Ed helped put her in his arms and while Daddy sat in the rocking chair next to my bed, I fell asleep.

When I woke up it was dark and our new little girl was in her bassinette sleeping and Ed was splayed out in the chair next to my bed dozing.

**

The next morning Daddy came again and also brought Aunt Clem and Jeffrey and Allen. Lisa had stayed home to be with Olivia because the hospital said she was too young to come in.

"So what are you gonna name her?" Jeffrey asked as he helped pass the baby to Aunt Clem as she sat in the chair next to my bed. Aunt Clem looked utterly in love with her as she held her and cooed to her and ignored everyone else and it gave me an idea of what Aunt Clem must have been like when the twins were born.

"What's her name?" Aunt Clem asked.

Ed and I looked at each other and held our breath. We had been up in the middle of the night with me nursing her while Ed watched. We had been wide awake even though it was nearly midnight and we couldn't bear to put her down while her eyes were wide awake and she was turning her little head and looking at everything. She would look at me and blink and then look at Ed and blink and then back at me and smack her fat beautiful lips and blink again. Ed and I had spent a long time just watching her do this, until she began to fuss.

Then Ed had helped change her diaper and he put her into some jammies that Daddy had brought. He was making me laugh the entire time he was doing it.

"Little foot goes in here and little foot goes in there," he had sang as I watched him put her footed yellow pajamas on her.

"Her toes are too small, Ed," I had said and sunk back into the bed and all the pillows and smiled and closed my eyes for a bit.

"She is so tiny, we are gonna have to work hard fattening this baby up!" Ed said in a squeaky little voice as he flicked up the zipper over her belly as she breathed slow and her chest rose up and down in the dim hospital light.

"What are we gonna name her?" I had asked Ed and I looked around the room to make sure no one heard me.

"Something special," he whispered to me as he leaned in close to me with her sleeping in his arms. "Something that will protect her," he said and when I looked in his eyes he had tears on his lashes.

"Like what?" I asked, curious to what he was thinking.

"Something that will always go with her, that will always be part of her, which will always keep her safe."

"Like Smith and Wesson?" I said and smiled and winked at him.

"Huh ahuh!" he laughed quietly, his chest shaking and made the little baby nestled there quake and complain a little in her sleep.

"No, not Smith and Wesson, jeepers Blondie, you are such a redneck at heart," he said and laughed silently some more. "No, something like your mom's name, Baby. Something like that. If she had your mom's name, I'd feel better."

I didn't know what to say. I sat and thought about it and said it a few times in my head. It didn't sound right but I didn't want to say that to Ed. Instead I said, "I don't know, I think your mom should be part of it too, don't you?"

Ed just looked at me with confusion in his blue eyes and a question on his lips.

"So we would call her?" Ed trailed off and waited for what I would say.

"Genevieve June," I said and nodded my head at hearing it out loud.

"Genevieve? But that's my mom's name," Ed said and scratched his head.

"I know."

Baby Small

I looked down at her to keep from looking at him. She had Ed's thick lips and my little chin.

"Genevieve June," I said now to Aunt Clem as she held her.

"That's perfect," Aunt Clem said and kissed her on her little pink forehead.

That afternoon just as Daddy left and Ed dozed off, I heard the unmistakable whine and whir of Petra's scooter. I was holding Genevieve and had just finished nursing her when Petra nosed her scooter into my room and came to a stop far from my bed.

"Oh. My. God," Petra breathed.

"Hi," I whispered back to her.

"Is she sleeping?" Petra asked quietly, her eyebrows disappearing right up into her hair.

"Yes. But you can come in."

Ed was snoring in the big squishy lounge chair next to the bed with his socked feet up on a little table.

"Had lots of visitors?" Petra asked as she came closer to the bed and gestured to the table near the window which was covered in gifts.

There was a pink teddy bear and yellow flowers from my Daddy and a dozen pink balloons from Ed and small sunflowers from Mrs. Small's very own garden and a dish of African Violets from Jeffrey, Allen, and Aunt Clem.

"Just family," I told her and waved her to get closer to me.

Petra got as close as her scooter would allow and leaned over as far as she could without losing balance and looked at the baby.

"This is Genevieve."

"Hi, Genevieve."

"Want to hold her?"

"Nah, not now." Petra backed her scooter up an inch with a jolt and the baby's eyes popped open and she began to frown and began to work up a cry.

"Now I know you're not gonna turn down holding my kid," came from a sleepy, croaky voiced Ed as he slowly sat up.

"Well," Petra said and looked nervous.

"You can do it," I told her as Ed took the baby from me.

"Where's them tiny diapers the nurse brought, Baby?" he asked me as patted the crinkly diaper under the jammies and then he laid Genevieve down in the bassinette.

"Ed changes diapers?" Petra asked and drove her scooter around to him to get a closer look.

265

Baby Small

"I'm her daddy, ain't I?" he asked as he began unzipping the tiny jammies and slipping them off. "She's wet clear through," he said over his shoulder at me.

"There's dry sleepers in that bag my dad brought," I told him.

After Ed got her changed and happy again he let her lay in the bassinette for a minute. I could see her feet kicking above the lip of the bassinette as she stretched her legs up in the air. She looked bowlegged from here and I smiled.

"All right there Miss Kooky," Ed said to Petra, "I'm going to help you get in this chair here and help you hold this baby. Otherwise Blondie is gonna be upset for a long time and I'll never hear the end of it."

"What? What?" Petra asked as Ed helped get her over to the chair.

Her face was pure crimson by the time Ed got her settled in the chair.

"Here put this pillow on your lap," I said to Petra and I put one of my pillows on her lap.

She got her arms ready for the baby and of course the pillow was there to help her and of course Ed was right there too.

Petra held Genevieve for almost an hour. The little baby was alert and curious and she stared and blinked at Petra the whole time while Petra talked to her.

"Your mama tends to stay at home, so it'll be up to you to make sure she gets out and just as soon as you're big enough, we'll walk you down to Cloyd's and get you some hair bows. You need some hair first, but all good things to those who wait as they say," and on and on Petra went until Genevieve began to suck on her fist and then get fussy.

Ed helped get her latched on to me and then before Petra could try to leave he said, "I'm heading down to find a cup of black coffee. I'll be back in a bit." And he was gone. I think he knew Petra and I needed to be alone.

"She sure is slurping," Petra said after a while.

"You should hear her poop!"

"Oh my gosh, you can hear it?"

"Yes!"

"She must get that from Ed."

"Oh lord!"

Petra sat with me while I nursed Genevieve first from one side and then the other. And after I got her settled on the other side, I finally asked, "So, who brought you to the hospital?"

She didn't answer for a while. And she wouldn't look at me.

"Allen?" I finally asked.

"Yes."

"What's going on there?"

"Nothing. Nothing on my end. He's nice to hang out with but I'm not looking for that, for, you know."

It was my turn to raise my eyebrows at her for once.

"Really," she said and then she relaxed back into the deep chair.

"Where is he now?"

"In the cafeteria."

We were both quiet a while and then I remembered something.

"How did you get home? Where's my truck?"

Petra smiled.

"Sandy drove me back home. I'm not sure how she got back out to her home, because she left your truck at your place. She cleaned it up inside too, is what Allen said."

"Oh." I remembered my water breaking and making such a mess and was again glad we'd taken the old truck and not the new Bronco.

"It was so cool watching you fly off in that helicopter. No one will ever have a birth story like that," Petra sighed. "Everyone in town is talking about it."

"How do they know?" I asked shocked and embarrassed.

"Oh they know. I think half the town's got scanners and they told the other half," Petra shrugged.

"So I'll be going home to more rumors and talk?"

"Well yeah, that and kittens! Don't forget the kittens!" Petra brightened.

Chapter Thirty-Six

My worry about what the town was saying about us was replaced by worrying that the hospital would never let me and Ed take the baby home. But they did. Two days later Ed packed up everything we had acquired in the little hospital, and somehow it had grown to be a lot of stuff, and he packed up the car and brought it to the front door of the hospital where the nurses had me and Genevieve all ready to go.

Her car seat was waiting in the back of the Bronco and I got in the back with her and as Ed drove away from the hospital I said, "I can't believe they're letting us go home with her."

"She's ours Baby, and we will take good care of her."

And we were ready for it. I don't think either of us felt uncertain by the time we got her home. It felt natural to pull up the long drive in the Bronco to the back of our little white house with a baby in the car.

When we got in the back door we were greeted by Applesauce and Thunderhead and a flock of black and gray and white kittens who were all growing bigger already.

"I married you Blondie, and suddenly I got all these mouths to feed," Ed laughed as he held the door open for me and Genevieve.

"Make room, mama's comin' through," he told the animals and then he turned to me. "We're home baby girl," Ed said down to the baby as we came into the living room together.

"We're home Genevieve June. This is where it all happens. This is where your life begins. This is where our family lives," I told her as I showed her around the living room.

"This is where we'll teach you to write that long name of yours, huh ahuh!" Ed said as he sat down at the dining room table.

"This is where you will always live no matter what," I said to her but I was looking at Ed.

"No matter what," he echoed me.

"No matter what," I said again as if to make it stick for eternity but was interrupted by the ringing of the phone and Genevieve woke up crying just as Ed went to kiss me on the cheek.

"Shit mother fuck," he mouthed against my cheek as I handed him the baby and I couldn't help but laugh as I picked up the handset.

THE END

DEDICATION

With much love to my husband Craig and my sons Henry and Stuart for allowing me and encouraging me to write and be creative. For understanding that I need to do this and that I love this. Thank you for sharing me.

With much thanks to the readers for being patient, for investing your time and love in Baby and Ed and Petra and all the family and friends of LaRue, IL.

Thank you dear readers for taking a chance on me, a writer without an agent and without representation. Thank you for all the reviews, kind words, emails, facebook likes, and word of mouth you give my writing.

Without the readers, there would be no Baby Small.

Printed in Great Britain
by Amazon